NOVELS BY MORRIS PHILIPSON

BOURGEOIS ANONYMOUS
THE WALLPAPER FOX
A MAN IN CHARGE

A
MAN
IN
CHARGE

a novel by

MORRIS PHILIPSON

SIMON AND SCHUSTER • NEW YORK

PUBLISHED BY SIMON AND SCHUSTER
A DIVISION OF GULF & WESTERN CORPORATION
SIMON & SCHUSTER BUILDING
ROCKEFELLER CENTER
1230 AVENUE OF THE AMERICAS
NEW YORK, NEW YORK 10020

DESIGNED BY EVE METZ
MANUFACTURED IN THE UNITED STATES OF AMERICA

1 2 3 4 5 6 7 8 9 10

LIBRARY OF CONGRESS CATALOGING IN PUBLICATION DATA

PHILIPSON, MORRIS H   1926-
A MAN IN CHARGE.

I. TITLE.
PZ4.P55MAN   [PS3566.H475]   813'.5'4   79-299
ISBN 0-671-24818-9

FOR
SUSAN ANTONÍA PHILIPSON

Pleasure comes not from things in themselves, but from our enjoyment of them; happiness lies in the possession of things not dear to others but to ourselves.

—*François VI, Duc de la Rochefoucauld*

PART 1

WORKS AND DAYS

THE DAY SOMEONE TOLD CONRAD TAYLOR that his wife was having an affair with another man turned out to be an inordinately eventful one for him. But he had felt equal to it.

The first working day of the new year. The sidewalks had not been shoveled, the streets were not yet cleared. Four inches of snow had fallen during New Year's Day, and the wind had blown great drifts against the parked cars, over the shrubs and the hedges around the large houses along Hillhouse Avenue, frosting the tips of all the leafless twigs and branches of the elm trees along the quiet street. Conrad Taylor walked to his office, bundled up in a brown leather coat lined with chocolate-colored curls of sheep's wool. His black rubber overshoes left potholes of footprints in the snow. He felt alone in the early morning light, the first man up and doing. The sky was a clear blue, the sun shining bright on the white froth. He watched the fog of his breath come and go as he strode forward in the biting cold. He felt the hairs in his nostrils freeze into metallic pinpoints that twitched against each other as he breathed. He was invigorated. He would start the new year right. He usually reached his office at eight-thirty; this morning he would be there by eight.

Isabel remained asleep in their bed. He could see the gold of her hair spread about her head like a sunburst on the pillow. Conrad prepared his own coffee; there was a special pleasure in that, for only from the time that he awoke until he arrived at his office could he enjoy anything like solitude. During the rest of the day, most of his time would be involved with other people. But there, grinding one cup of roasted French coffee beans and one cup of Kenya, he prepared the mixture he preferred, set it to percolate. Soon enough the heat of the coffee radiated through him. He turned on the radio for the early morning news, and surveyed the kitchen as he listened. By what an unexpected fluke his lonely and rather disheveled life had become rich and well-ordered. Isabel had arranged for the kitchen to be remodeled. It was all stainless steel and white Formica, with ovens at chest level, toaster, and poachers, and roasters on counters; clear jars of colorful spices on circular trays, china cups suspended from brass hooks in cabinets painted sea green to match the pebbly look on the covering of the floor. Neat as a pin. The servants arrived close to noon—unseen by Conrad—and left after dinner, invisibly having restored every cleaned thing to its proper place. In the morning he found the large, efficient room as bright and fresh as on the moment the construction men had first left, and Isabel saw that everything was where she wanted it to be. Once she had things organized, she showed almost no further interest in them. "I have to pay my own way," she had said when she agreed to marry him. "I'll take care of all household expenses—and my personal expenses—out of my income. You take care of everything else." As a result, Conrad was able to deposit most of his salary in his savings account. He was a middle-aged man whose hair was still chestnut brown, whose deep-set brown eyes were still clear, whose passable good looks and vigorous body excited a wife young enough to be his daughter. He was more than ready to start the new year. He volunteered.

Conrad never took anything other than coffee before noon. He thought of himself as a stoic—but "a sybaritic stoic"— which made him smile.

Having put on his coat in the front hall, he had bent over in the foyer to pull up the overshoes, when he noticed a letter lying in the mail-drop cage on the inside of the front door. Ordinarily mail wasn't delivered until the middle of the afternoon at home. Someone must have dropped it off during the night. He drew it out: a plain white envelope without postage, let alone a special delivery stamp, addressed merely with his name in penciled block letters. He shoved it into his overcoat pocket, opened the door, ready for the arctic air. He moved out with his spine straight and his chin thrust forward.

He was aware that people thought of him as a haughty man, which irritated him because it was not the case; but a certain aloof pride was a useful mask—it put people off and he was more comfortable with distance from others. He knew that people thought he had a sharp tongue, which he enjoyed; and he thought he knew when to keep his mouth shut—but he wasn't right about that all the time. At a reception for the Board of Trustees, after being introduced to Mrs. Baird-Lloyd, a direct descendant of Peter Stuyvesant, and her husband, the chairman of the board of the Clayton Bank, a man in his late sixties, bald, waxen, frail, almost blue-lipped, he had whispered to the provost, Clifford Rostum: "We've just met an extraordinarily wealthy woman and her late husband."

Clifford Rostum wasn't amused. In a not unfriendly manner, the provost said, "Conrad, you have an all-pervasive irreverence."

"I resent that," Conrad said lightly.

"Now, now, don't be touchy. You are a prima donna."

"I resent that even more."

"Ah, but there are real prima donnas and false prima donnas. At least you're the real thing." The provost smiled. "I admire that."

The memory of the encounter still rankled.

Actually his reputation for hauteur troubled him. He thought the main difficulty was dealing with people who have too little sense of humor and therefore can't learn to put things in manageable perspective—without which no one can ever hope to achieve a disinterested judgment.

Recently, at a cocktail party, just before Christmas, a young member of the faculty of the English Department, who had undertaken to teach a course in psychoanalytic interpretations of literature, sententiously asked, "Has anyone ever developed so profound a theory of human psychology as Freud's?" Conrad Taylor replied, "Yes. La Rochefoucauld."

"But surely you can't compare the author of the *Maxims* with Freud . . . ," the young man said in disbelief.

"Naturally," Conrad Taylor condescendingly stroked him, "of course not. La Rochefoucauld was a duke, a prince of the realm in the reign of Louis the Fourteenth, and Freud was only a twentieth-century, middle-class, Viennese Jew."

The small group around them laughed, for whatever reasons of their own, but Conrad knew he believed what he said and no one else imagined that he did. They would interpret his remarks as anti-Semitic instead of trying to understand what he implied. The extent to which he didn't give a damn about that was a kind of snobbism, although he hadn't meant it that way; but the faculty of the university was in no position to acknowledge that one of the members of the administration had a mind of his own, a thinker to take seriously. That would have been too much. The concept of specialization of labor was paramount in their preserve. If they were not empowered with his budgetary and administrative controls, at least they assumed a monopoly of the right to be taken seriously. They were the certified public intellectuals.

Conrad Taylor was executive vice-president for the college. He watched the course of the reputations of the scholars rise or fall. The young men or women of promise shot off their fireworks or fizzled out. Either they hardened into rocklike certainties, or they dissipated their chances—and spent the rest of their lives like old-time gold miners, sifting through one pan of silt after another, searching for hard, valuable ore they were convinced was to be found in themselves, sometime, somewhere. It struck him that there was a useful image in thinking of starting out on an academic career as undertaking a kind of gold rush. Then it occurred to him to ask one of the younger faculty members in American history, just then using computers to quantify their data, about what the statistics actually were as to how many went to California and the Klondike and how many found how much gold. It was the kind of question he could drop casually at the Faculty Club, walking out after lunch, stopping briefly at the table of an assistant professor—and expect an answer within a few weeks or so, from a young person, if he knew how to make a friendly gesture.

The walk through the empty, snow-blanketed streets in the early morning light filled him with a private satisfaction akin to proprietorship. He was a guardian and a servant of a great institution. He was a stalwart; he helped keep the foundations strong. Without people to do that—anything can crumble. He passed the Georgian buildings of red brick and white trim, passed the stately Woolsey Hall of pale gray granite, the college houses of mellow beige stone. A large black Newfoundland hound romped in the snow; a girl in a navy pea coat called to the dog from the far side of the quadrangle. He barked a delaying action. Conrad passed the Beinecke Rare Book and Manuscript Library, and then the Sterling Memorial Library, through a high snowdrift between the street and the wall along the sidewalk. When he reached the college building that housed his offices, he nodded at the porter inside the gate of the yard, mouthing a silent "Happy New Year" that could not have been heard through the porter's window, and went up the stone stairs to the suite of rooms that were his domain.

He was in his own element, and he had arrived there before anyone else. To the left of the long corridor was the waiting room, his secretary's office, and Tom's, his assistant's; beyond them, the comptroller's office. To the right were his rooms. He walked through the conference room to reach his study. It was a peculiar arrangement. His office—or study—was, in a sense, secreted. He could always meet people first in the conference room, with its long table surrounded by ten captain's chairs: a room with walnut paneling carved in a traditional medieval linenfold design, the liturgical residue of the sources of higher learning in the Western world. The room was spare, if not Spartan, without decoration, without draperies on the windows, a workroom where the labor was problem-solving, where the goal was mutual understanding—compromise, not conquest. But then he could always retire into, or invite into, the privacy of his own study the special visitor or the special problem, for the intimacy of considering more subtle issues, or for the softening of a more difficult encounter, in the elegance—not to say grandeur—of his inner office. It was an eighteenth-century-looking room with leaded bay windows with a view of the quadrangle; there was a large silk hanging on one wall, and, on the others, books from floor to ceiling; a Chinese velvet carpet of the early nineteenth century, brought back on a Yankee clipper just after the War of 1812, covered the floor; a long sofa upholstered with silk brocade in a red-and-gold pineapple pattern stood opposite the doorway. Two large wing chairs, covered in the same fabric, faced each other across a walnut table—Conrad's worktable with its neat stack of forms to be filled out, reports to be read, proposals to be evaluated: the place where the paperwork of his job was done. He worked with a pencil and a long yellow legal pad. All of his files were either in the secretary's or the assistant's office. There was a telephone on a cabinet behind his chair. These were the necessary tools. The rest of the work took place in the mind. He hung up his coat and scarf and placed his boots in the slender closet against the back of the door. He sat down in the wing chair and looked out of the window. Moving slowly along paths that cut diagonally across the quadrangle, a figure in a hooded coat—a loden coat of church-mouse gray, with a peaked hood like a cowl—held a book open between gloved hands and read as he, or she, gradually walked along through the snow. Conrad thought that the figure was identical with one that might have been seen in a medieval cloister. It was for such love of learning that the university existed.

Conrad had been in charge of the college for nearly ten years. If he were to die now, he could die content, he thought. At fifty-three, he recognized that, while he had not made the significant contribution to psychology that he had hoped to produce when he was in graduate school—and never would— he had carved out for himself, nevertheless, a career as an administrator, worthwhile to this university and therefore to the world; that was to be respected, appreciated. It was as if he were trying to reassure himself against being considered haughty. He was a worldly man and he was aware of how few people know what that means. The vast majority of humanity imagines that things cannot be other than they are; only worldly people know how wide the range of possibilities is for each decision that may affect the future—how flexible, how unpredictable, how intuitive and subjective the decisions that bring about the shifts, subtle as the quarter-inch alteration in a kaleidoscope which rearranges the elements involved into an entirely different picture.

As a public figure, Conrad believed himself to embody a certain set of high standards regarding the virtues of a liberal education; he was there to strengthen them, to resist their adulteration for faddist purposes. He was the defender of the values of a general undergraduate education against the narrowing pressures of graduate school demands for specialized preparation; he was the defender of the college against the naive criticism of elitism. He knew how to grab a desirable opportunity in good times, and how to make unpleasant but necessary decisions in bad times. He had preserved the facts, not just the image of the importance of the college against the superiority complex of the graduate schools. He had added men and women of impressive caliber to the faculty, as he had gradually cleared out some deadwood. He had helped make the college more self-respecting, at a time when most of its peers were disoriented and merely self-defensive. Under

17

pressure to become more "relevant" they had diluted their essence. If the college took pride in its good works, it was to a considerable measure made possible by him.

An aggressive newspaper reporter had once asked him if the university wouldn't be better off without an undergraduate college and he answered, "Of course it would—but only in the sense that the Garden of Eden would have been better off without the tree of knowledge of good and evil."

As a private person, Conrad Taylor had not been so successful. His first marriage was a disaster. He had married Anne when both of them were graduate students at the University of Chicago, and when he thought so little of himself that he imagined she would be the best match he could make. But, then, she had married him out of the same lack of self-confidence. It was during their years together that he wrote *The History of Psychology in France: From Diderot to Piaget*, and she had come to loathe the academic world. That book, his only book, was dedicated to his mother. When Anne discovered that, she summed up her contempt for their "struggling" years together by weighing it in both hands, spitting out "Our first child!" and hurling it across the room at him. The book was still in print. It remained dedicated to his mother. His French mother. By a peculiarity of mind, he found, in recent years, that he never thought of her as "my mother" anymore, but always as "my French mother." It was from France that she had come and to which she returned.

A few years after they had arrived in the East, his first wife ran off with a Broadway producer. Conrad had no difficulty in securing a divorce and being granted custody of their daughter. Caroline was then eleven years old, and he failed her. He had been unable to prevent her from dropping out of college, from taking drugs, and becoming promiscuous, from bumming around, from hating him even more than she hated "his" capitalist-imperialist-sadistic society. She had said she wanted to become an actress; he thought of her as nothing but playacting one role after another in real life. The last he had heard from her, just before Christmas, in a letter asking for money, of course, was that she was working her way down the east coast of Africa by playing her guitar in village marketplaces. But she had an allowance to buy her safety.

His ulcers ate away at him; surgery contracted the scope of his physical existence, leaving him with only half his stomach. Then the gods saw fit to comfort him with Isabel. She was more than twenty years younger than he, only a little older than his own daughter. They met in Aspen, in a ski lodge, and she made him feel like an eagle, fearless and powerful—and he had caged her, if not tamed her. He had pursued her and won her. She was beautiful and she was rich, and he was in awe of his own good luck. But he could not domesticate her. After three years of living together, he acknowledged that she was a wild bird and flew to her own instincts and early imprinting. They would always send messages to each other across distances, occasional messages. He felt that they had achieved one distinction: they *talked* with each other when they had dinner alone together, although they might not talk much with each other at other times. Most couples, long married, eat in silence. Conrad remembered the speechless dinners with Anne, when they were in graduate school. But then, Anne prepared and served the dinners. Isabel brought with her a cook and a maid.

He looked at his wristwatch. It was 8:30. Isabel would be asleep. He could imagine her soft breathing. He could imagine the silken blond hair like a halo around her head on the pastel-pink pillowcase of their double bed. It made his heart heavy to think that she should never have been his. She should have married a Texas cattle baron with an estate the size of Albania, where she could ride her horse all day in one direction without ever leaving her own land. He stunted her. Her freedom was a source of endless concern to her. There was no making her happy as he was happy. He made things happen, and always for a purpose outside of himself; whereas, she endured whatever happened as obstacles to her only purpose—her own pleasure. But there was so little outside herself that gave her pleasure.

He stood up and looked out of the window again. The monklike hooded figure had reached the corner of the quadrangle almost below Conrad's window and stopped to look up. Conrad could see the open book held in the gloved hands against the chest of the figure. Recognizing the black and green series design of the paperback cover, Conrad realized that it was a book of hard-core pornography, and he laughed out loud.

At that moment, he remembered the letter folded in his overcoat pocket and drew it out, smoothing the envelope, and slitting it open with an ivory-handled letter cutter on his desk. Pasted separately on a plain white sheet of typing paper were words of different sizes cut out of newspapers and magazines. Run together they made up the sentence: "Your wife is having an affair with a man she meets whenever he comes to the hotel here." There was no signature. He examined the envelope. There was no return address. There was only this ice pick to be thrust into Conrad's heart. He folded it into a small rectangle and shoved it behind him into the trouser pocket that held his folder of keys and buttoned it. He crumpled the envelope and threw it into the wastebasket. He closed his eyes and felt his heart pounding.

Is there any reason to believe that what it says is true? he asked himself.

Isabel and he had never sworn eternal fidelity to each other, but it was implicit in their marriage contract. He had not been unfaithful to her once since they met, not once since she married him. There was no one else he desired. But they were separated often enough from each other. . . . There was always time when she could . . . But she had never given him the slightest hint. He thought of telephoning her. But that was absurd. Should he even mention it to her? What validity did it have, this anonymous attack? From a sniper, a hidden enemy. Completely concealed, unknowable. What rights did such an unidentified accusation have upon his credulity? Even if it were true, did he have to confront Isabel with it? Did they have to talk it out? He did not know how to handle it. He would have to think about it later.

Mrs. Todd, his secretary, knocked and entered the study without waiting for a reply.

She was in her fifth month of pregnancy, so their days together were numbered. Her husband was a student in the Law School, and she had been working for Conrad nearly three years, an excellent secretary. Why couldn't they have waited a little longer? She would leave him in the spring, before her husband graduated. She wore black slacks and a white homespun linen blouse from India, slightly starched to stand away from her figure. Her long brown hair, parted in the middle, fell straight down to her shoulders. Two enameled scarabs decorated the pins that held the hair away from her forehead. She was pert, pretty even, in a no-nonsense way. There were no salutations, no wishes for the new year.

She blurted out, "Bad news," nervously, "Very bad news." She was almost shivering.

"The baby?" Conrad asked without looking at her middle.

"No. Here in the office." Her hands were formed into fists at her hips. "There's been another robbery!"

"Oh, hell."

She began to tremble. "I'm so sorry."

Conrad stood up and put his arm around her shoulder. "Why should you be sorry?"

"It was my calculator. I had it in the center drawer of my desk. It's worth about two hundred dollars." Tears blurred her bright brown eyes.

"It's not your fault."

She confessed: "The desk wasn't locked."

"But the door to the offices was." He paused. He remembered: "Cameron's office wasn't locked when the Dictaphone

21

was stolen from there. But we can't live as if this were a fortress."

"This is the fourth thing that's been stolen since Christmas. All during vacation. There isn't a single student around."

"There are always townies around."

"We'd notice anyone who shouldn't be wandering around these offices."

"I think the robberies take place at night."

"That's worse. Then it must be an inside job. Someone who has keys." She shuddered.

Conrad stood close to her and stroked her back. "It's all right. They're only *things*. People aren't being hurt." No one's told you, he thought, that your husband is involved with another woman.

"I'm hurt. I feel violated."

"That's hypersensitive. We're talking about a typewriter, a calculator, a clock, and a Dictaphone."

"It's the feeling of being exposed, of being preyed upon. There's someone in the world who is pawing through our desks, handling what's private to us, taking off with things that we're responsible for. It's dirty! I was upset when the other things were taken, but now that my own calculator is gone, I feel degraded." She was wiping one hand against the other, like Lady Macbeth trying to rub out the damn spot.

"Call campus security. Tom spoke to them about the other things. I'd like to meet with them myself this time. All right?"

"Yes, of course. It's just the thought that any one of us . . ." She turned and left the room.

He was left with the palpable vibrations of her sense of defilement. No doubt, he imagined, Mrs. Todd is all the more sensitive for being pregnant. But the facts touched him, too, in a depressing way. They came with the awareness of the forces in the world that were out to take, to get, to rip off what did not belong to them, what was rightfully someone else's, or worse still, no one else's but belonged to the institution—for the benefit of many. What could one get from the resale of a stolen desk calculator? Twenty dollars? Who can be so desperate? Who, that is, who had access to these offices?

The buzzer of the telephone intercom sounded. Mrs. Todd asked if two- thirty would be a good time for Conrad to meet with the campus security people. He checked with the daily calendar on his desk and said, "Yes." Conrad had no sooner put the receiver back in its cradle than one of the outside telephone lines rang.

"Long distance from Washington," a secretarial voice announced. "Is this Mr. Taylor?"

"Yes."

"Senator Stonefort calling. Hold on, please."

Echoes of childhood, Conrad thought. Old Stoneface. It was difficult for him, even after all these years, to think of his boyhood playmate as the senior senator from Missouri. Still, it was true. They'd grown up together in a suburb of St. Louis. Double-dated in high school—Stoneface was the first in his class to have his own car, a 1933 Ford—and he was the most adventurous. Or was it "programmatic"? He figured that if he had his own car as a junior in high school he would—surely—get laid before he was a senior in high school. He was always a good planner.

"Conrad?" The voice of the senator was intimate and confidential, not commanding.

"Hello, you old goat."

"That's no way to talk to a member of the United States Congress."

"It weren't no accident you got to be called 'Stoneface,' " Conrad replied in a dialect that spread lard over each word.

The senator laughed. "Touché, old buddy. God, it's good to talk with somebody who's not a yes-man. How are you?"

"Sitting up and taking nourishment," Conrad responded.

"You always were a square! Now, tell me: How's the new wife?"

"Great, great. How's the old one?"

23

"Ruby? She's a gem!" A dreadful joke he never tired of. "She runs Washington. How's the family?"

"Now, let's skip the small talk. This call's on taxpayers' money. What's up?"

"I don't need to tell you that the Administration is in difficulty, do I?" the senator began. There was no joking in his voice now.

"Well, I heard on the news this morning that Mr. Nixon's tax returns are going to be reexamined . . ."

"He has to do everything he can to improve his image."

"How about improving the country?"

The senator was silent. When he spoke again, the tone of his voice was more intimate. "The White House has under consideration a proposal that would have very far-reaching consequences, if the bill they have in mind is approved."

Conrad Taylor was listening to the shorthand expressions, thinking that phrases like "the Administration" and "the White House" applied only to institutions with lives of their own; were no people to be mentioned? He said, "You speak as if you think your line is tapped."

When the senator continued, he said softly, "Conrad, I need to talk with you. I can't tell you more over the phone. I appeal to you as an old friend. Come down and spend the day. How soon can you make it?"

Conrad began to finger the pages of the appointment calendar before him.

"You could come down one afternoon. We'll meet during the evening, stay overnight, and then get together with my staff the next morning. It won't take you away for more than twenty-four hours. What do you say?"

"How's next Wednesday?"

Senator Stonefort was obviously consulting his schedule. "Yes," he said finally. "That will work out very well. I'll make a reservation for you. You like to stay at the Hay Adams, don't you?"

"Right."

"You're a Hay Adams type," the senator said cheerfully.

Conrad wrote the initials "D.C." onto his calendar and closed off the space for the twenty-four-hour period.

"You'll have dinner at our house."

"I'd like that. Thank you."

"All right, I'll have my office call yours on Monday or Tuesday to confirm everything." He hesitated for an instant and then added, "You'll see how important this is."

Conrad said, "I believe you."

"I'm depending on you. Thanks." And then he hung up.

Conrad shivered. The senior senator from Missouri. We are the grown-ups now. When we were little boys, country boys, there were great men in the Senate: Norris and Borah and Vandenberg and Wagner. Leaders of our fathers' generation. And now there's Stoneface. We used to play practical jokes together. Conrad thought of the time they made telephone calls at random. The telephone was still a new experience. They would pick out a name from the phone book and pretend to be a distant relative who'd just arrived at the railroad station in St. Louis. They'd pretend to be offended that their voices were not recognized. They had done it two or three times before someone believed them and promised to get into a taxi and come to collect them at the station. But after they'd hung up and had their loud laugh, they felt so guilt-ridden that they phoned back quickly to confess it was a joke. Then they phoned the local tobacconist to ask if he had "Prince Albert in a can." And when they heard the answer, "Yes, of course," they begged, "Let him out! Let him out!" How old could they have been then? Twelve? Thirteen?

And now Stoneface was Senator Stonefort, a man of probity. A member of the Foreign Relations Committee. He would probably end up on the Supreme Court. The great men were gone—the older generation was gone. Now, men like Stonefort and Conrad Taylor, in their early fifties, were wearing their robes, sitting at their desks, trying to make the kinds of decisions that their fathers used to make, their heroes used to

25

make. Why did it continue to feel like a masquerade? As if they were still trying on costumes for size? What they had seen in their heroes was their certainty, their self-confidence, their assurance; and they themselves knew what it felt like to *appear* that way. But in their own practices, they knew the degrees of uncertainty, the margin for lack of confidence, the innumerable arguments for alternatives to undermine assurance. Would it never be the same for them? Although they might appear as sure of themselves to the next generation as their predecessors had appeared to them, what they felt now was the challenge and the lack of certainty from the inside. They knew the strokes of reassurance that come with responses to their exercise of power. But it was never enough. It was the secret of men in positions of authority: to maintain the appearance of resoluteness, despite all of their own qualms which must be concealed. In the realm of action, reservations to one's own decisions are like poor relations who have to be paid off and kept hidden from view.

During the previous decade, Conrad had been in and out of Washington, in and out of dealings with federal agencies, negotiating grants, participating on commissions; he was familiar with the bureaucracies of the National Science Foundation and the Library of Congress and the Smithsonian Institution. While much of such experience engaged him and pleased him, there was always a depressing undertow—a kind of ill-concealed paranoia—that permeated almost all encounters with government. The necessity for checks and balances, of watchdog agencies, of affidavits and receipts and sworn statements for reports—all were based on the lack of trust, on the assumption that everyone will be deceitful unless there is elaborate machinery to prevent abuses. He was always left with the feeling of having been called before a criminal court and presumed guilty until proven innocent. It was because the stakes were so high, the amounts of money involved so enormous, and the possibility for abuse so easy that the principle of justifying every expenditure had been established.

But the procedures had become so complex that they resulted in making one feel smaller for having undertaken to ask for the moneys made available solely for the purpose of being asked for. So it was when he went to the government for help. Now the senior senator from Missouri was asking him for help, but in a situation where the President of the United States himself was the object of the distrust that permeates not only Washington but the nation as a whole. A year after Mr. Nixon had defeated Senator McGovern for the Presidency, Dr. Connolley could tell the joke: "We thought the choice was between a knave and a fool, but you see, we got both."

Conrad brought a picture of Senator Stonefort to his mind: he had aged well. Although his hair was all white and he had become a heavyset man, he carried himself with an impressive bearing, as if he were conscious that, at any moment, a photograph of him might be snapped. Conrad recognized that he looked forward to seeing Stoneface with pleasure. But, along the margin of uncertainty, he wondered how different was the "he"—who looked forward to that pleasure—made by receiving the melodramatic letter about Isabel?

The buzzer sounded. Mrs. Todd said, "Mrs. Kirkill is here . . . She doesn't have an appointment, but she wonders if she can see you for a few minutes?"

Conrad's eyes turned to the stack of forms marked Personal and Confidential, the interoffice communications, his calendar, wishing to escape into work that he liked to do. He asked, "Did she say what it's about?"

"Only that it's personal."

Conrad felt trapped. "All right. Will you show her in?"

Conrad had no liking for the Kirkills. They were a weird family. Brom Kirkill was an extremely tall, thin man with a face like a greyhound's. He had emerged from some back-

woods town in northwestern New York State, won a fellowship to Oxford, and studied in India. He was a Sanskrit and
Persian scholar who had remained in academic obscurity until
recent years when one of his courses, on the mystical poems
of Rumi, which happened to suit the desires for the bizarre of
the flower children generation, made him into a popular lecturer. He acted out the caricature of the absentminded professor—of which it seemed there remained precious few (and he
was very precious indeed). The only evening that Conrad had
ever eaten dinner at the Kirkills' home, some eight years before, ended with Brom appearing to pour brandy into little
silver goblets for each guest, despite the fact that the bottle
was empty; and, although Brom went through the charade for
each of the six people present, not one of them called him on
it.

Vivian Kirkill was a robust, brassy woman who probably
would have been happier married to an automobile salesman.
She had no more interest in her husband's work, or in the life
of the university, than she would have had in the study of
anything. But she took a stance as if she were a barmaid in the
presence of the gathering of Saturday-night, lower-class revel-
ers who wanted nothing but to get drunk as quickly as possible, whereas she was the sober dispenser of pleasures and
the bouncer as well. She always presented herself as the only
sensible person in a gathering of irresponsibles. A most unlikely couple. Where had Brom ever found her? Conrad imagined that she literally had been a barmaid, somewhere in Buffalo, when Brom taught at the university there.

Their son, Christian, was an early college dropout, and Conrad remembered with distaste that he was one of the influ-
ences that had suborned his daughter.

As he opened the door into the conference room, where he
had hoped to talk with her as briefly as possible, Vivian Kirkill, walking past the conference table, presumed that his posture at the door was an invitation for her to enter the study—
which she did, directly.

"I've never been in your office before," she said accusingly. "What possesses you to break the record, then?" Conrad forced a smile across his lips.

"Personal business," she said in a flat tone, lowering herself into one of the wing chairs and appraising the room like an auctioneer who has been called in to fix price tags on each item. "Yes, this is the kind of posh office I assumed you'd have."

Conrad seated himself behind his desk and slid his chair backward, trying to put as much space between them as possible. She made him feel vulnerable. She was a bulky woman in a heavy coat of violet-colored nubby wool, seated with her feet crossed at the ankles, wearing white galoshes that made Conrad think of spats. Whatever became of spats? She placed one black-gloved hand in her lap and the other on her large bosom. She sat erect, as if she were the last woman in the country to wear whalebone in her girdle. The yellow scarf that had covered her head was now draped across her shoulders, and her pink and white face was crowned with a garland of tinted blond curls that must have been set as "her style" by the phenomenal success of Shirley Temple as a child movie star. Only the network of thin red lines across her cheeks and around her nostrils gave a clear indication of her actual age.

Conrad repeated, "Personal business."

Barely turning her head, she continued to scan the objects in the study, pausing at the draperies and then at the carpet. "Are these your own things? Or do they belong to the university?"

"The books are my own. Does that have anything to do with . . .?"

"Well, yes," she interrupted him. "You see, it's personal property I'm worried about. For our declining years, you might say." She smiled narrowly, as if to mock the thought of any possibility that she might enter a decline. "Brom is not getting any younger, and his salary check is not getting any fatter." She looked him squarely in the eyes, as if he alone were responsible for that.

Conrad realized that her eyes were a clear green; he had not remembered them that color at all. Perhaps she changed the color of her eyes by wearing tinted contact lenses. He broke away from the thought by asking, "How can I help you?"

"Well, it's rather awkward." She threw up both her hands and then leveled them on the arms of her chair. "But I'm not one to avoid the awkward. I'll lay it right on the table. It's because of Christian."

Conrad realized why her appearance made him feel vulnerable. It tended to open all the wounds of resentment he felt against the boy. When he had first seen Christian, the child might have been about eleven years old—good-looking, with long, flaxen-colored hair, strongly interested in athletics but not a good student and something of a cutup. Good-natured enough. As a teenager, he became surly and slovenly. He would come to Conrad's house to pick up Caroline on a summer afternoon wearing filthy blue-jean cutoffs and showing his dirty bare feet.

"How old is he now?" Conrad asked.

"Middle twenties."

"Is he here?"

"Yes," Vivian said petulantly, "aggravating the trouble."

"I hadn't heard that he'd returned from London." Conrad forced himself to face the painful memory of the last time he had seen his daughter. He had agreed to pay for her to study at the Royal Academy of Dramatic Arts and sent her off to London, but she dropped out from that, too, soon enough. When Isabel and he stopped in England on their way back from Switzerland, he found that she was sharing a three-room flat with Christian Kirkill, an Irish girl, and two male blacks from Africa. Caroline played a guitar on the steps of the Cupid fountain in the center of Piccadilly Circus.

"What does Christian do?"

"He *lives* on a Kirkill fellowship. A self-study fellowship. What he *does* is privileged information. At least, I'm not privileged to have it. He says he's an artist."

"Yes, he *says* he is an artist." Conrad relived the walk from Piccadilly Circus, between Isabel, elegant and taciturn on one side of him, and Caroline, slatternly and taciturn on the other side, through Leicester Square, down a side street toward the National Gallery. They were to pick up Christian where he "worked" and take him along to dinner with them. Outside the iron railing on the sidewalk near the entrance to the National Portrait Gallery, Christian sat on a campstool before his easel among the half-dozen or so "artists" making pastel portraits of the tourists seated opposite them. He remembered Christian's work as two-dimensional, vaguely approximating the face of the sitter, insubstantial, thin, as if he saw only the impression of the face on a veil between them. By the end of the evening, after the dinner on Greek Street in Soho, and the gruesome view of the "pad" that Caroline shared with Christian, the Irish girl, and the two blacks, Conrad had tried to crush all of his resentment into a hard ball and cast it away from himself. He said to Isabel, "I could take the moral decay, I even think I could stand the sexual ambiguity of that 'commune'—but what I really can't bear is *no talent*. People who think they are artists and who've never been told they have no talent, who aren't even potentially artists enough to know what talent would be." The measure of his failure as a father was that, when he came to see her for the first time in half a year, all Caroline wanted to do was to rub his nose in her degradation and to get rid of him and his new wife as quickly as she possibly could.

Vivian Kirkill recalled him to the present situation. "Christian came over last night—to eat—and to tell us that he needs more money. He's thin. He says he's losing weight. He's afraid of some disease. He wants extensive medical examinations." She barked out a hollow little snicker. "What he wants is to take up permanent residence in some kind of rest home.

31

You know," she snapped out, "the only child syndrome. The only spoiled child, that is."

Sadly, Conrad said, "Yes, I know." He did not want his daughter to become the subject of this conversation. "Why are you telling me all this"—then he added gently, using for the first time her given name—"Vivian?"

"We give Christian an allowance. He wants more. What he threatened last night is that, if we *don't* give him *more*, he will go to the university and ask to garnishee his father's salary."

"I don't believe that's possible."

"That's what I thought. Although he says he'll plead his medical needs."

"I don't think that would make any difference. I've never heard of such a thing. He could go on welfare, or even more outrageous—he could get a job."

"He says he can get a court order to enforce our support."

"I think that's preposterous."

"Well, I'm very relieved to hear it. I'm glad I came to you." She heaved a heavy sigh of relief.

Conrad said, "Now look: I'm not in a position to give you legal advice, but from my experience of the way the university operates, it seems to me out of the question."

Vivian repeated, "I am relieved!" Tears began to well in her eyes. "It's not that this is my only problem . . ." she began.

Conrad stood up. "Don't take it so hard."

Vivian remained seated. She resisted being dismissed. "There are other things I'm worried about . . ."

Conrad came around his desk, stood by her side, and put his hand on her wrist with a reassuring squeeze. "You're a strong person," he said. "We all have to live with disappointments."

She looked up at him through green eyes that were clearing now. Strengthened by the feeling of being equal, she agreed. "Yes, we all do."

He helped her up and opened the door. She squared her shoulders and took a deep breath. "I won't bother you again," she said, with a certain brassy satisfaction, as though it were he who was leaving and she who remained in charge.

He closed the door from behind, grateful to be freed of the burden of her presence but struck by the hollowness of the truism that we all have to live with disappointments. Cold comfort. Why can't life be perfect—which means without any disappointments? And if not, why do we have to suffer from knowing how imperfect it is? If we had no idea of perfection . . . He smiled to himself. That would be like saying—if we had no heart, there would be no chance of having a heart attack. What makes for one man's "perfection" is the cause of the other's disappointment.

Conrad was more disturbed by the conversation with Vivian than he realized. He wanted to steady himself. He stood in front of his chair, resting his weight on broad hands pressed against the surface of the desk. He thought of the bottle of malt Scotch in the cabinet under the telephone, but it was too early in the day to take a drink. He lifted his head and gazed at the silk hanging on the wall opposite. There was nothing especially distinguished about it, either in rarity or beauty. It had been woven in Turkey about one hundred years before: a repeated pattern of golden flowers and green leaves tilted in one direction against rows of similar flowers tilted in the opposite direction, on a background of a rusted-red shiny thread. A six-foot-long, four-foot-wide piece of fabric cut from a bolt of cloth that might have been meant for a great lady's evening gown. He had taken the idea of hanging such a piece of fabric in his office from seeing something like it in the consultation room of a friend of his, Jerry Rosenblatt, who was a psychiatrist. "What's it for?" Conrad had asked.

His friend had replied, "I find it restful to look at. The rhythm of the repeated pattern makes me think there's always another chance. And then, depending on where the repeated image hangs, either high or low, and how the light strikes it, I'm shown that, no matter how strong the similarities are, no two experiences are identical."

It was all true. It relaxed him to study the repeated pattern; and the morning light, slowly moving downward along the length of the fabric, gave each flower its individuality, making the upper ones recess into the background and the middle ones shine out, reminding Conrad of the uniqueness of entities and encounters, and strengthening his desire to appreciate the particular value of each experience.

For a number of years before Conrad bought the piece of tapestry, there hung at that location on the wall a portrait of the Duke of La Rochefoucauld. It was a fine steel-point engraving in black and white, based on the original enameled miniature, smaller than the palm of one's hand, that for centuries has belonged to the royal family of the Netherlands. In the engraving, the portrait was surrounded by an oval frame that appeared to be carved out of marble, surrounded by carved flowers and ribbons, all above a carved mantelpiece holding up the ducal coat of arms, a sword, medal of honor, a single book, and laurel wreaths. The head of the nobleman showed a fashionable seventeenth-century wig all waved and curled, a high forehead, a long, slender carved nose, the lips decorated with mustaches briskly combed outward toward the cheeks, and under the lower lip just a hint of goatee stopping short of the rounded chin. The eyes that dominated the face were of a man reserved in the presence of an artist, not riveted on the sight of something outside of himself more than contemplating the condition of posing for a portrait. The effect was that of a man who had taken his own measure and was not entirely displeased. He wore a suit of armor, layered along his right arm like an armadillo, and over the coat of metal lay a wide collar of intricate lace fastened with tassels of gold thread: a variation on an iron hand inside a velvet glove.

On a whim—to take pleasure in the secrecy of it—Conrad decided to leave the picture there and hang the piece of fabric over it to conceal the portrait to all but himself. Suspended from a rod held out by hooks, the silk brocade stood a few inches away from the wall. The thought of La Rochefoucauld stimulated him; when Conrad let his mind focus on any one of the *Maxims,* he could feel his thoughts begin to race. He kept the engraving hidden, the way one keeps a pornographic picture hidden and goes to look at it occasionally to stimulate one's erotic imagination. Thus did La Rochefoucauld stimulate Conrad's intellectual imagination.

Now the interview with Vivian Kirkill was behind him. He phoned Mrs. Todd.

"Cameron would like to see you," she said.

Conrad looked at his calendar. "I don't have an appointment until ten. Would you ask him to come in now?"

"Difficult to get back to work?" Conrad asked of his old friend and colleague.

"No. It's such a relief to get through with the holiday season." Cameron McNeill was taller than Conrad and thinner, a sandy-haired Scotsman with a handlebar mustache and a broad, engaging smile. He had been brought in as chief accountant and subsequently became the comptroller. When Conrad hired him, he had said, "I need a man who can count—and I can count on." They had been through good times and bad together, and they were as dependable for each other as they were appreciative of each other. They stood in the center of Conrad's study and shook hands.

In his left hand Cameron held a letter and a check. "Do you know anything about this?" he asked.

The letter, from the National Science Foundation, was brief. It was obviously a covering letter in reference to the fact that the three-thousand-dollar check enclosed was in payment of a bill presented for consultation services. There was no reference to the name of the consultant. The check was made out to the university. But there was a project number referred to on both.

Cameron said, "I can't find any reference to such a project

35

in my files on the NSF. Do you happen to know anything about it?"

Conrad said, "No."

"Just thought I'd ask you first."

"Sorry, it doesn't ring a bell."

Conrad handed the check and the letter back to Cameron, who said: "Well, I'll call the NSF and track it down." He turned toward the door and stopped to look back. He winked at Conrad and added, "Have a good day."

For nearly half an hour Conrad worked on the documents before him. All payments of bills required two signatures; the forms were to be signed first by Cameron McNeill and countersigned by Conrad. The forms for faculty appointments and for changes of status were initiated by chairmen of departments and countersigned by Conrad. He had never understood why people who are responsible for keeping records, and for the authorization of changes, thought of the physical procedures to bring about such results as "paper pushing." He enjoyed the mechanics of changes and the manipulation of records as a carpenter appreciates his tools. The instruments for such processes seem impersonal, but they always require the human touch to make them effective. These were the orchestrations that enabled the music to be played.

But then other sounds were heard. The radiator under the windows began to knock, as if a hammer were being played along the pipes. Conrad went over to turn the knob and cut down on the heat. He saw Theodore Evats approaching through the snow-covered quadrangle. At that instant, he was passing in front of the bronze sculpture of the first president of the university. Professor Evats wore a gray fur-trimmed hat and a gray woolen coat. Everything about him is gray, Conrad thought. Pale gray. A bloodless man, but punctual. The chairman of the History Department. It was he who had made an appointment for ten o'clock that morning. At just about this moment, he thought, Isabel would be waking up.

Conrad met him in the conference room and they sat down

facing each other across the table. Mrs. Todd had taken Evats's hat and coat in the waiting room, and he appeared in a gray flannel suit and a university necktie against his white shirt. He carried a briefcase, which he put down on the floor. He took off his glasses to shine them with a white linen handkerchief. He was very neat. His almost entirely bald head was shiny, and the flesh of his face was scrubbed clean. He wove his fingers together and placed them primly on the table before him. He was a very modest man, Conrad thought, but in him that seemed presumptuous, as he had so little to be self-effacing about. His academic reputation had been made in his mid-forties by the publication of a two-volume work on the effects of the enclosures of public grazing lands on the economic development of England in the eighteenth century.

"I hope you've had a good morning so far," Professor Evats said, "because what I have to say will not add to your pleasures."

"As a matter of fact, I have," Conrad replied. "But then I have very low standards."

They both smiled. There was nothing haughty about Mr. Evats. He was a short man who seemed to wish he were smaller so that he could get by without ever having to be observed. Conrad had been a guest at his home only twice, once at a cocktail party, and once for dinner, at which he was astonished to discover that it was Mrs. Evats who sat at the head of the table, and the chairman of the History Department sat at her right, like a favorite child. Mrs. Evats came from Czechoslovakia. Conrad assumed that whatever it was had crucially inhibited Mr. Evats, it had probably prevented him from ever making love with a woman of his own country.

"You will remember Mr. St. Cyr," Evats began.

"Of course. The department recommended tenure in November."

"Yes." Mr. Evats's eyeglasses were hit by the morning light in such a way that Conrad saw him like a comic strip character

37

who has only two large white disks where his eyes ought to be. "I'm afraid that was a mistake."

"Oh?" Conrad said coolly. "What has happened in six weeks to make so much of a difference?"

"You will remember," Evats repeated, "that the problem over his tenure in previous years was caused by the minimal number of his publications."

"Yes."

"Only a few articles . . ." Mr. Evats's face was moved toward the expression of a sneer, but didn't quite get that far. "And then, about six months ago, the university press brought out his magnum opus, a book on *The Diffusion of Civility in the German Principalities from 1685 to 1820.*"

"Yes, and it was well received."

"In the *Times Literary Supplement,* in *The Annals of the American Academy of Political and Social Science,* and in the *Library Journal.*"

"They were very important, as I remember, in the department's recommendation for tenure."

"True." Mr. Evats bent over toward the floor and brought up to the table from his briefcase the book and a copy of a journal. "The winter issue of the *Journal of Modern History,* however, did not appear until just after Christmas."

"Is there a negative review in it?"

"There is a one-sentence review. Let me read it to you." He fingered the journal open to where he had left a place mark, and spread it flat on the table before him. "It says: '*The Diffusion of Civility* by Henri St. Cyr, 532 pages, $23.00, is a translation of *Das höfische Zeitalter in seinen Popularformen* by Eugen Dischgauer, published originally in Dresden in 1936 by the Hecht Verlag.' "

Conrad reached for the journal, turned it around on the table, and read the sentence to himself. "Is it true?"

"We have a very great library, Mr. Taylor," the chairman of the History Department assured him, reaching down into his briefcase again, and proffering the German tome.

"It looks as though it's never been taken out."

"As far as I can make out, it hasn't been."

"And you compared the texts?"

"I have. Mr. St. Cyr's 'book' is simply a work of plagiarism."

"Well . . ." Conrad said slowly, resting one hand on each book, "that is very sad."

"It is most regrettable."

"And no one in the department had any suspicion of this?"

"Not as far as I can make out. But then, St. Cyr is the only member of the department in German history prior to the twentieth century."

Conrad added, "German social and cultural history. What about the people in German literature?"

"I've asked. None of them had ever heard of the German original. It was one of those books that got lost because of the time at which it appeared. Just before the war began. Apparently, there weren't even reviews in German or British journals, let alone in the United States. St. Cyr must have believed that it was a lost book and that he'd get away with this."

"Won't he?"

Mr. Evats showed his amazement. "How can he?" he said, pointing to the *Journal of Modern History*.

"Have you confronted him with this?"

"No, I wanted to talk with you first." He became meek. "I wondered what you thought we ought to do, but I didn't want to get in touch with you before the holidays were over."

Conrad thought: He wants a gold star for good behavior, whereas the fact is the department had voted to grant St. Cyr tenure on the basis of an inadequate evaluation of his book.

"I wasn't particularly happy about his appointment . . ." Evats began again. "He does have a fair reputation as a good teacher, but I was never impressed by his scholarship. You know those articles of his were really on nonproblems. For example, that one on the ode by Schiller in honor of the Duke of Weimar—where he sets up the question of whether it is truly laudatory or whether it is meant ironically, and then goes

39

on to prove that it was meant ironically. I've been told that nobody ever thought it was purely laudatory."

"Did your colleagues share your reservations?"

"I believe so."

The fingers of Conrad's left hand began tapping along the cover of the book before him. "Then why the hell were you so eager to grant tenure as soon as his one book was published?"

"We don't have anyone else in that period."

Conrad said, "Hopeless."

"What do you want me to do?"

"He will have to be let go for cause, but we have to find some way to save face, too."

"I hoped you might talk with him."

I'm sure you did, Conrad thought. You coward.

"This is the kind of thing that happens when you don't make judgments on the strength of your convictions, but by default."

Evats tried to make light of it. "I thought you might speak to him in his native language."

Evats knew that Conrad was bilingual. St. Cyr had come from the Sorbonne in the late sixties; he had learned German as a child during the Nazi occupation of France.

Conrad said, "The only common language we're supposed to speak here is the integrity of scholarship." It was the kind of remark that made people think him stuffy. On the one hand, he had no desire to let Evats think he could butter him up and, on the other hand, he actually meant what he said. "Why don't you leave these things here with me, see if you can get hold of St. Cyr, and let's meet together later this afternoon?" They were both standing now. "Try for three o'clock, will you? If I don't hear from you before then, I'll presume he can make it."

"Yes. Certainly. By all means," Evats said. Conrad was afraid he was going to add, "sir." In another life, he would have been happier as a footman to some colonel.

Back in his study, Conrad asked Mrs. Todd to get the director of the university press on the phone. In a few minutes he was told that the director was at their London office; would he like to speak with the assistant director?

"Brian," he began, "what would you do, if you found you had an illegitimate book on your hands, in order to make it legitimate?"

Cautiously, he said, "I'm afraid I don't know what you mean."

"You published a book about nine months ago, *The Diffusion of Civility*, that purports to be by Henri St. Cyr."

"Oh, you've heard about the review in the *Journal of Modern History*."

"Yes. If this is a translation and not an original work, I suppose you can expect to be sued by the original publisher?"

"Well, actually we have looked into this and found out that the publishing house no longer exists. It was Hecht Verlag in Dresden, and they were destroyed during the war. There's no such firm left anymore, with anybody to make any claims. Bombed out. No records, no contracts. No press left." He sounded smug.

"That takes care of your obligation to the original publisher. What about the author?"

Brian said, "He emigrated to England in 1938. Taught at Reading, outside London, until the war came. He's dead. There was no family." Out of the kindness of his heart, Brian added, "Pity."

Conrad asked, "What about your obligation to the buyer of the book?"

"In what sense?"

"So that he knows what he's buying." He began to show his irritation. "In other words, how can you make it clear that this is a translation?"

After a pause, the assistant director of the press said cautiously, "I suppose we could insert an erratum slip."

Conrad laughed. "Quite an error! What about the possibility

41

of removing the title page and putting in a new one? And putting on a new binding?"

"Yes, I suppose that can be done."

"Giving the true author's name."

"Yes."

"How much will it cost to change the title page, binding and jacket?"

"I'll have to find out."

"Do that, please, and let me know. You'll call back this afternoon, won't you?"

"I'll try to," Brian conceded.

At eleven o'clock, Mrs. Todd brought in a cup of coffee along with the morning mail. "Tom would like to talk with you," she said, "about the enrollment studies."

Conrad looked at his watch. "Ask him to come in at eleven-thirty." She nodded and left him alone. This fragmenting of time . . . Conrad thought, this breaking up of a day into scheduled appointments, meetings, conferences, consultations, telephone interruptions—so that a day ends up like a mosaic of many different-colored, tiny stones mortared together to form a picture that can be seen as a whole only at a distance or in retrospect—is so unlike what one imagines waking up in the morning. I am going to live my day, he thinks. *My* day. But that ends up meaning only I will try to hold my own, maintain some kind of equilibrium, continue to be myself, whatever happens during this day. Every day. No matter how routine the sequence of fragments might appear on the surface, an appointment with the chairman of the History Department at ten, squash at noon, lunch at one, the security guards at two-thirty—those are only labels on little bottles. The taste of each is unpredictable. It would be so easy to lose balance, to lash out, to shout "Don't bother me," or "Fuck off! you asshole"—if it were not that it is not *my* day alone. It is a day in the life of the institution, and my personal responses are tempered by my judgments of what is good for the university and not just for myself; or what is good for the long haul and not just for the moment. There is a musical term—what is it?—descant? decant?—for a line of melody played against a theme, the origin of counterpoint; my concern for the life of the institution is the one, my consciousness of myself—interior conditions: thoughts and feelings—is the other. And only I can hear the counterpoint, or the disharmony.

He went through the morning's interoffice memos and letters from outside. There was a preponderance of mail for the admissions office, complaints regarding criteria for acceptance, mainly from alumni who had assumed that their qualified children would be given preference. But there was so much more than that to determine priority. Complaints from foreign applicants claiming that they needed to know a year or two in advance whether they would be admitted in order to arrange for passports and fellowship grants. Complaints justified and unjustified. It was that time of year. Then there was a curious letter from Salt Lake City saying that the under-signed—Mr. Chancellor Drake, a positively Elizabethan name—writing on the embossed stationery of a legal firm, would be telephoning that afternoon; a letter dated six days before, obviously delayed by the logjam of mail between Christmas and New Year's. An announcement of a mystery. Mr. Drake wished "to discuss a matter of the utmost confidentiality and of considerable substantial value to the future of the university." Conrad reckoned that either "considerable" or "substantial" would have been enough. But in the West they tend to exaggerate. *Ten*-gallon hats?

Cameron put his head through the doorway. "Mind if I come in?"

"Not at all."

He placed a note on Conrad's desk, between the neat stacks of mail, and laid his large hand over it. "Let me tell you what this says. The mystery of the three thousand dollars is solved. The NSF tells me that the check is for the consultation fee for

David Bach. It was made out to the university because the bill had come in on university stationery. Now, I've checked back on Bach's salary. He didn't take any leave of absence, any time off, during October. In other words, he got paid his full salary for the month of October and he also sent the NSF a bill for one week's consultation during the same month."

"*Merde*," Conrad said.

"We could return the check," Cameron said, straightening up and folding his arms across his chest.

"We have to."

"The university has already paid Bach for that week's work."

With a heavy sigh, Conrad said, "I'll talk to him about it."

"I don't envy you." Cameron snorted, patted Conrad on the shoulder, and turned to leave. "I'll keep the check in my office." He walked through the doorway sideways, letting Tom Spofford enter as he left.

Cameron doesn't envy me, Conrad realized, but is there some man who does? who wishes to take Isabel from me? whom she would want to leave me for?

"Eleven-thirty," Tom said. "Happy New Year!"

"And the same to you." Conrad smiled. It was easy to smile at Tom: the eager youth, the embodiment of being bright-eyed and bushy-tailed. The protégé. "You wanted to talk about the enrollment figures."

"Well, maybe you ought to look them over first. You might have some questions. You'll need them for the budget meeting tomorrow."

"What questions should I have?"

Tom laughed. "They're pretty much what we went over last week. What I get from the admissions office makes me think they're right. The projected income is simple multiplication. The only question is the percentage of grant support."

"Big enough question. But I'll go over the figures after lunch." Tom laid a folder down at the edge of the desk. "Time to play?" he asked.

"The court's reserved for twelve."

"Let's take off."

Separately they loaded themselves with the scarf and gloves, the boots and hats and overcoats of winter, and met at Mrs. Todd's office.

"I'll be back about two," Conrad said. Mrs. Todd had brought her own lunch in a paper bag.

After entering the gymnasium building, they separated—Conrad to the faculty dressing room and Tom toward the student and staff lockers. "We have court number four today," Tom said. "Meet you there." And then, over his shoulder, threw the challenge, "Bet I beat ya." At which Conrad smiled tightly, thinking he should say something like, "There's no race on." For Conrad, a drawback was threatening their sympathy with each other. He enjoyed the pleasure of the boss-and-subordinate relationship, which had become a teacher-and-pupil rapport; but the intimations of equality between them, as when Tom suggested a direct competitiveness, irked him—the younger man was overstepping the bounds, taking liberties. Conrad disliked being aware of this judgment on his part, which implied a resentment against youth pushing itself forward in general rather than criticism of Tom in particular. Conrad Taylor was a middle-aged man who had no son; he chose to submerge even the hint of resentment under the pleasure he took in helping the young man grow up. Tom is my son substitute, he told himself, and relaxed the tightness of the smile, saying nothing, indulging youth.

The faculty locker room was not crowded. Conrad nodded to the few men he recognized. He opened the green steel locker and began to undress. Conrad had never been a serious athlete and never enjoyed the locker room machismo of the devoted jocks, but he liked to keep himself in good shape. When he was an adolescent and his father worried about his becoming a bookworm, an intellectual without a satisfactory social life or an adequately trained body, he had once confided to Conrad, at the time insisting that his son go out for the swimming team—"Many more girls are seduced by having their hands run over hard abdominal muscles than are won by running their hearts over a sharp brain." Conrad snorted at the recollection; he had made it both ways, though not with all that many women. As he pulled on his sweat socks and sneakers, the white shorts and tee shirt, he thought of his wife. Isabel would be at the riding stable now, exercising her horse. Both he and Isabel kept in good shape. They would make love that evening. She had said, last night, that she'd like to dress for dinner.

Tom was in the squash court. Through the framed glass window Conrad could see the young man slam the black ball with his racket. He was practicing his aim to strike just above the lower foul line. What an attractive young man, he thought: well proportioned—with strong shoulders, a lean, flat chest, and powerful legs. His squash left a great deal to be desired— he had much more strength than he had skill, but training is what produced gracefulness and cunning. He was a raw youth, a diamond in the rough, and Conrad meant to polish him.

When he entered the court and they took positions to volley for the serve, Conrad caught in the corner of his eye the vision of the boy crouched and ready—eager to be tested, his long black hair parted in the middle with a sweatband around his head, the smooth flesh over his high cheekbones already flushed, his mouth open in anticipation, all of his muscles tensed—and he was filled with admiration. He felt he was right to try to help the boy make something of himself that otherwise would never come about. They began to play. Conrad won the serve.

From Conrad's point of view, Tom Spofford had appeared out of nowhere. He had responded to an advertisement for an assistant to the executive vice-president for the college that called for training in statistics. The ad had been placed in *The New York Times* for three days during one week and twice in the Sunday edition, and Conrad had received seventy-eight applications. Tom was the only one who delivered his letter in person and asked if he could wait to be interviewed as long as he was there. Conrad felt that everything about Tom was shining: his fresh-scrubbed, clean-shaved face, the newness of his mail-order green plaid suit. He was such a hick, such a country boy, unlike the sophisticated students at the university: so ready to do the job that was waiting rather than impose his demands on the world to make it do what he wanted. He actually said, "I want to be of service." He was at the ready: from the neatness of the square-cut nails on his long strong fingers to the polish on his new black shoes. Within five minutes, Conrad knew he would hire him.

Tom came from South Dakota, where his father was a lay minister in a Pentecostal church. He had gone to a Bible college in the Midwest and shown an exceptional aptitude for mathematics, which won him a scholarship to a technical and engineering graduate school in New Jersey. But, while he excelled in statistics, he had no desire to become an engineer. As he was completing his master's degree and wondering about which way to go, he discovered Manhattan: spent his weekends there, haunting all the museums of New York, standing up at theaters and concerts, crashing the pads of mere acquaintances. It was during one such weekend that he'd seen the ad for the job Conrad was offering and took the train to New Haven the next day to present himself. He felt certain he could work up the kind of reports, make the kinds of analyses, interpret the data, and carry out the comparative studies that the job required. That he "felt certain" came through to Conrad as a plea: try me, give me a chance. Conrad regarded him with incipient affection. He drew a cigarette out of an inner pocket in his jacket and before he had raised it to his lips, Tom had produced a lighter and lit the cigarette for him. Of course, he was hired.

He worked well. Not only did he fulfill the assignments given to him quickly and efficiently, he was always ready to ask, "Is there something else you'd like me to do?" He understood machinery and could fix a car motor or a television set; he would take the draperies to the cleaners, or work a better linseed oil treatment into the table in the conference room than the janitor ever thought of using. Conrad took him to lunch, began to play squash with him, talked with him at the end of the day—an hour or so over Scotch and water. Their offices had been converted from a floor of dormitory suites in a nineteenth-century building. Conrad's was without a bathroom or even a washbasin of his own. In Tom's office, behind a hinged panel, was a sink and a small refrigerator. At about 4:30, he would bring Conrad their glasses, ice, and water.

Tom was twenty-three years old and had a passion for success but no sense of direction; he was good-natured and hopeful, which Conrad took to be unassuming and without delusions of grandeur, although Mrs. Todd did not warm to him, for she was to be a lawyer's wife, whereas Tom lived with his girlfriend, who had a menial job, together with two or three others in some loose kind of commune and talked with Mrs. Todd about expanding her consciousness.

Within the first six months, Conrad discovered that the self-assuring attitude of "God will provide" which seemed to be Tom's inheritance from his father—strengthened by his having been hired for this job—was counterbalanced by a greed for salvation. At least for extreme experiences. As their late afternoon conversations became more personal, Tom confessed to having lost his faith in his father's church, and sought for substitutes in LSD and other drug-induced dreams of release or of community. Still, in contrast to his daughter's chaotic life, it seemed to Conrad that Tom had those experiments under control; performing his job—not only adequately but with cheerfulness—was an anchor into the real world that his daughter lacked. She had not made her connections with other people's needs; she lived out her fantasy of being a free spirit, which was radically different from being engaged in life. She

wanted to live on a plane above the world's corruptions—
somewhere in midair. Tom seemed willing to float free only
on his own time.

When Tom spoke to him about money problems—because
of his car, for example—Conrad arranged for a loan from the
university's credit union, thinking that it was entirely unlike
his daughter's appeals for money. Tom had a salary as security
against the loan; his daughter was only a drain and a spend-
thrift. Conrad thought the boy's appearance ought to be im-
proved. The green plaid suit would have to go. He gave
Tom a check at Thanksgiving so he could buy a new suit,
and the young man came back a few days later in a dark
blue outfit with an almost imperceptible red stripe in it,
high waisted without a belt, which Conrad thought handsome.

"I knew you'd like it," Tom said.

"How did you know that?"

"I saw it with your mind."

Conrad smiled broadly, with the thought that this is the
measure of influence.

Late one afternoon, sitting down to a drink, Tom began a
line of questions with "How did you become . . ." Conrad took
the invitation to outline a program for him. "You'll have to
continue graduate work," he said. "You ought to get your
Ph.D. It's like a tuxedo. There are some places you just don't
go without a tuxedo—or a Ph.D."

"Do you think I can get to become—you know—an administrator, like you, someday? . . ." Conrad sensed that Tom used
the words "executive" and "administrator" like a jeweler fondling loose precious stones in his hands, trying to imagine the
proper setting for them.

They had lunch in the office one noon when Conrad had
brought goat's cheese and red wine and black olives, and he
thought, This is a lunch such as a protector and his protégé
might have eaten in ancient Greece or Imperial Rome—for
three thousand years in Western civilization, an older man

49

might have sat down to a midday meal with a fresh-faced younger man he hoped to instruct and influence to follow his footsteps—and these were the foods they shared: the goat's cheese, the red wine. "You plan to start work on your doctorate next fall," Conrad began, meaning: Follow my suggestions, take my advice. . . . All that you desire will come in time, and I will help you formulate those desires. Right now, all you desire is amorphous; I will give it shape, names, conditions for achievement. So much in life is a matter of luck. All you can do is make yourself into someone good luck will come looking for.

Only one incident had annoyed Conrad, just after Thanksgiving. He had left for a meeting but, having forgotten his reading glasses, returned to his office five minutes later to enter his study and find Tom there, holding back the patterned-silk wall hanging, gazing at the portrait of La Rochefoucauld. "What are you doing?" he asked brusquely.

Tom was flustered. He dropped the fabric back into place. "I thought I saw you look behind this once and I wondered what was there."

"Why didn't you ask me if you could see it?"

"I thought you might say no."

"I might not have wanted you to, right?"

Tom was ashamed of himself but countered by asking, "Why do you keep it covered like that?"

"To remind me of hidden resources," Conrad snapped out. He collected his glasses from the desk and left Tom standing alone in the study with the farewell remark, "Don't be afraid to take no for an answer," thinking—You can't have everything at once. But he left him alone, walked out without telling him to leave. In fact, he closed the study door behind him, leaving Tom stranded in it.

Conrad never referred to the incident again. But Tom brought up the question, "Who was La Rochefoucauld?" soon afterward at lunch.

"You've never heard of him?"

"No. I take it you admire him."

"He was a good friend to me earlier in life." Conrad stopped himself with a laugh and brushed aside the private joke.

"What is it you admire?"

Conrad thought for a moment before answering, "He never lets us forget how little control we have of our lives."

"You have plenty of control!" Tom replied.

At your age, it looks that way, Conrad thought. Then he told him something of the life and writings of La Rochefoucauld. ". . . In his middle age he gave up dreams of political power— a man of action manqué—and became a thinker . . . unsparing of all wishful thinking. He named the limits of human powers and showed how narrow the margin is where we can struggle with them." Tom regarded him blankly. "It's all crystallized in the *Maxims*. You should read them."

"I will."

Conrad imagined that everything he had said was as remote from the young man's experience as if he had been talking about the physiology of amoebas. Then it occurred to him that he could make a connection. "When you discovered museums in New York, did you ever go to the Cloisters?"

"Yes."

"Did you see the series of tapestries of the Unicorn?"

Happily, Tom answered, "Yes!"

"Well, they belonged to La Rochefoucauld's family for generations. They were on the walls of his mansion in Paris when he died." He left Tom to contemplate the fact that his eyes had played on works of art that had once hung before La Rochefoucauld's eyes as his private possession.

"But why did you say he was a friend earlier in life?"

"Oh, that was a joke. What I meant was I took him very seriously when I was in graduate school. I wanted to write my dissertation on him. But I was talked out of it."

"How come?"

"Fashion. He was completely out of fashion. I could work on the history of psychology—and scope would make up for depth—but I couldn't concentrate on him alone. Actually my adviser was contemptuous of the idea. He wouldn't take it seriously."

"Why not?"

"Well, frankly—from my prejudiced point of view—for two reasons. La Rochefoucauld was an aristocrat, a nobleman, and in a democracy only professionals are taken seriously. And secondly he was not a 'systematic writer,' and in twentieth-century scholarship, to be systematic is all. Besides, there are no 'happy endings' in La Rochefoucauld. Nobody wins. It was the wrong taste for the times."

"Everyone wants to win something," Tom said wistfully.

The squash game was intense; they were drenched in perspiration within a half hour. They began to play more slowly and yet there was an accident. Tom stood close to the back wall as he shot the ball fiercely into the corner of the walls opposite; the ball came back toward Conrad and bounced so close to him that he leaned backward and thrust the racket well behind him to meet it, but Tom had come forward and the racket hit him squarely in the chest and knocked the wind out of him. He moaned and his shoulders slumped; he crossed his arms over his ribs. Conrad grabbed the young man with both hands. "Lie down," he said, and held his shoulders until Tom was down on the floor stretched out on his back. "I'm so sorry!"

Tom said, "My fault."

The feel of his body, through the heft of Tom's shoulders, held in his hands, amazed Conrad with its solidity and its warmth. That extraordinary firmness and fullness of youth. Conrad had never touched him before. If you have no son, when would you have occasion to hold a youth of twenty-three by the shoulders? It gave Conrad the most oddly revitalizing sensation. He patted the boy's muscular arm until he felt embarrassed, as if he were misappropriating something. It made him think of Tom's girlfriend who had come to the office four or five times; she conveyed such a sure sense of possessiveness about him.

"It's okay," Tom said, slowly raising himself up on one elbow.

"Take your time."

Tom breathed deeply. Then he said with a smile, "I'm all right now." He got to his knees and gradually stood up straight.

Conrad could not restrain himself from patting him on the back. He wanted to feel the thickness of the body again. They left the squash court together. Alone in the faculty shower, Conrad considered Tom's girlfriend; her name was Ronda or Rhoda, he couldn't remember which. Not an attractive girl. Too thin. With long, straight, pale hair and chubby cheeks. A strange-looking girl in a flat brown jumper without gracefulness. She squinted, which implied to Conrad: She ought to wear glasses but refuses to do so. Tom said she felt he was under Conrad's "spell." There was something peremptory about her. She was always ready to needle Tom, as if she were a governess come to pick up her charge at the end of a visit— knowing that he must have misbehaved or been given too much latitude in her absence. When Tom spoke of her to Conrad, extolled her, saying how bright she was—she'd won a scholarship to Columbia—and Conrad asked why she hadn't taken it, Tom answered that she wanted a scholarship to Radcliffe. Conrad drew the implication that she was one of those "rule or ruin" creatures who must have things exactly her way or would make it hell for everybody else.

"How did you meet?" Conrad once asked Tom.

"On the Green. I was sitting on a bench—last summer— playing my recorder. A friend of mine was playing the bongo drums when she came over and sat down next to me. She said, 'My name's Rhoda. I'd like to be your friend,' and I said, 'You will be. You are.' That's how it began."

How simple, Conrad thought. And then they screwed. Well,

not all that different from how he came to meet Isabel. But of a different order of complexity. Tom had nothing to lose.

And now, if there was any truth in the anonymous letter, how much did Conrad stand to lose?

Precisely at one o'clock Conrad Taylor arrived at the door of the Faculty Club. Everything about the building pleased him: the eighteenth-century white clapboard exterior, the brass plate on the door, the fact that the renovated interior was far larger and more modern than the exterior gave any reason to expect—the new inside of the old and the large inside of the small were paradoxes that engaged him; his club, his village inn. He was "at home." No, Professor Webster had not yet arrived. Conrad told the majordomo he would wait in the bar.

There were a few acquaintances standing up at the long, polished, mahogany railing and half a dozen members seated at small tables around the room. Conrad nodded and smiled. He ordered a Bloody Mary. He felt bodily enhanced by having played squash, charged by his physical contact with Tom, cleaned by the shower, and renewed by having gone back to work after the long holiday weekend. He let his gaze wander about the familiar room.

Brom Kirkill sat engrossed in conversation with a female student of his; David Bach waited restlessly—his legs crossed, one foot swinging out and back like a pendulum. Conrad was particularly amused by seeing two people who happened to be sitting back to back, oblivious of each other. One was Julian Hügelmann, a visiting professor from the Jung Institute in Zurich, and the other was Lord Lisle, formerly governor-general of Jamaica and then of Cyprus, a British diplomat, sometime ambassador to Washington, there to deliver a lecture that evening as a guest of the Department of Political Science. It was the fact that they had their backs to each other that delighted Conrad. Their lives were spent looking in opposite directions. Hügelmann, as a Jungian analyst, looked inside people to find a community of archetypes, The Wise Old Man, the Anima—all that sort of thing—so no one need ever be alone; each had everything he needed for a community in his unconscious; all the necessary players of any human drama were within each one of us. And Lord Lisle looked beyond individual people to nations, "families of nations," as he so often put it, in order to argue for the cooperation of the abstractions called peoples and countries to make a community, a single unity for mutual advantage. With the two of them rested the introvert's and the extrovert's solutions to all the problems of the world; one would save the World by rescuing the Self, and the other would rescue the Self by saving the World. What would happen if they were face to face rather than back to back? Conrad chuckled.

He took a sip of the drink the bartender made just the way he liked it. Then remembered that he ought to speak with David Bach. Ah, David Bach. The man was unbelievably vain. He had been exceptionally good-looking when he was young, very much the Nordic ideal: tall and blond with a ruddy complexion, straightforward and seductive. His weakness was for adolescent girls. He would marry an eighteen-year-old and divorce her by the time she was twenty-one. Each next wife was seventeen or eighteen. He had been married five times, and his affairs were numberless. Conrad had once said to Isabel, "I'm sure that when he uses the phrase 'My better half,' he means his left profile." With time, the good looks had faded, he had paled. He was a scientist of accomplishment, but he looked washed out, bleached, self-consumed. With his drink in his hand, Conrad moved toward Bach's table and stood above him for a moment. "David," he said, interrupting the silent meditation, "Happy New Year; how are you?"

"I'm fine. And you?"

"Swell. But I do have a question for you. Any chance you could drop by my office later this afternoon?"

"What's it about?"

"I have to ask you about a . . . a confusion." Conrad was suddenly aware of how much their conversation would embarrass both of them.

"Ask me now."

"This is hardly the place," Conrad replied. "Could you come by at about four or so?"

Bach rubbed his forehead with long, bony fingers, trying to remember his schedule. "Yes, I think so. I'll call you if I can't make it."

"Fine. See you later. Enjoy your lunch." Conrad returned to the bar, continuing to think of David Bach—the geologist, one of the few scientists in the world who had been granted the privilege and the pleasure of analyzing samples of the surface of the moon brought back by astronauts, a connoisseur of eighteen-year-old girls and the surface of the moon. . . .

Brita von Bickersdorf of the Law School approached the bar and ordered a Scotch and water. She was an odd mixture and had come to the university, in a sense, by accident. Herself a Swedish lady of the Staël-Holstein minor nobility, she had married a penniless Prussian prince in the early thirties, and, as ardent anti-Nazis, together they fled Germany for England shortly after Hitler came to power. Her husband became a renowned biochemist at the Medical Research Council unit outside Cambridge. The only way the university was able to lure him to the States in the early 1950s was to offer a position on the faculty to his wife as well, although she had no reputation through publications but was established as a lecturer in jurisprudence. Their transplantation took an entirely unpredictable turn. He seemed to dry up and then fall apart in this alien atmosphere. During the half-dozen years in which he felt his originality increasingly spent, and grew despondent, she came into her own as a leading theoretician of international law, a teacher, and a consultant, influential at both the university and the United Nations. She blossomed, she flourished. Her husband took early retirement at sixty, and within a few months committed suicide.

Brita Staël-Holstein von Bickersdorf stood next to Conrad, a large woman, without makeup, her gray hair pulled back into a bun at the nape of her neck, a middle-aged woman in a tweed pantsuit and a sporty print shirt open at the neck, standing erect, as if an inner censor shouted the order "Good posture!" to her every few minutes, so that her nearly military bearing reminded Conrad of a white goddess, a woman whose breasts stood at attention, with hands on her hips, jutting her elbows outward to make sure that others kept a respectful distance. She had the appealing rounded face of a woman who is overweight by choice.

"You're looking splendid," Conrad said.

"I can't imagine why. I am overworked and undersatisfied." She was not complaining, only stating her facts.

"Then it must become you."

"I don't know." She sipped her drink. She shook her head and shrugged her shoulder in mock worry. "I have three courses this semester, five doctoral candidates, I must submit a brief to the World Court at The Hague in March, I am on the Board of Advisers for the UNESCO Human Rights Review Committee, which meets once a month in New York, and I am working on a book that I've been trying to finish for three years. I don't think I'll survive." Her smile invited compassion.

"Well, if you don't survive," Conrad said, "you will go directly to heaven, having endured purgatory here on earth."

"Oh, I don't think I should like that," Brita von Bickersdorf said, "I wouldn't find any of my friends *there!*"

They laughed, and then she excused herself, recognizing her luncheon date entering the lobby. When she swept away from Conrad she scattered behind her the scent of a sweet perfume—as if a gust of wind had pelted a handful of apple blossoms on his face.

Brom Kirkill laughed a high, shrill laugh and slapped his knees, attracting Conrad's attention away from thoughts of Brita. The female student who sat opposite Kirkill looked to the floor shyly as if she should never have said anything so wicked or witty; or was she embarrassed that he simply over-appreciated whatever it was she had said? Conrad had never overcome the resentment he felt toward Brom Kirkill. Four years before, he had been invited to participate in an international conference of university administrators to be held in Bombay, and when he told Kirkill he was going to India, Brom said, "You must see the cages."

"What are they?" Conrad asked.

"That's not for me to tell you," Brom Kirkill replied. "Go see them. Just ask to be taken to see them." He was kittenish and know-it-all at the same time. "It's something you have to do, if you're in Bombay." Conrad assumed it was the local zoo.

But it turned out to be one of the most chilling experiences of his life.

Everything about Bombay oppressed him. He was there in the month of April when the air was heavy with the fetid odor of burning cow dung all the way in from the airport. Thousands of people of all ages lived on the streets, ate, urinated, and slept on the sidewalks all the way up to the very steps of the big and well-appointed hotel he was put up in. Everywhere he looked there was an excess of humanity: tidal waves of dark people moving together as a crowd, many of the women pretending to make themselves invisible in billowing black dresses and black veils that allowed only their bright black eyes to appear; all those pairs of piercing eyes moving among the slender men in white, young or gray-bearded, men in homespun muslin drapery or in European-style business suits; all of which created the almost continuous fear that to walk the streets of Bombay was to live in perpetual danger of being trampled to death by an endless crowd that might go berserk at any moment. It was a place where there is a sect of believers who leave their dead exposed to carrion birds, to be consumed by vultures. Conrad could not escape the thought that the air smelled of death—even on the campus of the University of Bombay, with its Victorian brick buildings, where the conference took place, incongruous-looking, as if the buildings of technical schools in Sheffield or Manchester or Birmingham had been transported to this tropical campus a few blocks from a harbor on the Arabian Sea.

Conrad wore summer clothes made of seersucker and still felt oppressed by the heat even in his air-conditioned hotel room, and he slept badly during the entire week he was there. He had made the gross error of forgetting to declare himself an alcoholic on passing through customs, and therefore without a visitor's license and ration book he was unable to buy a drink of alcohol. He was afraid to drink the water. He felt particularly fragile and likely to contract some grotesque disease. On entering the emigration shed at the airport, he had seen the blackboard listing the countries where cholera was rampant and from which travelers had to submit to special examinations. Bombay itself, he could see, was a huge modern city, a creation of British imperialism, not an ancient native city like Lahore or Delhi, hardly older than Chicago or Denver; but for him it was the end of the world.

The conference itself was a source of depression. The representatives of underdeveloped countries in Asia and Africa saw their problems of higher education as unsolvable: trapped as they were between the dream of giving every one of their millions and millions of citizens an education equivalent to that at Oxford and Cambridge, and the total impossibility of realizing such a desire. They were incapable of taking compromising steps, gradual, practical steps to achieve limited goals that were within their limited powers. Even though they could not have the best for everyone all at once, they felt it was a betrayal to propose anything less. They were content to bemoan their plight; they did not want to be given practical advice—which is why Conrad thought he had been invited—they wanted a shoulder to weep on. Then, at night, they behaved like Shriners at a convention in Los Angeles.

On the evening before he was to leave, Conrad gave a dinner at his hotel for the host of the conference, Bahadur Lal, and his wife. Lal was a university administrator who had traveled in Europe and in the United States; he apologized profusely for the fact that the hotel would not serve wine with the meal because Conrad did not have a permit. They drank bottled ginger ale. Mrs. Lal asked if he could send her some American lipsticks when he returned home; she was especially partial to shocking pink. She wore a sari the color of beach sand, and the movement of her hand whenever the garment began to slip down from her left shoulder, the gesture of throwing it back with her right hand, a limp-wristed, silken-smooth movement of her hand and arm, Conrad thought the most feminine action in the world. The gesture expressed something seductively negligent, within the self-consciousness of being vulnerable. What made it so feminine, Conrad imagined, was the manner which implies being prudent without urgency. Lal and his wife, who came from the south of India, were both dark-skinned and heavyset and generous with each other. Theirs had been an arranged marriage, he was told, in the classic Indian tradition; it was his sisters who had known best how to choose a bride for Bahadur. The bride and groom had never seen each other before their wedding. But the sisters had been right. They had made an excellent choice. The Lals were obviously happy with each other.

Over dessert, Conrad said, "I was told to ask if I might see the cages while I'm here. This would be my last chance."

The Lals were silent, until Mrs. Lal said, "I've lived in Bombay eight years, and I haven't seen them." She turned to her husband, "Yes, let's do that."

Mr. Lal was uncomfortable but said, "I suppose we could."

"What are they?" Conrad asked.

"It's . . ." Bahadur groped for the appropriate term, "what you call the red-light district."

"Oh!" Conrad uttered, embarrassed. "I didn't realize what I was asking about." Conrad Taylor hadn't been in a whorehouse since he was eighteen years old and hitchhiked to Florida during a winter vacation.

"But I've always wished to see it." Mrs. Lal's tone was that of a "modern" woman. She took advantage of the situation. Apparently Bahadur would never have agreed under other circumstances. Conrad didn't want to imagine their conversation when they were alone in their own apartment later that night.

Bombay is a sprawling city, and Conrad had no sense of direction as they drove away from the hotel and past the university buildings. The car was air-conditioned and the chauffeur silent. Mrs. Lal sat in the middle of the back seat with her husband on one side and Conrad on the other. At length, Bahadur said, "Here we are."

The car moved very slowly in the thick traffic along where the streetlights were brighter than elsewhere, as if the whole scene were floodlighted in the dark night. It was like a long row of side shows at an old-fashioned carnival. Each doorway of the two-story buildings was brightly painted blue or green or yellow; the girls stood before the doors, wearing sleazy satin dresses in European styles, tight fitting—and they looked and strutted and shouted as their own barkers, caricatures of 1930s movies. Through each of the doorways, one caught a glimpse of a narrow room with a narrow bed. Sometimes old women were seated on the bed, sewing, or playing with a nearly naked infant. Some of the doorways were covered by a thin curtain; the lights remained on inside and one could see the silhouettes of coupling. The car carried them on around a corner, along a similar display, back and forth through the network of streets, slowly enough to see the grimaces of the whores, the come-on gestures, to hear the taunting calls to swarms of men wandering the sidewalks; some of the appeals were made directly to them through the closed windows of the automobile. "Depraved" was the only word in Conrad's mind.

Their car was halted for a few seconds by a group waving the passengers out to join them. A gaggle of flat-chested whores in red and orange dresses, even more heavily made up than the others: rouged and lipsticked, their long lashes and dark eyebrows accentuated with kohl, with many bracelets on their arms, their long black hair brushed back in high pompadours. "Those are boys," Bahadur said, half amused, half appalled.

"How awful," Mrs. Lal sounded, as if, perhaps, thinking of her own children.

"Who uses them?" meaning all of them, Conrad asked.

"The poor," Bahadur replied, happy to put some space between himself and the scene before them. "Sailors, country people. The lonely."

"And where do they come from?—these girls and boys, I mean. How do they come to this?"

"Many of them are sold into service by their parents," Bahadur answered. "But some of them are kidnapped."

Those words rent through Conrad as if he was made to see social life before civilization began. One can have one's life stolen away. Bartered. Perverted by others. Never live one's own life.

The car came to a sudden halt, throwing the passengers forward.

"I'm sorry," the driver said. But an elderly bearded man in a dirty dohti had stepped heedlessly in front of the car and continued to move through the traffic of the street, oblivious of danger. Played along the singsong melody of Indian speech, using English words, Bahadur liltingly explained, "If one does not fear the coming of death, one shows no caution. It is the curse of our culture to be fearless."

Why had Brom Kirkill said, "You must see the cages!"? Conrad looked at him now in the bar of the Faculty Club, in the safety of this kind of civilization. What regression to primeval passions did the cages appeal to in Kirkill?—with his gawky, hee-hee, small-town kid's guffaw, the elbow in the ribs of the little boys behind the barn having discovered sex. Was it the fantasy of slavery, of being able to buy or sell a person, of total irresponsibility to others as human beings: the thought of having boys and girls *in cages?* Conrad could see again their lurid faces in the middle distance between where he stood at the bar and where Brom Kirkill sat at a table drinking with one of his female students, flattered by having lunch with her professor in the Faculty Club. No doubt they were talking about the mystical poems of Rumi—about mystical release from this-worldly bondage through hashish and dervish dancing and the self-hypnotic words that lead one to the ultimate Word. That this elaborate institution of a many-faceted university should have been gradually constructed over centuries in order for Brom Kirkill to instruct a girl born in Duluth or Atlanta or Oklahoma City in the 1950s into the meaning of religious utterances practiced by a pack of drugged Persian priests in the thirteenth century was mystery enough for Conrad. He finished the Bloody Mary as Walter Webster entered the bar, and they went into the nearest dining room. The table reserved for them was next to the fireplace, under the rough-hewn beams of the high ceiling.

A large, barrel-chested man, Walter Webster looked like a Roman patrician, but he was, in fact, mostly Boston Irish. A man of sixty-two with a huge head, his once copper-red hair faded to wisps of sandy white, his gray-blue eyes bright but reserved, his fair complexion mottled with faint brown spots the size of raisins. His big mouth opened into a broad smile, always sideways, always ironic and confidential. His once irregular and unattractive teeth had been replaced with admirable artificial substitutes, but there was something about them that caused him discomfort. He spoke as if he had to make the effort continually to keep his teeth in their proper place. As in most seasons, he wore a camel-colored sports jacket with leather patches on the elbows, and today his silk shirt was pale blue and his necktie was woven umbra and azure. He was a bachelor and could afford to treat himself well.

"Let me tell you how I spent the morning," he began.

"If you promise not to ask me how I spent mine," Conrad replied.

"I was preparing my income tax return. I always do that the first working day of the new year. It reminds me of some of my more worldly responsibilities." He stroked his commanding nose.

Walter Webster, formerly dean of the Division of the Humanities, was one of the world's leading authorities on Renaissance painting, especially French painting, from Clouet through Poussin. He spoke in a tone of voice that belied the grandeur and authority of his appearance; his tone was self-depreciating, tender; it did not make pronouncements, it pleaded to be given credence, it appealed for sympathy.

"I went over all my canceled checks for the past year, putting them into different batches to add up the ones for deductible items. You know how it's said that your life flashes in front of your eyes in the few moments before you are about to die? That's what it was like. Just for the past year, of course. All those canceled checks—each representing some boring necessity, a mistake, or a delight. All that evidence of expense of spirit . . ."

". . . in a waste of shame?" Conrad asked.

"Not always," Webster chuckled. "Almost always in shame, but not always a waste."

"You went to Paris for the Christmas vacation?"

At this point they began to talk in French. "Yes, I did," Webster replied, looking around to see if anyone within earshot was likely to understand them. "That is why I phoned you at home yesterday to ask if we could talk."

"Did you have a good time?"

"Superb!" Webster kissed his fingertips and shot them out above the lunch table in a gesture of fireworks. "Unexpected. Unimaginable. Truly: a glorious time."

"*That* good?" Conrad said coolly, spooning up the first of his cottage cheese. We are heading for a fall, he imagined.

"Yes, I meant it when I said 'superb.' "

"The theater?"

"Well, of course, there was Barrault and Renaud at the Théâtre d'Orsay; the new Ionesco; the new production of Beckett's *Godot;* and then there were the galleries, the ballet, the opera. I hardly had time to change my clothes."

Conrad looked at him slyly, remembering that, in their separated lives, there were strong elements that they shared in common, but that the greatest point of divergence rested on the fact that since the Second World War, Conrad knew that France was no longer *the center of the world*, whereas Walter Webster did not. He was still under the illusion that the details of every event that occurred in Paris were of world-reverberating consequence; whereas Conrad had come to believe that if France fell into the Atlantic and ceased to exist, no one in the rest of the world would feel the loss, and few would lament.

The center of the world, at the moment, was unknown. And "the moment" might last for a decade or half a century or even more. The United States and the Soviet Union each played at the pretense that it was within their domain, but neither was self-satisfied enough to feel the reassurance of indifference if they were wrong. There was no center in the sense that mattered to Walter Webster. He, who had once believed in a pope, now believed in Paris in a similar way—for him there was one infallible judge, and his decrees determined the accuracy of evaluations throughout the world. The artists of Paris and the critics of Paris created fashions and reputations and enunciated assessments of trends that mattered more than those of any other place in the world. It would be a heartless joke on Walter Webster, in his presence, to speak seriously of the existence of Guatemala, or Ghana, or New Guinea. He was in his sixties. When he was twenty-one, it was true: The French outshone all others. But everything had changed; only he didn't know it. France, Conrad thought, was the size of Texas, smaller than Zaire; it was one of those European principalities that had lost its sex appeal; it manufactured perfume and wine and literary critics who said that literature exists in order for a critic to tell readers what the author had concealed, for nothing was to be taken at face value, nothing could simply be what it appeared to be.

"But it wasn't only the theater," Walter insinuated.

"All that good food!" Conrad replied.

"That goes without saying," Professor Webster answered. "The truth is that something much more important happened."

"*Tiens!*"

Their hamburgers arrived.

"I fell in love."

Conrad said, "I'm so sorry ...," with a smile, but archly. They were by now old friends, old allies, old companions at arms. They had fought more than one university battle on the same side and more often than not on the winning side. They shared the same passion to maintain the excellence of the university. Conrad respected Webster's talents and achievements as both a scholar and an administrator, appreciating the basic fact that he was as hardworking as he was bright; and Walter respected Conrad's integrity. They had become friends, as it were, before they'd realized it. Late one evening after a lengthy Curriculum Committee meeting, they went to a bar on Chapel Street together. It was shortly after Conrad's divorce and he was withdrawn, not to say embittered and morose. Walter Webster tried to console him. "We all have to live with disappointments," he said. "It's necessary to remember that. It might be good for you to think of the disappointments of others, so you'll know you're not the only sufferer in the world. Let me tell you of the greatest disappointment of *my* life." They sat in a sheltered booth toward the back of the bar, which was not filled with people, and still Walter whispered. "I want you to know what it is. I know I can trust your confidence." After another silence, he made himself say it: "I am not able to make love with a woman. I am attracted only by men. I have kept it a secret. I have lived a life of oppressive discretion. But I have borne it." He paused. "The world is changing gradually; this isn't the sin or the crime or the shame that it used to be. But *I* haven't changed. I was formed in an earlier world. And I have my family to consider."

That revelation had been one of the most unnerving surprises in Conrad's experience. He knew that Webster, a man of independent means, had lived with his mother and his sister in a sprawling Victorian house on St. Ronan Terrace ever since he came to the university. Even after the mother had died, the brother and sister continued to maintain the orderly life of solicitous consideration for each other that characterized their style under the matriarch. But Conrad had never given any thought to Walter's private life. He seemed a member of a vanishing species, an old-fashioned bachelor—a completely masculine man, to all appearance, simply too absorbed by his studies and his teaching to engage in romantic affairs; gracious, but a monastic type. The declaration amazed Conrad as much as if the big, athletic-looking man had unexpectedly told him that both his legs were artificial.

"I said," Walter repeated, assuming that Conrad had not understood him, " 'I fell in love.' "

"And I said, 'I'm so sorry.' "

"Don't patronize me."

"I was only joking."

"No; you just don't want to take me seriously."

Conrad felt chastised and asked somberly and sympathetically, "What can it lead to?"

"That's what I wanted to talk with you about. You know that I am not a promiscuous man. I have had few satisfying relationships in my life and all of them have been abroad. I have kept that part of my life totally separated from my responsibilities to my family and to my professional life—in the university."

"Yes, I understand that."

"Such affairs are short-lived. Two months, three months is the best one can hope for."

Conrad nodded in agreement, not trusting himself to say anything.

"I am now sixty-two years old. In all probability this is the last affair of my life. I can't let it escape." Tears welled in his eyes. He brought the linen napkin up to cover his face and remained silent for a few seconds. Quietly he went on, though his eyes were moist: "I want to be with the boy. I want to live to the fullest the pleasure of this last chance. You're probably too young to grasp the meaning of that belief—my *last* chance."

"But you came back . . ."

"I had to for a number of reasons. I couldn't have discussed this with you on a transatlantic telephone call, could I? I want to go back. I want to spend the next few months with him— maybe six months," he said in yearning hopefulness.

"Couldn't you bring him here?"

"No," he replied sadly. "He can't come. He's a fireman."

It was impossible for Conrad to keep from laughing. "What difference does that make?"

"Civil service," he answered. "He couldn't take time off. Besides, no one knows about him either. He lives with his family. It wouldn't make any sense."

"A fireman? For you? You, who deserve at least a young marquis?"

Now it was Walter's turn to laugh. "You sound like the millionaire's wife who discovers her husband's having an affair with a chorus girl. She doesn't object to the affair but thinks it ought to be with a girl at least her equal in the Daughters of the American Revolution. It has nothing to do with what other people think one 'deserves.' "

"It has to do with what you like," Conrad said supportively. Gently, he asked, "How did you come to know a fireman in Paris?" He touched just the right chord; Walter was happy to answer the question. He relived the exceptional event.

"It was on a Sunday. I went down to Blois in the morning and spent the day in François Premier's palace. The last train back that night was a slow local and it was crowded: you know those carriages with four passengers to a bench facing each other? The fireman sat at the window and I took the only empty seat, next to him. It was night, and chilly and crowded; the train made numerous stops and starts. He was in a dark blue uniform, apparently asleep, his head back against the cushion, his mouth slightly open—a beautiful mouth. Youthful! Oh, my God—he's nineteen! An Apollo! Well, I settled myself in between him and the rest of the travelers. He excited me instantly, but I was perfectly restrained. The train jostled us all. He woke up and we talked for a few minutes; after he smoked a cigarette, he closed his eyes again. But then I felt his body shifting toward me, curling toward me, making an advance to me. It's an unmistakable sensation, unique— someone offering his body to you—like a child climbing up on your lap, wanting to be cuddled. He rested his head on my shoulder. All under the pretense of being asleep. But then I felt, through the cloth of my jacket, that he kissed my shoulder."

Conrad was embarrassed: You are telling me more than you ought to, more than I need to know.

"At the last stop in the suburbs before Paris, we were left alone in the compartment. I put my arm around him and drew his face to my chest. I stroked his cheek. He opened his eyes and looked lovingly into my eyes. I asked if he could come to my hotel with me for a nightcap when we reached Paris, and he said 'Yes!' That's how it began. As simple as that. But, Conrad—feel the joy within me—that look on his face when he said 'Yes,' that gave me the most gratifying moment of my life. But to say that means you won't believe me when I tell you it became only better and better from then on."

"I believe you," Conrad said with compassion. Where was Isabel at the moment? he wondered.

"We had one week together. Every night. I would not have

believed this could happen. At my age. But it did. Surely it will never happen again. I must go back!"

"Why not wait for summer vacation?"

Walter seemed suddenly deflated. "I can't. I just can't wait. I told him I'd be back within a month. Conrad, I've never begged you for anything before this."

"You are chairman of the Art Department. You are scheduled to teach three courses this semester."

"The major administrative decisions were made in the fall. You could ask Gabor to be acting chairman for six months. Could you find a substitute to teach the three courses?"

"On one month's notice?"

"As a visiting lecturer, coming in a couple of days a week." He was pleading.

Conrad stroked his arm. "Calm, now, calm. Yes. I'll try. I appreciate how important it is to you." He was straightforward and sincere.

"Bless you."

"What would you say to my asking John Drexel at the Museum of Modern Art? He doesn't have a permanent teaching position."

"Marvelous. Marvelous." Walter was indifferent. He was in love and nothing else, not even the quality of who might substitute for him in his absence, held a candle to that. He was sixty-two years old and reveling in the prospect of enjoying his "last chance." All he wanted was six months' freedom. He would come back unhappy but grateful.

"Like some dessert?" the waitress asked.

"Not for me," Walter said quickly, and stood up. "Conrad, please stay. Finish your coffee. If this is rude, please excuse me." He was obsessed. "I want to run. I want to send a cable!"

"Certainly."

"Bless you. You are a friend! I am deeply obliged. I'll never forget this." Walter Webster strode out of the dining room like a Roman senator charged with the command of a military expedition.

Conrad slumped in his chair and sipped the hot coffee slowly.

All of us have to live with disappointments, he thought. But how do we do it? That's the more important point: How? How do we cope? His eyes played over the faces and figures of the other diners at the club this lunch hour, this day: Brom Kirkill—giggling with his lady student, knowing that his son is an ingrate and a parasite, knowing that his wife is a brassy, self-serving broad. Brita von Bickersdorf—chatting with a dignitary who looked like a Russian diplomat; does any day pass without her reliving the moment when she entered the bathroom and found her husband dead, his left wrist slit by his straight razor, the bathwater turned crimson with his blood? There was David Bach at a table with three graduate students who were nervously rocking backward and forward, each of them talking and gesturing at the same time, like children in a rowboat, without oars, in a rowboat tethered to a dock, playing at moving across the surface of a lake. He could hear only the music of conversations but none of the words. David Bach's disappointment is that eighteen-year-old girls become nineteen and twenty and twenty-one; and must be replaced. He was like a man growing deaf who continually needs a more and more powerful hearing aid. But then what does he listen for other than his own heartbeat? Walter Webster, an art historian of superior taste and an author of subtlety and tact, acting like a moonstruck adolescent over a pretty boy in a fireman's uniform. All of them knowledgeable in their disciplines, authorities in their fields—but no less chaotic in their private lives than the waitresses or the janitors of the club, possibly more so, self-justified by a more sophisticated set of rationalizations: still nothing more than getting even for their disappointments. Stability was indispensable in their professional lives, but as husbands and fathers or wives and mothers they seemed to recognize no such predictability as desirable. If they didn't happen to like the way things were going, they would pack up their bags and slam the door behind them—as wild a reversal as if a forty-year-old professor of chemistry suddenly announced that he'd prefer from now on to teach courses in sociology.

Conrad felt a moan rising up toward his throat and the need to swallow it. What *if* his wife *were* having an affair with another man?

To attract his attention, Evats touched him gingerly on the shoulder. "Conrad? I just wanted to tell you that three o'clock will be all right. St. Cyr will be in your office then."

"And you?"

"Me? You want me there, too?"

Conrad stared at the bald, pallid man with disbelief.

"Of course, I'll be there," Evats said, nodded and withdrew.

Administrators are appointed, Conrad thought to himself, because faculty members don't want to do any of the dirty work themselves.

Tom Spofford stood in the corridor as Conrad opened the door from the hall. He reached into Mrs. Todd's office and brought out the yellow slips of telephone messages, ready to hand them to Conrad when he approached. A man from Salt Lake City would phone again later in the afternoon. The president of the university had called. The assistant director of the press had phoned.

"All right?" Conrad asked Tom, in shorthand for what had happened on the squash court.

"Perfectly," the youth replied.

"That's good," he said kindly.

Back in his study he tried to put through a call to the president, who turned out to be on another line. He reached the press.

"Do you have figures for me, Brian?"

"Yes. We printed fifteen hundred copies of St. Cyr's book. It's on a specialist discount, so there've been very few orders so far—about three hundred; and about fifty review copies have gone out. We have approximately eleven hundred copies in the warehouse. To replace the binding, print a new title page, remove the old one, tip in the new, and repack—that's a lot of handwork—it will come to a total cost of two thousand, two hundred dollars. You see—twenty cents per copy."

"And how do you propose to pay for it?"

Brian laughed nervously. "I don't propose a thing. You're the one who asked me to find out . . ."

"Well, let's split it. It has to be done. I can cover half the cost out of discretionary funds. Will the press cover the other half?"

"Is that really a question?"

"No." Now Conrad chuckled. "You will pay the other half."

"I see."

"Let's say half the mistake is the press's responsibility. My budget will make up for the other half. How soon can this be taken care of?"

Brian sighed. "In about three weeks."

"All right. Do *not* ship any more copies from the warehouse—is that understood? Wait until the changes are made before filling any more orders."

"I understand."

"And prepare a statement of correction—of information—to be mailed to all the places where you've already sent review copies. Got that?"

"Yes."

"And send me a copy of that statement for my files."

"Yes."

"Is there anything else to do? Oh, yes. Have you placed any ads?"

"Ah . . . I think so; in the scholarly journals."

"Can the ads be changed?"

"I don't know."

"Well, for Christ's sake, man, find out!"

"Yes."

"And get back to me when you know. Maybe you can kill an ad if it's too late to change it."

Brian was not a man accustomed to acting with dispatch.

73

Scholarly book publishing was carried out at a more leisurely pace than that of journals, let alone newspapers. Executing a decision on an instant's necessity was not a common occurrence for him. He said, "I'll see what I can do."

Gently, Conrad insisted, "All of these corrections will have to be made."

"Yes."

"Thank you."

He had no sooner put down the receiver than Mrs. Todd called on the intercom to say that the president of the university was on the phone.

"Hello, Conrad!"

"Mr. President," Conrad replied comfortably. Gregory Blackwell was a good man, industrious, only slightly bumbling. He had made his career at M.I.T. in particle physics, and won a Nobel Prize for his fundamental insights and discoveries concerning nuclear structure. Binding energies and things like that. He was hardly an irresistible fund raiser, but a moderately successful one. He was not an innovator for research projects or teaching methods at the university; nevertheless, he struck the appropriate chord of dignity and he embodied the significance of the enterprise all were engaged in. He stood for the well-being of the institution and got along swimmingly with the trustees. Besides, a Nobel Prize winner is a kind of secular saint.

"I have bad news for you, Conrad. Bad news for us all."

"What's that?"

"Clif Rostum's had a heart attack."

"Oh, my God."

"He's in the intensive care unit right now."

"How serious is it?"

"They say the first twelve to twenty-four hours are the most dangerous."

Conrad was speechless, then he asked, "How did it happen?"

"Well, you know, he's a jogger. Half an hour before breakfast every day."

74

"In this weather?"

"Today he decided to make it forty-five minutes. At sixty-two. Imagine!" Then he added, "I'm only sixty. I haven't run for half an hour in ten years."

"What happened?"

"He was in my office at eleven. That's when he told me about making it forty-five minutes a day starting with the new year." He paused. "Clif began to feel 'peculiar.' That's the word he used. I made him lie down on the sofa and poured him a glass of water. But he couldn't get it down. He began to feel pain and I said, 'Let's get over to the hospital.' He pooh-poohed the idea and tried sitting up. He was clammy and sweaty. Then he began feeling nauseated. That's when he admitted as how it might be a good idea to go to the hospital after all. My secretary called for the car and then alerted the emergency room. He *walked* to the car. Only when we got to the driveway of the hospital he confessed: 'The pain is a hell of a lot worse.' Calder was waiting for him, right at the entrance, with a bed, and they wheeled him off immediately. Calder's supposed to be the best cardiologist around."

"What have you heard since?"

"Half an hour ago, Calder phoned. That's when I tried to reach you." He stopped for a moment as if to read from notes. "Clif's had a massive coronary thrombosis. The infarction damaged much of the right ventricle. His heartbeat is still radically irregular. He's not in great pain. But that may be because some of the heart nerves have been 'killed.'"

"Does Elsie know?"

"She's at the hospital now."

"Do you think I can see him?"

"No, no. Even I can't get in. No visitors. Just the immediate family. Elsie told me she's reached the children. They'll be coming in tonight."

Conrad tried to imagine how much of a scare it would give him if he were "attacked" and surrounded by doctors and nurses in "intensive care" and his daughter were suddenly to

75

appear out of nowhere. The ultimate signal. The angel of death is an estranged member of your immediate family who appears unexpectedly at your bedside in a hospital. All he could say was, "It's that bad?"

"Calder says there's no way of knowing how it'll go. And, if *he* doesn't know, nobody can."

"I'm terribly sorry." How feeble, he thought.

"We'll postpone the budget meeting. Let's not do it tomorrow. We'll wait a couple of days to see what happens."

"Yes, of course," Conrad said. "I'm so sorry." He was looking forward to the meeting on next year's budget. "Is there anything I can do?"

"Pray," said the president, the Nobel Prize winner, the agnostic. And added, "I'm sorry to be the one to tell you about this. We'll talk again tomorrow."

"Thank you," Conrad said weakly, feeling a strange rising of good spirits. He hated this reaction in the very instant of experiencing it. He was the next one in likely succession to take the position of the provost. If Clifford Rostum died, it was better than a fifty-fifty chance the position of provost would be offered to Conrad. He didn't *want* him to die. He expected Clif to continue until he retired at sixty-five or sixty-six. There was time . . . Rostum was sixty-two. Webster was sixty-two. Each asking for one last chance. So different. Clif Rostum had lived a full life. He was no monk, taking his occasional revenge for disappointments with a fling in some foreign country, his gratifications kept secret, the routine of his life cool to the point of dullness. Clif Rostum was a public figure. Married to Elsie for forty years, father of two daughters and two sons, all grown up, married well, doing good things. His own accomplishments as dean of the Law School firm behind him; his own books used as texts throughout the country. For a decade he had been provost for Gregory Blackwell, as European prime ministers are chief executives for heads of state, for titular presidents who are figureheads. Blackwell represented the university to the rest of the world; Rostum ran the

university as if it were a world. Conrad wished himself to be
the next provost, and the sooner the better. But now he was
struggling at a disadvantage—as if he were overwhelmed with
a lust that he had not chosen, a desire he did not sanction, for
something inappropriate and shameful. It was not simply his
own wish but an ambition thrust upon him, as if it ought to be
his, whether he liked it or not. Would being provost prevent
Isabel from having an affair with anyone else?

He wanted a drink.

He bent down to the cabinet behind his desk to take out the
bottle of Scotch. There was no bottle in the cabinet.

He felt shoved back into his desk chair more than that he
decided to sit down on it. He had been robbed. He bent forward from the seat and opened the door to the cabinet again.
It was empty. There had been nothing else in the space but
one bottle of malt Scotch, three-quarters full, and that was
gone. Of course, he should not have kept it there to begin
with. The prohibition against liquor in offices at the university
was still on the rule book, still grounds for dismissal. It didn't
matter that many of the faculty and staff ignored the rule as if
it no longer existed; the fact is that the ruling had never been
changed and probably never would be. Customs may have
changed but the regulations had not been altered. Conrad considered himself at fault for ever having brought the bottle into
the office. He felt winded as if he'd been slammed in the chest
with the whip of a squash racket.

Then he was ashamed at being startled when Mrs. Todd
stood in the doorway and announced the chief of the security
guards—as if the guard had come to "take him away." He
stood up and shook hands and asked the man—Terry Baker—
to take a seat and requested that Mrs. Todd sit down as well.
Baker looked like an efficiency expert: modestly dapper,
clean-shaven, his dark hair cut close to his head, his steel-
rimmed glasses shining bright. He leaned back in the chair,
comfortable, an authority being consulted on his specialty. He
crossed his arms over his chest and declined the cigarette

Conrad offered him. "I gather there's been another incident," he said calmly.

Mrs. Todd described the calculator that had disappeared from her desk drawer. Then Conrad asked her to list the other recently missing objects, thinking, They are things, people aren't being hurt, while feeling the sting of how he hurt at the moment, both found out and punished. He could not remember when he had used the Scotch last. Surely before the long holiday weekend. He was not certain that the bottle had been in the cabinet that morning. He thought of it just after Vivian Kirkill had left the office, but he hadn't looked to see if it was still there at that time. In all the years he could remember, nothing had ever been taken from his study before this.

"What?" he asked Baker. "I'm sorry. I didn't hear that last remark."

"You could have all of the keys changed."

"Actually, Cameron—Mr. McNeill—had a new lock put on his office door just *before* the Dictaphone disappeared."

"Where did he keep the key?"

Mrs. Todd answered that his secretary hid the key under her typewriter at her desk just outside the office.

Mr. Baker laughed out loud. "Now, where would a thief look for a key? First he'd go to the center desk drawer and second he'd look under a typewriter. Like under the mat on the front steps. They're just as smart as the rest of us, you know."

"That makes the rest of us sound more stupid than we'd thought we are," Conrad replied.

"Well, it's an endless battle . . ." Baker offered from the wealth of his experience. "You figure out some clever way to keep him from getting into an office, and he figures out a more clever way to outsmart you."

"You do make it sound endless, indeed," Conrad said.

"It is," Baker replied conclusively.

"Can't you give us any suggestions . . .?"

Baker became very businesslike. "If I were you, I'd change

all of the locks and make only one key available for each office and keep it with the gateman downstairs, with a checkout roster so that he knows at all times who has each key that's not in his possession."

"All right. I suppose that can be done."

Conrad longed to tell them of the missing Scotch. But he could not bring himself to it. He could not confess to the efficiency expert that by bringing a bottle of liquor into the office he had broken a basic rule. There was a palpable lack of sympathy on Baker's part, as if he saw no reason for the sense of outrage or of being despoiled; it appeared as though he respected the thief as much as he lacked compassion for the robbed.

Conrad broke the conversation short by standing up, thanking Mr. Baker for his help, and apologizing for a pressing appointment with two men about to arrive. Mr. Baker said he was awfully sorry about all this—unconvincingly. Mrs. Todd showed him out.

Alone in his study for a few minutes, Conrad knew not which private wound to run his fingers over first: the provost's heart attack or the robbery of the liquor. Somehow, both threatened him with "exposure." He wanted no one to know how he felt about the prospect that the provost might die within the next twenty-four hours, and he wanted no one to know that he had made available to himself a bottle of Scotch during office hours. He felt ashamed of secreting a bottle of liquor in his office and belittled by having been robbed of it; and he felt corrupt at his hopefulness regarding the provost's death. He would have to make of himself a more honorable man to overcome both drawbacks. How could he make himself more certain of Isabel?

Through the intercom, Mrs. Todd announced the arrival of Mr. Evats and Mr. St. Cyr. Conrad sighed, and went out to meet them in the conference room. They shook hands formally, in silence, and seated themselves stiffly: Conrad at the head of the table and one of them on each side of him—facing each other as if they were the adversaries and he was the judge. But there was no accusation and no defense. Conrad simply said, "This is extremely unfortunate."

And St. Cyr acquiesced. "Yes. I am very sorry for the university—for the department, and for the press—but I am also very sorry for myself." Conrad stared at him objectively. St. Cyr had dark blond hair and a mustache and beard that showed increasingly darker brown hair as it grew down and under his chin. His gray eyes were narrowed, almost Oriental. His left ear lay close to his head, but his right ear stuck way out as if an invisible hand pressed it forward like a horn in order to hear Conrad better.

"We have all been put in embarrassing positions," Evats offered. He was gauche. Conrad presumed he meant to be sympathetic, but between the words and the tone, what he said appeared to be self-protective, and abusive of St. Cyr.

Conrad took a different tack. "We will do what we can to repair the damage. I have found out that the original publisher is defunct, that the author is dead, and that he left no heirs. I think it is our responsibility to make the correction public: alter the information on the book itself so that your name appears as translator rather than author. Do you agree?"

St. Cyr nodded his head, accepting, impotent, passive.

"Is there anything in the work that you added to it, that wasn't in the original German edition?"

St. Cyr shook his head, no.

"Is there anything deleted?"

"No."

Conrad paused. "Is it a good translation?"

For the first time during the interview, St. Cyr looked grateful.

Conrad went on: "It is no small achievement to publish a good translation of a worthwhile book that wouldn't be read widely enough only in German. That is something to be proud of."

"Let us not speak of pride," St. Cyr said almost under his breath.

"Still, it is an accomplishment and that can be respected in itself. Nevertheless, because a misrepresentation was involved, I'm sorry to say that the administration will have to rescind the department's confirmation of tenure."

"I understand."

"You should complete the academic year through June, but, without the possibility of continuing here beyond that time, you ought to begin to look for a position elsewhere." Conrad felt the razor-sharp edge of the fatal words. He spoke calmly and quietly, but with firmness, wondering if the man would burst into tears, or bang his fists on the table, or attack him.

St. Cyr was docile, defeated.

Evats looked at his watch. "If you'll excuse me," he said, pushing back his chair and lifting his briefcase from the floor, "I have a class. I have to leave." He bent his head toward Conrad, waiting for approval.

"We'll talk later in the week," Conrad said, dismissing him.

When the pale-gray, bald, self-effacing chairman of the Department of History had left the room, Conrad contemplated St. Cyr: a man close to forty, a fairly popular teacher, a pleasant-looking man wearing a tan herringbone tweed suit, a yellow-colored shirt, and a necktie crocheted of walnut-colored wool dotted occasionally with a touch of coral. Conrad remembered that St. Cyr's wife crocheted. She had made the elaborate shawl he had complimented her on at a faculty reception a few months before. He had a wife, a child, and back in France, no doubt, he had parents, siblings, cousins, old teachers, friends. A whole life. Only get beyond the surface, or the label, of any human being and there is another network as intricate as one's own. The thought of a "label" reminded Conrad of the bottle of Scotch missing from the cabinet in his study. He felt the weight of the absence as if the disappearance made the empty space heavier. He thought of the provost breathing oxygen and of his own shameful response to the news of the heart attack. "Most of us do things we come to feel ashamed of," he said.

"And destroy a career?"

81

"It isn't that bad."

"In this economy? Do you think I can find a comparable teaching post in this country—now—or in France?"

"And after we become ashamed of them, we try to do better, and not make the same mistake."

"I will never be forgiven, will I?"

"You could be, if you emphasize that you made a good translation of an important book." Conrad saw the weakness of his argument; he added: "I am only suggesting that you consider how to rescue yourself from an ugly situation."

"I suppose you mean well . . ."

"Why did you do it?"

"Do you have to ask? Isn't it obvious? For years I have been told I must publish a work of research. My own research. I have no taste for it. I am not a scholar like that. I am a teacher. A good teacher. And I see all around me, here, decrepit old boys who once upon a time produced one work of original research and have gone to pot since then—they are neither good teachers nor good scholars, but they are tenured! And so it doesn't matter. They are beyond reproach." The venom in his high-pitched voice appeared to be spent. "I thought I could get away with this one sleight of hand and earn my place as a good teacher alone. . . ."

"But it is the worst thing an academic can do: to plagiarize."

"Don't say any more!" St. Cyr shouted and stood up, shaking the table as he rose suddenly.

"Stay calm. I'm not your enemy. I only want to know that you are aware of how serious a mistake you made—so that you understand why you cannot stay on here."

"Oh, I understand." He walked away from the table, having turned his back on Conrad, and stared out of the window toward the whiteness of the winter scene.

"Isn't it possible that, elsewhere, under less pressure you will be able to pursue your interests and produce the kind of research that will . . ."

"What interests?"

"In German history."

"I hate German history." St. Cyr actually chuckled. "There, I've said it. You are the only person in the world to whom I have told the truth." He turned back from the window and faced Conrad squarely. "I wanted to be a teacher. It was my family and my professors who pushed me into German history. There is an opening there, they said. Nobody is rushing into it. People find it distasteful. Leap in. Make yourself indispensable."

Conrad was reminded of Evats's simpleminded explanation of the morning: He was the only man in that period. . . . "But you yourself had no taste for it?" he asked.

"None. It was a way to a job, like becoming a mechanical engineer. I wanted to be a teacher, but I had to learn about something to teach."

"I'm very sorry for you," Conrad said.

"I think I'd better go now."

Conrad stood up. The chair scraped the hardwood floorboards under him. "Sometimes, if one loses a job early in life, it's like having a heart attack early in life. From then on you take a lot better care of yourself than you would have taken otherwise."

St. Cyr replied: "This is not like a heart attack. It is like a stroke. I will have to learn what else I can do—now that I will be paralyzed."

Conrad Taylor opened the door and let St. Cyr out. Tom stood expectantly in the doorway of his office. Conrad shook his head and then waved his right hand, no. He could not meet with Tom. His capacity for concern was fully engaged. St. Cyr turned and nodded in a simple European manner, without expression of any emotion, with the formality of departure as if they had spoken of the most ordinary of affairs, as if he might be back in the morning to continue the conversation—rather than display any measure of the fact that, in all likelihood, his academic career was ended. No expression of feeling at all, not even the faintest indication that Conrad had been kind and that he was grateful. The interview might have gone entirely in a different manner; there might not have been any expression of human sympathy. But it appeared as if Conrad's behavior hadn't mattered to St. Cyr. When one has hanged himself, no human kindness—afterward—does matter. But not having been kind would have mattered to Conrad.

He closed the door behind him and stood alone in the conference room, alone in his territory. He felt his heart pounding; he thought of the provost's heart. Of a heart that had been "attacked." Clifford Rostum was strong in his convictions, but he was over sixty years old; how strong was his constitution? Conrad wanted to be alone so that no one else—and not even some aspects of himself—might guess the mixture of his emotions. Why must he feel this willful acquiescence that the office should become his upon the provost's death? He did not truly, not passionately, suffer that ambition. As if to wish it was expected of him, whether he cared about it or not. But expected by whom? His parents—long since dead themselves? Did they call forth this desire? Would that have satisfied them? They would not have wanted him to benefit from another man's disadvantage, but then they wanted him to take his rightful place—whatever that was.

Thinking about a man as if he might die any minute is very different from thinking that same man might go on living for years. The provost was a man of *gravitas*. He had filled that position for nearly fifteen years—for about five years before Blackwell became president. Rostum himself was passed over for the presidency in 1963. His devotion to the university, to the institution, was rarely mediated by loyalty to individual human beings who made up the institution. He took safety in his grasp of standards and goals and his knowledge of the rules, unimpaired by the presence of faculty or staff bound to fall short of the ideal. He lived more in his intellect and his intuition—his judgment of the effectiveness of people—than in any passionate attachment to people. He did not have to like or dislike anyone; he had only to estimate their professional value. He felt that he could do that best if he never became attached to any of them. He had been a tactician in the law, and, as an administrator, he was an efficient strategist. He lived off an income of a minimal sense of humor, resenting Conrad's good spirits, and took solace from the rectitude of his fulfillment of a duty. Conrad Taylor suddenly recognized the fact that he had never loved the man. For all the years that he worked with him, for all that he was indebted to him, he never felt close to him, warmed by him any more than he had ever been invited to comfort him as a man who had misgivings and needed a friend. Their relationship had been strictly official, as though the provost had no time left over for social or private life. He was a very old-fashioned Puritan. Conrad closed his eyes and tried to imagine the provost in the intensive care unit: the long, slender, neat body would be covered by a white sheet; only the head on the pillow would be visible—the bony, narrow face; the thin white hair would be brushed back in proper place; the cool blue eyes would dart from one side to the other. He would not exert himself; he would follow doctors' orders scrupulously. He did everything scrupulously. When it was appropriate, he would even smile scrupulously because—Conrad guessed—his little rabbit teeth embarrassed him; he did not show them more often than he had to.

Conrad realized that he wouldn't mind if the provost died, painlessly, quickly, and that Conrad would become his successor. But he writhed against the offense that it was *he* who was having such feelings. He did not choose to have them. They had him. He felt guilty, as if he'd involved himself as a coconspirator with nature to undo the man, to do him in. He wanted to assure himself that no one would ever know that he felt this way, and he calmed himself with the realization that the secret would remain with him.

For all the years he had been the university administrator in charge of the undergraduate school, he was responsible to the president through the provost. But as provost he would become overseer of the college and all the graduate faculties, all the professional schools. He wanted that, and he deserved it; he had been primed for it. By this movement of his thought, this operation of his mind, Conrad led his consciousness toward justifying his instinctual elation at the thought of the provost's death. He was startled when the intercom buzzer sounded. Mr. David Bach had arrived.

"Tell him to wait just one moment, and see if I can talk with Dr. Rosenblatt or his secretary."

The image of Jerry Rosenblatt appeared before Conrad's mind: the body of an owl, with the head of a blue jay. He was with a patient. Conrad's message was to ask Dr. Rosenblatt—when he has any news of Clifford Rostum—to please call Mr. Taylor at home during the evening. Then he signaled for Mr. Bach to be shown into his study. After Mrs. Todd had left them alone, Conrad gestured for him to sit in one of the wing chairs, "Please." They faced each other in silence.

"What did you want to talk about?" Bach asked.

For a couple of seconds, Conrad felt disconcerted, as if he didn't recall the topic of conversation himself. He longed for a drink from the missing bottle of Scotch; he ached with hidden tensions; he grasped for a temporary escape into the issue at hand. He took a deep breath and blurted out, "It's a matter of three thousand dollars."

"Really? Whose?" Bach was curious, uninvolved.

Conrad looked at the pouches under Bach's eyes, the whiteness of his complexion. His gaze trailed down, over the crossed legs to the foot that moved back and forth like a pendulum. "Well," he said, "it's either yours or the university's."

"You're being too indirect. I don't see the point yet." Bach's voice was tinged with the control that barely concealed his growing impatience. He declared himself A Busy Man.

"The National Science Foundation has sent to the university a check for three thousand dollars. We had no record to account for such an amount, so we got in touch with them. It turns out that the check is in payment for a consultation that you billed them for."

"Oh, is that all?" Bach leaned back, drew out his cigarette case, and lit up. "What were you being so mysterious about?" He chuckled. "Hand it over."

"I can't do that."

"Why not?"

Conrad realized that the man opposite him had no idea of what was about to be said. And Conrad was in no mood to be tactful; he wanted the situation to be resolved quickly so that he could get back to his own thoughts. "No check made out to the university can be transferred to an individual without proper justification. On the contrary—there's a discrepancy."

"What the hell does that mean?"

Conrad paused for an instant, lifted one finger of his right hand on the arm of the chair, but did not say, "Don't swear at me"; it didn't need to be said, he assumed, reading Bach's expression and the calculated self-anger with which he crushed out his cigarette in the ashtray. "These are the facts," he began. "You are employed by the university."

"*Employed!*" Bach's voice shot out. "I'm a tenured member of the faculty."

How touchy, Conrad thought. Under other circumstances, this would have been the right moment to recall why the president of a Midwestern university said he believed the faculty would never unionize: "They wouldn't admit that they work." Instead he didn't even let himself smile.

Conrad continued: "You were on the faculty during the month of October of last year. Your salary was paid to you for the full month of October. There is no record of your taking any time off."

"I didn't take any time off."

"But you billed the NSF for one week's work as a consultant during the month of October."

Belligerently, Bach said, "So what?"

"You can't have it both ways."

"I worked for them on my own time."

"There is no such thing," Conrad replied.

Like a dart, Bach's lips twitched toward his left cheek. "*What?*" he demanded.

"Professors don't punch time clocks. There can't be a question of dividing the time you work for the university from your 'own time.' You're not paid by accounting for a specific amount of time. You are paid for Full Effort. If you wish to withdraw your effort from the university for a period of time, of course, you may do so. But you have to sacrifice a week's salary to justify earning a week's consultation fee from the NSF. You cannot both get your salary paid by us and bill them for the same week's work."

"Don't lecture me," Bach said so softly it sounded like a snarl.

"I didn't intend to." Conrad looked at the man who was angry but not regretful or embarrassed—aware only that he could not know whether Bach was angry for making the mistake of trying to pull a fast one or because he had been caught at it.

"I've never heard the phrase 'Full Effort' before," Bach said. "Where is it written . . .?"

"Read your contract. Actually," Conrad added, "no one would have known but for the balls-up over the bill. You sent it to the NSF on university stationery without giving your home address."

"My secretary sent it."

"And she's a university employee," Conrad couldn't refrain from noting. "Or let's assume that a bright clerk at the NSF would have recognized this payment was for you personally, and had the check made out in your name, even if sent to you at the university. Still, all would have been well for you. But instead it may have been handled by a *dull* clerk, and, since seventy-five percent of such bills are paid to the parent university, made it out that way rather than to you."

Bach remained stonily silent.

"What is the university supposed to do with the check?"

"Want me to tell you what you can do with it?" Bach asked, with all the sneering promise of a vulgar cliché.

Conrad disregarded the remark. "We didn't create the problem. You did. Now, we could return the check to the NSF and ask them to have a replacement made out to you—and you could forfeit one week's salary; or you can sacrifice the NSF fee and leave your salary unaffected. Your ordinary week's salary can't approach the week's consultation fee . . ."

"Why are you being so righteous?" Bach asked coldly.

To compensate for my own shortcomings, Conrad thought. But what he said was, "I am an officer of administration in this university. Administrators handle," instead of "unsavory" he said, "complicated or tangled situations. I am merely fulfilling my duty."

Calmly, Bach asked, "Is scolding me one of your duties?"

"I am not scolding you."

"Don't you know that this sort of thing goes on all the time?"

Indirectly, Conrad answered, "I deal only with those problems that I know about."

Bach stood up and began to pace the office, his hands thrust deep into his trouser pockets, his shoulders slumped, rounded; back and forth he moved from the window with its view of the winter quadrangle to the opposite wall with its dressing of a thousand scholarly books. Conrad was unable to read the expression on his face, thinking: how very different from the experience with St. Cyr. He had expected to hear a verdict. David Bach arrived unaware of having been discovered by accident, tripped up by an error that revealed double-dealing—over which he felt no guilt—whether he cheated the university or the taxpayer. He imagined he hadn't done anything wrong because he told himself the tall story that begins: "This sort of thing goes on all the time. . . ."

At length, Bach stopped pacing, stood still in the middle of the room. It had grown dark. Conrad got up and switched on the desk lamp. Its soft light implied the start of the day's work all over again.

Bach announced: "Send back the check. I'll cancel the bill for the fee. Everybody can forget the whole thing. Right?"

"All right," Conrad said, appreciating the grand gesture. He offered to shake hands, but Bach glowered; his hands remained buried in his pants pockets. He turned where he stood and left the study without shutting the door behind him.

Bach feels that I've made a fool of him, Conrad thought; whereas I think he made a fool of himself.

Unsettled, Conrad lowered himself into the wing chair and looked out to the empty, darkened conference room. At least the problem had been faced, the terms stated, a solution arrived at. Still, Conrad felt not so much drained or spent as he felt that he'd played the scene badly. He had not put it in the best light. The same points of the argument could have been stated more diplomatically, more gently. Couldn't they? If he had not been at the moment so uptight himself—about himself. The facts were indisputable, but there are shades of values and motives, so the way this conversation had gone was distorted by irrelevant circumstances. The actions were known and the rules were named, but the tone was not right. He needn't have come on so strong. Needn't? What were *his* needs? To readjust some internal balance that had been thrown off keel—by the robbery of the liquor and by the response that overcame him at the news of the provost's heart attack; by anxiety over whether the "sniper's" note about Isabel had any truth in it. In his effort to recover from feeling foolish, he had dealt with Bach heavy-handed. He should have been sympathetic, appealing to Bach to help get the university out of an awkward situation; understanding, compassionate. Instead, he was almost vindictive, self-justifying. Of course he wanted to experience again a sense of being in the right, untrammeled by actions that were improper or thoughts that were only self-serving. He wanted his record clean again. He wanted to do The Right Thing. As a result, he overstated the case, appeared a prig, or a drum-beating evangelist calling out for "Purity! Purity! Let's each of us be pure again! Come clean and all will be forgiven." How all behavior—even such as this interview—is "situation dependent," conditioned by circumstances. The facts may be simple and the rules may be clear, but what made for touchiness, on Bach's part as well as on his own, distorted the human qualities engaged—and had nothing to do with the problem. St. Cyr had done something much worse, but Conrad did not make a fool of him. He tried to face the facts with human understanding. When a man has been found out there is no need to be vindictive: the necessary consequences will result in chastisement enough—perhaps more than enough. Oh, Christ! how he disliked himself at this moment. He must do something generous or altruistic to regain his self-respect.

He asked Mrs. Todd to place a call for Dr. John Drexel at the Museum of Modern Art in New York. He walked back and forth in his study, waiting for the call to go through. Mrs. Todd had to inform him that Drexel was out of town for the rest of the week and would return his call the following Monday. Walter Webster was to be served. In secret, in confidence, like a friend for whom one can arrange a bank loan, so that no one will know it has been taken out until long after he has paid it back in full. If Drexel could not take Webster's courses, someone else of camparable stature would have to be found.

Thus did Conrad meditate, slumped in the wing chair, looking through the open door of his study, through the conference room, to see Tom Spofford enter with the usual end-of-the-afternoon tray, holding two glasses, a small bucket of ice, and a pitcher of water.

"I'm sorry, Tom, there isn't any Scotch here tonight."

"Oh, that's all right. We can drink the water."

Conrad thought: You will go far.

"You look bushed."

"I've had one crisis after another. Not exactly a run-of-the-mill day." He had regained his composure, sat up straight in the armchair. Tom set the tray down on his desk and poured the water into the glasses.

The telephone rang. Tom offered to answer it and Conrad nodded. "It's Mr. Chancellor Drake from Salt Lake City."

Conrad looked at his watch. It was ten of five. He came around to the far side of the desk and took the phone from Tom—beckoning him to sit down and listen; he is to be instructed, as the provost used to initiate Conrad: learn how things are done, how I think things ought to be done.

"Conrad Taylor here," he said.

"Well I'm mightly glad to connect with ya," the voice offered. "This is a very happy occasion indeed."

"I'm glad to hear you say that. But—what is the occasion, Mr. Drake?" The sound of the voice made him imagine a two-hundred-pounder with his feet propped up on top of a desk, a Havana cigar in his free hand. Was he wearing a ten-gallon hat? Conrad knew next to nothing of the Far West.

"I'm calling ya from the heart of the intermountain region." It sounded like the beginning of a speech to the Rotary Club. "I am the chief legal counsel for Mr. Clement Hugo." There was a long pause. "I presume ya're aware of who Mr. Hugo is?"

"I hate to confess my ignorance, Mr. Drake, but I have to admit that I don't know the name of Mr. Clement Hugo. We're a long way from Salt Lake City here in the East."

"I aver that I am somewhat pained and surprised that his name is not familiar to ya, Mr. Taylor. But, then," he sighed, with a certain endurance, "you are probably not all that familiar with financiers." He actually laughed, patronizingly, as if that would put Conrad at ease. "Mr. Hugo is the most distinguished citizen in the intermountain region."

Conrad suppressed the desire to ask, "Precisely which mountains is he inter—?" Instead he asked, casually, "In what way?"

"Well, sir, Mr. Hugo's accomplishments are many. It is true that he inherited a fortune as a young man, but he has multiplied it many times—I mean, *many* times over—in his own long career: first through banking, and then construction. You know whose company built the Glen Canyon Dam on the

Colorado River for the federal government of the United States? Mr. Hugo's! You know whose engineers are at work on the Alaskan oil pipeline? Mr. Hugo's." But then the sweetness of the tone of voice was gone. With a pedagogic meanness, Mr. Drake said, "Apparently you don't know that Mr. Hugo was a Presidential ad-viser from 1939 to 1942."

"No. I'm truly sorry that I didn't know." Conrad Taylor calculated that Mr. Hugo must be in his late seventies. "But, Mr. Drake, I wonder how I can help you?"

"I'm glad ya asked."

"I don't know what it is you're calling about."

"Did you get my letter? I said I'd telephone you."

"Yes."

"Well, I indicated this is a matter of considerable importance to the university."

"Yes, I found it very intriguing. I'm extremely curious to learn what it's about."

"I should think so," Mr. Drake said in tones of self-satisfaction. "It has to do with *a million-dollar gift* to the university."

Conrad stood upright, fully at attention. Quietly he repeated the phrase: "A million-dollar gift to the university. That would be a very great kindness on the part of Mr. Hugo. We would be enormously grateful."

"Hold on. Not so fast."

"Is Mr. Hugo an alumnus of the university?"

"No. Mr. Hugo never went to college. He's a graduate of the school of hard knocks." Mr. Drake began to laugh. "You know the school colors?—black and blue!!" He laughed himself into a paroxysm of coughing.

When Drake had quieted down, Conrad asked, "Well, then, does he have any connection with the university? Or is there some special program at the university that he wishes to support? Or . . ."

"Hold on!" Drake interrupted. "I didn't say he *is* giving a million dollars to the university. I'm talking about something he *might* do."

"Oh." Conrad waited, but, as nothing more was said, he asked, "Might do, under what conditions?"

"Well, conditions are just what he thought I might discuss with a man in your position."

"My position?"

"You run the college, don't you?"

"To an extent," Conrad replied cautiously.

"Enough—I hope." Mr. Drake laughed again.

"Enough for what?" Conrad's voice was no longer without an edge of defensiveness.

"To make a deal."

"What would be the conditions for the gift of a million dollars, Mr. Drake?" Conrad asked, wary.

"Mr. Hugo's grandson is on the waiting list for admission to the college next fall, Mr. Taylor, Mr. Hugo's grandson, Vincent—that's it: Vincent Hugo—doesn't like standing in a waiting line at the box office, not knowing if all the seats will be taken or not, if you get my drift—any more than his grand-daddy Mr. Clement Hugo would like that, ya hear? Ya know what I mean? Sure ya do. Well, if Mr. Hugo could have your assurance that Vincent was not on the waiting list, but would become an honorable member of the entrance class starting in the fall of this year—why, then, Mr. Clement Hugo would be in a position to express his satisfaction for that assurance with a gift to the university for one solid million dollars. Ya understand?"

"I understand," Conrad said slowly. "I understand very well." He took a deep breath. "Mr. Drake," he began, "I am in charge of the undergraduate school in many respects, but I do not control the decisions of the admissions office."

"They are responsible to you, aren't they? They could bend a little to your wind," he laughed. "They might be influenced by a little 'directive' on your part. To the advantage of the university, of course."

"Ah," Conrad said coolly, "and I see the advantage to the Hugo family, as well: the tax-exempt, philanthropic 'investment.'"

"You are very fast, Mr. Taylor."

"Well, I'm afraid we've hit a snag."

"What's that?"

"A sort of conflict of interests."

"Really?"

"You see, I can't exert any influence on the selection process of the admissions office. If I did, people might get the idea that admittance was up for sale, that one could buy one's way in. So the development office, which accepts generous gifts of funds for the university, is kept strictly separate from the admissions office."

"But both college admissions and college development offices are responsible to you, personally, aren't they . . .?" Mr. Drake left a smile in the sounds of his insinuating words.

Conrad was ready for him. He began: "If Mr. Hugo made a million-dollar gift to the university it would be tax exempt, but I would not be able to guarantee anything about his grandson's admission."

"But there is ya personal influence, Mr. Taylor. Only you know what goes on in both offices; the people in development don't need to know what the people in admissions decide, and vice versa. Right?"

"That's quite possible, Mr. Drake. But I'm afraid you don't see why it's wrong. The whole system is an attempt to be objective, and to satisfy a range of purposes—independent of this kind of financial influence." Conrad suffered a sudden backwash review of his thoughts about David Bach and the difference between the facts or the rules and values or extenuating circumstances. We are forever trying to achieve objectivity—dispassionately—as if it were ever possible to see clearly and judge accurately unaffected by being a passionate person who is seeing and judging.

"I'm afraid," Mr. Drake began like a country boy scratching the back of his head, "I just can't figure out why ya wouldn't make an exception to that system, when it'd be for so much advantage to the university."

"It would cost me my job," Conrad said, "as soon as it was

found out. And that kind of thing can't possibly be kept secret."

Incredulous or disingenuous, Mr. Drake asked, "It would be that bad?"

Conrad now became uncertain of how he would get off the phone. He made no response.

"What *are* you prepared to do for Mr. Hugo?" Drake began again.

"I tell you what, Mr. Drake. I'll make you a proposition. If Mr. Hugo will write a check in my name—pay the million dollars to me personally—I will guarantee that his grandson is admitted. Then, I'll resign from the university; I'll take early retirement. Only—the money will be an expense of Mr. Hugo's, for services rendered, not a philanthropic gift to a nonprofit institution. It won't be tax deductible."

There was no sound from the Salt Lake City end of the line.

"I'm sorry," Conrad added. "Which way do you think Mr. Hugo will go?" He smiled. "His decision will make all the difference for the rest of my life—as well as for Vincent's."

Mr. Drake replied, "I suspect ya won't be hearing from me further. Vincent's on the waiting list at Harvard, too."

"There are some things even money can't buy."

Mr. Drake's parting comment was, "The hell ya say!"

Conrad didn't laugh aloud until the receiver was back on the cradle of the phone. He had regained his composure; he had done The Right Thing deftly, without being vindictive. He had not lost his cool.

"Wow!" was all that Tom could say.

"You have to see it to believe it," Conrad replied, thinking: The young man still has the power to be shocked and to be impressed by how a shocking proposal can be dealt with.

"Is there anything I can do for you?" Tom asked, standing up. What Conrad liked most was Tom's good manners—the habit of showing respect without being obsequious.

"No. Thank you." He finished his glass of water. He smiled, seeing that his watch read five-thirty. "Why don't you take the rest of the afternoon off?"—a standing joke between them when they remained after hours. After all the jolts he had felt through the course of this day, standing in the presence of the young man refreshed him. He gripped Tom's shoulder, remembering the body blow with the squash racket. "Feeling all right?"

"Fine." He seemed as fresh as when he first arrived in the morning.

"You'd better go now. Say good night to Cameron and to Mrs. Todd for me, please. Have a good evening."

Conrad wanted to be alone, even if only for a few minutes. He had not mentioned to Tom the provost's heart attack or that the budget meeting had been postponed. He wanted a little breathing space without people, without the need to communicate anything or worry about other people's problems, to sense again that he was in charge of himself, at least in a small way. He turned off the lamp and stood near the window in the dark office, looking out at the quadrangle. The buildings he could see on three sides were silhouetted in the early night light. The lamps on their posts did not glow as brightly as usual; they shed a faintly blue, milk-white light through frosted glass. Perhaps it was a new policy of the Plant Department's to conserve energy. Black paths were pressed down in the pale snow by those who had crossed the quadrangle during the day.

He would go home and make love to Isabel.

The anonymous letter was buttoned away in his back pocket. If it contained no truth, then some enemy meant to wound him without any risk of reprisal. But if it was true, how much would it endanger his marriage? Theirs was not a profound marriage of psyches matched as neatly as their bodies complemented each other; their marriage was a comfortable accommodation of surface satisfactions. He had never deluded himself about that. And, therefore, much of importance to Conrad went unsaid between them; he assumed the same was true for Isabel. How important could an "affair" be? Should he confront her with the anonymous letter? They were not accustomed to "confrontations." They were accustomed to doing favors for each other. Still, he was uncertain. Another man would have dropped the letter in a wastebasket and never given it another thought. But he was not another man. He was unsure of what he should do.

He tried to invoke Isabel's presence. He had always considered it a failing of his sensory organism that he could not recall in mind a fragrance at will. He could say the name of her perfume, he could see her dabbing it behind her ears or between her breasts; he could recall himself inhaling the scent; but he could not recapture the fragrance. His nose had no memory. But his hands did. He could close his eyes and trace the shape of Isabel's shoulders and breasts in his mind until it was almost possible to imagine the actual sensation against his fingers and the palm of his hand. He could not invoke the pressure of her body against his. The visual memory was clear but insubstantial. Seeds of yearning. He was ready to go home. From the corner of the desk he picked up St. Cyr's translation of *The Diffusion of Civility* to take along with him.

The sky was clear and the air was cold, pinching at the flesh of his face. Not hurrying, he walked along the freshly shoveled sidewalks of Whitney Avenue, trying to recall other physical sensations. In midwinter he attempted to make the skin of his face relive the heat of summer sun. He thought of himself as a teenager, during all the years that his parents kept a summer house at Charlevoix; his mother loved it simply for the French name. He could relive sensations of lying on his back on the raft in the lake opposite their cottage, soaking up the sun; beads of sweat oozed from every pore, his bathing suit still wet but his body baking. He could see the rose light through his closed eyelids, but he could not recapture the warmth of the sun on the surface of his face. Is that, too, a failure of memory only on his part? Can other people do it—recapture the actual sensation? Make a memory of sunlight warm them in winter?

Less than a half block before him, Conrad recognized the lumbering hulk of Marvin Flower—the Norris and Hastings Treadwell Distinguished Service Professor of English Literature—ambling along ahead in the same direction, a somewhat disheveled, bulky silhouette. His arms jerked out punctuating gestures; he was obviously talking to himself, possibly out loud. Marvin Flower was a funny fellow—both amusing and a figure of fun—who seemed always totally engaged in whatever was distressing him at the moment. He played it both ways, entertaining others and setting himself up as a source of entertainment; he caricatured himself. His lumpy figure continued in its slouching, sidling gait until he crossed Trumbull Street and arrived in front of the redbrick building just short of the Historical Society. He stopped and stared at the house, which was now used as offices for architects and engineers. Without increasing the speed at which he walked, Conrad caught up to him.

"Marvin," he said with surprise, "have you run out of gas?"

"Oh, woe, Conrad," Flower exclaimed with the pleasure of a wail. A moan was Professor Marvin Flower's most characteristic form of expression. It sounded somewhere between a muezzin chanting from the balcony of a minaret and the implications of "The world is too much with us, late and soon . . ." He asked, "Do you know whose home this used to be?"

Conrad replied, "Yes."

"Listen to me." Flower grabbed Conrad's arm and turned him slightly so that both of them were staring at the handsome Georgian house.

"Are you going to tell me about Coleridge at the waterfall and the meaning of the word 'sublime'?"

"No. I'm going to tell you what just happened to me. Besides, I told you about the waterfall before." They stood side by side, Flower peering at the building through his thick

99

glasses. His face was pudgy and red-cheeked in the cold air. "I was walking along, minding my own business," he began, addressing the house, "thinking about the loss of awareness of tradition—you follow? Considering that so many Jews like me have become prominent literary critics because we are the people of The Book, with a thoroughgoing reverence for the written word—you follow? and descendants of millennia of Talmudic scholars who lived for the ingenuity of making textual interpretations—you know? and that most of them—not me! not me!—are devoid of consciousness of how they come by that passion and that skill—you follow? Wondering if it could be transmitted by genes to the new breed who don't believe they even know what a Talmudist is. Could it be? They"—he rocked his head back and forth continuously— "think they're descended from Dr. Johnson by way of Matthew Arnold. You follow? Not me. I revel in it. The thought is as clear and as sweet to my mind as vodka is to my palate."

"That's a good line," Conrad smiled. "You must use it someday."

Marvin Flower coyly glanced away to the snow-covered lawn, as if to conceal a blush, then he confessed, "I have already. It's in *The Gilt of Inheritance*, published in 1969, a somewhat too autobiographical work—you know?"

Conrad chuckled. He had not meant to needle Flower even affectionately, but then he assumed that his friend heard very little of what anyone else said.

"So there I was," this ancient mariner continued, hugging Conrad more closely to his side, "contemplating this curious question, when lo and behold, I found myself in front of this house. You know whose house this was?"

"Yes: William Lyon Phelps.' "

"Oh, woe, Conrad. You know! You know! But do you know what I just realized, what has just struck me with the force of a revelation? I won't say I'm Saint Paul knocked off his horse, but—believe me—I know an insight when I see one." Now he let go of Conrad and brought his two thick-gloved hands together, as if in prayer, pointing them accusingly back and forth to the dark brick house. "He was The Villain. William Lyon Phelps," he called out, "it is all your fault!" Then he turned to face Conrad: "You don't follow," he said, "but you will."

"What was William Lyon Phelps?" Flower asked. "The beloved professor of English literature, the most popular teacher of his generation. What would you say—1900 to 1935? The admired academic who became the leading literary critic in the ladies' magazines. Right? The arbiter of taste. Author of *The English Romantic Movement*. Well. What did he do? He argued for the cause of studying *modern* American fiction in university courses. Imagine! He wanted students to study contemporary American writers. But what did he mean? He meant Howells, and Mark Twain, and Henry James. Right? And he won the argument. So *he* was the perverter of American literature in the twentieth century!" Flower was inspired, orating. He took from his overcoat pocket a large handkerchief, lifted his Russian fur hat, and mopped his brow.

"Phelps," he said, with resignation. "Phelps! If you have to study modern writers as if they need to be interpreted because they are as complex as Shakespeare and Coleridge and Shelley—you lose all the fun. You follow? You think Shelley wrote in order to be taught in a college course? Never. He wrote for a public. So what happened when contemporary writers discovered that they might be—they could be!—the object of study at a university? They stopped writing for the public and wrote for the professor. Writers aren't supposed to know how they will be interpreted in the long run. But under the new dispensation they would be invited in the spring to listen at seminars to interpretations of what they published last fall. They ceased to be professional writers; they became professorial writers."

Another good line, Conrad thought. Has he used it already?

"You know what? For the past forty years, American writers who aspire to being literary artists don't live for popular suc-

cess, for a public. They live for the chance of being interpreted by a professor. They don't understand what they've
written, so they live in the exquisite hope that an academic
scholar will explain them to themselves. Like a god who'll
make the final judgment. 'Oh, to be explained!' they cry. At
the bottom of every page they write they imagine the explan-
atory footnotes that will appear in the edition of the year 2074.
Once they got the idea that they were worthy of 'study' they
were ruined. Whose fault? William Lyon Phelps's!" he proclaimed, pointing the damning finger at the house.

Conrad laughed heartily.

"Of course, Phelps lived to regret what he'd done, poor
fellow. But still he was The Villain. He was the cause of it all.
You know—there ought to be a moratorium on contemporary
literature at the university. There ought to be a minimum requirement. An author has to be dead twenty-five years before
his books can become required reading in a course—let alone
the subject of a dissertation. That might turn the writers
around—you follow? Turn them back to face an audience, a
public, away from writing in code because they like the idea
of a game that makes professors into spies to decipher their
messages. Right?"

"You are priceless," Conrad said happily. "I'll suggest it to
the Curriculum Committee."

Looking appreciated, Marvin Flower nodded his head in a
self-depreciating gesture, brushed the compliment aside with
an, "Oh, woe, Conrad . . ."

Conrad Taylor turned the key in the front door and entered
his home as if he were the guest of honor at someone else's
party. It was not his own house; he neither rented it nor
owned it. It was a perquisite of office, as an administrator of
the university, to occupy this heavy, neoclassical wooden
mansion on Hillhouse Avenue. It was like the use of the
chauffeur-driven limousines that were at his disposal; they

did not belong to him but they were in recognition of, an expression of, his status; they facilitated his job. When he had moved in with his first wife, the house was almost fully furnished with the remnants of the tastes of its previous occupants. Most of the furniture consisted of reproductions of eighteenth-century English antiques. It was that wife who gradually replaced all the tables and chairs, the desk, the bookcases and mirrors with the severely simple designs and thinly upholstered cushions of modern Scandinavian teakwood furniture, disharmonious with all the reproductions of Boucher and Fragonard in their ornate imitation French frames, which she was also attached to. After she had left him, Conrad removed all the reproductions—he hated reproductions—and left the walls bare for years. It had not been necessary for him to entertain at home most of the time, and on the modest scale on which he did it—usually for drinks at the end of the afternoon—he could invite a guest or a group of guests into his study, or into the room he called the bar. When his daughter was no longer living at home, he found himself making use of his bedroom and bath, the kitchen, and his study, as if he was meant to occupy only four rooms in this sixteen-room house.

With his marriage to Isabel, all of that changed. Well through the first six months of their marriage Isabel was almost entirely engaged in renovating and redecorating the house. She brought out of years of storage the furniture she had inherited from her parents and arranged to have draperies made and new carpets laid for the halls and the main rooms. The inherited furniture was luxurious, deep, and smooth. Isabel and Conrad purchased only original contemporary paintings and etchings and woodcuts; they shared a passion for the genuine. Bright colors sprang from the blank walls. And so there was a whole new experience of life initiated by their marriage in this house that had harbored many other lives unknown to them. At the same time, the outer shell of the house itself, and all the decorations remaining from prior generations—the mid-nineteenth-century moldings around the doors, the plaster decorations in ovals on the ceilings in the main rooms, the thick walnut newel post and the banister that ran up the stairway to the second floor—gave Conrad a curious sense of longevity. Living through the three changes of the appearances of the house contributed, also, to a sense of transiency; and that heightened his pleasure in it, for, as he was aware, when thinking, this too shall pass, that a situation or condition is only temporary, of undetermined brevity, he tended to appreciate it more and tried to recognize it more sharply for what it was at the moment.

Rosalie, their Chinese maid, in a black dress with a white apron, stood at the far end of the hall as Conrad took off his coat and galoshes. "Mrs. Taylor is in the sitting room."

As she should be, Conrad thought. Their behavior had gradually become patterned into a ritual. Unconsciously, without articulating any plan, they had begun to repeat the actions that gave them their most direct satisfactions. They had lucked into it. One evening, toward the end of their first year of marriage, they had dressed for a dinner party. Conrad was ready well before Isabel and sat in an armchair in the living room in his black tie and dinner jacket, smoking a cigarette, not quite leisurely, but rather eager to leave in order to be on time, when Isabel entered the room as if she were a mannequin demonstrating an exquisite new gown at the opening of a couturier's salon. She was wearing a silver lamé evening gown with long sleeves that came to points over her wrists like arrowheads aimed at her fingers, and an artificial camellia made of white silk pinned at the center of the deep cleavage. She wore silver dancing slippers and paraded around the room, sometimes with her arms stretched out to both sides, sometimes with them held against her head, and sometimes hidden behind her back; she walked around the peach-colored sofa and in front of the glass coffee table, a foot in front of where Conrad sat, past the fireplace, sometimes showing herself from the front and sometimes from the back. Her fingernails were polished the same Chinese lacquer red as inflamed her lips. When she had stopped the mannequin parade, and sat down in the armchair facing his, Conrad knew that he must have her, must make love to her within the next few minutes— all the care and time that had gone into preparing to be beautiful and to leave on schedule must be overwhelmed and ignored. They must each make a mess of the other, and then start all over again. They would be late for the dinner party; that didn't matter in the least, compared with the mutual satisfaction they took in knowing that this pleasure came first. Without ever saying it to each other, it showed they placed their personal happiness above obligations to anyone else. By then, it was clear that, in their marriage, sexual satisfaction was the essence of their personal happiness. How long could that last? They did not have a great deal to do with each other in the rest of their lives.

On the following evening, they had each needed to attend to something that kept them apart. But the night after that, Conrad came home to find his wife in the sitting room as carefully made up, and in as elaborate a gown as the silver lamé. The ritual gradually confirmed itself into their basic habit. They would have cocktails before the fire in winter, or in Conrad's air-conditioned study in summer, and they would make love before they came down to dinner.

Conrad left his hat and gloves on the table in the hallway and entered the sitting room. Standing before the fireplace, Isabel had struck a pose. On the large, square, glass table before her lay a silver plate with caviar canapés, the shaker with dry martinis, and two long-stemmed glasses catching the yellow and blue flickers of the flames. She herself seemed gilded by the fire behind her, the dark burgundy color of her velvet dress gilt-edged by the light. She held her hands interwoven before her at the level of her stomach. The long blond hair had been pulled to one side and brought over her left shoulder like a giant tassel. Her cheeks were blushed by the afternoon encounter with the winter air. She was a treasure prepared to dazzle. Conrad approached her without a word, raised her clasped hands toward his face, planted a kiss on each palm, and then licked the interwoven fingers.

"Have I got you eating out of my hands?" Isabel asked.

Conrad replied, "That is where I eat my heart out."

Isabel laughed. "And you don't even love me anymore!"

Conrad stood erect, just a fraction taller than she, looking at her golden eyebrows, the sapphire eyes, and asked, "Why do you say that?"

"All you want is to keep me from others. All you want is to lock me up here. And take your own pleasure. All you want is for me to yield to your wishes so that you won't think you've made a great mistake."

Hesitantly, Conrad said, "I don't know whether you're joking or not."

"You don't have to. You don't have to know. There's so little I can keep you guessing about, I shall have to keep it a secret whether or not I'm joking."

Conrad let go of her hands, thinking that she was playing a role in a drama that he could not identify at the moment, playing a part, and he was unsure of what character in the play he was expected to be at this time. It is not that she reads my mind; I will not have words put in my mouth. But she is testing me for something. For reassurance? Could she have any idea that he'd received the anonymous letter?

Isabel bent low, scooping the floor-length velvet gown back under her as she kneeled at the side of the glass table and poured the martinis into the glasses. From her position at his feet, she raised one glass and offered it to him. He lowered himself to the floor and stretched out perpendicularly to her, never taking his gaze from her face. They sipped their cocktails in silence until, starting anew in a different tone of voice and at a higher, freer level, acting unselfconscious and genuinely interested, she asked, "What did you do today?"

"I turned down a million-dollar bribe."

Isabel smiled. "Well, I guess you can't top that one."

Conrad decided not to mention the provost's heart attack until later, perhaps at dinner, and determined to put the letter out of his mind. Then he added, "Oh, woe, Isabel . . ."

"You ran into Marvin Flower."

"Yes. He's working on the hypothesis that American novelists—who aspire to 'literature'—have all been ruined by the desire to be interpreted, explained, by academic professors to their graduate students . . . rather than to have a popular following. 'Oh, to be explained, interpreted.' "

"Don't you?"

"Don't I what?"

"Long to be explained, interpreted?"

"As if I didn't understand myself?"

"Of course you don't. Nobody does."

"I don't believe that."

"Well . . ." Isabel said, "I figure that nobody does, but there are people like me who don't want to know and people like you who do long to be explained . . ."

What he longed for was to stop talking and to hold her in his arms. He studied how carefully the wine-red lipstick had been painted on her full lips. He watched the rhythmic rise and fall of her bosom as she breathed. Extending his right foot lightly, he began to rub the point of his shoe up into the arch of her foot.

"I had a devil of a time driving through this weather out to the stable," she said, never taking her eyes from his eyes. "I had to exercise Champion only in the stable ring. I couldn't possibly take him out in this cold. But I didn't use the saddle. I rode bareback. I love the feel of his huge body between my legs."

Conrad deposited his half-empty glass on the table and reached out to grab Isabel's shoulder, saying, "I don't think he can give you half the satisfaction you need. . . ."

"But I'm all dressed," she said. "Dinner's almost ready. Rosalie's waiting to serve it . . ."

He stood up and cupped her under her left arm, making her

rise along with him. "I think you'd better come with me. Now."

After lovemaking, Isabel was talkative and Conrad quiet.

In a few minutes, Isabel interrupted herself and announced, "I'm starved. I'll go down and tell the cook we're ready for dinner." She threw on a pair of blue jeans and a large knitted sweater.

He sat up in bed against the large pillows and took a cigarette from the end table where the one lighted lamp allowed him to see the room: its Biedermeier pattern of vertical stripes on the wallpaper of the room, on the fabric of the draperies that covered the windows, on the bedspread. All of this had been chosen by Isabel. Conrad was content with the knowledge that the furniture and the draperies and the blankets were not his but to make use of. He protected himself against the danger of confusing himself with possessions. He was not attached to most of them, in the sense that he would sacrifice anything for objects. They could not anchor him down. Still, he loved certain objects of beauty that encaptured some emotional experience of his own—such as the jade tree on the mantelpiece that caught his eye at the moment. It was the symbol of their commitment to each other. Conrad did feel committed to Isabel—and yet he was aware that, for all his thinking of her as an independent and competent person, who lived her life along the specific lines she chose for her pleasures, it was difficult to believe in her existence when he was not in her presence. Perhaps it was because most of the things she cared about were so remote from his own interests that he could not actively imagine how they felt from the inside.

He brushed aside these thoughts, roused himself from the bed, and got back into his clothes. Descending the front hall stairs, he thought how quaint of Isabel to have preserved certain old touches that identified the house despite her renovations. For example, there was one gas jet preserved on the wall next to the entrance to the dining room. The gas flame glowed through the opal-like bowl that surrounded it, a reminder that, when the house was originally built, there had been only gas illumination in it. And then there was the old-fashioned wire basket on the inside of the front door, into which mail deliveries were dropped through a brass slot. A black wire basket, like a cage, with a slide latch on the top. The memory of the letter in his back pocket sent a chill through him.

Isabel had redone the dining room in white and blue—with a vengeance. The ceiling and all of the woodwork around the doors, the windows, the shutters, too, were bone-white, but the walls were painted a royal blue, the same color as the carpeting and as the tablecloth and the cushions on the white dining room chairs. The porcelain was an undecorated white, as were the candlesticks and the candles themselves. Before he sat down, Rosalie had poured Chablis into the first wine-glasses, and now she brought in the tureen of onion soup. For some inexplicable reason, Isabel found that she liked to maintain a habit of her mother's, which was to have the table set for at least four, even when only two were having dinner; but Conrad and she sat facing each other at the middle of the table rather than be as distant as they would if they sat at the head and the foot.

Isabel began a monologue by saying, "Let me tell you the dream that woke me up this morning. It's that recurrent memory-dream of myself as a girl on my Arabian gelding, alone in the woods in the early morning, about three miles away from boarding school. I feel my heart trembling during the long canter across the meadow. And then I walk the horse on a sandy path. Thin rays of sunlight slant through the maples and the pine trees. I lean forward to stroke the wet flesh under the horse's mane and then I catch sight of the deer. A young buck at the side of the trail, beautiful, with velvety antlers. When a coral snake slithers on the path in front of us, the horse rears up unexpectedly and my forehead is whipped by the limb of a tree. I lurch forward in bed, as if to thrust against the blow, and I find myself shocked awake, alone, no longer thirteen years old, no blood running down to my left eye."

Conrad said, "Your unexpected blow."

"I've tried to figure it out, and this time I think I have. I sat there in bed realizing I was dissatisfied about something and feeling that it had to do with Ellen Connolley. I remembered how two weeks ago she invited us to their New Year's Eve party. 'Just the couples of the golf foursome,' she said; 'let's make it black tie. But no decorations, please.'" Isabel chuckled. "And I said, 'You mean Conrad can't bring me?' Ellen stopped laughing and I explained, 'I'm Conrad's decoration.'"

"Even I don't think that's funny anymore," Conrad said.

"But *that* wasn't what bothered me," Isabel said. "It's something that happened at the party."

Conrad recalled without pleasure the incident of Dr. Connolley's flirting with Isabel while they were dancing to Glenn Miller records from the 1940s—turning her smoothly on the polished floor of the large living room, where the rug had been rolled away.

"At the end of the evening," Isabel continued, "really just before we broke up, Henry Warner, who was obviously drunk, blurted out, 'I'm the only man in the room who didn't marry for money.' Of course, when he realized how rotten that sounded, he tried to change it. Remember? He said, 'That is, who didn't marry money.' Ellen Connolley tried to save the situation by saying, 'How fortunate for all of us,' and she put another record on the phonograph."

Conrad could remember the moment vividly now; it had stifled the unselfconscious pleasure of the evening, and the party broke up after one more dance.

"The point is, I didn't say anything to you about it then or the next day; I thought it was too silly. But I couldn't shake it. And then I got hit in the head by that tree just before I woke up this morning."

Conrad laughed. "Isn't it still 'too silly'?"

Isabel chose to sit in silence while Rosalie cleared away the soup bowls, served the salmon soufflé, and poured the Moselle into the second glasses. When the maid had closed the door behind her, Isabel said, "The question is whether you married me for my money."

"But that's the curse of all rich girls. They're afraid it will happen to them."

"And for good reason," Isabel said quickly. "You see, you refuse to answer the question."

"I refuse to answer the question, not on the grounds that it might incriminate me, but on the principle that it's unworthy of being asked. Either you trust me or you don't. And if you don't, then nothing I say will change your mind, will it?"

"Then why *did* you marry me?" Isabel asked.

In a rasping, nasal imitation of W. C. Fields's flippant voice, Conrad said, " 'Cause you fuck so good." Then he moved on quickly to, "Why did you marry *me*?"

Isabel turned her attention to the soufflé—but before savoring a mouthful, she answered, "It was a new pleasure to try out." Then she looked up smartly, caught his eye as a smile began to play on her lips, and said, "I *do* know why you married me. I seduced you, and, for revenge, you took me captive."

"You are not a captive. You come and go as you please and you do what you want to. . . ."

"Except when you need me here. As a hostess. As a companion. As a decoration."

"Are you unhappy most of the time?"

"No." While Rosalie served the endive salad, they remained quiet. When she was no longer in the room, Isabel added, "It's just that I feel I ought to be doing something else—only I haven't the faintest idea what. Don't make a long face. I don't hold you responsible. You are blameless"—she smiled—"and I am shameless."

All that Conrad could think of saying was, "You shouldn't

have taken Henry Warner's remark seriously. He had too much to drink and he was simply congratulating himself. He inherited a lot of money."

"*In vino veritas.* But I'm not harping on that." She rang for Rosalie to remove the dinner dishes and bring dessert. While the maid was in the room, Isabel asked, "Did you play squash today?"

"Yes. And I knocked the wind out of Tom Spofford. Banged him right in the ribs. He was doubled over." He shook his head in apology.

"I don't know what you see in him." Isabel visited Conrad in his office only infrequently, but Tom had come to their home at least a few times and she thought of him merely as wet behind the ears.

What did he see in him? Conrad wondered. A chance to experience those Pygmalion moments when he thought he was remodeling the youth in his own image? Did he want to exercise that much influence? He stared at Isabel; had he wanted to mold her into something other than she was? He would never be able to change her in that way. She was so accurately herself. Still, he found it disturbing that they could so easily rub each other the wrong way. He recognized himself to be literal-minded and therefore easily thrown off balance. If, at five o'clock, Isabel wanted to drive to the Silvermine Inn for dinner and they showered and chatted pleasantly until they were ready to go, only for her to say at the car that, no, she preferred to drive up to the Chinese restaurant in Hartford—he behaved as if she'd just walked out of the United Nations. He wanted people to mean what they said. But, then, people mean so much more than they say.

What he was afraid of in himself was having too little flexibility, almost no sense of being "free and easy," the way she was. He was considerate, thoughtful, kindly—but not much given to "a good time." He was uxorious to a woman who hardly wanted to be married. Every now and then he would break out of his sense of obligation to her and say, "What I want to do is—X, or Y, or Z." If she answered, "Well, then, you do that yourself" and he was prepared to go without her— that was liberation for her. She could join in or not, as she chose, but at least she was unburdened of feeling his unre- mitting indulgence of her, his endurance of her whims, that out of his consideration he was always forbearing.

He regretted believing she was right to assume she would never be at home here, among a community of people she had inherited by marriage, not chosen. Conrad's friends, Conrad's colleagues, Conrad's acquaintances' *wives*. The ultimate be- lievers in the work ethic: salvation by doing. Each of them breast-feeding four children, raising them according to the latest theories—was it Spock or Piaget? Or Getzels and Jack- son this month? But that was only with the right hand. With the left hand, they played recorders and violas at soirées mu- sicales, volunteered in hospitals, corralled women voters, supplied coffee to picketers, sewed their own clothes, did macramé, made gourmet meals, made Isabel sick. They knew nothing about sports, or about fashion; nor were they generous enough to tolerate what Isabel cared for. They had no men friends; they were no longer women, they were wives, the way some females were nuns. The vocation was total—al- though often enough they would get divorced and change partners, continuing to work for their salvation by doing everything just as earnestly as before. Isabel got along with none of them; not that she hadn't tried. But she turned them off. None of them was "free and easy" either.

There was a cocktail party, for example, at which she found herself trapped among a clutch of faculty wives deploring David Bach's separation from his latest spouse, carrying on about "serial polygamy." Isabel tried to deflect the conversa- tion. "Have you ever considered," she asked, "that if you re- member having had sex with three or four other men, and think of them as if they were present, participating with you, while you're having intercourse with your husband—that could be called a 'serial orgy'?"

Vivian Kirkill's brassy voice announced, "No," definitively.

The others were petulant with disapproval. Isabel would never become one of them. She was too much of a threat to them. They had to work so hard to be admired at all.

Among Conrad's acquaintances there were a few exceptions—those who were not faculty wives—whom Isabel had come to know and not dislike: Dr. Connolley's wife, Ellen, who was not good-looking, but high-spirited and amusing. And Kate Warner, whose husband owned the so-called "Tiffany's of New Haven." Isabel liked playing tennis with Kate Warner at her home in Woodbridge. Kate was a handsome woman with three children who preoccupied her. Although she was charming, there was an intensity at the core of her that made Isabel uncomfortable. It was as if there were a destiny dreaded, which made Isabel worry about herself, for she did not wish to ask questions like: What will become of me? Where will I meet my fate? She loathed the idea of pulling herself up by the roots to see if she were growing. She had stopped growing. She was fully formed.

Conrad said, "Senator Stonefort called this morning. He's asked me to come to Washington for a day next week."

"Your friend at court."

"Would you like to go down with me?"

"Which day?"

"Wednesday."

"Maybe."

Conrad tried to imagine what alternatives came to her mind. Would she be choosing among such possibilities as participating in the Junior League horse show in New York sometime this month, or skiing, or visiting her brother on the West Coast? Did she have a lover?

The dessert was fresh fruit in kirsch and on another salad plate came wedges of cheese and crackers. And then espresso in demitasse cups.

At length, Conrad said, "The provost has had a heart attack."

Isabel chose her words carefully: "Do they think he will live?"

"It's touch and go. If he is still alive in twenty-four hours, there might be a good chance for survival."

"You know there's no love lost between us."

"How can you dislike him so much? You barely know him. You've had next to nothing to do with him."

"I know him. He just doesn't know I'm alive. Every single time we're together, it's been necessary to introduce me, as if he'd never seen me before."

"He's nearsighted."

"I'm a sight for sore eyes. I've always been amiable to him, and I've always been disregarded by him."

"He's a very limited man."

"And now he may come to the end of his limits? If he dies, will you become provost?"

Conrad felt that his inner thoughts might be revealed unless he was very cautious. He replied: "There's no way to know—yet. And it is premature even to think about it."

"Would we have to move into the provost's house?"

Repressing all of his own mixed feelings, Conrad stood up and said, "What a delicious dinner. Thank you."

Isabel rose, and said, "I'll give your compliments to the cook."

Conrad opened the double doors of the dining room and walked into the hall as the telephone began to ring. "I'll get it," Conrad called out toward the back of the house as he walked into the living room. Beyond the piano, before the archway that opened onto the few steps down to the sun porch, there was an alcove. Isabel had placed a love seat into it: a classic S-curved double chair, for lovers to sit facing each other, but not touching. The telephone stood on a pedestal just behind the center of the curve. "Conrad Taylor here," he announced into the mouthpiece—as the representative of the telephone company had once instructed the staff of his office to do.

"Jerry here," came back at him.

"Oh, Jerry, thanks for calling. Have you found out anything?" Conrad's fingers nervously played against his back pocket.

"Yes, I have." The voice was somber. "I happened to walk in at a very bad moment."

"In the intensive care unit?" Conrad asked, as if the antiseptic words themselves were supposed to be preventive of something worse, if not healing.

"Right. Believe it or not—there were two residents in cardiology taking turns pounding away at his chest with their fists." Conrad felt a cold shiver run through his spine. "His heartbeat's that irregular."

"That irregular . . ." Conrad repeated, distressed to be hopeful. "What will they do now?"

"They're going to force in a temporary pacemaker."

"How?"

"Well, they make an incision in the right arm and send a catheter up through an artery to the heart."

Conrad was silent.

Dr. Rosenblatt continued: "They're giving him oxygen, and intravenous feedings." His voice was flat, reportorial in the conventional broadcaster's manner—in which, without passion, the worst flood disasters and earthquakes are recounted along with announcements of political coups and society marriages.

Conrad asked, "What do you think his chances are?"

"Few," Jerry replied.

"Oh . . ."

"I'm sorry."

"Yes. Well, I'm grateful to you for calling. Thanks a lot."

"I'll check in again tomorrow," Dr. Rosenblatt said.

"I'd appreciate it."

"I'd do it anyway," Jerry said crisply. But then he added, "And I'll call you. Wait a day. Wait twenty-four to forty-eight hours. Then you'll probably be able to see him."

"I hope so," Conrad forced out of himself.

"Good night." Conrad put the phone down and remained still against one of the curves of the love seat. He drew the anonymous letter out of his back pocket and unfolded the paper—thinking of two interns alternately pounding on one's chest.

"Who was that?" Isabel asked as she entered the living room and started to look for the latest Agatha Christie she had just been reading.

"Jerry," he replied. "He's been to see the provost. It sounds very chancy; he has a slim chance of surviving."

"I was going to say, 'I'm sorry for Elsie,' but then I don't know her well enough. I don't know anybody well enough . . ."

"Nobody knows anybody well enough."

Isabel chuckled. "You can make the most commonplace notion sound profound."

Conrad thought of the editorial in *The New York Times*, in which James Reston suggested that the secretary of state, Dr. Henry Kissinger, ought to marry again. Having everything else, he implied, he needs only a wife "to keep him in line."

"Does Jerry sound worried?" Isabel asked, trying to be sympathetic.

"He sounded professional. Doctors don't let you know if they're worried. They just make you feel they're aware of more than you are. It's supposed to generate confidence in them."

"What's that you're holding?" she asked. Conrad was recalled to the letter lying on his lap.

Isabel approached him, gliding across the high pile of the smooth beige rug, past the sofa and the end tables, relaxed, comfortable. She stared at Conrad's pale face and, without a word, reached toward the letter. He could have prevented her from reading it, but, instead, lifted it to her hand, knowing that the important decisions of one's life are not made in the moment they're acted out, but by how one has lived all the years of his life up to that moment.

"It looks like a blackmail threat in a 1930s movie," she said, before reading. Once she had taken it in, she let it drop to land in front of Conrad's feet. She snorted. He watched her face. She frowned.

"You're accustomed to hate mail, aren't you?" she asked.

"Most of that sort of stuff doesn't touch me."

"Is this different?" She sounded unperturbed, uninvolved, only curious about why this should bother him. He sat immobile, and then lit a cigarette. "It's just hate mail," she repeated.

"Someone who knows where I live, knows that I'm married, maybe even knows you, has gone to the trouble of patching up such a lousy letter and coming out on a cold night in winter to drop it into our mailbox. Someone who wants to hurt us, stood on our front porch, and dropped that letter into the mailbox."

"But someone with no guts. No face. An anonymous guerrilla. No one who would ever stand up to you or me and say it. Some nasty smart-ass."

Conrad stared at her from where he remained seated. He looked up at the beautiful, strong, independent woman who was his wife and asked, as casually as he could make the words come out, "Is there any truth in it?"

As though having been given license by him, she replied, "That is not a question worthy of being answered."

He sprang up and grabbed her by the wrist. "But if *I* ask the question—'Are you having a love affair with another man?'— then it's because I think it's worth asking."

"Let go," she said quietly, standing her ground. When he dropped his hand from her arm, she turned away toward the hall and stopped at the credenza where the maid had laid out the after-dinner drinks and poured a brandy for herself. At length she said, "You think it's worth asking. You imagine someone might know something about me that you don't know. That's beneath you. It has nothing to do with us." Isabel sighed. "It's a matter of trust. And nothing I say will make any difference, will it? I'll be goddamned if I'll respond to such an accusation—even if I *weren't* having an affair!" She laughed.

"Then you *are*," he said, crestfallen.

Her reply was clearly self-protective but made with dignity and the detachment of her self-esteem. "Even if I were, it wouldn't concern you and I wouldn't discuss it." She paused. "And if I weren't—I wouldn't admit it. I thought you and I were above this. I'm very sorry if I'm wrong." But the tone of her voice said she wouldn't be sorry at all. She poured another brandy from the decanter and handed it to Conrad. "I'll be in bed, darling," she said. "This is such a good Agatha Christie, I can't put it down." She stroked the side of his cheek with her cool palm and then she left the room.

Conrad rested the brandy glass on the piano and rubbed his hands back and forth over both eyes, closed to block out all sight. He felt sweaty, as if the heat in the house had suddenly jumped up ten degrees. He walked around the sofa to throw himself down on it lengthwise, and try to let his body relax, let the tension seep away. He had behaved like an adolescent told by his girlfriend that she didn't want to go steady with him. Lashing out, grasping her by the wrist—that was puerile. Or is there so strong an instinct for fidelity, *demand* of faithfulness on the part of the wife, that the body orders the action, the desire to dominate, independent of the mind? Oh, the mind, the mind! the weariness of the mind's arguments that adultery doesn't matter, it makes no difference—when the body still says it does.

She had never dropped a hint of involvement with any other man. There were times when she was away without him, but no word had ever reached him—through anyone he knew— that she was carrying on with someone else.

Anyone he knew? He thought of the vicious letter, lying somewhere behind him on the floor, pasted together out of printed words. Whoever sent it knew him, probably knew him *and* Isabel; but did he know the person who had put it together? An enemy. The thought formed in his mind: a faceless enemy. Someone who wished him ill, who wished to hurt his feelings. But the countermovement of his mind formed the thought of a friend, a misguided friend, someone who thought he was doing the honorable thing by Conrad to let him know that Isabel had a lover. A naive friend.

Conrad got up from the sofa, pulled the meshed fire curtain apart and lifted another log onto the embers, stirred the fire with a poker, shoveled some of the embers up onto the wood in the grate, and left the fire curtain open, turning his back on it to look for the letter. He found it under the piano, and reread it as he returned to the fireplace. Why did it say "the" hotel, the way he said "the" university—as if there were only one? He threw it onto the fresh flames, watched it turn brown, then black, shrivel up and fall apart, disintegrate into the ashes. He hated it; he hated the fact of it, whether it spoke true or false. He hated the thought of someone trying to second-guess him, of someone who took it on himself to pry into his private life and to "inform" him: an informer. No one had that right— even if he's invited to exercise it. It is the one thing no one must ever allow himself the liberty to do; spies should always be shot.

His mind was wandering. He turned out all of the lamps in the room, settled himself glumly in one of the armchairs, and stared into the fire. The thought of his first wife came to attack him—like indigestion. They had thought they were in love, but they were children holding hands to minimize their fears. They became disabused of love early, but neither of them had the courage to confess the failure. It was a sheer accident, a deus ex machina, that a Broadway producer—what was his name?—seduced her and, mercifully, she ran away with him, abandoning their child to him. Had they remained married? He knew nothing of what had become of her. Caroline never spoke of her. He knew only that, when she was eighteen, Caroline had spent a weekend with her mother at Southampton. He rejected the thought of his first wife—with her tight little mouth, her mannish suits, her intellectual pretensions.

Isabel was the ultimate opposite.

Conrad got up to look for the brandy snifter, poured more of the powerful liquid into his glass, and returned to the armchair. Isabel was his reward. He had never expected to marry again—let alone to find himself happy in bed with so young a woman. And if he was happy in bed with her, enjoyed talking with her over dinner when they were alone, proud to show her off in company, at the university or among private friends—then, what more did he need? The seal of certainty that she would never be unfaithful to him? Why? For his vanity. For the illusion that there could be no other man more desirable than he. That would not be realistic. One knows too much to hope for it. But one hopes that it will not happen to himself. It is amusing and inconsequential only when it happens to someone else. He had more than enough in his own life and in his new marriage to be satisfied, to be content. When would *more than enough* be enough? He chuckled silently to himself.

There are so many levels of faithfulness. And sexual fidelity is only one—perhaps less important than all the others. The others are sensed, felt, judged, all of the time, day in and day out. Besides, it can't be policed. He snickered. He remembered vaguely a story of Rabelais's. Where was it, in *Gargantua* or *Pantagruel*. The *dream* of the newly married man. And the magician or the witch. There was some supernatural power in it—a magus of some sort. And the young husband begs to learn how he can make certain his wife will always be faithful to him. The Wise Old Man slips a ring onto his middle finger and says, "As long as you wear this, your wife will not be unfaithful to you." —What a joy!— But when the husband wakes up he finds that the finger is his penis and the ring is his wife's vagina. Only while they are coupled together can he be certain that his wife will not be unfaithful to him. Now Conrad laughed out loud.

Then he allowed himself the luxury of recalling how Isabel and he came to be married.

PART 2

HOW HE CAME TO MARRY HER

A<small>T THE END OF THE SUMMER</small> before he was operated on for stomach ulcers, Conrad arranged to take a six-month leave of absence—the only protracted absence from his position he had ever requested—on the hidden assumption that he might not survive the operation and, even more secretly, in the self-pitying belief that, in any case, his life was no longer worth living. He had been under surgery before. This time even more of his stomach would have to be removed. He took the diagnosis as a prediction that he must gradually starve to death: a melodramatic extrapolation from a medical point of view, but consistent with his sense of gradual shrinking of the nourishment available for his well-being in general. As things were, he had come to live on very short rations. His first wife deserted him—literally. His daughter had abandoned and rejected him—figuratively. She had made herself a thorn in his side, a constant abrasion, a mirror of the knifelike pain in the center of his chest. It remained true that he felt admired and appreciated for the job he did at the university, but he did not mislead himself into imagining he was indispensable. There was no other person for whom he was irreplaceable, and being level-headed about that knowledge allowed him to turn his thoughts to his own nonexistence, to anticipate death.

Still, out of the inertia of good habits of appropriate behavior, he could not allow the ulcer to kill him without putting up a fight, without doing—allowing to be done—all the things that doctors recommended, as if it mattered to him whether he lived or died. Surgery did not frighten him. The image of a knife, a scalpel, was ever present in his mind; it was what he felt at all times—the slowly twisting, insinuating, sharp edge of the cutting knife below his heart—stabbing, pausing, jabbing. The torture allowed for no position to put it to rest, no condition to alleviate it; it stabbed through the strongest painkiller, kept him awake at night, and forced him to double over in the privacy of his study in the middle of the day. He could drug himself into senselessness, which is a form of nonexistence, or he could run the risk of further surgery which might result in his death—despite all of the optimistic prognosis of the doctors. The plan for the operation and a long rest, a recuperation and a vacation, justified the request for the leave of absence. He saw his daughter fly off for at least a year to study acting in London, and then entered the hospital with all of his papers in order—his bills paid, his last will and testament witnessed properly, the utilities turned off in his house.

Almost to his chagrin, the operation was a success and his recovery assured. He became, rather by accident, a free agent, with nearly half a year in which to do whatever he wanted to—only to discover that there was nothing he wanted to do. His friend Henry Warner made an arrangement with his older brother who lived on a yacht out of Palm Beach to set him up in comfortable quarters in Florida and, when he was strong enough, to take him on long quiet cruises through the Caribbean. To Saint Maartens on one run and, then later, to Cosumel and along the coast of Yucatán. Conrad dragged himself through these pleasures as if he had cheated death but had no life to return to. Warner's brother was not his kind of man— hard drinking and wenching, a man without conscience—a man with whom Conrad had nothing to talk about. On the other hand, he no longer wanted to talk. He wanted to be all alone. Brought up in the heart of the Midwest, the nearly flat lands of Missouri, educated on the perfectly flat land of Chicago, comforted for years by the gently rolling hills of Connecticut, bored by the sand and stumpy palmettos of Florida, Conrad longed for towering, snow-covered mountains, for Rockies, for jagged edges, for crisp, cool air, for solitude. Early in January he left the Warner yacht for Aspen, Colorado.

On the plane flying west, he sat next to a nine-year-old boy and his mother. The child was kept entertained by putting together a small jigsaw puzzle on the little tray that jutted out toward him from the seat in front. Conrad watched the mother begin to organize the pieces for him, urging him to start with the straight-edged ones that must make the outer border and then work inward from the frame to complete the picture. It was a reproduction of the painting of Washington crossing the frozen Delaware. Conrad fell asleep—and entered into a dream in which he was a jigsaw puzzle. That is to say: the dream told him that he would be able to see the picture of his life, to see his life as a whole. He worked very hard to get the pieces to fit—they were curved-edged, old-fashioned, hard wooden pieces that had to fit perfectly; there was no chance of fudging or compromise. Each one belonged in only one place. He sweated with eagerness to make each one join with another to build up the picture he longed to see. There were his mother and his father, the suburb of St. Louis, the University of Chicago, Anne, his former wife, the university to which he had devoted himself for so many years, his daughter Caroline—all moving inward from the frame to locate him, to allow the picture of himself to come into view—when he discovered that there were no other pieces left, no unused part to be set in place: all of the surrounding conditions were established and he was the missing piece that should be set into the center. He became panicky, terrified that he had lost the piece that counted most if he were ever to see the picture of his life. He searched on the floor, through his pockets, in his carry-on luggage looking for the missing piece and could not find it. Then, suddenly, fallen back in his seat, slack, staring at the incomplete puzzle on the small tray before him, he saw that the shapes of the pieces were alive, were changing before his eyes, they were molten, malleable, rearranging themselves, squeezing toward each other as if to fill the empty space in the center—and the thought terrified him that he was only the way in which all the other pieces converged—and nothing else. That he was only their pressures on him and his invisible resistance to those pressures. Calling on all his reserves of strength to exert himself against them suddenly jolted him awake. The plane began its descent. He brought out his handkerchief to wipé away the cold sweat from his face and his neck.

The first few days in Aspen satisfied his need for solitude and rest. He was alive, released from pain, quiet, and out of touch. But the effect of the dream on the plane did not dissipate for a while. His mind frequently forced him back to the image of the jigsaw puzzle of the conditions of his life without revealing the picture of his life as a whole. At the center, among the living, self-moving, enlarging, and shrinking pieces of the puzzle that surrounded him, Conrad felt unable to see himself at all if he tried to understand his life only in that frame of "conditions." It was like trying to comprehend himself through the expectations of others, which was not more than half the picture. He had lived up to those expectations, but what was he independent of them, of all of them? The sense that he was nothing without them irritated him. He felt the need to exert his own pressure not in response to the demands, or by fulfillment of expectations of others, but freely out of the eagerness to identify and affirm himself. Nevertheless, he could not find the strength to exert such pressure.

He was drifting, He drifted along the pleasant streets of Aspen, Colorado, with the loose aimlessness of a man unaccustomed to enjoying vacations. He stopped at the window of a haberdashery store and stared at a handsome, chocolate-brown corduroy suit with leather buttons that would have been slightly sporty for him, thinking that he ought to go in and try it on—he had only a minimum amount of cold-weather clothing with him—but he postponed entering the store. He felt that reading every page of the local newspaper over an hour-long breakfast was an accomplishment. In one of the bookshops, he came across a set of *Remembrance of Things Past* and imagined that would be a project worth undertaking. He had never read Proust in English. But then he remembered how many times he'd been told by friends who were seriously ill, in their hospital rooms or as they were about to leave on lengthy cruises in order to recuperate, that they were taking along *Remembrance of Things Past,* with the implication that if they were to die soon, they wanted at least to have reread Proust. Those associations left an unpleasant taste in his mouth. He had not been given bad news about how little time he had left to live. He had been given bad news about how much time he still had. He turned quickly away from the shelves of books and walked out of the store and tried to make himself concentrate on the faces and figures of passersby along the sidewalk.

When he had been very unhappy as a child—he couldn't remember how old, or what it was he had been unhappy about—his mother consoled him with this advice: When you are very sad, and feel you are trapped in a room walled with mirrors so that all you can see is reflections of your own unhappiness, then you must cut a window right through one of the mirrors—because the only way out is to concentrate on something other than yourself. You must give yourself over to a piece of music or a work of poetry, contemplate a painting or a piece of sculpture; turn yourself over to it, and it will rescue you. Thus did Conrad try to concentrate on the faces of the passersby: mostly youthful, mostly healthy, and almost universally cheerful. This was a place people came to revel in, to enjoy their own well-being. A "resort." It occurred to him that longing to be refreshed by basking in the presence of such people is what had lured him to Aspen rather than the sight of the rugged mountains, which had been the signal image in his mind.

At this time of the year, well after the height of the Christmas season, there were fewer tourists in Aspen; mainly serious skiers filled the hotels and lodges. The weather was glorious. The sky gave no hint of depth. There was no cloud in it to offer any benchmark for distance. There were no layers in the uniform cornflower blue of its endless clarity. Conrad took a deep breath, decided to buy ski pants, a sweater, and a jacket on his way back to the hotel, and to have his hair cut.

The next day he saw Isabel for the first time. It had snowed heavily all day long. Whereas the lobby of the motel where he stayed was usually empty during the day, it was now crowded with frustrated skiers. He took the elevator to the top floor where the large, glass-enclosed room that was a bar in the evening served as a coffee shop during the day. A fire burned on a platform, surrounded by the circular bar, and shot its flames up toward a bright copper funnel that carried the smoke away out through the top of the building. Conrad had taken a cup of hot chocolate and strolled to the glass wall to look at the snow falling like balls of cotton against the pale gray sky. When he idly turned his head to look back toward the fire, his gaze fell on Isabel—then a nameless female— seated at the bar, looking toward him. She wore tapered black ski pants and a bulky sweater of oatmeal-colored wool woven into elaborate braids across her chest and down her arms. Around her neck was tied a silk scarf of turquoise blue. She had a radiant complexion, suntanned, and the warmth of the room had heightened the pink glow in her rounded cheeks. He thought her eyes might be reflections of the turquoise scarf she was wearing, but he could not see them well from where he stood. It was her hair that made him keep staring at her. Her long, golden hair had been swept casually but smoothly up over the crown of her head and all the outer lines of it held the light from the fireplace behind her, so that they seemed to flicker and quaver as her face remained immobile. The word "exquisite" formed in his mind. He hoped that she could see the disinterested look of admiration on his face. It occurred to him that she must be accustomed to that look, and that it was probably one of the joys of her life to watch that look be gradually transformed into lust. He did not respond to the gift she offered; he did not acknowledge the fact that she was looking at him with a Mona Lisa smile. He imagined she was thinking of someone else as he turned his eyes again to the falling snow.

The next day was clear and sunny. Conrad rented boots and skis and spent half the morning on the beginners' slope, reassuring himself that he could try the intermediate slope, on which he spent the rest of the morning. But by noon he was fatigued, ate a very light lunch in the lodge, and then lay out on a deck chair on the terrace. He could see for ten miles from that side of the mountain, and the air tasted delicious.

Conrad slept for a while. When he woke up and bought himself a cup of coffee, he stood against the wooden balcony along the terrace gazing out at the sparkling scene. The late afternoon sunlight on the snow dazzled, as if millions of diamonds were scattered across the surface of the fresh whiteness. Pine trees in dark green and apple green contrasted sharply with the paling blue of the sky. The lowering sun gilded the faces of the healthy young people as they came to a halt at the base of the lodge some ten yards beyond where he stood. High above them other skiers appeared, having come down from the highest point on the mountainside, visible now on the crest of the last slope as each of them curved the way down to the end of the run. One of them moved with such verve, he thought of her dancing with an imaginary partner. She zigzagged her way down toward the base with such exhilaration, such joy in the movements she made over the sleek, white-covered earth, the purity of the smooth snow, that she conveyed the thrill of flying, silent, lifted off the snow and coming down again to the fulfillment of the final run, filled with such satisfaction in her own ecstatic grace that, as she drew to a halt, thrusting her spiked poles into the hard snow, and looked around her—at the young men and women drinking hot chocolate from paper cups—it seemed to Conrad she was looking them over as if trying to locate someone she could hug, to share her pleasure with. He recognized the beautiful blond girl he had seen for the first time the day before.

She gazed up at the terrace and caught his eye. He felt as though she might call out to him, as if they knew each other, but she didn't let herself do that. She smiled a broad smile and stretched her limbs. This time he smiled back. He lifted his paper cup to toast her. She made a curtsy, awkwardly, sliding on the skis under her, and then bent down to unbuckle her boots. He moved away from the terrace and entered the lodge. He did not want to be there if she looked up, but not at him.

The next evening after dinner, Conrad wandered over to the Jerome Hotel, to watch couples dancing in the nightclub there. It was as if he had been waiting for her, when Isabel arrived arm in arm with two ski instructors. She was dressed in a long-sleeved black velvet gown that fell just short of her ankles and revealed elaborate patent-leather shoes with crossed straps like the ones Joan Crawford wore in 1930s movies. Around her neck lay a circle of great chunks of amber, large as golf balls, tobacco-stained translucent gold. Conrad felt like a spy. He skulked among the tables surrounding the dance floor and gradually allowed himself to believe that she became aware of his watching her.

Isabel danced with one of the ski instructors and then with the other, but she did occasionally look in Conrad's direction. When it grew late, and the combo played its finale, a pianist took over. Wheeled alongside of the dance floor, his piano was edged with a dark leather shoulder to serve as a bar, and stools were brought up for drinkers to huddle close and listen to him play Cole Porter and George Gershwin. Conrad rose up onto the stool to the pianist's right. Isabel took a barstool on the opposite side, facing him. Each of the ski instructors kissed her good night and left the room. Alone, in the dimly lit, partly filled lounge, she stared at him directly across the piano. He thought of her as flushed with uncomplicated physical satisfaction, relaxed and happy inside her skin, and that, as a "reserved older man," an almost pale, middle-aged fellow in a business suit, he thought of himself as an intruder.

She smiled at him, a friendly, open smile; in Aspen, people who've never seen each other before ask, "How you doing today?"

He looked over his shoulder to see whether she intended the smile for someone else.

She shook her head and snickered. He beamed, he relaxed, he sent her a very kindly look.

She tilted her head to the right to contemplate him better.

He tilted his head to her right in response.

With one hand, she stroked the amber balls at her neck—a slow and cautious gesture. The index finger idly slid along her throat.

He felt for the Windsor knot in his necktie and let the index finger stroke his Adam's apple.

She raised her glass and drank a sip without taking her eyes away from his face.

He drank from his glass and studied her hair, her throat, her shoulders.

When the pianist began the next song, Isabel rose from her stool and walked to the middle of the almost empty dance floor, raised her arms, and stood still, waiting for him to join her. He approached—in his neat dark suit, white shirt, burgundy-colored tie—taller than she, excited, suspicious. He took her in his arms.

"The last dance was lovely," she said, "but I thought we might enjoy it even more without the piano between us." Her voice had both a high-pitched tinkling and then a throaty quality.

He held her firmly and led them into the smooth movements of the dance. Isabel touched her nose to his chin—which made him imagine that she wafted her perfume toward him as if it were a caress. He assumed she could feel the tension in his body.

"You don't know what to make of me, do you?" she said.

"You're right. I don't."

"I won't bite," she replied.

"But I might," he said, despite how unsure he felt of himself.

She laughed out loud. She threw her head back and looked at him with pleasure, saying, "What fun!" She was not threatened. She had lured him out of his silence, she had given him freedom to let desire seep into his gaze at her. She let her body move against his to the rhythm of the music and against the hardness of the floor, as she had skied during the day, pitting her skill and grace against the conditions of the sport.

"You're very good-looking," she said. "You remind me of a movie star. . . ." She smiled. She couldn't remember the name of the actor.

"How many hundreds of times have you been told how beautiful you are?" he asked. There was nothing sarcastic in his objective question; she must realize he was actually humble. She simply yielded herself more willingly into his embrace.

When she said, "I'd like to go to bed with you," she felt the tremor run through his body. "Are you shocked?" she asked, not looking at his face.

"It's culture shock," he said slowly and then added quickly, "but good."

"You're shy!"

"No. It's just that I'm a lot older than you and not accustomed to gifts from the gods."

Isabel stopped moving at the edge of the dance floor. She took his face in her hands and brought it to hers—her lips open for the readiness of their first kiss.

Then he said, "I don't even know your name. Let's sit down. Let's talk."

"You are old-fashioned." She smiled approvingly.

They took their drinks from the piano and hid themselves at a small round table with light only from the stub of a pink candle. They stared at each other as if stroking each other's face. It was then Conrad saw her eyes were the burning blue of sapphires.

At length he said, "Tell me the story of your life."

"I can give you the facts, but I don't know if they make a story," she replied. She told him of boarding school in Rhode Island, of winter vacations in Jamaica, of the death of her parents. Of becoming a ward of her uncle, of college at Vassar, of her apartment in New York. She enjoyed horses and horse shows, skiing, swimming, travel. She told him of her brother Kevin—the sculptor—and of his home overlooking the Pacific at Carmel. Of fashion shows in Paris. She hardly listened to herself; she was no more involved in what she was saying than if she were filling out an application for a passport. She cared only for the expression of interest in his eyes. And then suddenly she asked, "Is there a story in it? What makes for a story?"

"Consequences," Conrad replied. "Discovering what seemed to happen for its own sake brings about something unexpected."

"You have all the answers," she said, more appreciatively than critical.

He brushed that aside with, "No, no, no." He didn't want to be taken for a pedant. Isabel held his hand in hers, on his lap, under the tablecloth.

Briskly he asked, "What are you doing with your life?"

"Getting over my parents' death," she answered, not flippantly but without relish for the question.

"You make it sound as if they died together."

"Yes. They were killed in the same accident. I was fifteen." But she was not to become morbid. "Do you realize," she announced with a laugh, "that we still don't know what to call each other?"

They exchanged names as if each slipped the other the keys to their hotel rooms.

Conrad sketched for her the outline of his life. He touched lightly on the painfulness of his first marriage and how his daughter had become estranged from him. He mentioned his recent operation.

"But you look in such good shape," she interrupted him.

He told her of squash in wintertime and golf and tennis the rest of the year. He indicated how much he enjoyed living in New Haven; of his no longer teaching, and of writing less than before. But most of all, of his satisfaction with being an administrator.

"What does an 'administrator' do?" she asked, as if the word were not easily digested—a foreign dish, too highly spiced.

"He's a combination impresario and stage manager. Administrators arrange things so that the show can go on, then the actors and the musicians are able to perform."

They studied each other's eyes for signals of interest, appreciation, desire. Isabel fondled his hand in hers.

In a gentle, warning voice, Conrad pointed out: "I'm old enough to be your father."

"But you're *not* my father . . ." Isabel replied passionately and kissed him on the lips. Then she sighed. Suddenly she asked, "What are you drinking?"

"Scotch."

"I have some very good Scotch in my room."

"Here?" he asked.

"Won't you come up?"

She never did turn on the lamps in her suite that night. They walked through the sitting room to find the draperies drawn away from the French door to the balcony in her bedroom. A full moon shone its pearly light through the pines and the birch trees and fell between shadows on the carpet. He undressed her carefully in the quiet of the darkness, placing her clothes upon an armchair. She began to undress him, but he balked at taking off his undershirt because of his recent operation.

Between the sheets of the double bed, they fondled each other and kissed—kisses that seemed to last an hour. Stroking and caressing, kisses of delicacy and sensuality. Isabel caught her fingernails in the fabric of his tee shirt. He was so sensitive an explorer, so simply fascinated, he felt that his sense of wonderment was what enchanted her. There was no explosion of frenzy, only the exquisite approach to pleasure and then to ecstasy. His hands amazed her—the patient explorations of his extraordinarily sensuous hands. He was both experienced and modest.

In the days that followed, Isabel confessed to him that she had enjoyed sex from the age of eighteen. She had known men determined to impress her with their prowess: intercourse with such well-made males was tinged with calisthenics, as for athletic competitions—testing for admittance to an Olympic team out to set world records. She had known only a few timid or insecure men, for she attracted the self-confident and ambitious almost exclusively. Conrad was not shy, he was not without self-assurance; but neither was he in any kind of contest, nor was he more interested in his own pleasure than in hers. She realized that he did not strike her as ambitious because he was already accomplished. He didn't have to make his way in the world any more than he had to prove that he could excite her erotically. He was established in the world, and she had offered herself to him freely. With him she was both erotically excited and psychologically safe at the same time. His modesty was her aphrodisiac. She craved to show her appreciation by satisfying him with gratitude for the ways in which his self-possession exalted her. She almost broke into tears. It was only with the greatest effort of self-control that she said only, "That was wonderful." And he said, "You are magnificent."

They fell asleep in each other's arms, awoke to make love again. They separated reluctantly, saying as little as possible to each other, promising to meet in the evening.

They kept their rendezvous in the bar at the Jerome Hotel. He rose from his seat as she approached; he kissed her hand. She was the first to speak: "Haven't I seen you somewhere before?"

"Only part of me," he answered.

"I like the tip of your iceberg."

They spoke slowly, cautiously, with the uncertainty of whether the pleasure of the night before had been merely imagined. They were testing their memories against a sense of probability.

"Is this actually happening?" Conrad asked.

The room was crowded and noisy, but they concentrated only on each other's eyes and lips.

"You look tan," she replied. "You must have sat in the sunlight all day long."

"You skied."

"I thought of nothing but you."

"Who are you?" he asked. "I wish I could know you."

"If I were a fabric, I'd be moiré silk," she replied. "If I were a stone, I'd be an emerald. If I were a flower, I'd be a peony." She laughed. "You know that game?"

"Of course. If I were a stone, I'd be a Petoskey."

"What is that?" she asked with surprise. He felt he could always introduce her to new things.

He told her about the state stone of Michigan—fossils millions of years old found along the northern beaches of Lake Michigan. Oval-shaped rocks, dull as gray flannel when dry but, wet by the lake water or polished by grinding, they reveal the intricate honeycomb patterns of internal configurations laid down in prehistoric times. The fascination of an extraordinary treasure disguised as an ordinary rock. "Will you keep me from drying out?" he asked. "Keep me moist so that all the elaborate internal designs can be revealed?"

In the course of that evening, they tended to speak again after longer and longer intervals, fearful of losing the justification for being in each other's presence. It seemed to Conrad, at that time—there was so great a gap between the attraction they felt for each other and the differences between their personalities—that their sexual interests had lives of their own, like naked children allowed to play with each other, but only in the company of their adult guardians, hovering close to them to keep them from hurting each other. Conrad's sexuality remained an endless mystery to him. In the first years of his marriage to Anne, in his early twenties, he knew his sexual appetite to be indefatigable—despite the growing evidence of his wife's indifference. But after she had run away from him, rejected him, he felt that his sexuality was essentially crippled, shamed, belittled. In some sense he had never recovered from the feeling of being publicly branded "not man enough—to keep his wife." The fact that on an intellectual level he did not believe that at all made no difference to his loss of self-confidence. He rarely felt the desire to seduce a younger woman and he never attempted to do so, even when such feelings were aroused in him. He had been satisfied for years by occasional, but infrequent, affairs with other men's wives, each of which had been initiated by the woman and none of which had led to a continuing relationship. Otherwise, he relaxed himself with a regularity of masturbation.

But making love with Isabel released in him what must have been long, long suppressed passions to possess; to *keep her* unto himself and to repeat the experience of joy that he took in making love with her.

That second evening she went back with him to his motel and stayed the whole night.

During the next morning, after they had skied together for a while on the intermediate slope and Isabel went off by herself to the higher, more difficult runs, Conrad returned to his motel room and placed a call to Poughkeepsie, New York, asking to speak with the provost of Vassar College. They were old acquaintances from a variety of intercollegiate councils and conferences. The provost of Vassar was a lady of the same age as Conrad, with a sharp mind, an easy manner, and a heavy, guttural voice.

They exchanged insignificant chitchat to begin with, although Conrad did explain that he was on leave of absence because of his operation and recuperating at Aspen. He then came to the reason for his call and asked her if she remembered Isabel, who had graduated from the college about eight years before.

It did not take her more than an instant to reply.

"Of course I do. She was a famous beauty among the beauties. I recall her as absolutely gorgeous."

"What else do you remember about her?"

"Horses," she said. "She was very big on horses," and then she chuckled. "As I remember—she was a very good student and got fine grades but, then, she didn't seem to give a damn about the work. I think she had no sense of being competitive as far as her studies were concerned, but then she didn't have to try to excel. She simply was good at her work and let it go at that."

Then as in a rush, what followed was, "Of course, you know, she is enormously wealthy. Her parents left her millions. And she is constantly sought after."

Conrad said only, "Oh," flatly, in the same instant that he felt he must try to marry her.

"Now it's my turn for a question," he heard the voice at the other end of the phone declare. "Why are you asking me this? Have you met her?"

"Yes. She is here in Aspen. I met her a few days ago."

"Ah, Conrad . . ." He heard the voice stroke him gently. "Isn't she much too young for you . . .?"

Conrad laughed lightly. "I'm trying to find out how young I am."

"I don't know which way to wish you luck," she said.

"That makes two of us," Conrad lied in conclusion. He already knew exactly what he wanted.

It is not a matter of how young I am, Conrad corrected himself. A few months ago, I had thought I might be dead by now. Instead, there is a charming, youthful spirit who makes me feel intensely alive—not because I play at being as young as she; just the opposite. She makes me feel desired by her because I am old enough to be her father. Instead of a youth her own age, a boyfriend in the playpen with her, I am an older man, dependable as a father. She makes me feel worthy of her gifts—because I make her feel secure.

The next evening they met for dinner at the Crystal Palace, to drink margaritas and dine on frog's legs. Isabel seemed withdrawn and cautious.

"Are you unhappy about something?" Conrad asked.

Pensively, Isabel said, "The better you get to know me, the less you will like me."

"Will you ever tire of my telling you how beautiful you are?" Conrad asked.

"Never!" she answered flippantly, but added, "Won't you tire of saying it to me?"

"I want to know you better. And I want you to know me."

"What shall we do about it?"

Conrad thought for a moment. "Let me tell you a story."

"I love to hear stories."

"In Paris, in the seventeenth century, one of the great ladies who had a salon famous for sophisticated conversations was the Marquise de Sablé. The Duc de la Rochefoucauld was one of her regular guests. She started a 'parlor game' for them; each of the guests was to write three descriptions of themselves. First, what they believed to be the way other people saw them, second, the way they saw themselves. The third was to be the truth."

"Did they do it?"

"Not all three. They discovered that they could imagine what other people thought of them, and that they could attempt to be honest about how they thought of themselves, but the 'objective truth' is a mirage."

"A kind of make-believe," Isabel said.

"I think the idea of objectivity is another name for the fantasy of God's knowledge of us," Conrad smiled.

"Are you a believer?"

"No."

"Then you don't think there can be an objective judgment of a person?"

"No, I don't. Unless you try to think with God's mind. But there is no God."

Isabel sighed. "What a relief!"

"From what?" Conrad asked.

"From imagining that anyone will ever know everything about you—including yourself."

"Does that please you?"

"It supports what I've come to understand and believe." Her face was grave but not unhappy. "The truth is," she began, "that I was in treatment—in psychoanalysis—for five years after my parents were killed. Do you want to know how it ended? I came to the conclusion that nobody can make any sense out of life; there's no sense to be made of it. And if I could live with that, then I could come to enjoy it." When she finished saying that, a shiver ran through her body.

Conrad reached across the small table and patted her bare arm. "Can you live with that?"

"I do. . . ."

He stared at her nose, at the tiny curved line that was her nostril, her eyelids almost mauve, and her smooth forehead. He was arrested by something on her forehead.

She asked, "What is it?"

"A thread?"

Above her left eye there appeared to be an inch-long white line on her tan forehead.

"Oh, that," she said, brushing his hand away. "A scar. From childhood." She told him of riding her horse, of stopping in the woods, of the deer and then the snake, the sudden strike of the maple limb, the stitches over her eye. "Ordinarily, I use makeup to cover it. I'm not wearing any makeup before you."

"Neither am I," he replied. Tenderly, he ran his finger along the line of the scar. "I wish I could protect you," he said, "when a snake appears from the bushes." Then, cautious as a gambler placing a bet, he said, "This could become serious."

She brought her hands up to both cheeks and stared quickly around the dining room of the Crystal Palace, as though to deflect the conversation, and admitted in a low voice, "I'm not a serious person."

That night in her bed they recaptured that first experience together—the excitement and the mutual concern. The quiet intensity, the fulfillment, and the restfulness after joy. Conrad said, "This is happiness."

Isabel said nothing. But they slept in each other's arms.

In the course of the next few days, they took long walks in the late afternoon, speaking of the far-flung places they had traveled to in the world, of books they had loved, of their childhoods, and their parents.

"My mother was something out of the remote past," Isabel said. "She played the harpsichord and did needlepoint, embroidery, painted watercolors of landscapes. She never said a harsh word. She lived out of touch with any real feelings: completely absorbed by how things *ought* to be, how they *should* be. . . . She was as ethereal and sweet and otherworldly as my father was robust and gutsy and outgoing. He was a happy warrior." She laughed at a private recollection. "My brother and I called Mother 'the Princesse de Clèves.' "

"You know that book?" Conrad asked with surprise.

Then it was Isabel's turn to act astonished. "I said I am not a serious person. I didn't say I was uneducated."

"I apologize. But it's such a strange book."

They were sitting on a sidewalk bench near the secret garden of the Paepcke estate, looking up toward the distant mountains. Isabel said, "I'm sure I don't know what that book means, or if it was supposed to be a joke. Poor Princesse de Clèves: the dutiful daughter, the honorable wife refusing the ardent lover. The totally ethical lady. Was it Madame de La Fayette's purpose to show that you can be just as unhappy if you are moral as you can be if you're immoral?" She threw up her hands in ignorance, "Could she have been that cynical?"

"Or realistic." He smiled. "You know she wrote it under the

influence of La Rochefoucauld, or they collaborated in writing it."

"No, I didn't. Will you always bring me news from the past?" she wondered out loud.

"She was his last love affair. At least, it's known that he visited her every day during the time she was writing the novel."

"Tiens!" He felt her stare at him as if trying to imagine what they might make of each other if their affair did not evaporate. She asked, "How did you become a serious person?"

He did not like the question, but he answered, "I always took it for granted—that I'd do something worthwhile. My grandfather was the mayor of Bruges, a Socialist, and in France a well-known writer on atheism. My mother was very much 'a literary lady.' She named me after the contemporary writer she most admired—Joseph Conrad. My father's people were leaders among the pioneers to the Midwest. He was a lawyer who ended up elected judge of the probate court."

"Are they still alive?"

"No. He died just after I started college. My mother disappeared during the war."

"Disappeared?" She laughed. Then corrected herself: "I'm very sorry, but I've never before heard anyone say, 'My mother disappeared'—except with another man."

"Well, she had gone back to France in the spring of 1939. When the Nazis invaded a year later, all of her family were forced out of my grandfather's house during the night. There's no trace of what happened. I spent a lot of time in 1947 trying to find out. Either they were killed on the spot and left in an unmarked grave, or they were sent off to a concentration camp. There are no records."

"I'm so sorry."

Alone, he wondered if he were hallucinating the whole affair. Could there actually be such a woman, who made him feel respected at the same time that the touch of her fingernail against his wrist made him want to rape her.

The following week passed for them in a glow of euphoria. Conrad recognized that Isabel was the envy of her acquaintances, who felt that they must each find a new partner to go to bed with as night fell after a day of skiing, the sauna, the pool, and the good dinner; whereas *she* was *involved:* and with an excellent man, no ski bum, no fly-by-night. He felt fresher and more cheerful each day. She reveled in his recovery. "I shall keep this Petoskey stone moist . . ." she told him. "And polished."

Wistfully, he asked, "When do you plan to leave? Where will you go from here?"

"I promised my brother to visit him in Carmel." She smiled. "*He's* having a new affair. He wants to show off to me."

"What's he like?"

"Kevin? He's very entertaining, engaging; always interested in something unexpected. And then there's his sculpture. He's had that since he was a teenager. He says he likes to make things smooth—he turns stone into skin."

"Does he exhibit and sell his sculpture?"

"And how," she responded with vigor. "He's very enterprising. And he's usually successful at whatever he turns his mind to. He wrote a book once that sold pretty well."

"What's it called?"

"*In the Footsteps of Jesus, on Camelback.* For a while there he thought he had the call. He'd gone to a very high church prep school. But he didn't want to be ordained. Thought he might develop his own splinter church. That's when he decided to retrace the life of Jesus all over Palestine. And he wrote the book."

"How did he find out he *didn't* have the call?"

Isabel laughed. "He woke up one morning and realized he cared more about the camel than about the footsteps of Jesus."

Conrad basked in the brightness of her eyes.

"He's a great traveler." She continued: "You know: Fiji, the Seychelles Islands, Rhodesia. He picks up people . . ."

Just like you, Conrad thought.

". . . and brings them home. He brought the camel driver back with him from Palestine—to run a cattle ranch in the San Fernando Valley."

"Is he still there?"

"I don't know. Kevin sold his shares in that ranch sometime later. I didn't say everything he touches is successful."

"Is he married?"

"Divorced. He was married for a couple of years to an Italian countess. At least she became a countess by a previous marriage. Then, when Kevin and she were divorced," Isabel chuckled, "one of the conditions of the settlement was that she could revert to using the title rather than her maiden name or Kevin's name."

"Did they have any children?"

"One. A boy. They live in Rome. Kevin sees him about once a year."

Conrad felt the pain of the lives that fly apart into fragments: two hours for a son here, three weeks for a trek into the mountains there, a new mistress, always a new scenario, nothing worth controlling, repeating. Adventure.

Isabel actually said, "He fell in love with the travel books of Richard Halliburton when he was a boy. I think Kevin's trying to retrace *his* steps more than those of Jesus."

"And Halliburton was always reliving someone *else's* adventures!"

"Who lives his own life?" Isabel asked as a joke.

As the end of her stay at Aspen approached, one day was so overcast and threatening of snow that Isabel decided not to go up on any of the runs. Conrad and she wandered around through the main streets and the back streets of the town, like children playing hooky. They came upon the Alpine Jewelry Store set back around a courtyard with birch trees in the middle, a dark-brown brick building, neat and inviting, and decided to enter and look around. They noticed and quickly passed the display case of engagement and wedding rings; they looked at place settings of porcelain from Staffordshire, Limoges, and Copenhagen. They toyed with trinkets of crystal and silver, and then their eyes were riveted on an object on the surface of a glass counter—a tree of black wire, heavy with leaves made of Monterey jade, with one perfect pearl, like the moon, caught in its highest branches. It was set on a base of a wide, oval pool of malachite in which the different shades of green irregularly circled about the center as if a stone had dropped in the middle of a lake to make ripples out toward the far edge, or as if the pearl as moon was reflected at the heart of the green stone. At the moment they stared at it, they squeezed each other's hand so that, without a word, both of them knew they felt the same shock of joy at being in the presence of an object of such charm.

"How much is it?" Isabel asked.

The salesman behind the counter translated the symbols on the tag and said, "One thousand dollars."

"It's marvelous," Conrad said, beginning to finger it, moving it in different directions on the top of the counter.

"It's unique," the salesman said. "We've never had anything like it before."

"Neither have I," Isabel said, looking at Conrad.

"Would you like it?" Conrad asked her.

"Of course!" Isabel exclaimed.

"Then it's yours," he said.

"No, no." She put her hand on his arm. "One doesn't buy a trinket for a thousand dollars *just like that.* . . ."

"We'll have to mull it over," Conrad said to the salesman.

Isabel asked, "Where is the nearest bar?"

The salesman replied, "Around the corner in . . ."

"Oh, yes, I know it," Isabel interrupted. "I must have a drink."

Conrad looked at his watch. "Well, it's three-thirty," he said. And then, looking at the salesman, added, "Don't let it get away."

They walked arm in arm out of the jewelry store and down the side street around the corner until they found the bar. The lounge was dark and nearly empty: very rustic, lined with weathered wood from the sides of an abandoned barn. The bartender came to their table and took their order. A slow song full of haunting loneliness came from the muted mouth of the bright jukebox in the far corner. They sat opposite each other at a small, square table. Conrad said, "Why don't you marry me?"

Isabel laughed. "I'm not the marrying kind."

"No one is. But almost everyone is willing to try."

"I'm not a gambler."

"Why not let yourself go?"

"Why don't we simply have an affair?" Isabel asked. "No strings attached, and we'll go our separate ways when we've had enough of each other—?"

Conrad said, "It wouldn't do for the world that I live in. It's like a tuxedo: there are some places one doesn't go without a tuxedo."

Isabel laughed again. "You see, I'd be just a decoration for you."

Their drinks were brought to the table.

With boyish self-assertion, Conrad said, "You need me."

Isabel's mood changed instantly. "I don't want to talk marriage!" Her body had tensed; her relaxed, easygoing manner disappeared. She was visibly distressed.

Conrad reached across to touch her, but Isabel drew back. "I can't leave you alone."

"Please, leave me alone!" She spoke in a hoarse whisper as if under physical pressure. "You upset me."

"I see. I'm sorry."

"I think I'd better be alone for a while. I want to go to bed and sleep for a day. Forgive me, darling." She tried to smile, but she seemed to be drained of energy. "I want to go now. Please don't get up. I want to go by myself." She pulled on her jacket, prepared to leave without touching or kissing him, backing away. "Perhaps we'll see each other tomorrow," she offered tentatively. "I just can't . . . anymore . . . today."

In a second she was gone.

Conrad rested his elbows on the table with his eyes closed against his fists. First he drank her drink and then he drank his, and ordered another round, to share with the missing partner. At the same time that he felt he had lost her, he could not resist hoping that what disturbed her was a breaking down of her reserve. Was that what upset her? It was not impossible. She had been in charge of her own life for so long; now, perhaps, she was unnerved by a weakening in her resistance. Was she frightened to discover that she might want to say yes?

But, then, how could he have asked her to marry him? What voice was speaking through him? She was a treasure and he'd never felt more alive than this—reveling in being her lover. The question had meant: can't I preserve these pleasures?

He imagined she thought of him as a man her father would have admired. He believed that he was in love with her, and that, even if it lasted only a little while, she was experiencing a certain state of grace or a condition not of uninteresting calm but of peacefulness that is all alive. He did not challenge her to "change her ways," only to couple her ways with his. He tried to sell himself the bill of goods that she did not have to be defensive with him.

Conrad vacillated between hopefulness with one drink and despair with the next. She was upset by her wish to take marriage seriously; he was doomed to lose her. And then he remembered the jade tree, with the pearl caught in the upper limbs and the reflecting pool of malachite below. He must buy it for her. He must give it to her as a gift. But he had not left a deposit. He suddenly felt attacked from the middle of his intestines by a great, spreading chill that threatened to freeze his chest and his arms with the unexpected fear that the jade tree might be gone when he got back to the Alpine Jewelry Store. What if it is sold? he asked himself. The salesman could not have known whether they were serious about buying it.

He wanted to own it—to give it to Isabel. He *needed* it for her. What if it's sold? He felt hollowed by the fear of the loss, of the possibility that he might have lost his opportunity. What will I do if it's gone? He had never felt this way about *a thing* before.

He left money on the table and moved quickly out of the bar, down the corridor, to the street, beginning to run toward the jewelry store, when it struck him so forcefully—as with huge, invisible hands grasping him at the shoulders—that he stood still suddenly in the middle of the sidewalk: I am in love with her! How could I possibly feel this way unless I am truly in love with her? He began to move again, at a slower pace, though more rapidly than his ordinary walking stride, beginning to pant, anxious to arrive at the store in time.

He was too late. It was after five; the front door was locked. Clerks were putting out the lights. The jade tree no longer appeared on the surface of the counter where he had seen it last. He turned away from the glass door, bereft, as if he could not deny the validity of the bad omen.

Alone, that night, he tried to fall asleep despite the self-pitying thoughts that intensified his sense of loss. He had never known a woman who made him feel so comfortable with himself; that fact stood in contrast to the torture he recalled in the effort to put on a good face before women he was not comfortable with. The more he thought of Isabel, the greater value he put on her virtues; she was not only beautiful to look at and comfortable to be with—she had intelligence and charm and joie de vivre. He clutched a pillow and tossed back and forth in the dark, resisting the demand of one part of his mind to make the rest believe that, just as he had been unable to take ownership of the jade tree, so would he be unable to keep Isabel from withdrawing herself from his future.

As Conrad entered the breakfast room off the lobby of the motel the next morning, he recognized her instantly. She sat at one of the small central tables—looking for all the world as if expecting to keep an appointment. But their conversation was stilted. "I didn't know whether I'd see you again," he said.

"I'm sorry about yesterday. Please sit down."

"Have you had breakfast?"

"I have a present for you."

"You have a present *for me?*"

Isabel reached down to the floor at the side of her chair and brought up to the table a large, smooth, wooden, Japanese-looking box and slid the front panel up to reveal the jade tree.

"I wanted to buy it *for you*," he said.

She asked, "May we share it?"

"We do share it!" He smiled. He wanted to ask: What made you change your mind? But he would not be reckless with so delicate a moment. What he said was, "I adore you."

She replied, "Don't leave me."

She made him feel exalted. He did not mention marriage again, while he thought of nothing else, at the same time knowing he could not think it through, could not imagine it beyond the fact of wedding. He had asked her to marry him before realizing how intensely he loved her. Conrad considered himself some sort of throwback, a man for whom the idea of marriage legitimated a passion of loving. How the many years ahead would be shaped by their making a marriage together lay hidden beyond a gate he wished to enter with her alone. All of his energy was concentrated on forcing that gate together with her, on taking her with him. But, a few days later, it was she who took him with her—to San Francisco.

As the plane began to lose altitude, aiming its descent across the breadth of the state to the airport on the western coast of California, Isabel raised one arm and stopped the steward in the aisle next to her seat. "How much does this plane weigh?" she asked.

The steward said, "You mean, like, right now?"

"Yes."

"About a hundred and fifty thousand pounds," he said, smiling.

"And," Isabel continued, "what rate of speed is it flying at?"

"We're doing about four hundred and fifty miles an hour right now," he said.

Isabel turned away from him toward Conrad. "Can you imagine what the impact of a hundred and fifty thousand pounds at four hundred and fifty miles an hour would be if we hit the earth right now?"

Conrad had no time in which to answer. Isabel shut her eyes and grabbed his hand over the armrest that separated them. "Hold my hand," she said, keeping her eyes closed. "I can't stand landings."

"What do you do," Conrad asked, in a whisper, "when you're traveling alone?"

"It's a great way to meet people."

When they had rented a car at the airport, Isabel said aggressively, "Mind if I drive? I know the way."

With a snort, Conrad replied, "I have no male chauvinist piggishness against being chauffeured."

Isabel said, "I'm a very good driver."

"My manhood isn't threatened."

Isabel had every reason to believe him.

She took her right hand off the steering wheel and squeezed his left arm appreciatively.

The density of highway traffic south of San Francisco thinned out soon enough and, as they approached the ocean, the landscape was transformed. Away from the cities and the suburbs which have conquered the flat land and redecorated the hills, nature asserted itself: the hills said moss green velvet, the next hill proclaimed avocado green pastures, horses grazed along the weathered boards of boundary fences. Fluffy clouds, roaming separately in the light azure sky, cast shadows of cool dark pools that moved gradually across the smooth fields in the direction that Isabel drove the car. At Santa Cruz they saw the Pacific Ocean beyond the winter stubble of wheat fields—their first sight of the vast expanse of the slate-blue ocean—but soon they were driving between tall old pines as if one must not take too much of the endless ocean view all at once. They drove in silence with the car windows rolled down, breathing in the tang of the fresh air, separately measuring the distance from Aspen: this would be the first time they would find themselves together in a different scene, under different conditions. Isabel knew what to expect. Conrad did not. She respected his quiet. Only at Castroville did they simultaneously laugh out loud together. In that flat land where artichokes neatly grow on sharp stalks for miles in every direction, they drove through a dusty hamlet, where the sign on an archway over the main street announced: Castroville, The Artichoke Capital of the World. They did not have to exchange a word; they shared the same sense of the absurd. They distrusted self-congratulations. The "World's Greatest" Anything must always be laughed at.

At one point, Conrad asked, "Will your brother and I get along?"

"Honestly, I don't know," Isabel replied. "But it doesn't matter. We're each here to enjoy ourselves, aren't we?"—by which he took her to mean: here in life or here in the world, not just here at my brother's home.

After Monterey they drove along the millionaires' mile, a curious realm of pompous houses, half hidden in woods, but not so far removed from each other that their owners could not enjoy the reflections of their glory; houses of people with great wealth, secluded among their well-tended trees and gardens, between golf courses and the endless ocean, a fortress enclosure, a policed peninsula: all that money could buy. At the gas station, the young attendants were so healthy-looking, so friendly and efficient, they gave the impression that, at least on this spur of land, this end of the world, even the automobile exhaust fumes were fragrant.

They reached Carmel, the jewel, in early afternoon sunlight. "I'll show you around the town," Isabel said with pleasure, playing tour guide as they parked the car to stretch their limbs and take a stroll. This was one of the places at which she alighted; she left a wardrobe of clothes in her brother's guest room. The cleanliness of the streets made Conrad imagine that a brigade of wardens rushes out to pick up a candy wrapper from the sidewalk the instant a child makes the mistake of dropping it, or snatches out of the gutter a cigarette butt if an adult is inconsiderate enough not to use an ashtray. He admired the flowers planted in the islands that run down the length of the main street and the cream-colored, two-story buildings, the elegant shops making one imagine that here people ate only gourmet foods out of cans shipped from France or delicately painted pottery jars from the Far East. Even the hardware store seemed to feature only brass doorknobs from Italy, kitchen gadgets from Finland. In the windows of the clothing shops, the liquor stores, the tobacconists —always modestly, unostentatiously presented—were the best that money could buy. Flawless weather, a slight breeze from the ocean, handsome people beautifully turned out, well-behaved children: all added up to an unexpected instance of perfection. "What do people do here all day?" he asked.

"Play," she answered.

"Playland!" he said, without rancor. "It's too rich for my blood."

"Not for mine," she said casually. He recognized that she would not be put down, whatever the differences of style between them. They got back into the car and drove out of the town, past the seventeenth-century Spanish mission, the cathedral and the cloisters forced up out of the golden tan of the earth, the stucco earth made into a tall house of worship turning its back on this life, sheltering cactus and calla lilies within its fortress.

They drove along. The road curved between the rounded

green hills on the east and the sun-silvered ocean on the west, along cliffs dropping down to the beaches of white sand, or down a sudden drop in the land, bringing them along the level of beach so close that they could nearly reach out to the foam of the ocean waves finally coming to rest, seeping away into the beige sand. "It's very near, now," she said. "Just beyond Point Lobos." The hills grew higher on their left as they continued to drive south, hills like the highlands of Scotland, heather-covered, and barely inhabited, unspoiled, the realm of cows and silent children on chestnut-colored horses.

But when they parked the car in the driveway to Kevin's house, they were in another world: as if they had come to harbor at the other side of the ocean and stood on the remote hillside of a cove in Japan. The rockiness of the enclosure predominated, the sparseness of the vegetation, the horizontal branches of the cypress, windblown into postures of caution, set the notes of foreignness. The ocean sounded against the beach far below and above their heads the strange, wide-winged dark birds with small heads signaled to each other. The house itself seemed to express the wish not to intrude on this extraordinary seclusion: one story high, vertical planks of redwood and long, slender windows of plate glass partly concealed by the gray-blue junipers, an odd arrangement of cubes each at a different level, as if one room led to another by afterthoughts, implying that only very hesitantly the owner had suggested: perhaps we might extend ourselves slightly toward those rocks over there, if we do it very quietly, asking permission of the bushes and the moss. Stretching her arm through the open window, Isabel leaned into the car and pressed her hand against the horn on the steering wheel. The shriek of sound blasted into the quiet scene. Birds flew out of hiding from some pocket of the flat roof of the house and dashed away toward the ocean. An Oriental opened the front door.

"Isabel?" a rich, deep voice shouted from some distance, as through a tunnel. "Isabel?" They could not make out where the call came from. Through the door held open by the house-boy, they passed into the main room—another transformation. The building appeared to be incomplete, as if it had three sides only: at the far end was a wall of glass that opened the space to the distant horizon and the cove below; the rocky precipice falling sheer as a canyon down to the beach exposed the room to the breadth of the ocean. Beyond the glass wall was a terrace of redwood planks that jutted out over the gulf, a platform in space. The room itself was organized around the huge stone fireplace. On the hardwood floor mounds of over-sized pillows, covered in Far Eastern silks of purple and or-ange, were curved in a semicircle around the open hearth.

The man who stalked into the room came toward them with a slight limp of his right leg—his arms open wide to embrace. He was a masculine mirror image of his sister. "Darling!" Kevin shouted. "Baby! Honey!" Broader and taller than she but clearly out of the same mold, well-formed and pleased with himself. His eyes a deeper blue from the same lode of sapphires. He was covered by a white smock half open in the back like the ones patients are made to wear in hospital beds, and his face and hands were lightly coated with a fine dust white as cornstarch. "I've been sanding. Marble," he said. "In the studio," as he dropped the smock onto the floor, took Isa-bel in his arms, and hugged her without pressing their faces together. He must have worn something on his head. None of his short blond hair was coated with the fine dust. He brushed away at his cheeks for an instant and then kissed Isabel on the lips, not noticing Conrad. "How are you, my darling?"

She hugged him, laughed, and answered, "Attacked by swans! And how are you?"

"Drowned by sturgeon!" he shouted back. And they both laughed, standing there with their arms around each other. Isabel was aware of how Conrad must feel left out by their private language, for she glanced at him as if to say that she would explain later. Then she introduced them, and Kevin gave him his full attention, shook hands with Conrad and pat-ted him on the back at the same time. "Delighted," he said.

"Awfully glad to meet you. To see you here. Welcome." With the white smock lying on the living room floor, he was suddenly conscious that he stood there barelegged, wearing only a pair of cutoff blue jeans and a polo shirt. "You've got to get out of your clothes." He shivered in mockery. "No winter here. There's still time for a swim." He turned to the houseboy who stood half hidden against the wall next to the large fireplace. "Yato," he said, "come here. Yato and his wife are from Thailand. This is my sister, Isabel. And this is Mr. Taylor."

The houseboy had a sweet smile, black hair, and dark eyes; his flesh, tawny as a lion's, was hairless and smooth on a boyish body. He wore a woven skirt, the seaweed color of Hong Kong grass, tied into a knot at his waist like an ancient Oriental warrior. He moved silently and bowed from the middle.

"Yato, take the champagne out of the refrigerator, get the glasses, and take them down to the pool. We'll drink and swim," Kevin announced. He hugged his sister again. "You know the way," he said, indicating that she was to go to her room in one direction while he left the living room toward the opposite direction.

Conrad followed Isabel. The hallway was narrow and dropped to a lower level of the house. Doors along the way were made of rice paper and disappeared sideways between walls. She led him into a spacious bedroom, much larger than it appeared from outside, for it was built half into the ground. The bamboo-shuttered windows looked out into the middle of flowering bushes. She opened a drawer and took out a bathing suit of her own, a black jersey tank suit, and then extended to Conrad a pair of men's trunks, white boxer shorts with red piping. They were silent, sensing each other's thoughts. As he held the man's bathing suit in his hand, Isabel began to undress before him, meaning to erase the thought of other men she had brought to this bedroom, to erase any judgment of his by focusing all feeling into desire for her—without thoughts and without judgments.

He stripped off his clothes almost in anger and began to kiss her shoulder, her breasts, lowering himself to kiss her body, down the length of her legs, until he kneeled on the floor kissing her feet. He urged her onto the edge of the bed, and made love to her there. They put on their bathing suits and walked back to the living room. Not a word was spoken between them. Only twelve minutes had passed. Yato entered the living room with the luggage from the car. Kevin returned, wearing a tight, coral-colored bikini, displaying an incongruous potbelly. "The drinks are down at the pool," he said, carrying bath towels under one arm.

"Do you swim in the ocean?" Conrad asked out of a need to discover if he could speak again. He felt gagged with joy.

"Too dangerous," Kevin replied. At the far end of the room, he slid part of the glass wall aside and led them across the redwood terrace to a stairway on stilts over the deep drop in the canyon down to a lower level. The swimming pool lay like a lozenge of aquamarine in a frame of white marble, surrounded by a slim border of mossy grass. It was guarded on all sides by the pine trees with their long, horizontal branches in exotic postures, like abstract, sculptured images of Balinese dancers. The slate gray of the ocean turned into teal and then azure just before it kissed the beach at the bottom of the cove. They were halfway between the level of the ocean and the dome of sky. Kevin shot the cork of the champagne bottle away from them, toward Hawaii.

They did not plunge into conversation. It was not because Conrad was a newcomer and they seemed in any way inhibited by his presence; nor was he eager to assert himself. Conrad was impressed by the fact that Isabel and her brother communed with each other indirectly—through a casual joke about the style of bathing suits or a glancing remark about the high cost of a houseboy these days. There was no urgency to catch up on the news about each other, as if what remained unchanged was more important to them—until Kevin mentioned his latest showing of sculpture in a Los Angeles gallery and Isabel expressed her interest in seeing what he'd been working on lately. He promised to take them to the studio later or in better sunlight the next day.

"What kind of reviews did the show get?" Isabel asked.

"Enthusiastic—for Los Angeles. And a good sale. I sold eleven out of fifteen pieces. But the reviews don't matter much. And they're never what you hope for."

Conrad asked, "What do you hope for?"

"They can't praise you enough!" Kevin laughed. He thought for a moment. "You simply want to hear that you're the greatest artist in the world. No one is going to say that—so no review is everything you ever hoped for."

"I once heard Virgil Thomson," Conrad began, "tell a story about Gertrude Stein. In her middle years, before the Second World War, he bemoaned the fact that her writings were not adequately reviewed. 'You don't have the benefit of criticism,' he said. And she replied, 'Criticism? A writer doesn't want criticism. An artist wants praise. Praise! Praise!!' "

They were comfortable with one another. They sipped the champagne; they swam in the pool. They basked in the sun— Isabel on a hammock taut between Calderlike low trees of black iron, Kevin and Conrad stretched out on the white marble border around the water. The houseboy came down with a platter of hors d'oeuvres and an armful of fresh towels for them, and took away the wet towels. The birds flew low overhead, examining them. The sun began to lower in the western sky, spreading a lacquer of Chinese red across the surface of the distant horizon. Kevin excused himself and said he'd bring another bottle of "the bubbly" back with him when he returned.

Alone with each other, Conrad walked around the edge of the pool to stand at Isabel's side. With one finger, he gently smoothed the thread of scar on her forehead. She reached up and stroked the still sensitive flesh in the center of his chest. Then she swung her legs under her, making room for him on the hammock, and they rocked slowly side by side, looking out to the far sunset.

Cautiously, Conrad asked, "What does 'attacked by swans' mean?"

"It comes from something that happened to Kevin and me when we were children." She took a deep breath. "Do you want me to make a long story short?"

"No. I'd like a long story." He took her hand in his and kissed her fingertips.

"When we were young, our parents had a house in Jamaica. We went there for holidays in winter. The house was built on the side of a hill—nowhere near as steep as this—but in a secluded cove that was shaped like this one." He felt that she was looking at the memory of palms and the lush papaw trees over her head. She said those curved leaves cast shadows on the pink beach sand the shape of clubs in a pack of playing cards. Giant clubs. Her favorite tree cast the ten of clubs, and she loved to have the shadows fall on her bare arms and legs. The cove was just to the east of Ocho Rios, and her father would stand under the archway on the veranda of the white house after breakfast every morning and say aloud, "Christopher Columbus sailed into this bay." Now it was theirs. He loved swimming and sailing, her hale-and-hearty father, her barrel-chested father, who surveyed the glossy green leaves of his banana trees, and the smooth course of the apron of his lawn that ran down to the bright sands of his beach on the bay of turquoise and royal blue waters into which Christopher Columbus once had ventured to explore.

"My mother decided that something was missing. She wanted swans gliding back and forth across the bay, so my father bought her three of them." Her mother, Conrad thought, her frail, organizing, otherworldly mother, with her aesthetic Christianity. Her neat, systematic mother. "She collected shells all along the beaches of the north shore and used them as wall decorations for the halls in the house: name-tagged and arranged—as bivalves and univalves—the Ponderous Ark, the Incongruous Ark, the limpets, the Calico Scallop, and the cross-barred Venus; the nutmegs and bubble shells, the dog-headed Triton." The names of all the shells had thrilled her as a young girl. "My elegant mother," she remembered, "brought home one summer two long, flat Russian wolfhounds for our house in Westchester; they satisfied her sense of refinement. But they were so stupid—they chewed the legs of all the dining room chairs—that Mother had to get rid of them before long. The swans for our bay in Jamaica were to be her consolation that winter.

"Well," Isabel continued, "they *were* very beautiful. My mother adored them, especially the curve of their necks. She called that 'a milk-white question mark.' I loved the long, tapered heads. Their white caps and then the cat burglar's thin black mask around shiny black button eyes. And their beaks—those long, orangy-pink beaks with nostril slits like raisins. And the mound of snow-white feathers, turkey bodies painted fresh white. A huge loaf of whiteness. I remember how they'd arch those white feathers out, making themselves look like a graceful bowl with one curved flower sticking out of it, and the bowl would float, glide silently across the calm water—that unbelievably clear water. I loved the rest periods, too, when they'd stop moving and preen their feathers, sometimes with one webbed foot sticking out of a side."

Isabel laughed. "The gardener took care of them. We never even thought about what they ate, until one day Kevin and I took a picnic lunch to the beach and, when they approached the edge of the water, we began tearing our sandwiches up and tossing them pieces of our food. Their heads bobbed into the water and they gobbled up the bread and the ham or whatever we threw them. They had a good time and we had a wonderful time, until all of our food was gone. Then they began to make a gurgling sound and swam as close as possible to the edge of the water and made a honking noise. We explained to them that there wasn't any more. We showed them the empty lunch basket. Kevin was twelve or thirteen and I was about ten.

"Then two of them rose up out of the water and were transformed into something grotesque—abominable snowmen. They began walking right toward us on the beach, those armless turkey bodies waddling on skinny black legs, with big webbed feet like flattened, rubbery galoshes. They opened their beaks and honked and walked straight at us. Both of us screamed and ran faster than we'd ever run in our lives— scared out of our minds—back up the lawn to the house, screaming all the way, terrified that they were running right behind us. My father came out onto the veranda just as we got there and put an arm around each of us. That was the first time we dared to look back and see how close they were. But of course they weren't on the lawn at all. Panting to catch our breath, we could see them gliding away serenely—silent, no legs or rubber shoes visible—apparently harmless: nothing there but gracefulness, all danger invisible."

Isabel leaned against Conrad seated next to her, put an arm around him, and hugged him close. "That's the long story," she said.

"So it became a phrase in your secret language."

"It's shorthand for whenever something beautiful suddenly turns threatening."

It was beginning to grow dark. Only in the far distance was the sunset light still colorful; at this terrace of the canyon, twilight already veiled their view. Close together, they looked into each other's eyes. "And what message did Kevin take from your saying that today?"

She remained quiet before telling him the truth. "We are in love and that is beautiful. But you want to marry me and that is threatening."

"What is the danger?"

"That it will spoil the fun."

In the evening the temperature dropped, and warmth from the fire in the living room with its fragrance of cedarwood was just what they needed. Kevin supplied them with kimonos, and Yato and his petite wife served dinner Japanese style, on a low table brought up opposite to the fireplace; the three of them reclined on the big cushions on the floor around the table. The two Oriental servants wore white linen jackets from India, and rested on skirted knees each time they deftly brought or gathered up the dishes. The diners drank warm sake and felt drowsy and mellow although it was still early. "You've had a long day," Kevin said. "All that travel. And it's *what* for you?—one hour, two hours later?" He was still fresh and wanted the conversation to go on.

"I'm not all that tired," Isabel assured him.

"It's just this position—" Conrad said, "resting on an elbow—that makes it look as if I'm falling asleep." He had been taking in the character of the room. On the long wall opposite the fireplace were recessed glass shelves displaying collections of objets d'art: bowls of celadon from Korea, pottery from Burma, Malaysia, Indonesia; papier-mâché figures from India, carved wood masks from Polynesia, richly clothed dolls from Japan. None of Kevin's own sculpture appeared in the room. On the wall around the foyer hung elaborately designed prayer rugs from the Middle East. Only the golden glow from the log fire illuminated the room so that the light wavered, making the collection come alive, for the shifting of light on the objects made it seem as if they moved, rose up or down, trying to draw attention to themselves. The living room of an intensely visual man, Conrad thought, a plastic artist, a graphic artist. "There are no books in the room," he said almost as a question.

"They're all in the library. Everything here is nonverbal and non-Western." Kevin was a programmatic man.

Conrad thought of the rows of well-organized seashells, labeled and mounted along the hallway of Isabel's parents' house in Jamaica, the winter home she had not seen since she was fifteen years old, since her parents died.

When Yato had cleared the table and closed the kitchen door behind him, Kevin began: "The extraordinary thing about being in the presence of Orientals is to discover that you have no historical or cultural milestones in common. I mean—you can quote a passage from Shakespeare and they ask you if Shakespeare is still alive."

"But that's just a matter of education," Isabel said.

"Don't misunderstand; I like it. I like being with people who never heard of Praxiteles, or a Gothic cathedral, or Brancusi." He chuckled. "Who don't know the difference between Thermopylae and Waterloo, or who lived at the Gettysburg Address."

"But surely they could learn," Isabel insisted.

"It wouldn't matter. It would always be like using dirty words in a foreign language—you never know what the strength of the vibrations are because you were never punished for using them in childhood. Besides, I like it this way; it's the same as being with innocent children—in the bodies of adults—who have no idea of how they came about. It's liberating. They're just human beings. It reduces human relationships to the essentials."

Disingenuously, Conrad asked, "What are the essentials?"

Kevin grew reflective and chose his words carefully. "First to assert your will—to see how much of what you *want* you can *get*. And then to see complementarity, reciprocity, in all give-and-take relationships—the yin and yang of everything. To see that if I do something good for you, you will do something good for me."

"And if you do something bad?" Isabel asked.

"You will suffer. If not by punishment, then by the sorrow in yourself for having failed because you know it was not good. Everything is reciprocal: between people and within each one by himself." Kevin turned to Conrad. "Don't you agree?"

"Yes," he answered, looking first at Kevin and then at his sister.

"Isabel tells me you were a psychologist and then became an administrator. Why did you give up psychology?"

"Because I didn't believe I could become great at it."

"Ah," Kevin sighed, "then you'll never get the reviews you long for either." And they all laughed.

"Where's the new mistress?" Isabel asked abruptly.

"Landlocked," Kevin answered. "At her house—Big Sur, down the coast. Her mother arrived unexpectedly from Spain. Her mother lives in Spain. Something to do with income tax. Wants to guard her loot. They'll both come up for cocktails tomorrow evening. Emily—did I tell you her name is Emily?—is a sculptor, too. We have a great deal in common. That's how I met her. In connection with planning the peace rally."

"What rally?" Isabel asked.

"Don't you know anything about it? California Artists for Peace and Prosperity. Didn't I tell you? On the phone."

"No."

"Well, that's how it started."

Conrad asked, "The new affair?"

"No. Well, yes. One thing at a time. What started first was a group of people into music, films, et cetera—in L.A.—who began to draw up plans for a rally: California Artists for Peace and Prosperity. And they sent out feelers to get all of us together. I went to one of the organizing meetings. That's where I met Emily. But that's another story. Anyhow, I thought I'd go along with the idea for the rally as it was planned, just as a supporter. But once I got involved, I saw that it ought to be much more ambitious. I mean: it's not just the artists of California who want all the money going into Vietnam to go for welfare programs and cultural programs and urban renewal."

That brought a smile to Conrad's face, as he drank a sip of warm sake in this Shangri-la.

"So I agreed to become one of the organizers. This has got to become a national movement, not just West Coast. It's American Artists for Peace and Prosperity now. We're working on plans for a march in Washington."

"When?" Conrad asked.

"That remains to be seen. We'll have to do a lot of fund raising first. Cover all our costs. Bring together as many of the big shots—and not just the small fry—as possible. It'll take lots of planning." Kevin said this with the self-assurance of a man who had experience of carrying out elaborate plans. "Grass roots and grandeur!" he added. "Want to make a contribution?" he asked Isabel.

"Are you putting your own money into it?"

"Of course not," he answered her with a laugh. "But my time is money. I'll do the work. And I'll help raise the funds. I've got the right connections."

Conrad asked, "What will you get out of it?"

"The satisfaction of knowing I've done my civic duty."

How righteous we are, Conrad thought, when we find a new cover story for the lust to exercise power. How lucky we are, in America, that every Indian can aspire to become a chief.

Yato returned to say that the beds had been turned down. Conrad looked at Isabel with a gaze of "Deluxe service!"

Alone in the bed, with their arms around each other in the dark, alone with only the sound of invisible insects whispering in the neighboring bushes and trees beyond the shuttered windows and the rolling sound of the waves breaking on the beach, Isabel and Conrad realized to their surprise that they were not sleepy. The jade tree, with its single pearl above the malachite pool, stood on an end table under the window— their private icon. They sat up and lit cigarettes in the dark and began to talk like old friends. Conrad had been measuring the quality of the relationship between Isabel and Kevin. It struck him earlier, as he told her then, that they behaved as if they had been introduced as adults who were surprised to discover they were brother and sister. Isabel seemed to weigh the amount of truth in the thought; she remained noncommittal.

"A very bright and pleasant man, your brother," Conrad said.

"Not more intelligent than I," Isabel replied with a smile.

"I don't underestimate your intelligence."

"Do you love me for my mind?"

"No. But I couldn't love you without it. You sure as hell ought to be doing something more with it than—"

Isabel interrupted him. "You overrate intelligence. All academics do. It's their bread and butter. But people who don't make their living by mind power know that it isn't the be-all and end-all of life that academics think it is."

"Touché! That's an example of your intelligence."

"Will you always make me laugh when I go pompous?"

"Always. Marry me." He had his arm around her; he stroked her upper arm.

"No." She shook her head, resistant. "Why should I?"

"The yin and yang of everything. I'll keep you in line. When you panic, I'll calm you down; when you're in the doldrums, I'll snap you out of it. I'll keep you on an even keel. If you'll do the same for me. Reciprocity. Marry me!"

"Is that all you ever think of?"

Their laughter was tinged with a sense of the importance of this conversation to both of them.

"I'll be there for you to grab hold of when the snake suddenly appears on your path," he said.

"I don't want to be married."

"Why?"

"Marriages don't work. They don't make people happy."

"Happiness! Is that all you ever think of? Who said people should be happy?"

"Idiot!" The humor had gone from her voice. She threw back the sheet and blanket and got out of the bed. Chilled by the evening air she went to the closet where Yato had hung her winter coat and wrapped it around her naked body. The dark cloth coat had a sable collar that ran down both sides of the front and curved around the bottom in an unending tube of fur. She sat in the armchair at the foot of the bed. Only the moonlight through the shutters tried to make the scene visible. The glow from their burning cigarettes flared and faded like fireflies in the room. "Now I'll tell you," she began, "why we shouldn't get married. You admire my intelligence. You are an academic. You like 'reasons.' I'll give you my reasons."

"Please do."

"Most of the girls I went to college with have been married twice by now. They talk to me. I listen. Two people like to make love, so they think they'll like doing everything else together; then they discover how little else they like to do together—or at least how infrequently they like to do it at the same time. They think their sexual fascination will never wear out, but soon enough someone else would be fun for a change. Then Old Sacred Ego is Wounded and one of the two is made to feel Guilty, while the other one is Abused. It's all so ridiculous. Because the reasons for it are lost in the past and don't matter anymore. Monogamy is the ultimate joke our culture plays on a working girl."

"You're not a working girl."

"Don't admire work so much," she said vehemently. Then she softened her tone and said, "I don't have to work. And I don't have to marry a man who will be my breadwinner. I don't want to have children. I won't have children. And I won't be sexually 'faithful' to one man only."

"Why not?"

"I hate being distorted, I hate pain, and I don't like children. I don't need to feel fruitful like a sow—I won't have them."

"How about 'faithfulness'?"

She took a deep breath. She was speaking slowly and yet he felt as if she'd been racing, moving at high speed. "If I've learned anything from the experiences of my friends, it's that no one remains sexually faithful to any *one* person." Isabel became more strident. "Listen to me! For the past ten years at least, I've been expected to be alluring and seductive, to make men want me, and to take my pleasure from them. I'm very accomplished at it. Do you honestly think I can believe, if I were married to you, I would no longer feel that way about another man—ever?"

"You might *feel* that way . . ."

"But not act on it? Why, when I won't have children? Doesn't that close the circle? The only reason men didn't want their wives to take pleasure with other men is that they might have to bring up some other man's child."

"The other reason is wanting to be the only man in the world their wives desire."

Isabel hooted with laughter. "Vanity of vanities. Can't men learn anything from experience?"

"Vanity doesn't learn from experience."

"Would you marry me," Isabel asked, "knowing that I will probably not be faithful to you and that I will not have children?"

Their cigarettes were out. Conrad made no reply. The moonlight seemed to have grown brighter in the room; she appeared to him like a black and white dream figure. He sat in the bed propped up against the pillows, she huddled in the armchair.

At length, Isabel asked, "What are you thinking?"

He answered: "I don't care for ordinary pornography. But one of the most erotic paintings I've ever seen in my life is a Titian. I'm trying to remember it clearly. It's the portrait of a woman, probably supposed to be a Greek or Roman goddess. A beautiful woman with blond hair, naked but for a cloak with fur around her shoulders. I've always wanted to make love to a beautiful woman against warm, slick fur like that. And there she is—seated at the foot of this bed."

Isabel got up, clutching the coat around her, and returned to her place next to Conrad. They kissed as if they were entering each other's soul through the body. His hand wandered over her face and her breasts and then the sable collar of the coat and back again and again.

"Jupitor and Juno," he said.

"Neither of *them* was faithful," Isabel said.

During the morning, they rode horses out of a stable in the highlands through the wooded hills beyond and then drove into Carmel for lunch.

169

In the afternoon, they changed into bathing suits in their bedroom. It was clear and bright, although somewhat cooler than their first day there, and Conrad put on a blue terry-cloth bathrobe that hung in the closet. Isabel wore a beach robe of thin, silken fabric richly decorated with the blue and green bull's-eyes of peacock feathers. She couldn't find the belt for it. They walked through the living room and out onto the terrace holding hands. The breeze blew the beach robe away from Isabel. With her free hand, she tried to gather it up and hold it together against her chest.

They looked down to the pool and saw that Kevin was lying on his back in the hammock. His eyes were closed. Yato was spreading a colorless suntan lotion over Kevin's legs—with a long, stroking gesture, almost a massage.

"He's so spoiled," Isabel said, with affectionate indulgence.

But I'm not spoiled, Conrad thought. I don't have every-thing I need, let alone everything I long for.

Isabel continued: "He and I are *both* so spoiled," thinking aloud.

"You don't have a perch or a frame . . ."

"Free as a bird," she said quickly, almost sharply, and he could see her beginning to tense, withdrawing into herself.

"Birds have to come to rest too."

"In a cage?" she asked, avoiding his eyes.

"No. A nest."

A gust of wind lifted Isabel's robe out behind her and she went to gather it together with both hands. Her left hand held one side of it clutched to her stomach, and with her right hand she brought the right side of it up to her left shoulder and pressed it against her there.

Conrad perceived Isabel as the essence of femininity. She stood close to him with her right hand limp against her left shoulder like an Indian lady holding the loose folds of a thin sari that slips down so easily from the left shoulder, and he suffered all the imagined misery of a possible lifetime de-prived of such femininity, the company of such a woman.

"Marry me," Conrad heard his words pleading hoarsely, "I beg you."

The tone was all wrong for Isabel. As soon as he heard his own words, Conrad knew that they would push Isabel away from him rather than draw them together. It was a supplication. It was an expression of Conrad's own profound needs, which must frighten her, for it had not carried with it the promise of benefits to her well-being, of a lushness of satisfaction for her. It had been a mournful insistence, which must strike her as expressing only a self-serving need. They were exactly the wrong words for her. She acted as if the platform where she stood were turning to quicksand, as though she would be lost if she did not escape immediately. She turned her back on him and walked down the long flight of stairs to the level of the swimming pool.

Conrad followed her slowly.

Kevin had yielded the hammock to Isabel, and now Yato was spreading the suntan lotion over the backs of her arms and legs. Conrad swam and then dried himself off with one of the soft, large bath towels. Isabel had withdrawn into silence. And Kevin, sensing that there was an unnamed tension between them, proposed that he show Conrad his studio. Yato went up to fetch a drink for Isabel, and Kevin led Conrad up the stairs and then off to the side of the terrace, beyond the library and his own bedroom, to the far end of the house where the studio was built half into the earth so that the large skylight was no higher than the other ceilings of the house. As they walked across the terrace, Kevin—limping slightly—put an arm around Conrad's shoulder in a friendly way. But it only reinforced Conrad's fear of the possibility of being deprived of Isabel: friendship as consolation.

Kevin's sculptures were not realistic. They were "significant forms" out of marble or tree trunks that he had carved and smoothed into images of birds' wings or abstract fish.

"Stroke them," he said. "It's the texture I love."

Conrad ran his hands along the veins of pale marble and the

smooth-sanded cypress. "Lovely," he said softly. "Very lovely."

Then they sat in low wicker chairs from Hong Kong and faced each other. Kevin kept only club soda in the studio. He poured a chaste drink for each of them in glasses without ice cubes, as if by accident the correct plan had been made for them to be sober and come clean with each other.

"You're trying to get Isabel to marry you, aren't you?" Kevin began.

"How do you know?"

"Well, she said she was having an affair with you when she telephoned me from Aspen, and then when she arrived she said, 'Attacked by swans.' "

"And you said, 'Drowned by sturgeon.' "

"Oh, yes." Kevin smiled. "We speak in shorthand."

"What does 'drowned by sturgeon' mean?"

"My father told us a story when we were children. He was on Wall Street. Stockbroker. Once, closing a very important deal took him to Neenah, Wisconsin, to meet with the president of Kimberly-Clark Paper Company. He said that Neenah was a nice little town, on Lake Winnebago, but the lake was very dangerous in winter. It was filled with sturgeon, and the locals there would go out on the ice and cut a hole to fish through in wintertime. Sometimes the sturgeon grew so large and were so powerful that if they caught on a hook the fishermen might not be able to wind them in. In fact, sometimes the fish would pull the fisherman down through the hole in the ice and swim away with him holding onto the pole." He laughed. "Isabel and I thought the story was hilarious, so we use it to signal whenever we've gone after a big fish and end up getting caught ourselves."

Conrad waited for a further explanation, but, at length, had to ask, "How does that apply?"

"I thought I'd told Isabel about the rally. It meant that I got involved with California Artists for Peace just for the hell of it—the sport—but then I got hooked."

"Now *you're* organizing it on a national level?"

"We start out doing things for a whim, but we end up covering the bills. Even with Yato and his wife . . ."

"You got caught up?"

"I hadn't planned to bring them back. In September I went off to Bali and Singapore and Bangkok . . ."

Conrad remembered that in September he had been in a hospital having part of his stomach removed.

"I found him in Bangkok. He worked in the gallery of an art dealer I know; his wife was their cook. He was an indentured apprentice." Kevin chuckled. "I literally bought them from their master. Of course," he explained, "it isn't the same thing as slavery. You can buy slaves only in Yemen. But you can't take them out of the country."

Conrad said: "I don't want Isabel as a slave or even an indentured servant."

"I don't want Emily that way either," Kevin said, sipping the clear soda water. "But look at what happens. It all depends on who gets his own way most of the time. So all affairs are a seesaw between who is master and who is servant."

Conrad said, "I'd like to be married to Isabel without either of us being subservient to the other."

Kevin laughed out loud. "And I'd like to be thirty years old forever. But some things really aren't possible."

Conrad felt depressed by the cynicism of this man nearly twenty years younger than he, as though Conrad was the "naive" and Kevin the worldly-wise. "You don't think a marriage of mutual equality and reciprocal respect can work?"

"Mine didn't. But then," he continued brightly, "losing the countess and my son resulted in gaining my sister."

"How?"

"You see, Isabel wouldn't speak to me for years and years after the accident."

"What accident?"

"The plane crash. I was in the same plane when my mother and father were killed."

"I didn't know."

"Isabel wasn't on the plane because she had to get back

from Jamaica before the rest of us. Her school started earlier than mine. You may have heard about the crash years ago. It's the only one of its kind. The plane was trying to land in fog at LaGuardia but it crashed into the East River. My parents were killed, but I got off with only a broken arm and a broken leg. For years I thought that Isabel would never forgive me for being alive. But, then, the best thing that came out of it was discovering I could be a sculptor. It started out as part of physical therapy for my right arm. I had to exercise by making soap carvings. Can you imagine a hand so weak that soap felt like granite?"

"And then how did you and Isabel . . .?"

"Become friends again? Well, on the one hand, she went through five years of analysis." He laughed to himself. "On the other hand, my wife divorced me pretty quick. I think that's what made it all right. Isabel figured that was my punishment. I wasn't going to be allowed to live a conventionally normal life."

Conrad said blankly, "I'm sorry."

"There's nothing to be sorry about. I don't happen to agree with Isabel. I think my life is just fine. Isabel and I get along very well now. We understand each other."

"Well enough to tell me if I'm a fool for trying to marry her?"

"Yes," Kevin said, leaning forward and patting Conrad on the arm. "Love affairs don't have to lead to marriage anymore. Besides, although I can easily imagine that Isabel is very satisfying in bed, I don't believe she has much capacity to love another person for any length of time. She doesn't put up with frustrations easily."

"I would not frustrate her."

Kevin laughed. "You mean you aren't human? You'd never make a demand that didn't happen to harmonize perfectly with her needs or desires at that moment? You are an intelligent man, Mr. Taylor; you know that isn't possible." And he added, "Isabel is accustomed to getting her own way."

Conrad said, "I would not be stealing her life away from her." He thought of the cages in Bombay and of an indentured apprentice to the owner of an art gallery in Bangkok. "I would not make her into something she would not choose for herself."

"But that is what we all do to each other." Kevin expressed his amusement with a gesture to include all the pieces of sculpture in the studio. "It is what I do to chunks of marble, trunks of trees. It's what I am doing to Emily, and what you and I are doing to each other right now."

"How are we doing that to each other right now?"

"By telling each other stories. I am making a story of my past and Isabel's past. And you," he tried to laugh but no sound came out, "are trying to tell me a story about your future."

Kevin gave a cocktail party for them that evening. The living room was filled with neighbors of his, pleasant people, amusing and worldly men and women. Conrad watched Isabel pass in and out among conversations for what she was: a tourist, a visitor, a member of the audience, although she gave him the feeling that she could easily be the featured actress in the play.

Emily turned out to be somewhat awkward not to say ungainly, a woman in her early thirties, who seemed drab in a sand-colored pants suit next to her mother in a black satin evening gown. The mother was a full-blown matriarch who looked people up and down on being introduced, as if she reserved judgment until she knew whether their shoes were shined. She was magisterial and condescending, informing anyone who listened that Americans did not know what was going on in the world because their newspapers lied to them. "But in Spain we're able to find out what's really going on in the world."

"Through the official newspapers?" Conrad asked.

"No."

He imagined she implied a network of carrier pigeons flying to her from all parts of the earth with secret fragments of accurate information strapped to their skinny legs. Most of her life was spent in playing the stock market.

Kevin was protective of Emily but only as a Big Brother with an inexperienced debutante sister. It occurred to Conrad that their lovemaking must have the intensity of a mutual shower, each one soaping up the other's back.

Among the guests were men who spoke of tin mines in Bolivia and women who acted in television commercials. There was no center to which they all brought whatever they could produce; they were each free to go their separate ways at all times. There was no community; the room could just as easily have been filled with forty entirely different people and offered the same quality of "our gang" to a party at Kevin's house. There was Emily this year. Who would be the "current" mistress next year?

Conrad followed Isabel and some of the other guests who moved halfway down the hall toward Kevin's bedroom and found the spacious library; he spied upon her as she opened a large folio from Kevin's collection of artbooks and then, losing interest, stared through the glass wall down to the swimming pool; illuminated in the night light, the rectangle of aquamarine lay protected from the winds by the outstretched branches of trees in silhouette. She must have sensed him staring at her and turned around to look into his eyes. She wore an evening gown of taupe-colored linen and a heavy African necklace of silver bells around an elaborate locket. He felt that he was not to be gainsaid. He was not an unattractive man. He was not merely an established man who needed a hostess, a partner to go to ceremonial receptions with him, someone to read Henry James aloud to him in his living room on winter evenings. She was not there to fulfill a need for an appearance, or for what his society assumed was appropriate to his position. He was a man for whom the lust for life had been revived by her taking him to her bed. He never wanted to lose that joy, although he was not capable of calculating what it might cost him.

Conrad walked sideways between the guests in the library to approach Isabel, a glass in one hand, his free hand reaching out to touch her. "I've never seen you wear the same dress twice," he said.

Simply and directly she asked him, "Why do you want to marry me?"

"Because we should be better for each other than either of us ought to be for anyone else."

"Ought and should," Isabel repeated. "The Princesse de Clèves . . ."

"Moralists aren't always wrong."

"What if *you're* wrong?"

"We'd get divorced."

"What an invitation to a marriage!"

"The promise of an escape hatch." There was no tone of imprecation now. Conrad was promising Isabel her happiness, not begging for his. He was self-confident and hopeful.

She said quietly, "I think you want to marry somebody, but why do you want to marry *me?*"

He thought only of the yielding of the vigorous flesh of her firm body, of the warmth and excitement of her kisses, of the intensity of shared pleasure. He replied, "Why not let a lifetime of marriage gradually reveal the answers? Nobody knows all the reasons in advance."

She sighed. "If you won't stop talking about this . . . I'll have to stop talking to you." They sipped their drinks, looking at each other. Then she looked away. "I don't want to hurt you, but I don't want to hurt myself even more."

He asked, "When your visit here is over, where do you want to go?"

"I'm going to Switzerland. The skiing is marvelous there this time of year."

"I'd hoped you'd go east with me. Come to New Haven. See the house, the university, the town . . ."

"You want me to try out all the armchairs of your life," she said. "You'd like me to walk arm in arm with you past the windows of your boss's office." She looked at him sadly. "I just don't think I can do that."

They wandered back between the relaxed, chatty people, through the living room out onto the terrace, and turned to observe the guests. Isabel thought out loud, "It's just like a party I might go to anyplace in the world."

"You always see the same people?"

"No. Always new faces. Always the same *kind* of people."

"Birds of a feather?"

"Migratory birds. Always en route."

"No ties," Conrad said.

"No shackles." Isabel sighed heavily. "We're all free-floating."

"They seem so rootless," Conrad replied.

"I used to think of myself simply as footloose."

Conrad's hopes were excited by what she revealed in saying "used to," for he thought it was possible she no longer wished to be rootless. He offered her firm soil to take plant in.

"You are a gem," he said. "Come live with me. I offer you a setting to show you off to your best advantage."

She considered: "My advantage . . .?" and then suddenly caught sight of her brother, beyond Yato and his wife serving drinks and tea sandwiches to the guests in the living room. "Kevin!" she waved at him to join them on the terrace. When he approached, she confided in a whisper, "You know what I've been thinking about? Going home from a party like this— all the cars parked outside. Remember how they used to be lined up at school? Day school, in Westchester, when we were kids. You and I went home at different times. Remember? The Lincoln had to go back for you later. That was the loneliest time of all for me. Getting into the chauffeured car in the middle of the afternoon to be driven home alone. I used to *hate* it."

"Did you? I loved it."

"Strange . . ." she paused and finally spelled it out, "what one doesn't know about one's brother."

They sipped their drinks and looked out to the clear night sky over the unruffled ocean. Kevin asked, "Remember the time you had *two* birthday cakes? Mother and Dad each ordered a cake from a different bakery."

"They didn't talk much to each other."

"Strange . . ." Kevin concluded, "what a husband and wife don't know about each other."

When Kevin had gone back into the living room, Isabel shivered. She turned away from the sight of the guests, saying, "Birds of paradise." Conrad put his arm around her shoulder. For the first time he thought of her as vulnerable.

"Come live with me and be my love . . ."

"But when I'm old and ugly you'll have no use for me."

"I will be dead before you are old, and you will never be ugly."

She moved away from his caress and snapped back at him, "You are just as selfish as everyone else."

He gazed after Isabel as she moved gracefully among the guests and joined a conversation with Emily and the man in tin mining. Isolated tourists comparing travel notes. Could she be saved? Was she not tired of being isolated? If she could sigh with unhappiness remembering how lonely she had been in the afternoons of her childhood, couldn't he imagine that she was weakening in her resolve to escape his hold on her? He stared hard at her and the people who populated the world she moved in—fellow tourists who touched on each other's lives only as lightly as a butterfly on a flower for an instant. No responsibilities, no consequences. Contacts as fleeting as changing partners in a square dance. This was the ultimate benefit of their freedom: they made no claim on your tomorrow, and they would brook no demand, recognize no expectation leveled against themselves.

And yet, and yet . . . was she not sending him signals, hints, that she was yielding, tired of being footloose, weary of the Grand Tour, ready to find home?

Before Conrad awoke the next morning, Isabel had driven away in the rented car. She left a note for him and a separate one for Kevin. The lines to Conrad read: "Darling! Marrying you would be too much of a good thing. And that's bad. For a little while, we did love each other. I hope you will remember that with pleasure. I hate farewells. I'm a coward about that; I hope you'll agree this is less painful than a scene. You wouldn't like that either. I do care about what you'd like. . . . There are a thousand other things that might be said. I'm not equal to finding the words for them. Forgive me, if you can. That's silly. I know you can. You are much wiser than I am. All I can do is say—Thank you." She signed the letter "Love, Isabel." She had taken the jade tree away with her.

Kevin defended his sister and comforted Conrad at the same time. In the end, he drove Conrad to San Francisco to catch a plane east, having told him where Isabel would be skiing in Switzerland: she had accepted an invitation to stay with friends at the Palace Hotel in St. Moritz, after spending a few days at her apartment in Manhattan.

Conrad checked into the Hotel Carlyle in New York because it was a few blocks from her apartment, and skulked in streets around where Isabel lived. He waited for her to appear at the Whitney Museum and the Madison Avenue Bookshop. All in vain. He did not find it possible to let himself telephone her or to ring the doorbell at her apartment. He asked a florist at the Carlyle to find out if she were home, before sending a bouquet of flowers. Her maid responded with the information that she had just left for Europe, and that she would be away for at least a few weeks.

It is difficult to feel rejected and depressed in a room at the Hotel Carlyle. All the furniture and the fixtures of the room say to a guest: "You deserve the best; you are being served the best." Even the ashtrays on the desk and the night tables, white porcelain shells with decorations of colorful butterflies on each of them, announce: everything here is in acknowledgment of your worth. They reflect what money and good taste can buy, and the same message will be sent to anyone who could afford to stay in those rooms. But the only fact of importance to Conrad, at the moment, was that he was staying in the room, and the message was being sent to him.

Why should he not have Isabel?

What would it take to win her?

He lay on his bed in a room at the Hotel Carlyle, fully dressed, bathed in the cool winter sunlight that filled the room through two large windows, looking up at the ceiling, thinking of his parents and how his father had won his mother. It was the great romantic story of his otherwise unromantic family of plodding uncles and aunts and cautious cousins. His father had graduated from law school before the First World War broke out. When the United States entered it, he enlisted and was assigned to the Adjutant General's Corps. Toward the middle of the summer of 1918 he found himself stationed in Bourges in central France, an officer and a gentleman—and therefore invited to the home of the mayor of the city, whose grown-up sons were in the army but who had one handsome and high-spirited daughter at home, a girl of twenty, five years younger than the American captain. He fell in love with her, he courted her, he implored her to marry him. He was an atheist with Socialist tendencies—which endeared him to her father; he was cheerful, vigorous, and self-assured, which made him alluring to the young lady. But his name will William Schneider. He was a young lawyer from St. Louis, Missouri, whom she found attractive, enchanting; whom she could imagine embracing and following to a new world and founding a new life as his wife; but she told him—teasingly, in a sense only to test him capriciously, not seriously—that she could not possibly marry a man with a German name. After all that France had gone though, for all that the French had reason to loathe the Germans, it would not be possible for her to marry a man with a German name, even if he was a Scots-English-German-American from St. Louis, Missouri. It never occurred to her, she said later—but only later—that, because of her taunts, he would actually change his name. He was on the staff of the adjutant general; for him it was not a protracted or complicated affair. With relative simplicity, he was able legally, officially, and conclusively to have "Schneider" changed to "Taylor."

When he told her that his name had been antiseptically translated, she jokingly replied—"You don't even know how to spell 'Tailor'!" But she was profoundly impressed. Immediately after the war ended, in December of 1918, they were married in Bourges—her father, the mayor, officiating—and she embarked on her twenty-year experiment as an American wife. Theirs was a good marriage—even if it produced only one child, Conrad thought. They never lost the sense of being "engaged" by each other, although he could not imagine his father as a romantic figure. The story about changing his family name was always of the utmost importance—as if he'd changed his citizenship or had his face remodeled by plastic surgery—but it did not quite fit comfortably with the childhood impressions of the man Conrad lived with as "Father." For his father was, otherwise, a memorably prudent, reflective, and calculating man. A usually reticent—and frequently sententious—man. "You can fall in love with a rich girl just as easily as you can with a poor girl," he'd say.

It suddenly struck Conrad that he had been prepared, years before, in the seedtime of his childhood, by the manner of his father's brusque and terse statements, for his love of La Rochefoucauld's *Maxims*—for the succinctness, acerbity, and double-edged clarity of the duke's pronouncements—because such was the style of declaration that he had always heard at home as the most ordinary announcement made by his father. That discovery struck him as funny because he had always before then ascribed to his mother—out of her Frenchness and her feeding him from sources of the Gallic spirit—the origin of his love for the condensed and intense *Maxims*—whereas, he recognized then, it was his father's tight-lipped expressions that had prepared him emotionally and trained him rationally to be quick enough to appreciate the caustic wit.

Perhaps no son can imagine his father as a romantic figure. But having his inherited German family name translated and misspelled in English was most adventurous, the most daring, the most unimaginable thing that William Schneider could have been expected to do. He risked the displeasure of his own parents and all the rest of his large, close, proud family. It was his single reckless action, his most unanticipated gamble. But then the gamble had paid off; the daughter of the mayor of Bourges agreed to marry him. And, subsequently, other members of his family changed their names to Taylor as well.

What must I do to win Isabel? Conrad asked himself.

What would be the most daring action on my part that could sweep her off her feet? that could lure her into believing that, of all the love affairs she'd ever had, theirs was the only one worth trying to continue, to make into a marriage? Not that he thought there was any possibility, on the rational level of discourse, of trying to persuade her out of her arguments against having children or against sexual fidelity; argument would get him nowhere. But committing themselves to each other's happiness would gradually change those attitudes without any discussion at all—he imagined. Those were not matters to *talk* about anymore. It was not argument he was after; it was action. What act must he perform that would impress her as much as William Schneider's changing his name? An action on the part of a man who had spent the past half week within a few blocks of Isabel's apartment without allowing himself to telephone her or to appear at her door? Why was there a problem of what he could "allow" himself to do? He wanted her. He wanted her to marry him. She had run away from him. It was self-evident. He must go and get her. She had to be pursued. She had not wanted a scene. How serious had been the others who had courted her and from whom she had run away? The worst that could happen is that she would run away again, or that there would be a scene. The gamble was worth that. If he lost, at least he would have made an honorable try. It might end with his being cast out, rejected, spurned, but he could suffer that in private. Whereas, if he succeeded—if he brought her back as his "Prize"—he would have won a treasure. He was determined to place his gamble.

Conrad reserved a ticket on a plane to Zurich; he went to New Haven only to pick up his passport and gather some other clothes into his luggage. No one knew he was at his home on Hillhouse Avenue; he left again within a few hours of arriving. He did not think about anything else he was likely to do— other than to *appear* before her; but throughout the flight to Switzerland, and all through the train trip from Zurich to St. Moritz, he thought alternatively of his father as a "romantic figure," because he had changed his family name in order to win his French bride, and of himself as a "romantic figure"— for the only time in his life—for flying across the Atlantic, for being carried in a streamlined railroad coach upward along the sides of Alps to reach a village of Tyrolean chalets, and one enormous, elegant, old hotel to which Isabel had gone to seek her pleasure—her fugitive's pleasures—when she ran away from him.

He confirmed at the reservations desk that Isabel was, indeed, staying at the Palace Hotel. He made no move toward her until the next evening. In the vast dining room, Conrad sat at a small table by himself, barely eating, having watched the group of which Isabel was a member enter and be seated. There was a tall, commanding man with a bald head and a sandy mustache older than the other two couples around the table with Isabel. They wore black tie and evening gowns. He bided his time, looked around the great room—a semicircular room three stories high, with huge glass windows that offered the view of the snow-covered lawn beyond and the mountains in the distance. There were different levels within the dining room, leading down to the dance floor in the center, beyond which a pianist and a string quartet, their backs to the windows and the evening landscape, played slow fox-trots. Conrad's table was located almost directly across the dance floor from Isabel's and on a higher level, but she partly faced him and it would not have been impossible for him to catch her eye, although more waiters hovered around each table than there were diners at each table.

After he saw that dessert had been served at Isabel's table, and there were three or four couples dancing, Conrad descended to the dance floor. He stood there, immobile, alone at the center of the circular dance floor, with his arms raised, waiting for her to join him, until all the diners at her table noticed him; Isabel rose and began to walk toward him. She did not move quickly but she smiled. Everything in the situation was conducive to restraint: the starched, white, floor-length tablecloths, the heavy silverware, the formality of the clothes, the brightness of the chandeliers overhead, the solicitude of the waiters, the thickness of the carpet on the stairs, the high polish of the dance floor.

They touched. He brought one hand to the small of her back and with his other hand raised hers to his heart. "The last dance," he said slowly, "was lovely. But I thought this would be better—without the Atlantic Ocean between us."

"You must be mad!" Isabel said, smiling happily. "How extraordinary!"

He breathed in the sensual, sharp-edged sweetness of her perfume. Between that fragrance and the fullness of her physical presence—the joy of her body close to his—an electric charge ran down the length of his spine, through the small of his back, directly into his penis.

"How did you know where to find me?"

"Kevin told me."

Isabel tilted backward and stared at him. Suddenly, no longer smiling, she said, "I never expected to see you again."

Conrad responded with, "You don't believe that . . ."

"But I am flattered." Her smile returned.

"That isn't good enough. You've got to be overwhelmed."

She laughed, and then they danced in silence, cheek pressed against cheek.

He felt certain of the rightness of his coming after her. "You don't know what to make of me," he said, recalling her to their first dance in Aspen, "do you?"

"It's a question of what you want to make of me," she replied.

"I have some very good Scotch in my room . . ."

"Here?" she asked.

He backed away, withdrawing the pressure of his body close to hers, wondering if he were trying to move too quickly. Holding her at arm's length, turning her smoothly to the rhythm of the slow music, disregarding the few other couples dancing on the large smooth floor, he asserted rather than asked, "You do love me, don't you."

"Don't ask questions, don't tell lies."

Conrad countered with, "Don't be afraid."

At the beginning of the next song, they danced without speech. Only the clear pressure of their bodies in contact— hands held in each other's, her breast against his chest, their thighs touching—sent signals of welcome and messages of desire. She was everything he had remembered: her ivory and rose complexion glowing, her glorious golden hair swept up in a large, smooth curve over the crown of her head. She wore an evening gown of light brown chiffon softness. "What a beautiful dress," he said, as he pressed his fingers back and forth into the folds of it against her back. "I'll be very careful with it," he promised, "when I take it off you."

Isabel snickered and brought her lips to his cheek. "We'll pretend," she said, "that you're my uncle—just arrived to visit at my boarding school, and you're going to take me out for a hot fudge sundae."

At the end of the dance, she took Conrad by the hand and

led him up the stairs to the table of her friends. The pleasure she took in this surprise was so obvious that none of them needed any explanation of her "old friend." They simply had another chair brought to the table and insisted that they stay long enough to drink a liqueur together, then they promised to look for each other on the ski slopes the next day. They were planning to do Corviglia—one of the most challenging runs.

Alone in the elevator, Isabel said she'd prefer their going to her room.

"All right."

When they walked through the foyer into the bed-sitting room where one lamp stood lighted on the desk, Conrad felt the sudden rush of vindication in the sight of the pearl-moon held among the jade leaves over the malachite pool. In a husky voice, he said, "You brought it with you," as if declaring it in evidence to support his case.

"I know a good thing when I see it . . ."

He did not recall their having spoken another word again that night. At first, erotic passion engulfed all other feeling. In the calming embrace of gratitude and reassurance he felt himself unable to ask demanding questions. He longed to know if she had any idea of how daring and adventurous his coming after her had been for him, for in her circle of friends that might not be an unexpected action. But for him it was just as she had said—extraordinary. Still, he could not possibly frame it as a question to ask her. Their lovemaking was without reservation on either side, without restraint and without reflections on the future. But then he wished that he could know whether she recognized the effort of will on his part to reject her farewell note, the gamble against his pride that he had taken in acting as his own man against her injunction to give up his hopes. He could not dispel his unhappiness in his ignorance of whether she thought of him as a faithful friend, an insatiable satyr, or an opportunist. And then it did not matter any longer. They kissed each other into another act of love, and he fell asleep believing that she thought of him as her lover.

From the town of St. Moritz, an aerial tramway carries the skiers up to different heights along the side of the alp. Conrad admitted that he was equal only to the lower level run and said that he would take the lift back up to the guesthouse that Isabel would ski down to after she had done Corviglia, the longer run from higher up the mountain. They would meet at about one in the afternoon and eat lunch there. It worked out perfectly. She had skied down the precipitous trails, over jumps, and along narrow trails between tall evergreens, until shortly after noon when she came down to the level of the guesthouse. She washed up and was waiting for him at a table in the ample, low-ceilinged dining room when he appeared.

Both of them were flushed with satisfaction. Separately they had done the kind of skiing they were equal to. They sat side by side, with their backs to a window, happy to be in each other's company, surrounded by French, German, and British sounds played against the muted speech of languages from the Middle East, from Africa, and Asia, languages they could not even name. And yet, Conrad imagined that the men and women who spoke those tongues were makers and shakers— potentates, maharanis, princes. They were on top of the world. The bright sun in the clear blue sky shone on the satin of the white snow around them and rebounded into the warm dining room; the voices of their neighbors were subdued; they drank hot glüg and ordered cheese fondue.

Suddenly an Englishwoman appeared at the entrance into the dining room, in an azure ski outfit—a handsome woman, shaking her auburn hair out behind her head, until she caught sight of someone she was looking for halfway across the room, and shouted in a shockingly powerful voice the triumphant declaration: *"I've just done Corviglia!"* Like Tarzan pounding his fists on his chest, she blasted out the primitive announcement again: *"I've just done Corviglia!"* striding between the tables to an admiring gentleman standing up to welcome her. All eyes had to turn toward her; she had invaded their privacy, arrogated to herself the right to be the center of attention. Her self-concern was offensive because she disregarded the self-importance of everyone else in the dining room.

With a mock cringe on his face, Conrad said, "Attacked by swans."

Isabel grasped his hand and held it tightly on her lap. Quickly, as if expelling a deep sigh, all in a rush, she said, "Oh, my darling," and turned to stare at him full in the face. Tears came into her bright blue eyes and Conrad sensed that he had said exactly the right thing, that intuitively he had struck a chord that touched her more deeply than anything else he could have said or done. He felt her yielding to him as if her whole being were coming loose from moorings of self-protection and willingly presented herself to him. He marshaled all the strength of his self-control to keep himself from saying another word; the confidence in the steady gaze of his eyes and the firmness in his hand with which he returned the pressure of her hand were all his reassurance to her.

With his free hand he raised the napkin from his plate and wiped the tears from her cheeks. She looked at him then clear-eyed and recomposed, not turning her face away, measuring him with her eyes.

Very softly, almost in a whisper, she confirmed, "You do love me."

He nodded affirmation, never taking his eyes from her face. He was aware, in that instant, of the impossibility of ever knowing what went on in the secrecy of her mind; he would always have to piece together what he imagined she was thinking from what she said and what she did. But his mind was trying to race through hers: to discover what had happened when he spoke to her in the private language of her childhood. Had he called forth associations of pain and pleasure—the beauty of Jamaica, the childish terror, the comfort of her father's protection? Had those words made her feel she was appreciated as a whole, as a person with memories of her history that he would help her to preserve; that she was not just the surface of what her life appeared to be at the moment, and that he was equal to sharing not only the present moment with her? He had spoken to her in the language of her first family.

After long silence, in a steady, soft voice, she asked, "Will you marry me?" Through his hand and along his leg pressed against hers he felt a tremor run through her body. He took it to mean that this was the first surrender of her life, her first relinquishing of herself to a man. She did not submit in sexual intercourse; she was a liberated woman who had enjoyed sex since adolescence. She made love the way she played tennis; she was an equal partner in a game of pleasure; she never complied against her will in anything. She did not give herself up or hand herself over. She could always withdraw and preserve herself. Her bodily integrity was not challenged by sex; she was merely making pleasurable use of her powers. But to agree to marry, to wish to marry, for such a woman—*that* was to *yield* to a man; that was consciously to entrust herself to another, to let him take charge. She trembled with the uncertainty of even a willing virgin. It meant that she wanted to take the risk of putting herself in his hands, and that surrender of her independence was infinitely more fearful and exciting than any erotic stimulation alone. He suddenly understood: this is what is meant by *abandon*.

Conrad brought up both of his arms to hug her about her shoulders and draw her to his chest. Then he cupped her chin in one hand and kissed her cheek. "I will be your husband and you will be my wife," he whispered, "and we will live happily ever after." His heart pounded.

They separated, sitting side by side again, sedately.

"I do want it." Isabel sounded as if she was talking to herself. In a sudden movement she covered her mouth with one hand, as though otherwise she might take back what she'd just said. Slowly she lowered her hand to the table. "I don't know if I can be what you expect of me. What do you expect of me?"

Conrad replied: "What I expect of myself—that whenever you don't feel passionately in love with me, at least you won't forget to be my friend."

As awed and hushed as if she were swearing acquiescence before the altar, Isabel responded, "Yes."

A waitress approached with their tray, carrying the copper pot in which the fondue bubbled above a burning Sterno can, the basket of French bread chunks, the spearlike forks, and their wine. Conrad watched a playful smile animate Isabel's lips. As the lunch was being laid out before them, Isabel said to the waitress, in the most calm and ladylike tones of voice, as if to make up for the bad manners of another guest in the dining room, "I, too, have just done Corviglia." Under the tablecloth, Conrad reached for her hand, to find her reaching for his. This would be the beginning of their own private language.

The waitress said, "Congratulations," sweetly.

I not only love Isabel's good humor, Conrad thought, but I appreciate the good manners to be expected of a well-brought-up rich girl.

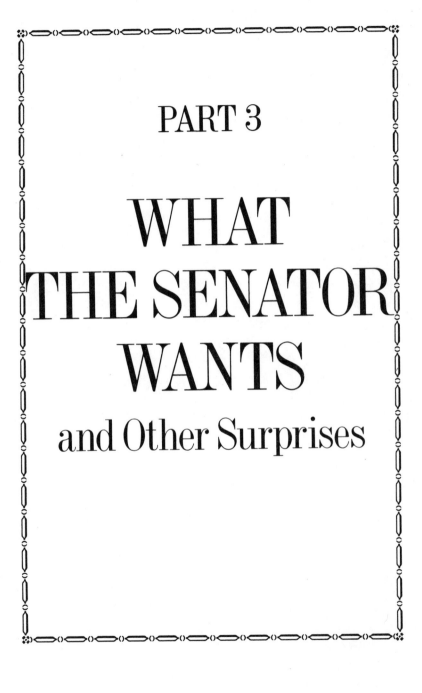

PART 3

WHAT THE SENATOR WANTS

and Other Surprises

As soon as Isabel and he were settled into their seats on the New York to Washington shuttle, Conrad's attention was caught by the presence of a horsefly on the plane. It alighted on the shoulder of the seat before him and appeared to be looking out of the window. He stared at the veins in the translucent wings and at the fly's arms moving over its head, as if to brush its hair forward. Conrad tried to swat it, but the fly escaped. "He probably knows I have my seat belt on," he said sarcastically. Isabel stroked his hand. "Reverence for life," she quoted. Albert Schweitzer had been a hero when Conrad went to college; he hadn't heard anyone mention the name since then. Conrad tried to smile and then he said, "Contemplate the fly—" which had returned to buzz above their heads. "He was born in Texas a week ago. Following his departing landlord to the airport, he found himself carried to Chicago. He went out through that sleeve of a corridor that comes to connect the 'aircraft' with the terminal and wandered through the labyrinth until he found his way onto another plane bound for LaGuardia. Here he is on his way to Washington, where—with any good luck—he'll transfer to a plane for Honduras. A jet set fly!" He made a silly smile and looked to Isabel for appreciation.

"It's the first time you've cracked a smile since the provost died," she said.

"Probably," he replied, letting himself slump down in the narrow seat.

"It's going to be all right," Isabel said, stroking his arm. "Everything's going to be all right."

She was cozening him; she behaved as if he were a sick child. She comforted him, not knowing why he appeared to be so unhappy. He seemed incapable of talking about it. There had been the shocking surprise that even "the best medical care in the world" had not been able to save Clif Rostum's life, then the sadness of the long, formal funeral, and now the fact that nothing whatever had been said directly to Conrad in the following few days about how the provost's position would be filled. Conrad was resentful and withdrew into himself. The trip to Washington would do them good. Conrad was aware that Isabel had no investment in whether the position went to him or not. He had no intention of appealing to her for sympathy, so her solicitude was all the more welcome. It made him believe that she did care for him, care about him. There was something more to him than his job and his ambition. He bent his head over toward his elbow and kissed her hand against his arm, where it was idly patting him. Then he shot both hands into the air and slapped the horsefly to death a few inches in front of his face.

"My hero!" Isabel exclaimed.

"You do love me," he whispered.

"You know I do," she answered calmly.

She has given her word. She will keep the bargain, Conrad thought. Take one day at a time.

Driving away in a taxi from National Airport, Conrad saw the same sight that affected him every time he arrived in Washington. They were moving slowly in thick traffic late in the afternoon along the Potomac toward the Fourteenth Street bridge, when the impression was so strong that he said out loud: "The Trylon and Perisphere!"

"What are you talking about?" Isabel asked.

"Look! You see the dome of the Jefferson Memorial and the tall pylon of the Washington Monument?"

"Yes."

"But seen together from this angle—the white ball and the tall, white sword-shape are exactly what the Trylon and Perisphere looked like at the World's Fair."

"What World's Fair?"

"New York, 1939." He was more reserved now, remembering that his wife had been born in 1943.

"Yes, darling. I've seen pictures of it," she said reassuringly. Conrad remembered once having to comfort a veteran of the Spanish-American War who asked if he recalled the battle cry "Remember the Maine." It was "information" for her; for him it had been an initiation into the Great World.

Conrad knew this was the symbol for his inability to take Washington seriously. For about five minutes on the drive along the Potomac, in order to travel from the Virginia side over a bridge to the District itself, every time he arrived he was confronted with the erect scepter and that regal globe, that image of the Trylon and Perisphere and memories of New York in the summer of 1939, his first trip east alone; and glowing through all the other recollections was the Cheshire cat— the permanently engraved impression of Grover Whalen's smile, the official "Greeter" of New York—the man who had no formal status, not an elected official, no other qualification for being the "Greeter" to the fair than that he looked like a man who ought to be an Official Greeter. America invented typecasting.

They were on the District side of the bridge now and the Trylon and Perisphere had separated into the Washington Monument and the Jefferson Memorial. The taxi took them along a series of six-story, sand-colored federal buildings, the printing and engraving section of the Treasury, past a crescent-shaped building like a Hapsburg Hof in Vienna, the Department of Agriculture building that thrust a bridge across a road to an annex of white marble in Palladian style. Then they were at the Mall, looking to the right down the long green esplanade to the Capitol building. Isabel was childlike with pleasure. For a world traveler, she had practically no experience of Washington—having visited it only once before, as a tourist in childhood. "The White House. The White House!!" she shouted in recognition as they skirted the Treasury Building with the statue of Alexander Hamilton before it. "And the magnolia trees—they're so large," as they drove past the appointment gate at the Presidential mansion, then around the statue of Lafayette. Her eyes darted everywhere as the cab curved into the short, semicircular drive and drew to a stop at the entrance of the Hay Adams Hotel.

"In *Democracy*, Adams once wrote, 'We could be vulgar and invite the President . . .' " said Conrad. But Isabel didn't make any effort to understand what he was referring to.

An efficient doorman took their luggage, a desk clerk signed them in, a porter rode up in the elevator and opened their room for them. It was not exceptionally handsome, but comfortable. A spacious enough room with a large bed, ivory and gold colored, with three closets along one wall, each with a full-length mirror on the door. The upholstery of one chair and the bedspread were decorated with a pattern of marigolds, and an armchair was covered in yellow pigskin; a desk without a chair before it stood near the window and in a corner there was a lady's dressing table. Isabel wandered to the window covered by lace curtains and framed by draperies of the same marigold-decorated material. Pulling the curtains apart she drew in her breath at the sight of the White House across the park—at the very idea of looking down on the White House. The window had many panes of glass in white frames without storm windows on the outside—the chill winter air came in as through a sieve. Beyond the casement stood a low, black, iron grille—a Southern touch—that went with the louvered transom over the door, as if to remind the visitor even in January that this is an almost southern city. Conrad stood behind her, peering down into Lafayette Square onto the tops of trees and the sight of redbrick paths through the chilled grass. He was surprised to see how many chimneys there were on the roof of the White House, implying that there must be a fireplace in every room, and by the sight of the flag on a tall flagpole in the center of the roof; does the flag fly only when the President is "in residence" as for any reigning monarch? Most unexpected, given this unique point of view, was the sight of the Washington Monument, perhaps half a mile beyond, which by a peculiar optical illusion appeared to be thrust up through the roof of the White House itself.

"You know," Conrad said after looking at his wristwatch, "the Stoneforts should be here in about twenty minutes."

"I'll freshen up," Isabel responded, carrying her cosmetics case into the bathroom with her.

Conrad continued to look out of the window. The sometime decayed handsome houses of the Federal period which flanked the square had been restored during Mr. Kennedy's presidency. He looked to Decatur House, the corner building at his right: Henry Clay had lived there. The huge trees around the White House must have been only saplings in his day. He'd rather be right than be President; what hogwash. The most American form of self-consolation. Conrad watched the light go on in the lantern-chandelier hanging in the middle of the high-columned portico of the Presidential mansion. Who would be calling this evening, he wondered, some head of state? or just one of the criminal lawyers representing so many of the staff of the untrustworthy Mr. Nixon?

Conrad was hardly aware of what Isabel had been wearing on the plane or in the taxi. He was conscious only of the silver foxes draped around her shoulders and the soft gray Italian fedora on her head—with a hatpin of silver and turquoise where a feather might have been perched. Now, as she came back into the bed-sitting room without her hat or coat or fur collar, he admired the tan wool suit by Chanel, the many long, golden chains of necklaces, and the high, brown-leather, Russian-like boots. "What a knockout you are!" he said appreciatively.

"Yeah, yeah, but would it get me elected?" She was aglow with the anticipation of going "onstage."

At that moment the telephone rang; the clerk at the front desk announced that Senator and Mrs. Stonefort were on their way up.

When they entered the room, introductions were made with handshakes and smiles. Stoneface took off his hat and coat and hung them in one of the closets. "Now this is the plan . . ." Ruby began. "I will take your bride away with me. It's only five thirty. And I'll drive her around some of the city for sight-seeing without any walking. That should give you men an hour and a half. At seven o'clock be down at the entrance and we'll pick you up. You'll have a drink at our house and then dinner at eight. Understood?"

"I understand," Conrad said, "that you run Washington, Ruby."

"I run only Senator Stonefort," she replied, trying to sound demure. Then she took Isabel by the arm and conspiratorially informed her, "I've found, from long experience, that if you let the men get their 'business' discussed first—without us around—conversation over dinner is much more civilized."

Isabel laughed; she was going to enjoy herself. The senator helped her on with her coat; Ruby helped her on with the fox collar; Conrad handed her hat to her. Sweetly, looking from one man to the other, Isabel said, "This is the loveliest bum's rush I've ever been given. I look forward to meeting you again."

Ruby actually giggled. She will like my wife, Conrad imagined. He had seen enough of Ruby over the years to know that she was not very bright but he wanted to believe she meant well. He never understood her reputation for being good-looking. She was well-built and had long, straight, dark hair and a long face, on which she never wore any makeup. But it was a

pale-skinned face with a long, thin nose—like a faded reproduction of a Modigliani portrait. Her manner was always cor-
dial and sometimes vivacious, but it was the behavior of a
woman who is fulfilling Her Social Obligation the way certain
Catholics Say Their Beads. What lay immediately under the
surface was so opaque a consciousness that it was obvious
nothing said or done in any meeting with her would be remembered or ever referred to again unless it dealt with her
ego directly. Isabel would flatter her simply by being so much
more sophisticated and beautiful while Ruby was cicerone-
in-charge. Ruby would remember all the gracious things Isabel might say about her and about Washington but would
screen out any other signal. Actually, Conrad was sorry for
Ruby in advance. Isabel was so much more a woman of the
world; Ruby was somehow essentially drab. Why was that?
He looked at her mink cape and her brocade, turban-like hat—
which on Isabel would have been brightened by her flair, her
"stage presence"—and he saw only a middle-aged woman
who had been married for a long time to A Very Important
Person and was a facet of his public life. But she was unlike
him. The senator cared about what you said and whether you
cared about what he said; Ruby did not. She appeared competent and self-assured but she possessed neither Isabel's
self-confidence nor Stonefort's ebullience. Stonefort had his
career; Ruby had their daughter, their only child, younger
than Caroline. The last time Conrad had seen the girl, a year
or so earlier, she was fifteen and suffered from a stutter. She
lived a circumscribed life between her mother's two thumbs.
If there was any ideal Ruby might be trying to realize in her
life it must be that of Good Form—a demanding abstraction
which needs no personality of one's own.

They ordered Scotch and water from room service and made
themselves comfortable. The senator took the overstuffed
chair with the marigold design and Conrad seated himself in

the armchair covered with pigskin, letting his fingers run from one wartlike nob to another along the surface.

"It's good to see you, Conrad," Stonefort began. "I'm grateful to you for coming."

"I'm glad to be here." He thought that Stoneface meant to continue for a while to be mysterious about this meeting, but, instead of plunging after the explanation, Conrad added, "Besides, I needed a change."

The senator picked up the melancholy in that remark. "You sound troubled."

"Not exactly. But uncertain of how things are going to develop at the university. You know that Clif Rostum died?"

"Yes. I read about it in the *Post*. Too bad. He was a good man, wasn't he?"

"In his way. I suppose I'll miss him more than I anticipate."

In his mind's eye, Conrad saw only the American flag on the tallest flagpole on campus flying at half-mast in memory of the provost. It remained so for three days, just as it would be lowered in his honor after Conrad's own death.

"Who will replace him?"

Rising to respond to the knock at the door, Conrad answered over his shoulder, "It isn't decided yet." As the waiter carried in the tray of drinks and lowered it to the surface of the desk, Conrad continued, "The president . . . ," meaning of the university, when Stonefort raised an index finger to his lips to silence him. In Washington one does not say anything about high-level governmental affairs in the presence of unknown waiters in hotel rooms. It amused Conrad to realize that the senator could not imagine there being more than one president. Neither of them said a word while the waiter poured out the highballs, Conrad signed the bill, and let him out of the room. But it was not amusing to recognize that Washington is the only European city in the United States. "European" in the sense of fearing that any hotel waiter might be a political spy, any sudden traffic accident might be the situation for the assassination of a foreign diplomat, any disappearance—even an unexplained absence of a few hours—might mean a political kidnapping. Intrigue was the essence of the official news and of the even more swiftly traveling gossip: the manipulation of power, the expenditure of the people's money, the marketing of ideas for attention, and the assessment of people for preferment. Washington was a barometer attuned to every variation of national and international pressure, in which every sign, no matter how trivial, was read with a magnifying glass. Civil and military politics were the air they breathed here, daily if not hourly: the way in Seattle the population lives for the daily count of how many porpoises got caught in the salmon nets. Civil and military politics were the only native products, and those activities consumed this Company Town, this curiously isolated small city. Unlike a European *capital* it was not embedded in the real world of finance and industry, high society and the arts; it was cut adrift, so that the rest of the United States could go about its private business while all the political action was siphoned into this one center which took on that burden of the public business for the whole country. This was the glorious delusion of the true Washingtonian.

"I was going to say," Conrad began again, "that the president of the university is rumored to be planning a Search Committee before choosing a successor to Rostum as provost."

"Oh? You sound suprised or disappointed."

"It's unheard of. The president doesn't need a Search Committee. The position of provost is an administrative appointment, not an elected one or one that has to be approved by the faculty. The president has only to recommend his choice to the trustees."

"Then why is he doing it?"

"I don't know yet that he will. It's only a rumor. Gossip. You're accustomed to rumors here that aren't true. . . ."

The senator laughed. He raised his glass in toast. Conrad said, "Cheers," and they both drank. They were seated in the lounge chairs facing each other. "It's beginning to get dark," Stonefort remarked.

Conrad rose, switched on the desk lamp, and resumed his

seat. He took this to be the end of chitchat. The mystery would be resolved now. "What would you like to talk about?" he asked.

The senator took a deep breath—not a weary sigh, but an infusion of air to fill the lungs of his broad chest in preparation for a sprint. He was about to go to work. He ran the fingers of one hand through his thick white hair; a smile appeared among the ruddy features of his pleasant face. You are about to finesse me, Conrad thought.

"The President," Stonefort began, nodding beyond the window of the hotel room toward the White House, "is under considerable attack."

"Investigation," Conrad corrected.

"To investigate the President is a form of attack. I believe he is an honorable man and wishes to do well by the country."

"I hope you are right," Conrad conceded, ". . . and, therefore, *my* assumptions are *wrong*."

"I know you have never supported him."

"And I know you are a good party man and have had to support him."

Stonefort brushed that aside with a flick of his hand. He brought out a pack of cigarettes and offered one to Conrad, implying that they were friends, old, dependable friends; they did not have to agree about politics. They had only to make the best of the situation.

"The White House had approached me to propose a bill in Congress."

"An executive bill."

"It would have to come from the White House. It has to do with the possibility of creating a new Cabinet post."

Conrad raised his eyebrows. Then he asked, "A lot more federal jobs?"

"Not necessarily. But the main thing is to extend support for the Administration among the intelligentsia."

"Mr. Nixon never sought their support before."

"That's unfair! Remember it was he who backed the National Endowments for the Arts and the Humanities when they needed it."

"Congress created them. He just didn't impound their funds. And he put an archconservative into the chairmanship of the NEH."

"Don't worry about him," the senator said confidentially. "He's getting enough trouble from Senator Pell."

"Well, more trouble isn't exactly what Nixon needs at the moment, is it?"

"On the contrary. He needs respect, admiration, the support of the country."

"Or, at least, of the 'intelligentsia.' "

"That's why this new proposal is under consideration."

"What is it?" Conrad asked. "Let's get to the heart of it."

"The White House is taking soundings on the proposal that a new cabinet post be created—Secretary of Culture."

Conrad let out a long, low whistle of incredulity. "In the You-knighted States of America?!"

"Don't give me a hard time," the senator said, one intimate joshing another. He stood up and poured each another drink.

"Secretary of Culture of the United States," Conrad said out loud—trying to pronounce the unlikely possibility without gagging on it. "Just as in Ruritania . . ."

"It's not so absurd. Most nations have it."

"Most nations haven't any separation of Church and State. Does that come next? A national religion?"

"You're being flippant and I'm being serious."

"I'm a weathercock for the rest of the nation?"

"For the rest of the intelligentsia."

"So that's what I'm here for?"

"No. It isn't. Why do you find the idea so strange?"

"You can't legislate culture."

"Cabinet officers don't legislate. They run departments."

"You can't 'run' culture."

"You can help pay for it!" the senator announced with a broad grin. "Look: all the basic mechanism is there already.

There's the Office of Education in Health, Education, and Welfare. There's the National Endowment for the Arts and the National Endowment for the Humanities. See? Education could be taken out of the Department of H.E.W., combined with the two endowments and *without* hiring a lot more people—you've got the basis for the Department of Culture."

Mocking, in a vaguely middle-European accent, Conrad made it into "Ze Ministree ov Kool-chure."

Stonefort looked around the room to see if anyone was listening before he whispered, "Your sense of humor is going to get you screwed someday."

The remark reminded Conrad of Clifford Rostum's saying, "You have an all-pervasive irreverence." And that wiped the smile off his face. "I apologize," he said. "I admit that the idea of a Ministry of Culture in the United States seems to go against what I take to be the American grain, but I'm willing to listen. I suppose my prejudice against Nixon has kept me from taking all of this seriously, but I was wrong. I'm sorry. I take *you* seriously."

"Now maybe we can get somewhere."

Conrad asked, "Where do you want to get to?"

The senator replied, "I want you to act as a consultant to me and my staff in preparing position papers that would be introduced in support of the bill creating a new department under a new Cabinet post—Secretary of Culture." He paused. "And, then, I want you to consider yourself as a possible candidate for that post if it is created."

Conrad remained silent.

"I must have your promise that you will keep this absolutely confidential. Not a word about it is to be leaked to anyone— especially the newspapers."

"I can assure you of that—whether I agree to act as a consultant for you or not."

Stonefort was momentarily flustered. "It hadn't occurred to me that you wouldn't," he admitted. "I'm assuming too much, of course. But—honestly—I hadn't imagined that you'd turn me down."

This time Conrad offered the senator a cigarette and they both lit up again. "Why me?" Conrad asked.

Stonefort leaned forward to pat him on the knee. "You're one of the keepers of the flame," he said, grinning.

"I'm merely the administrative officer in charge of the undergraduate college . . ."

". . . of a great university. One of the most respected institutions in the country." The senator revised the remark: "In the *world*. If you don't know what culture is—nobody does."

"What if nobody does?"

"Then I can't make a case for supporting it, can I? But there is a beautiful thing out there—isn't that true? American culture!" The senator had spread his arms wide as he often did to embrace the audience at a political rally. "A *beautiful* thing," Stonefort repeated.

It was the phrase "out there" that bothered Conrad. American Culture! All he could think of were the thousands and thousands of movie theaters scattered across the nation on the floors of which had been crushed a million empty cardboard containers of buttered popcorn. Conrad tried to take his bearings. He was seated in a room at the Hay Adams, across the street from the White House, listening to his old friend Stoneface, now senator from Missouri, tell him of a confidential plan. He was being asked for a position paper in support of a national Department of Culture and a new Cabinet post for which he should consider himself a nominee. Heady! he said to himself: heady stuff. Seductive, with all the unexpected allure of "This is really happening to me? . . . Do I deserve it?" How paltry the position of provost of the university seemed at the moment, suddenly shrunk to small potatoes. But the provostship was in the realm of stability and continuity, whereas a Cabinet post could be held for but a few years at most; a secretary was under constant critical survey and liable to instant dismissal. Didn't he have to sign a letter of resignation on being sworn in, so the President could use it at his discretion at any time? Conrad had known more than one academic who had spent time in a position of great power in Washington. It took them two or three years afterward to unwind, to return to normal, if they ever did. They kept retelling their stories as if that was the one form of decompression to avoid dying of the bends. They were like survivors of car crashes or the parents of a child they had helplessly watched die before their eyes. The shock to the system had to be overcome only by reliving it—telling the story over and over. Conrad brought his mind back to the present situation. "Who else have you asked?"

"To be a consultant?"

"Yes."

"I can't give out particular names," the senator whispered secretively. "But let me put it this way: we're going to get position papers on separate branches of American culture from specialists. I can tell you that. You know: on literature, theater, music, painting, architecture—all those sorts of things."

"Then, what do you want of me?"

"An overview. A sense of the whole ball of wax."

Disguising his dislike of the image, Conrad repeated "the whole ball of wax?" as a question.

The senator patted his knee again. "You're the man who can do it. You have a grasp of the intellectual and scholarly world as well as all those other things. . . ."

" 'Out there,' " Conrad quoted him.

"Right!"

"You want me to read all of the separate position papers before I write an 'overview'?"

"No, no. Not at all. We can't wait for all of them. We want to present the bill within a couple of months. Besides, if you do yours independent of the individual studies, it'll strengthen our credibility."

That pushed Conrad's shoulders back with firmness. No one in Washington these days wanted his "credibility" tarnished. "The separate studies will be a sort of 'current state of the arts' . . . and the overview you want has to describe . . ."

"The nature of the beast," Stonefort supplied, with pride.

"You can do it! You describe the character of American culture—and we'll make the case for a federal department to bring more of it to the people."

"And glory to the Administration?"

"True."

Not unkindly, Conrad asked, "Do you believe in this yourself?"

Stonefort slumped in his chair. Conrad refilled their drinks and looked at his watch. "It's almost seven."

"I believe we should try to do it," the senator answered.

"There are an awful lot of other people you could ask who would do a better job for you than I will. Have you asked Jacques Barzun or Lionel Trilling?"

The senator didn't say. He answered: "There's no one I both trust and expect to be as conscientious and cooperative as you. You're a pillar of American culture and you're a good friend." He smiled and added, "You know how to get things done efficiently."

"You mean—you expect me to meet your deadline."

Now they both laughed. Stonefort said, "Tomorrow, in my office, we'll talk about that with my staff. I have a file of materials for you, and forms to fill out. You know: for travel expenses and payment of consultation fee."

"I can't accept any money for doing this," Conrad said firmly.

The senator was startled at first, but, in an instant, saw his advantage. He thrust out his hand to shake Conrad's in mutual congratulations. "That means you *will* do it!"

Conrad paused before cautiously judging: "I suppose that's what I'm letting myself in for."

They were both standing now. Stonefort slapped him on the back. "That's what I like about you. A simple yes or no ain't got no class. You've got style!"

The evening passed in such a way that Conrad thought of it as "pleasant enough" but he felt sensitive to the impressions being made on Isabel for her to consider it "fascinating." The tone had been set by the conversation in the car driving from the hotel to the Stoneforts' house in Georgetown: the intention to draw each other out and to be entertaining. Ruby had asked, "Now, what were you two talking about?"—knowing she would not be given an honest answer.

The senator drawled, "Scholars, intellectuals . . ."

With a kittenish smile, Ruby asked Conrad, "What is the difference between them?"

"It's like the difference among jugglers, my dear—depending on the number of balls they can keep in motion at the same time," Conrad began. "A scholar can keep at least two different ideas in mind at the same time; an intellectual can keep at least three."

At dinner, the fact that no other guest had been invited, strengthening the impression that they were dining en famille, was a courtesy directed toward making Isabel as comfortable as possible and implying that whatever the senator had asked of Conrad was on the basis of intimacy, not simply official business. Stonefort addressed himself to Isabel as often as Ruby did, while Conrad, remembering that the senator had brought a briefcase out of the car with him, wondered how long he could keep up the small talk before he felt obliged to begin his evening's work. The Stoneforts spoke of diplomatic receptions they had attended and parties they had given—the word "party" sounded a synonym of Washington—of business and pleasure trips to exotic countries around the world, of fox hunts during weekend holidays at estates in Virginia. They lured Isabel into comparing skiing experiences in Europe with those in the Rockies or New England, into describing the latest fashion shows she'd been to in Paris and New York, into explaining what it was like to participate in the Junior League horse shows from the time she was ten years old.

It was not that Conrad felt left out—he contributed his share—and he was in fact grateful for the chance to be quieter than usual, half contemplating the scene he was part of at the moment, half meditating on the proposal Stonefort had made to him at the hotel. He had been asked to write the overall, the "main" position paper on American culture in support of an executive bill, and as bait he had been offered the suggestion (not to put it more strongly than that) of becoming the first Secretary of Culture. He was feeling his way through to the prospect without delusion. It had little to do with him, with his qualifications or competence for such a role. That is not how things are done in Washington. They are done on the basis of quid pro quo; what have you done for me lately, and what can you do for me next? If Stonefort had a candidate for the first secretary's position, he would put him forward, just as a dozen or two dozen other senators would do, fifteen members of the House, twenty governors. How would the chief executive and his staff rank them and decide? Not, for sure, by comparing the candidates, but by weighing the debts to, and expectations of, those who put forth the nominations. If Senator Stonefort put through a bill that brought any credit to the Administration during a period when it was being more discredited every day, would his nomination not have more "clout" than anyone else's? This was Conrad's way of telling himself to take no personal pride in the proposal. The absolute scale of Objective Merit for such a post was a mirage of the Rational Mind. It did not function in the actual world. The imaginary Most Appropriate Person for the job was as fanciful an idea as the unicorn. Some flesh and blood creature would be chosen and confirmed by the Senate and hold the post for a couple of years and go to his grave with the aura of having wielded extraordinary power—well or poorly—during a short span of time. The truth was: of all political officers, those who are elected "achieve greatness," those who are appointed "have greatness thrust upon them"; and the latter are taken in by thinking they earned it just as Malvolio was. But when one is rarely complimented in life, a little flattery goes a very long way. Thus did Conrad mean to keep himself from being carried away with self-importance over the proposal, by the same understanding that allowed him to imagine it was not preposterous.

The senator directed a question to him. What did he think of the increasing statistics of crime on and around university campuses?

"It's all very grim," Conrad replied, "and just like outraged citizens who form vigilante groups, universities are enlarging the number of their own security guards. But I'll tell you a story to brighten the picture. Our criminals can't be all bad." His voice became cheerful. "There were two mathematicians from Moscow visiting at the university last fall. They made the mistake of taking a long walk one evening and ending up in the worst part of town, near Wooster Street in the dark. A black hoodlum stuck them up with a switchblade and demanded their wallets. They handed them over, while speaking Russian to each other. The robber listened to them and asked, 'Where you from?' And they replied, 'The Soviet Union.' Well, he thought about that for a moment and then handed the wallets back to them. He didn't want the Russians to get a bad impression of our country."

The senator laughed heartily, but Ruby said, "As if there's no crime in the Soviet Union . . ."

She shrugged her shoulders and turned her attention back to Isabel. "If you stay on a few days," she said, "the Stuttgart Ballet is performing at Kennedy Center tomorrow night, and then there's going to be a marvelous party at the British embassy Friday . . ."

Isabel looked at Conrad inquiringly.

"I promised to be back tomorrow afternoon." Contemplating the two women, who faced each other across the dining room table, Conrad was struck by how much he respected Isabel—whether he liked her or not—and how little he believed in Ruby, though she did everything to make herself likable. Her lack of makeup and her plain clothes on her good enough figure were a pretense that she was a no nonsense lady, serious but taking it all in stride, whereas the effect on him was that she was incurious as every know-it-all is. No matter how many questions she asked in her capacity as Hostess to "draw one out," what came through the lackluster manner was her relief that she could carry off the charade at all.

Isabel was of an entirely different order of creation. She had all the courage of an egocentric without any of the drawbacks of false modesty. She did not need to appear earnest or "interested"; she enjoyed herself. Other people either bored her and offended her or contributed to her enjoyment of herself. What she offered them in return was a share in her own enjoyment: take it or leave it. Ruby Stonefort was not a source of enjoyment. Conrad smiled to himself at the thought that he had discovered what was concealed by her lack of makeup. She was nothing but a drab little Good Girl, aging poorly. The false front was a role in life that had been thrust upon her by marriage.

Isabel is free of that! Conrad recognized. Because of her money, her psychoanalysis, and her beauty. All her bluster about feeling that she ought to be "doing" something else with her life was mere static from the outside world. She was doing exactly what she could and wanted to do. The irritation she expressed over certain actions she performed to please him socially was in fact an expression of sympathy with women who did not have her freedom of choice and action. She knew she had given up very little in exchange for the comforts of Conrad's company. How she loved him or how much she loved him were not questions that worried him. Neither of them was a sentimentalist. They shared only what they could. But a person like Ruby was not full of her own life—only of what she must be and do for others—and that left her resentful and false, furtively testing her unassessable personal powers to find out where she stood in the eyes of others. Isabel was right out there. Ruby was a sneak. And even as he realized these thoughts, admiring his wife and downgrading the senator's, he was aware of the conversation over the dinner table through which Ruby was trying to lure Isabel into being overwhelmed by Washington. If the glamorous Mrs. Taylor could be made to envy Mrs. Stonefort, then Ruby's efforts would be validated. Poor Ruby. It did not occur to Conrad then that Ruby was going to get what she wanted.

He turned his attention to the senator. William Stonefort had appealed to him out of friendship. But how long had it been since their involvement with each other mattered to their minds or souls? There was only the memory of friendship to draw on. Once upon a time they had telephoned each other after dinner in the evening—talked for half an hour—even if they had spent the whole previous day with each other. How old had they been? Fifteen? Sixteen? They talked about everything: sex and politics, school, their parents, the Great World "out there." Conrad realized he had experienced no such friendship in his adult life. He lived with the support of warm acquaintances—Jerry Rosenblatt, Henry Warner, Walter Webster, Dr. Connolley—but not lifelong friends. Perhaps friendship is only a function of childhood when most "problems" are hypothetical: how will I behave in combat? How will I make out on the next date? In later years one is not so free with his fears. And then acquaintances are either people one knows and can make use of—or people one knows and can't make use of.

As things now stood, Conrad recognized, if he had met the senior senator from Missouri now for the first time they would never become friends. They did not care about the same things, they did not share the same loyalties. The crisis over the disreputable Nixon was only one aspect of it. He was looking at a man with a dramatic shock of white hair, large dark eyes under bushy eyebrows, high cheekbones, a wide expressive mouth, and a bronzed complexion. He must use a sunlamp. He had doubled in girth since the days when they ran on the high-school track team together. He had narrowed his dreams of what "making the best of a situation" could accomplish. But he was a successful political manipulator—who thought of "culture" as "out there." What to him was "in here"? He was under pressure to produce: what have you done for me lately? Conrad felt saddened as if he and his boyhood friend looked at each other from opposite ends of a tunnel that continually grows longer.

"I don't know what you're thinking about," he heard the senator say, "but I gather from your expression that you don't approve."

Conrad snapped himself out of his reverie. "I was just beginning to feel that we've taken up a lot of your time. Do you realize we've been two hours at dinner?"

"It was meant to be leisurely," Ruby explained.

"And you must have work to do, Bill."

"As a matter of fact, the Foreign Relations Committee meets at eleven. That's why I hoped you'd come over to the office and talk with my staff starting about nine thirty."

"Yes. Yes," Conrad agreed, standing up and moving to Isabel's side.

"I hate to go," Isabel said.

Ruby's smiling response was: "How kind of you."

Conrad became aware of the thought that estimating his wife high above Mrs. Stonefort was part of a process by which he was soothing his vanity for the possible truth that Isabel was having an affair with another man, telling himself that it was all right, even if she were, because as long as it did not impinge upon his self-esteem, deprive him, or detract from his life, he did not begrudge it to her—he remained grateful to her for the delight she brought him; not only their satisfaction in sex but the pleasures that come as dividends for having invested in someone who truly enjoys *herself*. There was the nub of his feeling at the moment! It was one thing for him to recognize that all people are rooted in self-love and must operate at all times to protect their pride; it was altogether different to estimate the degree to which they enjoyed it, or were torn by the idealistic belief that they ought to feel differently, ought to be some kind of impersonal altruist. Isabel was the exception; she was not torn. She was all of a piece. The senator was torn between what a senator ought to do and what a good party man is expected to do. How would he enjoy himself if he were free of both responsibilities? Was *he* having a love affair on the side?

Conrad unexpectedly perceived a twinge of contempt in Stonefort's expression and he suddenly realized that the senator had long since tired of his dutiful wife. He hoped Stonefort was having an affair. It was Justice Oliver Wendell Holmes's wife who once said to Theodore Roosevelt, "Washington is filled with fascinating men—and the women they married when they were young."

Ruby said, "I suppose Bill has asked you to do something for the government?"

That was a quaint way of putting it, Conrad thought. "Yes, he has," he replied noncommittally.

"I hope you'll do it," she urged.

"I'll try my best," he answered, hating himself for giving her an advantage.

She took it immediately. "I'm sure you will." Her manner was so gently and kindly patronizing that only a five-year-old would have failed to know her for an ass. How did Stonefort put up with it?

At last, alone in their hotel room, Isabel's first words were, "I don't want to go home."

"Why?" Conrad asked.

"It's fun. I'd like to stay for a while."

Looking around the room, Conrad asked, "Here?"

"No. Ruby's invited me to stay with them."

"Ruby?" Conrad snorted. "You'll mash her into the ground in forty-eight hours."

"She doesn't count," Isabel replied. She was removing the fur collar, taking off her hat and coat. She moved blithely, loosely.

"She's done everything she could to impress you," he said.

With her simple honesty, Isabel explained, "She's a natural-born servant."

Conrad laughed. "The only thing that keeps you from being a snob, darling, is that you already have what snobs aspire to."

"I don't 'have' Washington," she replied.

"You'll let Ruby think she's Lady Bountiful."

"I will."

"In order to experience Washington through her eyes."

"Through her 'perquisites,' " Isabel replied.

They both laughed. "Isn't she silly?" Isabel asked with delight.

"I don't know. Maybe she's vicious. Once she's sure she's done you a favor she'll want a reward."

"Like what?"

"Maybe she'll want you to go to bed with her." Conrad hadn't the faintest idea of why he had said that.

"You still haven't gotten over that anonymous letter, have you?"

"I didn't make that connection."

"Well, I did," she said casually. "But there's no point in being nasty. I'm being pleasant!" She had taken off her suit and shoes and flopped down in the pigskin armchair in her slip and bra, twisting the chair around to look out at the White House floodlighted at nearly midnight. "I won't stay more than three or four days. Do you mind?" she asked openly.

"No." He was unpacking the overnight bag they had brought with them. "But you don't have enough clothes with you . . ."

"I'll pick up a few things while I'm here."

Yes, Isabel can do that, he thought; she can return home in four or five days with a new suitcase and a new wardrobe. She was the only woman he had ever known who could buy a dress she never had any intention of wearing a second time.

"But you remember we're having guests for dinner on Tuesday."

"I'll be back before then."

"You're not the sight-seeing type . . ." he began, getting into his pajamas. "Museums bore you."

"I'm not staying for the museums. I want to see the high life. Washington so-sigh-it-tee . . ." she hissed.

"There is no society in Washington. This is a transients' town. People are only temporarily 'in place.' It's the American rotation system. Washington is more like a hotel than a city."

"I like fancy hotels," Isabel chuckled.

"I like you," he said, watching her take the pins from her long golden hair, benefiting from the contrasts he'd been considering all evening. She turned around in the seat with her arms still upraised and her hands on top of her head, as if in surrender. The peachlike blush of her high, rounded cheeks rose with her smile. Her eyes blinked: sapphires twinkling.

"Kiss me," she said.

He did, and lifted her from the armchair, and led her to the bed. They made love not as a challenge to each other or in a passionate farewell, but as colleagues who meant each other well and recognized each other's independence.

Conrad did not find himself alone until the plane took off from National for LaGuardia. He hadn't enjoyed even the privacy of a taxi ride. One of Stonefort's staff insisted on driving him to the airport in his own modest car. It was barely noon but Conrad felt worn out, as if he'd been working for ten hours. Stonefort himself appeared for only half an hour announcing to his "boys" that Dr. Taylor was willing to act as consultant—without payment—and to prepare the "over-view" position paper they needed so badly. It was then up to the staff to show Conrad the kind of thing they had in mind—samples of similar documents presented with other bills submitted to Congress. They indicated possible length, delivery date, head and subhead divisions; they concerned themselves with everything but substance. They were masters of form.

Isabel had kept the overnight bag with her. Conrad climbed on board the shuttle with nothing in his hand but the manila envelope containing the folder of documents—all the relevant information on the Office of Education, the National Endowments, and sample forms of other "enabling legislation." He opened the folder and began to read Public Law 209—of the 89th Congress.

AN ACT

To provide for the establishment of the National Foundation on the Arts and the Humanities to promote progress and scholarship in the humanities and the arts in the United States, and for other purposes.

Be it enacted by the Senate and House of Representatives of the United States of America in Congress assembled, That this Act may be cited as the "National Foundation on the Arts and the Humanities Act of 1965."

DECLARATION OF PURPOSE

SEC. 2 (20 U.S.C. 951) The Congress hereby finds and declares—

(1) that the encouragement and support of national progress and scholarship in the humanities and the arts, while primarily a matter for private and local initiative, is also an appropriate matter of concern to the Federal Government;

(2) that a high civilization must not limit its efforts to science and technology alone but must give full value and support to the other great branches of man's scholarly and cultural activity in order to achieve a better understanding of the past, a better analysis of the present, and a better view of the future;

(3) that democracy demands wisdom and vision in its citizens and that it must therefore foster and support a form of education designed to make men masters of their technology and not its unthinking servant;

(4) that it is necessary and appropriate for the Federal Government to complement, assist, and add to programs for the advancement of the humanities and the arts by local, State, regional, and private agencies and their organizations;

(5) that the practice of art and the study of the humanities requires constant dedication and devotion and that, while no government can call a great artist or scholar into existence, it is necessary and appropriate for the Federal Government to help create and sustain not only a climate encouraging freedom of thought, imagination, and inquiry but also the material conditions facilitating the release of this creative talent; . . .

219

Conrad stopped. He reread the last sentence. *"Release"* indeed, he reflected; as if talent were a genius in a stoppered bottle . . . and the long arm of a Secretary of Culture could reach benevolently across the nation pulling out stoppers here and there. It was all so naive. So appropriate to the "image" of a manipulator like Nixon. So transparent a ploy for cheers from the gallery. Creative talent doesn't need to be "released"; what it needs in this country is an audience. That's what's missing and cannot be bought with federal funds. He thought of the barber in Paris, at the barbershop near the American embassy where Conrad went to get his hair cut; the man was red-eyed, wiping away his tears as Conrad walked in, first thing one morning, and asked, "What's the matter?"

"Haven't you heard?"

"No. What?"

Then the barber rested both hands on Conrad's arms, as if it were possible to soften the blow. "Albert Camus," he said, "was killed in an automobile crash last night."

The plane gained altitude over the Potomac and headed north, circling wide around the Capitol. No, Conrad shook his head, forgetting Paris. I'm off on the wrong tack. The sky was overcast. Conrad looked down at the maze of new housing developments in Maryland, the developers' gaudy attempts at substitutes for natural communities; from the air they were to be appreciated more than on the ground. The idea was to create little whirlpools: to bring people together by curved roads rather than to separate them by sharp street corners.

Then the plane rose through a gauzy bank of clouds and the earth was hidden below; there was nothing but bright sunlight above the white mounds that concealed the land from view. Stewardesses—one black, one white—tugged a machine on a portable counter along the aisle, checking flight tickets. "American culture!" Conrad moaned to himself: a machine for selling "bus" tickets thousands of feet in the air, cocktails at noon, a shuttle between Washington and New York. ". . . material conditions facilitating the release of this creative talent . . ."

Where was he to begin? How was he to begin? He wrote the words "American Culture" across the front of the manila envelope. Do you know anything about American culture? He leaned back against the cushioned seat and recollected Dickens's joke about the man asked to give a lecture on Chinese philosophy.

"Do you know anything about Chinese philosophy?"

"No, but I can use a dictionary. I'll look up 'Chinese' and I'll look up 'philosophy.' It won't take long. It's called 'research.' "

Conrad counted it a blessing that his daughter Caroline unexpectedly appeared, and just as unpredictably left again, during the four days that Isabel remained in Washington. It was bad enough to confront her by himself; they would always be daughter and father. But Isabel had no patience with her and bedtime talk would have been burdened with trying to argue against Isabel's contention that the way a human being ought to behave toward anyone else is more important than the father-daughter relationship. The truth is that Caroline behaved like a blackmailer.

In the middle of Friday afternoon at his office, Mrs. Todd had buzzed to say, "Your daughter's on the phone, Mr. Taylor."

"Where is she calling from?"

Cameron McNeill, who was in the study with him, turned his back to look out of the window.

"From here in town."

"Put her on," he said. Cameron moved quickly toward the door saying, "We can continue this later."

"Caroline?" His voice was not cold.

"You sound so defensive."

"It's Friday afternoon. I'm in the middle of a meeting. I haven't heard from you in months. How are you?" He always found himself saying too much to her at once. "Where are you?"

"I'm at the train station. And I'm here to show you how I am."

He looked at his watch. "Well, can you stay overnight?"

"Of course."

He looked at his desk calendar. There was to be one more appointment that afternoon, and then cocktails at the club with Walter Webster. Conrad had phoned him before leaving for Washington, with the message that John Drexel at the Museum of Modern Art was willing to take over at least two of Webster's three courses. But on returning Thursday afternoon he found Mrs. Todd's message that Professor Webster had asked to see him at 5:30 on Friday. Conrad was eager to hear whether Webtser knew anything about the Search Committee; it was he who had given Conrad the rumor to begin with.

"Why don't you take a cab to the house, and . . ."

"Because I don't have enough money."

Right back to where we left off, Conrad thought. "Take a cab anyway. I'll phone the maid—Rosalie—to look out for you. She'll pay the taxi."

"All right." She sounded perky.

"As soon as I can break away, I'll find you there."

"When will that be?"

He decided to postpone the conversation with Webster. "I'll get home by five-thirty. Take a hot bath in the meanwhile."

"What makes you think I need one?"

Instead of allowing himself to snap back with, You always do, he answered, "I mean relax, make yourself comfortable. Everything in your room is just as you left it. I'll see you in two hours." She made no reply, although he thought he heard her humming faintly. "It's been a long, long time. I'm eager to see you," he said slowly and affectionately.

"You'll be surprised," she said sweetly, and hung up.

She filled him with dread.

He telephoned Rosalie to take care of the taxi fare and to welcome Caroline. Then he reached Walter Webster in his office. Webster was oddly evasive and said something unclear about not being available during the weekend and that he'd phone him on Monday. He was certainly tense and distracted. Conrad thought that, perhaps, more people had been thrown off balance by the provost's death than he imagined before. But he felt a falling away of others from—from what?—from support of himself. How much support did he need? All this is fantasy, he told himself. I will meet Caroline on my own.

She was not alone when Conrad walked into the living room. The fire had been lit, and Caroline sat on the large sofa facing it, with the maid by her side. Conrad had never seen Rosalie seated in the living room before. She tried to rise, but Caroline put a hand on her shoulder. "Did you know that Rosalie comes from Hong Kong?"

"Yes," he replied.

"And she isn't a refugee from Communist China. Her parents settled there as refugees from the Japanese. She was born there. Her father still works for a British bank."

"My father is a 'clark,'" Rosalie said.

"So Rosalie is neither a cop-out from Mao or one of the dispossessed. She just wants to be middle class. Right?"

Conrad saw the glass of Coca-Cola in Caroline's free hand as well as the second glass on the table before them. Caroline, the teetotaler, had been "drinking" with the maid. What a quaint idea, he thought, like being caught "kissing the chauffeur." She let go of the maid then and Rosalie stood up. "May I get something for you, Mr. Taylor?" she asked.

"No, thanks," he replied, "I'll do that myself," and he went off across the hall to the bar and poured out a long Scotch and water before returning to the living room.

Caroline remained seated, staring into the fire, her back turned toward him. Conrad thought she must have bathed. She looked fresh, almost pink, although that might have been due mainly to the soft shade on the lamp lighted on the end table between them, or to the glow from the fireplace. Her dark wavy hair was combed back and held in a ponytail by an elastic band. She was wearing a shapeless African dress, wide as a tent—a cotton thing loud with a pattern of pinwheels of red and green, fringed with gray feathers whose tips ended in vermilion points, all on a saffron yellow background. With a wide round neckline and sleeves that came down to her elbows, it seemed a garment made for a much larger woman. He could see that her face was longer and thinner, but perhaps only because he had caught sight of her in a moment of repose. She wore leather sandals without stockings on her long legs. "Are you warm enough?" he asked.

She turned her head and smiled at him condescendingly, with a look that insinuates, Isn't that just like a parent?

He leaned forward over the back of the sofa and kissed her on the cheek.

"Thank you," Caroline said, without finishing the sentence—with "Dad, Daddy or Father." Conrad reminded himself that she never called him anything, never called him by any name at all. At least she hadn't since she was thirteen or fourteen years old. But, once upon a time, she had been a little girl who liked to climb onto his lap and listen while he read her a story; a summer cottage child with four Band-Aids on each knee covering the scrapes from a fall on the rocks at the edge of the beach, near Kennebunkport. A long time ago.

"We have a lot of catching up to do," Conrad said, as he lowered himself into the armchair to her left.

"Yes," she said brusquely. "What have *you* been up to?" They both laughed. "The house looks very different."

It startled him to realize that, while he thought of her probably every day, she had never once been to this house since Isabel and he were married. "You've been away a long time." Before anything more might be said even to hint at a reprimand or lead to an argument, Conrad decided to get up and kiss her again, this time on the other cheek.

"Some things are the same, though," she considered, as he sat down again. "Like your perfume and your jewelry."

"Perfume? Jewelry?" he asked. "I put on after-shaving lotion and I wear cuff links." He pulled back the sleeve of his gray flannel suit to see which ones he was wearing—the oval of carnelian in a frame of gold, incised with his initials, given to him by his father on his sixteenth birthday.

"I never do have the right words for you, do I?" she said.

It's not that, Conrad thought; you just don't know how to make other people feel good; you know only how to contend, how to pick a fight. It was not the case that she didn't know the words "after-shaving lotion" or "cuff links." She *spurned* perfume and jewelry. She wanted him to know that she hadn't changed any of her antagonistic attitudes. Conrad was determined to keep his temper under control. "I have a word for you, however. Welcome. Welcome home, welcome back." He lifted his Scotch and water to toast her.

She responded with a sip of her soda.

"Where's Isabel?" she asked.

"In Washington."

Caroline snorted: "Fascist Army Headquarters."

"You have a tendency to oversimplify," slipped out before Conrad could prevent it from being said.

"You have a tendency to blindness."

Conrad stood up and moved around the glass table to the fireplace, his back turned to her, picked up the brass poker, and rearranged the flaming logs in the grate. Then he added three short birch logs like a peaked cap on top of the other logs and watched the bark catch fire in curls. By then he could turn around to her and ask, "What sort of dinner would you like? The restaurant at the country club is open. Chinese? You see, I told the cook not to bother about full dinners while Isabel's out of town."

"You have a full-time cook?"

"She's Isabel's."

Caroline laughed, but made nothing more of it. "How about cold cuts and cheese around the kitchen table?"

"Fine. I'll arrange things." He walked down the hall to the back of the house, thinking, That's exactly what I'll never be able to do as far as Caroline is concerned—arrange things. She is a case of cultural disorder. She is a casualty of the 1960s.

When he returned to his seat near Caroline, he held another Scotch and water in one hand.

"You drink a lot," she said.

Ignoring that, Conrad began, "I'm sorry not to have a proper spread for your first night back. It isn't as if I knew when you were . . ."

She interrupted him. "I flew in on Tuesday. Stayed with friends in New York. I didn't know how soon I'd be coming up, so I couldn't have told you in advance."

This is all such guff, Conrad knew. "I sent you off to London," he began, "because you wanted to study acting there. Instead, you've been studying Africa for over a year. What have you learned?"

"Ah, the Final Exam," she replied.

Conrad chortled. "No," he said gently. "I'd just like to hear something of your experiences. Your postcards didn't tell very much."

"Africa is beautiful. There is always snow on Mount Kilimanjaro. Lions wander freely in the Serengeti. They bottle capers in Mozambique," she said, as if by rote. Then she added, "Africans are phony."

"Oh?"

"At least in all the cities. They imagine they're either British or French." Conrad assumed that meant only "liberated," educated Africans would approach Caroline or allow her to approach them. "The real Africans are in the bush. But I couldn't . . ." She had trouble finishing that thought, and ended up with, ". . . stay there."

"Is that where you wanted to stay?"

"Yes. But there was no way."

"So you've come home."

"Oh, no," she announced sharply. "I'm just passing through."

Conrad had to admit to himself that he felt little pain. All the misery at the loss of her had been survived years before. He did not hope she had "come home" or would remain "home." She had nothing to offer him but cause for anger. He felt the drawbacks of paternal "duty"; that oppressed him. But she felt free and noble, having scourged herself of the bourgeois-capitalistic-sadistic culture he represented to her. She didn't feel deprived; she felt holier-than-thou, although there was nothing clear-cut about her; she faded into vagueness on all sides. She would live her life—as she had in that London flat—in the ambiguity of relationships like those with the Irish girl and the Africans. "By the way," Conrad said suddenly, "Christian Kirkill is back in town."

"Have you seen him?"

"No. I don't even know where he's staying. Do you want to see him?"

"No," she said with an unfeigned lack of interest. "What's become of him?"

"I don't know. What will become of you?"

"I thought you'd never ask."

"I'm asking now."

"I'm going to stay where I can be useful—among people who aren't phony."

"Are there any?" Conrad asked.

"The Hopi. In Arizona."

Conrad felt himself clamping his jaw together to keep from saying anything too quickly. He felt the pressure of his upper and lower teeth meshing together. When he relaxed enough, he asked, "How did you discover them in Africa?"

"On the plane coming back. A man got on at Dakar, sat next to me, talked to me all the way across the Atlantic. He was a Hopi. He went to the University of Arizona and then spent three years in the Peace Corps in Nigeria. He's on his way back to his people. He's going to run an agricultural station and an infirmary. He needs all the help he can get. I'm going to help him."

The fire was dying down and Conrad poked it again. Caroline was at last happy to go on talking. She described the reservation, the settlements, the children, the ceremonies— just as she had heard about them curving westward around the globe high above the Atlantic Ocean.

Conrad asked, "How can you help in an infirmary and at an agricultural station?"

"I'll learn!" She raised her voice for the first time.

It struck Conrad that he believed in salvation by rituals and Caroline by good works. It was as simple as that. He remained silent. She crossed her legs and finished drinking the soda.

At length, he allowed as how, "It might be a hard life."

"A soft life costs too much," she said. "Besides, with Sebastian, I can expect kindness. I stayed with him in New York."

"That's his name?" Conrad said dumbly.

"Sebastian Castillo. It's Spanish, but he's dropping it. His Hopi name is Lone Buffalo."

"Not like the Africans who think they're French or British?"

"No."

"People come in different-colored layers—like spumoni."

"All top surfaces are phony," Caroline said.

Ah, her father told himself, that is what she learned in Africa. "How about some food?" he asked.

"You haven't seen my surprise yet," she answered. As she moved to rise from the sofa, she spread her hands out at either side and pushed herself up from the seat. Her feet were unusually wide apart. Then she pulled the loose garish dress tight around her body, holding it with both of her hands behind her back. She seemed to be concealing a basketball between her hips. "I'm pregnant," she said.

"And unmarried," he responded.

She laughed comfortably. "You really are a stick-in-the-mud," she said. "That doesn't matter anymore."

"To whom?"

"To the rest of the world. Now you're going to ask me who the father is, aren't you?"

"Yes, I am. Who is the father?"

"I hoped you would ask." She tilted her head back, pointed her chin at him aggressively, placed her hands on her hips, and said, "I don't know."

"Lose count?"

"I don't keep count. It was someone between Nairobi and Cape Town."

"Some noble savage, no doubt."

"Who thought he was British or French."

They faced each other across the low glass table. Conrad put down his drink and thrust both hands into his pants' pockets. "Why do they always have to be black?" he asked bitterly.

She replied so quickly and viciously, she must have planned it in advance, as if she'd set the trap and he fell right into it. "Because their cocks are bigger, thicker, and stay hard longer."

He wanted to slap her across the mouth, which made his hands claw his thighs inside the trouser pockets. "How disgustingly vulgar," he said.

"It's not what anyone says that matters to you, it's how they say it. Would you prefer a more technical description, with words like phallus and erectus and tumescence and girth? Would that make it all right?"

"Nothing would make it all right. You're not all right, as far as I'm concerned."

"I'm a lot more all right than you." She turned her back on him and began to wander around the room. "Perhaps your wife's cook or your maid would be so kind as to serve the simple fare on a platter here by the fire."

"I told them to take the evening off," he answered.

"So that they wouldn't hear us? How considerate of you."

She *is* an actress, he thought. She is looking out through the archway to the darkened sun porch with one hand resting on her shoulder, her pouty mouth relaxed into a tender smile; she turns slowly to emphasize her thoughtfulness, her delicacy; she is here to taunt me.

229

"Why did you come here? Do you want me to arrange an abortion?"

She laughed out loud. "Of course not! I'm going to have this baby—your first grandchild."

"And spend twenty years bringing up your symbolic contribution to the betterment of racial relations?"

"You're a throwback," she said, not looking at him, running her fingers along the broad curve of the piano's wing. "You have no sympathy with what's happening in the twentieth century."

"What is it I'm missing out on?"

"People have stopped thinking in clichés. People have stopped living by the rules of family tribes."

"Do they live by any rules?"

"You bet," she announced enthusiastically. "By the promise to themselves to keep in touch with the depth of their existence, not to spend their lives merely skimming the surface."

Conrad smiled. "You may very well keep in touch with the depth of your existence," he said. "It's your paltry surface that worries me."

"Want to make fun of me? Go right ahead. I feel your equal now. And I say frankly, your life appalls me." She looked around the room as though to smash it. "You'll do anything for money, won't you?"

"I've earned it my own way."

"You're a hypocrite, and you want to make me into a hypocrite too."

"But I failed."

"Yes," she said happily.

"What have you made yourself into, then?"

"An honest person."

"What's so good about honesty?" He was growing weary. He wanted to allow himself to hate her.

"It keeps you from being purely superficial. . . . Like you."

"Let me put it this way," he began: "I don't know any more about 'the depths of my existence' than I know about the functions of my kidneys. And I never will. Only if something goes wrong with them, will I even think about them, and then it will be up to my internist to succor them. And if they kill me, that will be their revenge. I learned a long time ago that the surface of my life, as you put it, is all that's in my control—not my kidneys; and I was going to make as much of that surface as I do of my epidermis."

"You think there are things in your control that you have no control over."

"I know I haven't any control over you. I've tried to influence you. But I haven't succeeded."

"See what I mean?"

"How tedious," Conrad concluded.

Caroline screamed, "Why won't you take me seriously?"

"Because you are a dumb cunt," her father announced. "Now, aren't you happy to learn that I can speak to you in your native language?"

She looked up to the ceiling and heaved a tremendous sigh. "Let's go to the kitchen and eat something," she said petulantly.

He had to admit to himself that this was something to marvel at—this assumption on her part that no matter what she did or what she said to him, no matter how outrageous her behavior, he would feed her. He was to be depended on no matter how she abused him. So what her upbringing had achieved was to secure for her an unshakable sense of trust in him. But without limits, without any idea that she could go too far. That was the failure; he had lost the chance, somewhere in her childhood—or rather he had lost all the chances throughout her childhood—to make her incorporate into her conception of him that he had limits too. Why can't you take *me* seriously? he thought; reckon with *my* needs and desires; feed *me?* Or was the determination to take advantage of his trust a ceaseless probing to find those limits? Even at this age, with each new threat against him, was she, by any chance, trying to find some way to respect him and accommodate to him? No, no, he thought, rubbing his hand across his forehead, as they walked silently down the long hall to the kitchen, it is too late for any such wishful hope.

The dishes and silverware and glasses had been set on oval place mats that seemed to be made out of pressed seashells, shining opalescent and milky blue in the light thrown down by cones of milk glass from the ceiling fixture. This pleasant modern kitchen where Conrad happily prepared his morning coffee.

They sat opposite each other across the cool, Formica-topped table and helped themselves to the bread, the cheeses, and cold cuts spread out on trays.

"Milk?" was the first thing Conrad said.

"Coke," was Caroline's reply. He went to the refrigerator wondering why he hadn't told her to help herself. From the time of the divorce from her mother, Conrad had always thought of her and treated her as a victim, almost as an invalid; he served her. That was how he had lost the chance to make her a responsible adult. He had misled her into believing that she was to be served. He had thought he was being kind. It had been a fatal mistake.

"You are going to have this baby . . ." he began, not knowing how much of his distress came through the tone of his voice.

"Don't be sad," she said quickly. "It will be a wonderful experience." Then she added, "Lamaze."

"I wasn't thinking of the delivery. I was thinking of all the years that go into rearing a child."

"I want it."

"And you're accustomed to getting what you want. Pity you haven't wanted better things for yourself."

"That's a perfect example of how far apart our points of view are." She made a salami sandwich with mayonnaise on one slice of bread and mustard on the other.

"I can't believe you've given much forethought to raising a child—a half-black child—without a husband and without a job." He added, "In this country, today."

232

Caroline replied calmly, "I have a job on the reservation and that's not exactly 'in this country' because the Hopi have total independence from the United States Government in their own territories."

"What's the salary?"

"I'll get room and board, and I'll earn money playing my guitar."

Conrad began to gag on the piece of Vermont cheddar he had taken a bite of. He poured some of the rosé that he'd opened into the glass before him and drank a gulp, trying to control his fears for her. He quieted the tension in his throat and finally asked, "What if Sebastian gets tired of you—and somebody else's child—and kicks you out?"

"Hopis don't do that."

"You aren't a Hopi."

"They are the kindest and most gentle of all American Indians."

"How do you know?"

"Sebastian told me."

"You've been acquainted with him for how long? Two days? Four days?"

"Five days!"

"I wish you had a little more security for . . ." he concluded vaguely, ". . . what you're getting into."

"Do you?" she asked appreciatively.

"Of course."

She said, almost in a whisper, "I could have."

"How?"

"By bringing some capital into the infirmary and agricultural station with me. Investing in it. Helping to establish it."

Conrad began to rock back and forth on the rear legs of the aluminum kitchen chair, as if, surreptitiously, he might try to get farther away from her. He could feel her attack coming on. He asked, "It isn't established yet?"

"Well, in principle, yes, it is. Sebastian has the okay to start it and a building to use—offices downstairs and living space upstairs—but he'll have to raise the funds to operate it."

"I see," Conrad nodded. "And that's what he's doing now in New York, raising the funds?"

Evasively, she answered, "In a way . . ." She put together another sandwich and drank more of the soda.

"And that's why he sent you to see me?"

"Coming here was my idea."

"For old times' sake," he smiled bitterly.

"I thought I could count on you." She actually looked coy. "Your wanting me to be secure—and all that sort of thing. . . ."

"How much did you have in mind?"

"Twenty-five thousand dollars—just to start off with."

Conrad hooted out his laughter.

Caroline didn't crack a smile. She looked at him grimly, in earnest. "That can't be so much for the millionaire's husband, can it?"

"I have nothing to do with Isabel's money. Would you like to ask her for it?"

"You give me an allowance."

"Out of my own salary."

"You must be kidding. You've been giving me ten thousand dollars a year. That's out of your own salary?"

Now he was stolidly straight-faced. "You mean to say you haven't realized that? I'm earning fifty thousand dollars a year. I give you one-fifth of that."

"And on a very short leash, too. Eight hundred and fifty dollars a month."

"My salary is paid to me by the month."

"But you can let me have more than that, can't you? You must be banking the rest. Doesn't Isabel pay her share?" she asked, running her gaze over the renovated and refurnished kitchen.

Conrad said only, "No, I can't let you have more than that."

"You mean you *won't*?"

"That's right."

"Not even twenty thousand, or fifteen thousand a year?"

"No. Ten."

"Then let me have it now. Give it to me in a lump sum right now and I won't ask you for another cent until a year from today."

So this is what Caroline had come for; but she had learned to haggle in the markets and bazaars of Africa and would not have come out straightforwardly with what she wanted. She'd ask for something absurd in order for him to feel that he'd won something, too, when she got exactly what she wanted.

"You told me you were broke."

She affirmed, "That's true."

"How were Sebastian and you planning to reach Arizona if I didn't give you any money at this time?" He was hoping to hear of some kind of support that this Hopi offered her even if she couldn't bring money from her father with her.

"We'd hitchhike," she said casually.

Conrad tried to picture his pregnant daughter and a male redskin surrounded by backpacks and a guitar on the shoulders of highways thumbing their way across three thousand miles.

"Yes. Of course." They would like to think that they would make it all on their own, make themselves all on their own—they would be self-created, free from history, pure spirits—but it would be a little simpler, a little more comfortable, to have ten thousand dollars from somebody else to start with. Instead of suggesting that they leave the dishes for the maid, Conrad asked, "Why don't we both do the washing up?"

He put it the wrong way—a request rather than a requirement—and she declined, saying, "I'm awfully tired and I'd like to go to bed as soon as possible. I'd rather you made the check out right now." He agreed, knowing he could transfer that amount from his savings account first thing Monday morning. They left the cheeses and the cold cuts to harden and become inedible on the plates and trays.

In his study, Conrad switched on the desk lamp and brought his checkbook out of the center drawer. Following him into the room, Caroline ran her finger under the words he had written on the one manila folder lying on the surface of the desk. She read aloud, " 'American Culture,' " and barked out, "There ain't no such thing."

"And you," he snapped back at her sharply, "are a cultural transvestite."

Her hands shot up, hovered uncertainly in the air, and came to rest on top of her head as if to keep her hair from flying off. "Words!" she shouted. "It's a wonder I didn't become a deaf mute in reaction to your torturing me with words, your endless 'right' word for everything."

"If you can name it, it doesn't hurt as much," he responded coolly.

Lowering her arms and placing one hand over the other on her heart, restraining herself with effort, Caroline asked, "Why should my living my own life 'hurt' you at all?"

"It wouldn't. But you're not living your own life; you're acting out a charade—and you don't even know what it represents. You're playing charades and you're going to wait for the rest of your life to find out what it 'means.' " He took a deep sigh. "If it means anything."

"But *your* life *means* something, doesn't it!" she intoned with mockery.

"My life is self-explanatory. I am what I do. And I like what I do."

"You are the servant of a dying, exploitive civilization, and the minute it can dispose of your services, it will dispose of you."

"Do you want me to write this check, or don't you?"

They stood side by side before the desk, and Caroline looked down at the checkbook, opened now, half covering the manila folder, the three checks to a page neatly printed with perforations between them, the records column to the left, as her father slipped out his pen from the spiral binding in the middle of it. "Yes, I want the money."

"Blood money, right?"

"Paid out of your guilt for being a pillar of this cruel society."

"Gee," he said in small-boy wonderment, "and I was called a 'pillar' of something else just the other day."

She held her tongue. He wrote the check. As he freed it from the checkbook and handed it to her, he said, "If only we could find some humor to share between us, to put what's happened into perspective. . . ."

"That would make it better?" she interrupted. "Like calling me 'a cultural transvestite'?"

"Well, you have to admit there is something funny in your becoming an instant Hopi, don't you?" He smiled compassionately and tried to rest his hand on her shoulder.

She turned aside and moved away from him, answering flatly, "No, I don't."

"Can that be *your own life?*"

"I won't be a hypocrite!" she replied.

Conrad dropped his gaze from her eyes to the check she held in her hand. "What you call being a hypocrite, other people think of as being socialized."

Caroline snorted.

"And you can get 'acculturated' only once. Oh, you can inflict permanent exile on yourself; you can become an émigré; you can even imagine that you fully accept and are fully accepted by another 'people.' But deep down . . ."

"In my kidney?"

He smiled. "In the 'depths of your existence' . . ."

"I'll long for the banks of my fatherland?"—waving the check at him.

"Something like that." He was ready to give up.

"Well, I don't think so." She was calm and self-confident now. "All I want is to be myself."

"That's the one thing you can't be," snapped out of him. "Society abhors a vacuum."

Caroline left on Saturday as abruptly as she had arrived; Isabel phoned to say she was having a wonderful time and would return from Washington Monday afternoon. Sunday,

Conrad was alone, in an empty house, without servants, noises, wife, child, or friend; in respite, alone and heavy with thought, pregnant with thought, he said to himself, but that reminded him of Caroline. He stared out of the window of his study to the melting snow transforming itself into pools of dark water along the border of the sloping lawn and in parallel lines up and down the quiet street. His pathetic daughter, he told himself, was quite capable of managing something with her life. She had survived all that time in Africa; she would now take on the American Indian. She would be at home with anything exotic. She had strong guts, if soft brains. Her choosing to give birth to a half-black child meant to him that she had made the most important decision of her life without knowing it. She could no longer live for her whims alone; there would be another human being's needs to care for—and she had no idea whatever of how demanding that would be; she had no idea of how the dependency of a child would pervade the self-concerns of her life. That might change her in ways neither he nor she could predict—unless she abandoned the child, and that would change her life too.

He would have liked to despise her and forget about her, but he was not granted that peace. He felt sorry for her and knew that he could do nothing to make her into a person he would respect—after the models of people he did respect. Actually he tried to respect the independence of spirit and the determination to stay loose, stay free of the Establishment, stay true to principles of kindliness and unpretension; but in her they were pretensions, and pompous ones. She was a "savior" type and all saviors are ridiculous. Saviors retail nightmares and pretend they're bedtime stories. Everything in the whole world—as in every individual life—turns on what story one tells oneself. The story Caroline lived by was that "nature" was pristine, good, and then people perverted it with words that lie in order to take advantage of other people; she would not live with lies; she would take unfair advantage of no one and thereby, just incidentally, get even with everyone who did. It was her Fairy Tale, and, like Christianity, gave her the satisfaction of relegating most of humanity to hell or purgatory while planning to inhabit heaven with the small clique of intimates who were mirror images of herself.

And what story did he tell himself? Conrad asked, looking into the mirror over the fireplace in his study. That answers to the question of what life is "all about" are unfit to live with, unworthy of mature adults; that, like the benefit of Isabel's psychoanalysis, to know that it is *not* possible to "make sense" of life is acceptable—because "finding" Christ or Buddha, or Marx or Freud, or any other savior, is to fall under a spell, to be in the thrall of a teller of a tall tale, and to lose touch with the believable world before any story distorts it into make-believe.

Thus did Conrad turn his thoughts—with a heavy heart—to the question of an essay on "Culture in America," or "American Culture," or "The Culture of America"—for one's culture is the all-encompassing story one tells oneself in consolation for the disappointing facts of the real world. He looked over the books in his library to consider the sources he might consult: the essay on "Culture" in the *Encyclopedia of the Social Sciences,* the volumes of Kluckhohn and Kroeber, Herder, Meyer Schapiro, Ortega, Voltaire, Claude Lévi-Strauss, Hannah Arendt. But he did not take them down from the shelves. He knew what they had to say. He sat on the sofa in his study, in the silence and the solitude of that long, quiet Sunday at home, beginning to make notes until the telephone rang at twilight.

Gregory Blackwell said he'd like to have a few words with him before the budget meeting tomorrow. Conrad stood at the side of the love seat in the living room listening to the voice of the president of the university—a comfortable, relaxed, reassuring voice—suspecting that he was about to be conned.

"I certainly hope you don't mind me calling you at home on a Sunday," the president said.

239

"Not at all." This was not the only time it had ever happened.

"I think this is of importance to the university in general and to you and me in particular."

"What is it?"

"The problem of choosing a new provost."

Conrad stood alert and self-controlled, uncertain of what would follow—an offer, some form of temporizing, or the fatal word.

"You are one of the leading contenders for the position," Blackwell announced.

I hadn't thought there was any contending, Conrad said to himself. To the president, he said, "I'm very pleased to hear that."

"That's why I can't ask you to become a member of the Search Committee I'm setting up to consider nominees for the job."

"A Search Committee?" Conrad asked, flatly. "That's never been called for before—for a presidential appointment. If I understand it correctly the choice is entirely up to you."

"It's true that it's never been done this way before. But times have changed. There's so much pressure for 'group participation.' Of course the final decision will be up to me." He tried to chuckle, as if both to affirm his ultimate authority and apologize for it. "But after everything that's happened in the past few years, I don't think it would be wise to appear arbitrary. It's better to let as many members of the faculty and the trustees as possible feel that they're involved in the decision making."

"Ah, yes," Conrad affirmed—appreciating the duplicity of the thought that it was only a matter of not "*appearing*" arbitrary. "How many members of the Search Committee will there be?" he asked.

"Eight," the president answered. I've been setting it up during the past few days. It's firm now. I'll give you the list tomorrow."

"Thank you."

"Conrad, I want you to understand that you're one of the most likely people to be invited to take the job . . ."

He wished that Blackwell had said "obvious" or "desirable" rather than "likely."

". . . and that's the only reason I can't ask you to serve on the Search Committee."

"I understand that; I appreciate that." Conrad found that he could no more add "sir" or "Mr. President," than he could feel comfortable calling him "Gregory." He was clearly aware that this was a formal and official call and that a moratorium had been declared against all claims on friendly personal relations.

"Fine. I don't want this to make any difficulty between us," the president said. "I'll have to count on you even more than before—with Clif gone. But this procedure—this Search Committee routine—is necessary now. You'll bear with it, won't you?"

"Of course."

"Good man—I knew I could count on you!" There was an awkward pause in which neither could think of anything to say, and then Blackwell ended by adding, "Give my best regards to Isabel, will you?"

"Certainly."

"See you at the budget meeting tomorrow."

"Good night."

"Yes; good evening."

Conrad hung up the phone in the discomfort of ambiguous responses. He did not know Gregory Blackwell well enough to read this message accurately. He had always thought of Blackwell as a figurehead; Blackwell took his cues from the more experienced and more knowledgeable provost. Conrad had never expected that the president would outlast Rostum, that he would have to act on his own. He could not easily imagine Blackwell acting "on his own." Obviously, he had not called on Conrad for advice. And his favored colleagues, his peers, were not the faculty or other members of the administration—they were the trustees. In the old days—how suddenly they had become the old days—Blackwell was a man who had been led by the hand of Clifford Rostum. He was an elder statesman who had to be shown what seat to take, which hands to shake, what speech to make. Rostum used to send half a dozen dossiers into his office for the president to read every morning. How could Blackwell manage without that spoon-feeding? Or was it worth wondering: What did the dossier contain labeled, "If I should die unexpectedly . . ." or even, "How to replace me as provost." Rostum was not unequal to that degree of forethought.

Conrad felt distantly separated from Gregory Blackwell; he had never been intimate with him. Rostum was more significant to him and Rostum could have been expected to be there to oversee the transferring of his authority to Conrad in four years, just before Blackwell would be about to retire. It had not been a question in Conrad's mind of where he stood in Blackwell's esteem, because he felt secure in Rostum's esteem. But what if he had been wrong and the whole idea of a Search Committee had been Rostum's suggestion in order to make it easier for Blackwell to bypass Conrad? There was no way for him to know, any more than he could know whose advice Blackwell was asking for and taking these days. Of course, on the surface, it was highly probable that he was in line for the provost's position and that he should not be a member of a Search Committee; but, then, why have a Search Committee if the Obvious Man is present and ready to assume authority? What a lot of eyewash. Still, the sixties had conditioned administrators to a lot of eyewash. It was a wonder Blackwell hadn't said there would be students on the Search Committee.

Then Conrad turned on the lamps in the living room and went back to his study. He tightened the belt on the blue woolen bathrobe he had been wearing all day. He ran his hands through his hair and took a deep breath. Then he

poured himself a long Scotch and water, turned his back to all
the books on his shelves, and sat down at his desk—where the
manila folder lay on which he had written "American Culture." The thought of Caroline having said, "There ain't no
such thing," filled him with distaste.

He drew a long yellow pad out of one of the drawers, took a
ball-point pen from the pocket of his bathrobe, and began to
make an outline based on his thinking throughout the day and
on a lifetime of engagement and reflection.

It began: "The word culture originally meant worship: it
referred to the object of belief in a cult. What one person alone
believes—cannot prove, but intuits to be true—may be considered merely his fantasy; but what a group of people share
in common, come to believe of ultimate significance, so that
they shape their lives about it, is their culture, and, in turn, is
what cultivates them. The life-giving myth in the histories of
all civilizations is the basis of their spiritual experience. . . ."

All through dinner Monday evening, Isabel babbled on
with equal enthusiasm about the electronic experts' testimony
that five separate erasures caused eighteen and a half minutes
of gaps in the critical White House tapes, about the reception
at the British embassy, about Israel and Egypt agreeing to
remove their forces from the Suez Canal zone, about the ballet
at the Kennedy Center.

Conrad said, "You sound like the front page of the *Washington Post.*"

With that remark, she did calm down. "It gets to you," she
admitted.

"Exciting."

"I found it thrilling. Everywhere I went—people talking
about important things."

"In contrast to life at the university . . ."

"No offense meant, darling," she answered sweetly. "Yes,
in contrast to talk here . . ."

"I hope a little of it will go a long way."

"But wouldn't you like to be in on it too?"

"I don't think so. It's life in a pressure cooker."

"That's why it's exciting. So serious. Everyone concerned with matters of life or death."

"No. Only with war or peace. What's done here is concerned with what to live for."

Isabel leaned back in her chair and leveled her gaze steadily at her husband's eyes. "And how are the politics of power being played here these days?" she asked.

"In secret," he answered. "Pretending to make it more public; in a frame of participatory democracy—it becomes more hidden. It's just the blame that appears to get spread more equitably."

"What do you mean?"

"Instead of choosing the next provost himself, the president has determined that a Search Committee of trustees and faculty members be appointed *to advise* him."

"Oh. Do you know who's on it?"

"I just found out this morning. Baird-Lloyd of the Clayton Bank and Grant Hannover are the trustees."

"Do you know them?"

"I've met the old banker. He looks like Lazarus shortly *before* he was returned to life. But I've never met Hannover. I don't remember his ever attending a trustee meeting. He graduated from the college and then went to the Harvard Business School. Inherited a chain of newspapers in the Midwest, including the *Chicago Times-Herald*. Runs it."

"Who are the faculty members?"

Conrad sighed. "Evats, from History; Marvin Flower, in English; David Bach, for the Physical Sciences; Brita von Bickersdorf of the Law School; Jerry Rosenblatt for Psychiatry and the Medical School; and Walter Webster in Art."

"Walter Webster?! I thought you told me a week ago you were trying to find someone to take over his courses because he wanted to go back to France for a while . . . ?"

Conrad pushed aside his dessert dish and lit a cigarette.

"That's true. But he told me on the phone today that, having been asked to serve on this committee, he couldn't pull out now."

Isabel said, "Strange."

"Remarkable! What an act of loyalty. Understand that most of the faculty are far more devoted to their disciplines—like medieval monks—than they are to the parent institution that happens to house them at the moment. That's what makes a gesture like this on Webster's part all the more striking. Imagine giving up a private passion—a selfish desire—out of a sense of duty to the needs of the university. I'm impressed. Frankly, if the provost's position is offered to me, I think it will be largely because Walter made that sacrifice out of loyalty and stayed to serve on the committee."

"And if it isn't offered to you?" Isabel asked.

"I'll kick him in the ass."

They both laughed. Then Isabel said, "What will you do if someone else is made provost?"

He snapped out, "How about a job in Washington?"

Isabel clapped her hands together. "I'd love it!" she exclaimed.

Conrad felt his heart sink. Isabel had named the fear: What if someone else becomes provost? The conditions that made his life rewarding were bound to change one way or another: either he would become provost or someone else would—in which case, either he would have reached the end of his "progress" at this univerity or he would have to accommodate to a different, a not-yet-foreseeable future.

Throughout the month of February, the public life of the nation continued to weigh more and more heavily upon Conrad with its accumulation of news of incipient disaster in much the same way as the lack of news became oppressive regarding his professional life. Nothing whatever was said to him regarding the Search Committee. On the other hand, almost no one spoke of anything but developments in Washing-

ton. Nixon had been subpoenaed by the state court in California to testify at the trial of John Erlichman; no more Watergate
hearings were to be held to avoid interference with the
House's impeachment hearings; the former attorney general
of the United States went on trial in New York; the President's
personal lawyer pleaded guilty on two charges of illegal election campaign activities; the granddaughter of William Ran-
dolph Hearst was kidnapped from her apartment in Berkeley;
the British Conservative government fell in an election pre-
cipitated by a coal miners' strike; and the Soviet Union de-
ported Alexander Solzhenitsyn. It was ultimate *arbitrariness*
that Conrad saw everywhere: derived from the capriciousness
of some individual will—the President's, the commissar's, the
kidnappers'; it didn't matter in the least whether they pretended to be acting in the interest of national security, or the
well-being of the Supreme Soviet, or the Symbionese Liberation Army, not at all. It was forever and always some *one*
person's choice. That was the source of the private purposes,
either direct and obvious or devious with ulterior motives—
like Gregory Blackwell's motive in establishing a Search
Committee. The arbitrariness that bends and reshapes established rules and regulations, takes liberties with habits and
customs that are supported by a consensus. Still—it may *not*
be clearly *one* man's choice. There is a rhythmic pulsation of
responsibility between a group and the individual leader of a
group, such that individual and group forces wrestle with each
other and one cannot always be certain of the center and the
root of the arbitrariness. The reason why the complex Watergate scandal had riveted the fascination of the American people was that Mr. Nixon's character alone revealed itself as the
independently unique source of the despotic arbitrariness.
And now the most extreme example of all was Nixon's *world-
wide alert:* all troops of the United States Army, Navy, and Air
Force placed on combat-ready status—to threaten the Soviet
Union—which turned out to be incontrovertibly nothing but
the personal whim of a challenged President to divert attention from the investigation into his own corruption. An at-

tempt to draw sympathy and support, for which he personally commanded that a quarter of a million people, stationed in some twenty-five thousand positions around the globe, behave for three days as if they might be called to fight a war at an instant's notice.

"That is, without a doubt," Conrad said to Marvin Flower over lunch at the Faculty Club, "the most flagrant example of self-serving abuse of political power since Robespierre decided to kill off everyone else in the government because none of them was as pure and true to the Revolution as he was."

"Robespierre actually killed them," Flower said quietly. "Nixon just ordered an alert and then called it off."

"It was only one step short of pressing the button that drops all the bombs and starts the next war."

"Oh, woe," moaned Marvin Flower.

"And now we reach the lowest point of all," Conrad said in a tense half-whisper, squeezing the napkin in his tight fist. "For the first time in our history . . ."

"Our brief history," Flower interpolated. "We're only two hundred years old."

"For the first time, the President of the United States and his closest aides and advisers are charged by a grand jury with criminal actions."

"The President wasn't indicted."

"An unindicted coconspirator! Isn't that a magnificent phrase? Doesn't that enrich the subtlety of the hairsplitting mind? An unindicted coconspirator is like an anonymous rapist. The country's been screwed, the villain is caught, the police are now checking on his identity." Conrad suddenly laughed. "The newspapers will not be allowed to reveal his name until his next of kin have been notified."

"Do you know that there are people who believe the Duke of Clarence was Jack the Ripper?"

Conrad smoothed the napkin on his lap. "You'd rather not talk about it."

"No, no. I wallow in it. I bemoan it, I beweail it. It pours acid into my wounds. I think about it night and day. But there are other things on my mind as well. I have classes to teach. I have a deadline on a manuscript I've promised a publisher. I'm on the Search Committee . . ."

"Ah, yes. The Search Committee." Conrad thought of a diviner with a forked branch, tramping through a parched land, trying to locate a source of water. "How goes the *Search* Committee?"

Marvin Flower raked his stubby fingers through his thick dark hair. "Oh, woe! You have no idea of what Blackwell has done."

"No?"

"Are you aware of the announcement in *The New York Times?* The ad that lists the qualifications, asks for applications, states that the university is an equal opportunity employer, unbiased, open to either men or women, all that sort of thing?"

"Yes. I read it. I thought of applying."

Flower brushed aside that remark with—"You don't have to apply. You're on the short list. Then there's a long list. And you know how many applications there have been since the ad appeared? Take a guess."

"Two hundred."

"Three hundred and fifty, three hundred and eighty. Something like that." He brought out a handkerchief and wiped his brow.

Conrad smiled. "Will you interview them all?"

"Of course not! We meet. We talk principles, we talk ideals, we study vitas. The lists grow and the lists shrink."

"You will learn about people you're not already familiar with."

"Most of us are familiar with you." Marvin Flower leaned forward over the small table. "You're the one. You should be the provost." He looked around to see if he could be overheard. "This is such a waste of time. I have deadlines. I have classes."

"Am I to be interviewed?"

Flower sat back, silent. "Interviewed?" he asked himself out loud. "What for? Your past ten years here have been an open interview. Everybody knows where you stand. This Search Committee—you know—this isn't a Star Chamber; it's just an advisory group. We'll go through the motions."

"Not everyone on the committee is a friend of mine."

Flower replied, "I haven't heard a negative voice yet. I shouldn't be telling you this."

"Of course not. But just for the hell of it—what has Evats said?"

"Nothing. He hasn't opened his mouth. I don't think he can talk."

"David Bach?"

That gave Flower pause. "Actually," he said slowly, "Bach gave you a double-edged compliment. He said, 'Taylor has an excess of integrity.' Not that he explained what he meant, but it drew a laugh."

Conrad forced himself to chuckle, alone in knowing damned well what it meant. The waitress brought them chef salads after they had emptied their consommé cups.

"Tell me," Flower whispered conspiratorially, "if you're made provost, can you do something about improving the food in this club?"

"It will be the first order of business."

Brom Kirkill strolled past them, oblivious, wandering among the tables, trying to find his way out. Marvin Flower stared after the tall, thin figure, shaking his head. "Oh, woe, the suffering people bring on themselves . . ."

Conrad turned to see that he was following Kirkill with his heavy, sad eyes. "What do you mean?"

"Haven't your heard?"

"About what?"

"Vivian Kirkill. His wife. She's left him."

"Left him?!"

"Walked out. Ran out."

"Vivian?" Conrad felt dumbfounded.

"Took off with one of his graduate students. A fellow maybe fifteen years younger than she."

"I really can't believe it."

"Why not? Even hippopotamuses mate."

"But she's been mated for years. She has a son in his twenties."

" '. . . She sings each song twice over to prove she can recapture that first sweet careless rapture.' " Flower admitted: "Browning."

" '. . . to fly to troubles that we know not of,' " Conrad said. "Shakespeare."

"You actually are shocked."

"I'm appalled," Conrad said, and then added, "Wittgenstein."

"But why? A woman in her late forties . . ."

"Always so possessive of her husband. And I thought she was worried about *his* playing around. I thought them mismatched and always at each other's throat but—somehow—necessary for each other."

"There are no necessities anymore, my dear Conrad. Ours is the world's only culture dedicated to the purpose of *achieving* individual private fantasies of personal pleasure. Can you foresee the end result?"

"What?"

"Can't you guess? Ours will be the first and only society to legalize incest. The ultimate pleasure fantasy. Mothers will be able to marry their sons; fathers, their daughters; brothers and sisters will cohabit as happily as Egyptian pharaohs. In the meanwhile, the Vivian Kirkills run off with boys almost young enough to be their sons."

Conrad muttered, "Grotesque."

"Not at all. We like to take things to their logical conclusions."

"We? You mean Americans? I've been thinking a lot about American culture recently . . ."

"I knew a man once who actually did marry his mother," Marvin Flower said. "She wasn't his biological mother, but she raised him. His parents died when he was an infant and his mother's brother took the child. All during the years of growing up he told his stepmother she was the only woman he loved and the only woman he would ever love. He became a lawyer. He courted her. He persuaded her to divorce his uncle and marry him. And she did, by God!"

"Not 'by God,' " Conrad corrected.

"He is one of the few genuinely happy people I've ever known," Flower concluded. "And of course"—with a flourish of his hand—"more than a little crazy. Nobody sane is happy."

"It's reassuring that, in polite conversation, present company is always excepted."

There ensued a cool, quiet period, during which both of them attacked their salads. Conrad imagined Flower to be thinking about his friend who married his "mother," while Conrad was stuck with thoughts of Vivian Kirkill impeding him from fondling thoughts about the Search Committee. We are more or less hallucinating at all times, Conrad said to himself, carrying on conversations with some figment of our imaginations representing someone else. The more accurate we are to the other person under consideration, the more nearly crazy we are at the moment. He was, in that instant, imagining Vivian Kirkill seated in the wing chair in his office, facing him across his desk-table, pressing her right hand against her heart, while he, accusingly, demanded, "How could you?"

"Why shouldn't I?" she countered aggressively.

"Because there has to be some stability and continuity in life. Otherwise: chaos. There have to be people and relationships that can be counted on, depended on."

"Well, depend on others. I'm tired of being depended on. I've lived for years with this wild pack of yours—your scholars, academics, smart guys—indulging yourselves. I've been the one who sacrificed. I haven't had my own. It's not too late.

I'll get some of your selfish, your precious, 'private' satisfactions yet."

"What have you done for the world that justifies . . ."

"Don't bullshit me!" she shouted at him. "I've raised a child—while babying that perennial infant you think of as a big shot professor. . . ."

I never thought of Brom Kirkill as a Big Shot Professor, Conrad whispered to himself. But then surely she had to, she did. "Still," he asked, "what does justify throwing up everything and running away with a youth?"

"Passion, you fool! The real thing. I made a life with Brom— from the time I was eighteen and eloped with him. But what kind of life was that? Drudgery and an occasional facultywide reception. Sabbaticals for research in Iran. Do you have any idea of how nasty a sabbatical in Iran can be? When you don't speak Persian? Other people actually told me I must have a glamorous life. Can you imagine? Glamorous? I used to live for months at a time on that word. Until I woke up one day and looked a few facts in the face. I didn't like Brom Kirkill. There was nothing to like. He's a jerk. I didn't like my son Christian. He's a fink. So what was the shouting all about? Where was the glamorous life?"

"It doesn't have to be glamorous," Conrad said consolingly; "it just has to be worth living."

"Ha! A lot you know. You with your goddamned Boy Scout principles."

Marvin Flower pierced Conrad's reverie by saying, "You look very distracted."

"I was thinking about Vivian Kirkill."

Flower clicked his tongue and chided him, "You told me you were thinking about American culture."

"Ah," Conrad regained his composure, "that's somewhat less complicated. Yes, I have been brooding about it. Tell me what you think of this line of thought: in the beginning of the high civilization we're descended from, Western man took his spiritual life seriously and through its exercise, through its efflorescence, found his entertainment as well. But five hundred years later, *now*, with the death of religion, he takes only his entertainments seriously, as if they constitute all of his spiritual life."

"Entertainments?" Flower echoed, as imperious and ingenuous as a milord.

"Fun and games. Television. Music. Movies. Dance. Novels. Painting. Parties."

"Parties!?"

"They're all that's left of a 'communion,' the secular synod, the substitute ten wise men."

"That's a sacrilegious thought," Flower said pompously, but smiling.

"Right on!" Conrad exclaimed, not to be put down. "I don't mean anything so nineteenth century as the 'Religion of Art'; that's lost its sex appeal too. I mean Entertainment. *Low* culture is all that's left of culture. I mean, by turning the whole of culture upside down, the leaders of society would no more be caught having missed the opening of the latest smash hit today than they would have been caught missing Mass three hundred years ago."

"Well, it's so much easier to take," Flower opined. "Since each smash hit is different, whereas the Mass was always the same."

You do not hear me and you do not care about what I am saying, Conrad thought. You would rather be witty than sincere, of course; it's our curse. You are sincere only in your books. "I apologize for laying this on you—as the heathens say. But then," after a deep breath, Conrad continued, "you're partly the cause of it."

"I?" Flower was all innocence.

"Well, you humanists who have made entertainments into serious business. You know—once it was discovered that poems and plays and novels could be read for their *meanings*, because they 'teach' something about manners, or ethics, or politics—nobody can enjoy just a good read anymore, they're supposed to look for what the pleasure teaches."

"Ah, yes. The heuristic value. The pedagogic increment."

Conrad made a sour face. "Exactly. It's so much easier to read a novel for its philosophy than to actually study metaphysics."

Marvin Flower heard none of the sarcasm. He was nodding his head in agreement.

"Wasn't it you," Conrad continued, "who once told me that your students couldn't read Dickens or Trollope anymore because they didn't know what money is? They're so conditioned to look for symbolic meanings that they can't see literal meanings. Money to them was love or sexual prowess or political power."

"That's right. They couldn't believe that money was money." He snickered. "They find out later on."

"Well, that's my point. What has happened in our culture is that we're expected to take a novelist as seriously as we once took a religious leader or a philosopher. That's supposed to justify our escape from religion and our indifference to philosophy."

"But that *is* the New Wave."

Conrad slumped back in his chair and sighed. "The result is," he concluded sadly, "that as entertainments have become the substitute for spiritual life, an increasingly thick coating of veneer comes to conceal from us the 'depths of our existence.' " Conrad shivered at the recollection of Caroline's use of that phrase, of her wanting her raw nerves to be exposed at all times, her wanting to reinvent the wheel.

"What's wrong with veneers?" Flower asked. "The benefit of American culture is to sugarcoat every pill. It's not just *what* we tell ourselves is true that counts—that much might be international *and* timeless; it's *how* we tell the story that makes up our particular culture."

" 'Neither death nor the sun can be looked at directly.' La Rochefoucauld."

" 'Every profound spirit needs a mask.' Nietzsche."

" 'What is a chair?' Wittgenstein."

"Listen, Conrad, if you go on like this I'll be out of a job.

I'm here to connect your 'entertainments' with the 'depths of our existence.' Do you want to eliminate the whole division of the humanities? What else are we here for? To make connections, to interpret, to explain."

"So our culture is always at secondhand, once removed."

"It always was. Are you imagining a seamless whole in which even the lowliest peasant knew the same secrets as the high priests? There never was such a culture."

"I suppose you're right."

"Let us be serious. If I'm not right—you shouldn't be provost or I shouldn't be teaching. But then, what would I do? Get up on a soapbox and preach? I like my life. You—well, I wouldn't worry about you. You can always go back to clinical psychology, hang out your shingle, and treat patients, have a private practice. But have you ever heard of a literary critic with a private practice?"

Both of them laughed. But Conrad tasted the bitterness of the thought: "You shouldn't be provost." He could no more imagine himself going back to clinical psychology than he could return to his thirteenth year, sunning himself on the raft in Lake Charlevoix. At length, he said, "Everything depends on what *seriousness* means."

Marvin Flower whispered, "That's what all of us here are trying to find out."

It was a cloudy day. The sky was heavy with a milky-gray air as Conrad walked slowly back toward his office, alone. He felt he reflected the blanketed heavens in the heaviness of his spirit, shrouded, oppressed, overlaid. Why did he take the news of Vivian Kirkill's running off so seriously? Why did it affect him so?

Conrad was reminded of his own divorce. Is this why I'm bothered by the news about the Kirkills? It did not matter that his wife had run away more than a decade before. The sense of outrage came back up within him undiluted by time. On the one hand, there was the blow to his vanity: that *he* could have made such a mistake as to marry a woman so wrong for himself—that was the loss of self-respect and named his weakness. On the other hand, the sop to his pride was self-congratulations for the measure of strength it took to acknowledge that mistake, to break off the marriage; to declare "No more," it is finished. How tiresome, he thought; what I really long for is a world in which no one makes a mistake.

At the corner of High Street and Broadway, he ran into Rodney Booth, a British anthropologist prominent as an ethnographer of Southwest American Indians. They took off their gloves and shook hands. "Good to see you back here," Conrad said.

"I must say I love the rhythm of it," Booth began: "you know—six months or a year in the field, six months or a year at the university."

His sandy hair was receding and his long, leathery face— deeply lined like a Texan farmer's—was suntanned and cheerful. "It seems to do you a world of good," Conrad said.

"Anthropology is healthy." He smiled.

Suddenly, Conrad asked, "Is it true that the Hopi are the most peaceful and gentle of the American Indians?"

Rodney Booth laughed. "Only on the street corner of an American university campus might one expect to be asked such a question out of the blue."

"Well, I don't mean it as a challenge at a dissertation defense. Just curiosity. Not idle. A personal curiosity." He paused and then added, "I've been asked to make a contribution to a Hopi settlement . . ."

"I suppose on a scale of one to ten, the Hopi would rate about eight or nine for peacefulness and gentleness, about as high as any, with the Zuñi a close second."

"Is their culture a seamless whole in which the peasants know the same secrets as the high priests?"

Booth looked at him, wondering if his leg was being pulled. "Come now," he said, "that never happens. The gods speak only to the priests and the priests speak only to the initiated. But they do try to gather all of their people together through the rituals that define their culture."

"Exclusively?" Conrad asked. "Or are they agreeable to adopting an outsider, a foreigner who wants to assimilate herself—or himself—into the tribe?"

"They are peaceful," Booth explained calmly, "but they are very suspicious of outsiders."

"Could one who is determined to be adopted eventually overcome that suspicion? Become truly, genuinely one of them?"

Booth began to chuckle. "My dear Conrad, that would be about as likely as a Nubian slave marrying Queen Elizabeth the First."

"That likely . . ." Conrad echoed slowly.

In what Conrad took to be a tone of consolation, Booth added, "Perhaps because their laws are so rigid they have the stability that enables them to be peaceful and gentle."

"Rigid?"

"Well, I mean—so respected that no one would imagine breaking them."

"Unlike Mr. Nixon—I suppose you're thinking."

"It's hard to think about anything else these days, isn't it?"

"Yes." And then Conrad added, "What a bore." They saluted each other and then parted. But Conrad reprimanded himself for having said that; he didn't feel that it was a bore at all. It was a great national awakening to the facts of arbitrariness, of how, ultimately, every man in power—or every man in the exercise of whatever power he has—will break the rules, abuse the law, disregard the consensus, if he thinks he can get away with it, if he believes that his own wishes ought to be paramount, that self-serving is more important than serving. In any event, the interface between those two motives is so fine that the opportunity for self-delusion is constant.

Through the course of the afternoon, Conrad met in his conference room with the Curriculum Planning Committee, went over the budget revision figures with Cameron McNeill, looked over the computer printout of the list of students admitted to the entering class for next fall, and then played squash with Tom Spofford. At five he found himself gravitating toward the Faculty Club again on his way home. It was as if fated that he should run into Walter Webster at the bar.

"May I join you?"

Webster said, "Of course." He looked at his wristwatch. "I'm meeting Brita, but I'm a little early. How are you?" He was diffident. They had not seen each other since Webster announced his change of plans.

Conrad knew he must not skirt the issue. "I am aware of what it must cost you to be here now rather than in France. I'm sorry."

Webster tried to brush it aside with a gesture of his right hand, while he gazed at the floor. He was drinking vermouth. Conrad ordered a Manhattan. "I assume that the burdens of the Search Committee are onerous," Conrad volunteered, "if you have to meet Brita after hours."

"No, no. Not at all. But we're a subcommittee of two delegated to go through the correspondence. You wouldn't believe how many applications have come in."

"Oh, I believe, I believe," Conrad smiled.

"It's necessary," Webster said, "but—you know—all of this should have been avoided."

"In another life, in another day—before the 1960s . . ."

"It's a shame." He patted Conrad on the arm. "Not that I'm complaining, you understand. It's necessary now. But—for a foregone conclusion . . ." He winked and smiled.

Conrad evaded the conspiratorial implications by asking, "What do you think of the two trustees on the committee?"

Webster drew a deep breath. He was called upon to make judgments. Conrad reminded himself that this large, burly gentleman, ignoring the length of ash that dropped from his cigarette onto the vest of his black pinstripe suit, was a great art historian and critic, a man of discriminating sensitivity. His judgment mattered. Walter Webster pursed his lips and said: "Baird-Lloyd is like a fox, a wily diplomat, given to operating behind the scenes, a man whose lifetime of experience makes him express himself laconically, always in terms that can be given more than one interpretation when he's reminded of them."

"He *looks* fragile—weak or ill."

"Very deceptive," Walter said quickly. "He has an iron will. So far he talks only about the welfare of the university. But I suspect that he has a favorite candidate in mind, and I know that he has Blackwell's ear. We're not down to the wire yet. It will be fascinating to watch him operate when the time comes." Webster burst into a series of coughs and snuffed out his cigarette.

"What about Grant Hannover?" Conrad asked.

"Very attractive." Webster coughed again. "Dynamic. Full of questions. Taking it all very seriously. He wants to meet you. Flies in from Chicago for meetings." Then Webster paused to decide whether or not to make the next remark and, finally, said with some degree of awe, "Flies his own plane!"

Conrad raised his eyebrows.

"He's very good-looking—with long, deep dimples that wreathe a large, open smile, and the most extraordinary eyes. The color of polished cat's-eye, you know? a greenish brown at the center and golden around the outer circle."

Conrad said only, "Ah . . ."

"Are you aware of the fact that he ran against Mayor Daley in the election three years ago?"

"He's only about thirty-five, isn't he?"

"Of course, no Republican can defeat Mayor Daley, but it's going through the exercise that counts."

"He's out for political power?"

"I suppose so. He's got everything else. The *Chicago Times-Herald* gives him a national base to work from. And he's married to a Du Pont."

Conrad said only, "Oh . . ."

259

"But here's Brita," Webster announced, observing her removing her coat in the entrance foyer.

"I must be going," Conrad said, leaving his glass on the bar. "Take care." He went up to Brita von Bickersdorf at the counter of the cloakroom.

"My dear . . ." she said, leaning her left cheek toward him.

He kissed her and nodded toward the bar—"Walter is waiting for you."

"This is all so unnecessary," she complained.

Though it was still cloudy, the crisp, cool breeze on that early March evening was bracing as Conrad walked smartly toward the house on Hillhouse Avenue. I am behaving, he told himself, like aging French *littérateurs* who wanted to be elected to the Académie. They used to walk up all those stairs of all those apartment houses to call, in turn, on each of the members of the Académie, to present themselves. I must stop this. I must not ask anyone else anything about the Search Committee. I am making a fool of myself. If it is destined that I am to be offered the position of provost, it will come to me; if it is not, there is nothing I can do about it. Everything important in my life has come about in that way. I have not gone out and demanded it. It has come after me. As Isabel came to me, he told himself, thinking only of how they had met in Aspen, downplaying the fact that he had pursued her to Switzerland and that he would have changed his name to Schneider if that would have won her.

"How was your day?" he asked her over the dining room table.

Isabel answered, "Pleasant. I was able to take Champion out for a run in the fields. There's still snow on the hills, but the paths are all clear. Then I went to the florist's and I went to the hairdresser's."

"I see." Conrad looked at her shining golden tresses. He lifted his wineglass to toast her.

"Thank you," she said modestly, smiling her satisfaction. "I discovered the most wonderful plant at the florist. It's called gloxinia. It was created for *this* dining room. It has a horn-shaped flower that's royal blue in the center and white all around the frilled edge—but precisely the blue and white of this room. I've ordered a dozen of them and four wrought-iron stands. We can have groups of three in each corner of the room."

"Lovely," Conrad said idly.

"Incidentally, the florist talked about nothing but the President being indicted."

"He wasn't. He's an unindicted coconspirator."

"He's a conspirator. I wonder how Ruby and the senator are taking it."

"Phone her and ask."

"When are you going to Washington again?"

"I'm not sure. The paper I promised to write for Stonefort is due at the end of March. Which reminds me—I haven't got very far on it. I'll probably take it down and discuss it with him—about three weeks from now. Want to come?"

"Sure." After lamb chops, Rosalie brought in the Waldorf salad. "Darling," Isabel said when they were alone again, "the hairdresser was full of gossip. I wonder if it's true."

"What did he say?"

"That Vivian Kirkill has run away with a Mr. St. Cyr who teaches German history."

"Oh, my God!"

"Is it true?"

"I don't think so. I heard that she took off with a graduate student."

"That old bag!" Isabel actually threw back her head and laughed out loud. "She's such a bitch. Some poor boy must be desperate for a mother substitute to take up with her."

" 'Even hippopotamuses mate,' " Conrad quoted.

"What a lark, what a bedroom comedy. Vivian Kirkill playing Anna Karenina!" She laughed again.

Conrad stared at her, feeling vaguely how unfair it was that he could go through a day meeting with Marvin Flower, running into Rodney Booth, having a drink with Walter Webster—men of stature, rich and subtle minds; people Vivian Kirkill would call "Big Shots"—while his wife, a sophisticated woman, sees no one but the stable keeper, the florist, and the hairdresser. Still—it was not a question of fairness; she chose her life as he chose his. Well, to the extent that one has choice. And then there's Isabel's inverse snobbism; she *says* she prefers hairdressers to "Big Shots."

"How is Brom taking it?" Isabel asked.

"What?"

"Vivian's running out on him."

"I don't know. I saw him for an instant at the club this noon. He's still alive."

"You'll never leave *me*, will you?"

"Never."

"I didn't think so." Isabel added, "We have a safe life."

It could not have occurred to either of them at the moment that two weeks later Conrad would barely escape being killed.

The danger occurred in Conrad's office in the middle of March. It was the day the President of the United States was served with a subpoena demanding him, despite his refusal, to turn over to the Watergate special prosecutor more White House tapes and documents. Conrad and Tom Spofford were in his study when Mrs. Todd called on the intercom to say that a young man—who didn't have an appointment—would like to see Mr. Taylor.

"A student?" he asked.

"No."

"Who is he? Do you know what he wants?"

Mrs. Todd said, "His name is Vincent Hugo. He'd like to see you on a personal matter."

Conrad looked at the clock: a quarter to four. He felt an uncertain recognition of the name. "All right," he said, "in the conference room." As Tom and he were leaving the inner office, Mrs. Todd closed the opposite door behind her, leaving Vincent Hugo waiting for them in the wood-paneled room with the ten captain's chairs around the smooth conference table. The young man was tall and blond, so young that his full cheeks still had a baby fat quality to them, but he looked grim.

Conrad offered his hand. The young man still wore his camel's hair topcoat and a long purple scarf; he shook hands firmly. "This is my assistant, Tom Spofford."

"Hi," Tom said, without approaching the youth.

"You're not a student here?" Conrad asked.

"No," was the strong answer. "I want to be."

"Where are you now?"

"The Taft School."

"Very good," Conrad said sincerely. "That's very good." All three stood awkwardly near the center of the room, Tom resting one hand on the conference table. "What can I do for you?"

"I guess you've done it already," the young man replied.

"How's that?"

"You turned me down."

"I?"

"You're in charge of the college, aren't you?"

"I'm not in charge of the admissions office, if that's what you mean."

"Yes, that's what I mean. I just got the bad word from your admissions office. I'm not admitted."

"I'm sorry."

"A hell of a lot of good that'll do. You're sorry," he said mockingly. "I applied to Harvard, Yale, and Brown, and I haven't been admitted to any of them. And I'd like to know *why*. My grades are all in the fifth percentile at the Taft School. I'm a crack athlete, I'm on the debating team. I'm manager of the Dramatic Society. Why not?" His voice broke. "Why aren't I admitted?" Tears came to his small eyes. "What's going on?"

"Oh, a *lot* goes on," Conrad said. "There's a whole world of things going on. All kinds of needs are taken into consideration . . ."

"What have they got to do with me?"

"You're in the world. You're not being judged in some kind of 'controlled experiment' all by yourself. It's a world conditioned by circumstances. Many other conditions have to be considered."

"Why should I be the victim of circumstances? I want to be judged on my own and given my own chance."

"There's no such thing," Conrad said. "Much as you dislike it, being judged on your own is only part of the situation; there are other purposes that have to be served as well."

"Fuck them!" the boy shouted. "I want my chance! I've earned it. I'm good. I want to be admitted here. What the hell are all those circumstances keeping me out?"

Conrad was irritated but controlled himself, spoke slowly, crossed his arms over his chest. "Well, there's the problem of geographical distribution, of percentages of primary interests or likely majors, of extracurricular involvements, of financial responsibilities, of minority quotas . . ."

"Oh, bullshit!" the boy wailed. "Can't you just take me on my own? Does my life depend on being shoved up and down somebody's 'bell-shaped curve'? I'm not a goddamned circumstance. I'm *Me*. And I want *in!* Am I gonna be kept out so that you can say you've admitted two blacks from Georgia and four Jews from Chicago and seven girls from Texas? Is that what it comes down to?" He was panting, clutching his hands, one on top of the other, as if he might claw the skin off the bones.

"Yes, that's what it comes down to," Conrad admitted. "There are individual people in the midst of it all, but the many pressures around them are mostly impersonal." Conrad suffered an instant's recollection of the dream he had once had of seeing himself in the middle of a jigsaw puzzle, but while he could make out all the surrounding conditions—all the circumstances—he could not see himself. "There are just so many openings," he continued, "and a number of different standards are taken into account to make selections for admission."

"My intrinsic value isn't enough?" the young man asked.

That is a phrase he must have learned at the Taft School without ever wondering how to determine what it means. Conrad thought: Only God can know one's "intrinsic value." What he said was: "There's always the possibility of a second chance. You might start college elsewhere and, in a year or two, apply for a transfer."

"I thought," the boy began calmly, "you might consider a second chance right now." Then, with his right hand, he drew out of his camel's hair coat a small black revolver that he aimed directly at Conrad.

Tom Spofford said, "Where'd you get . . ."

"It's mine. It's legal. I come from a long line of people who know how to go out after what they want. And get it."

"Did anyone in that long line suggest you could shoot your way into college?" Conrad asked. It crossed his mind like lightning that never before had anyone pointed a gun at him.

Tears came again into the small eyes of the tall, blond boy with baby fat in his cheeks. "I really wish you'd reconsider . . ."

So that I won't have to make the mistake of firing this revolver, Conrad hoped he meant. "Well, if we're going to talk about this some more," Conrad said, starting to move toward Vincent Hugo, "let me take . . ." With both hands he reached for the gun. The boy jerked his hand upward, Conrad grasped his wrist, the bullet lodged in the plaster ceiling of the conference room. Conrad felt stunned by the sound of the shot and the relieving knowledge that no one had been hit. Tom stepped forward to grasp the boy's free left hand, and Vincent Hugo wrenched his wrist out of Conrad's grasp, whirled his right arm around, and smacked Tom squarely in the face with the handle of the revolver. The blow threw Tom to the floor.

Both of his hands came up to cover his mouth, and his eyes stared open wide with pain. Vincent Hugo looked at him with dismay. Conrad grabbed his wrist again in a tight grip and took the revolver away.

"I'm sorry," the boy said in a whisper, looking down at Tom. "Oh, my God!" he sobbed. "What am I doing . . .?" He was bewildered.

With the gun in his jacket pocket, Conrad gestured the boy toward the long table. "Sit down here. Don't do a thing while I see about Tom."

Vincent Hugo crossed his arms on the surface of the table and lay his head down against them as if to hide.

Conrad kneeled over Tom, whose face had gone greenish-white. He could see the bright-red blood oozing out behind Tom's fingers but could not make out whether it came from his lips or from his partly opened mouth. "Take long, slow breaths through your nose," he said. "I'll be right back." He needed water, ice, something to wipe away the blood with. "Call campus security," he ordered Mrs. Todd while he strode down the hall toward Tom's office, and he heard her answer in a low, frightened voice, "I already have," as he grasped the doorknob.

Alone in Tom's office he switched on the lights and quickly remembered where the pullman kitchen was hidden behind the folding panels. He turned on the water in the sink and half-filled a small bowl. He pulled open the low refrigerator door and found a tray of ice cubes, but he was at a loss to know where to look for dish towels or napkins. He tried the cabinets above the sink but they contained only glasses and a few dishes. Then he pressed the button to open a door next to the refrigerator and found three or four white dish towels stiffly dry, like shrouds over a gathering of pieces of sculpture. As he pulled them up into his free hand, he discovered that they concealed a bottle of malt Scotch, a typewriter, a Dictaphone, a calculator, the clock: instantly recognizing all of the things that had been stolen during the past few months. In a sudden charge of outrage, he slammed the door shut and stood there shaking with disbelief. He wanted to hurl the ice cubes at Tom, he wanted to kick him. Instead, feeling his blood run cold, he squared his shoulders, felt his lips tighten into a thin line of anger, and, imagining that he looked like a headwaiter, with the dish towels draped over one arm, carried the bowl of water and the tray of ice in his hands back to the conference room.

Tom moaned.

Vincent Hugo looked up with red eyes.

Baker, the head of campus security, with his dark, double-breasted diplomat's suit, his steel-rimmed glasses glinting, entered the room briskly. Together, Conrad and he bent down on either side of Tom, and removed his hands from his face. Carefully, Conrad washed the blood away from the chin, the cheeks, and the nose. Tom's upper left lip had been split and two teeth of the upper jaw were so loose they probably could not be saved. Conrad wrapped a handful of ice cubes in the one remaining clean dish towel and offered it like an ice pack for Tom to hold against his face. Then he wiped the chilly sweat off the young man's forehead with his palm.

"Think you can get up?" the security head asked.

Tom nodded, and they helped him into one of the chairs on the side of the table opposite Vincent Hugo.

"What's the trouble?" Baker asked, almost blandly. And, as there was no immediate answer from anyone, he added, "I hear there's been a shooting."

"That's not exactly the way to put it," Conrad began. "A revolver happened to go off—quite accidentally, that's true. Mr. Hugo was showing it to me and . . ." He looked up to the ceiling for an instant and added, ". . . it was only a blank anyway."

Vincent Hugo sat back in his chair and regarded Conrad's lie with wonder.

"Where is it?"

Conrad turned the revolver over to the security chief.

"Is this registered in your name?" he asked the youth.

"Yes."

"Where?"

"Salt Lake City."

Instantaneously, Conrad was flooded with the recollection of the telephone call from Mr. Drake, the memory of the attempted bribe. "Mr. Hugo's grandfather is an important man," he said, "in the intermountain region."

The security chief said to the youth, "Think you'll live long enough to be a grandfather?" The young man made no reply. Then he pointed to Tom holding the ice pack against his mouth and asked, "How did this happen?"

Conrad leaped in. "Listen. He lost his temper. Mr. Hugo was very upset about a decision that matters a great deal to him. He got out of control for a minute. It's unfortunate, but he didn't mean harm."

"What did he mean?" Baker asked.

Conrad said coldly, "He meant to show how unhappy he is."

Mrs. Todd came to the door of the conference room to say that Mrs. Taylor was on the phone and urgently wanted to talk with Conrad. "I'll take it in my office," he replied and gestured the security chief to go into the inner room with him.

"Isabel . . ."

"I've heard there was a shooting."

"How?"

"I called to talk with you. I had Mrs. Todd on the phone when she heard the shot. She had to hang up to call campus security. Are you all right?"

"Yes!"

"That's all I wanted to know. Can you come home?"

"Not yet. I'll take Tom to the hospital."

"Was *he* shot?!"

"No. I'll explain later."

"You're not alone."

"Right."

"Well, take care. Come home as soon as you can."

"Yes."

As he hung up, Conrad turned to Baker and said, "You can keep this out of the newspapers, can't you?"

"Is that an order?"

"That's a request. It would make very bad publicity."

"For the boy?"

"For the university. And for other universities as well. He wasn't granted admission—therefore this scene. But no one got shot. If the newspapers pick up the story, you know, within ten days the same thing will happen in a dozen other universities, only somebody else might not be as lucky."

"What about smashing up your assistant? What if he presses charges? It'll be out of my hands if he wants to report it to the city police."

"I don't think he'll want to do that."

"I have to ask him, you know."

"Yes."

Returning to the conference room, Conrad quickly said, "Tom, come into my office and lie down on the sofa." Turning to Baker, he said, "Talk to Mr. Hugo for a minute. I'll be right back."

As soon as Conrad closed the door behind them, Tom tried to ask, "When you got the dish towels . . .?"

"I saw the other things that were there."

Tom closed his eyes.

Conrad led him to the sofa. "Rest here. I'll take you over to the hospital as soon as I can." Tom stretched out on the sofa with one arm behind his head. Conrad could see the pale blood on the wet side of the ice pack now. "You'll be asked if you want to report this to the city police. To press charges for assault and battery."

"Do you think I should?"

"I don't think you're in a position to press charges against anyone else . . ."

Tom turned his face away to the back of the sofa.

From the conference room, Conrad saw Mrs. Todd peering in through the far door and walked over to speak to her. "Call Dr. Rosenblatt. Tell him that Tom's been hurt. His lip is split, and two teeth are loose. Ask him to alert someone in emergency receiving. Say we'll try to get there within fifteen minutes. See if there's a particular doctor we should ask for. That's a good girl." Then he turned his attention to the security head and Vincent Hugo.

". . . so I'd guess you're likely to be let off real easy," Baker said.

The young man only stared at him.

"How did you get here?"

"I drove."

"You have your own car?"

"No. We're not allowed to own cars at school."

"Whose car did you use?"

"Mr. Lake's. He's the resident head of my dorm."

"Does he know you have his car?"

Vincent Hugo hung his head.

Baker turned to Conrad. "I'll have to talk with your assistant before we decide what to do next."

"Of course."

While they were alone in the conference room, Vincent Hugo said softly, "I am truly sorry."

Conrad replied, "I believe you," thinking of all those Japanese students who commit suicide when they're not admitted to college.

The security chief returned to say, "He isn't going to press charges."

Vincent Hugo looked at Conrad and said, "Please thank him for me. And apologize again."

"I will."

Baker said, "Now, I'm going to take you over to the security office. You come with me and we'll try to get Mr. Lake on the phone and tell him you've complicated his evening a little bit. Maybe I can drive you over to the Taft School—and if somebody can drive me back here. . . . Or we'll work something else out."

"Oh, I can . . ."

"You're not going off on your own."

Conrad declared, "You won't be taking that gun back with you either."

"I don't want to."

The security chief said, "I'll have a nice long talk with Mr. Lake."

In the last second before disappearing through the doorway, Vincent Hugo turned to say, "Please forgive me."

Conrad nodded, thinking, I can forgive you. But how can I forgive Tom?

PART 4

OBLIGATIONS FULFILLED
Including a
Newspaper Interview

I SABEL WAS PECULIARLY RESERVED throughout dinner that evening. She asked Conrad to describe "the shooting," and then she asked him to go over it all again in more detail, while she gazed at him as if filled with a secret, wondering whether to reveal a word of it or not. So he told the story twice, leaving out only the discovery of the stolen objects in Tom Spofford's office. Conrad did not want to open that topic with her. He was afraid she would be unpardoning if not venomous about it, while he had not yet thought through his own feelings about it. He told the story, conscious of his nervous stomach— his foreshortened stomach—fluttering uncomfortably, as if at a restaurant in New York where he could feel a subway train rumbling underground, shaking through his innards.

"How awful!" Isabel concluded. "How terrible it must have been for you."

He tried to let himself realize that he might have been killed. Other people have been murdered under similar circumstances. And yet the danger escaped did not hurt so much as the anticipation of confronting Tom again, but he kept himself from saying anything about that. ". . . so Tom's at the hospital overnight, but he'll be all right. He'll be home tomorrow," thinking: where I'll have to see how he's doing. What can I say to him?

Conrad felt spent; the dinner wine made him lust for drink after drink that would put him to sleep in an hour. Isabel was silent, peering at him, hardly blinking an eye. He chose to escape into gossip. "By the way," he began, "that rumor about St. Cyr isn't true. He didn't run off with Vivian Kirkill. I heard he's going to work in a French restaurant in Boston, but he hasn't left yet."

"A professor of German history?"

"He's agreed to be maître d' for a cousin."

"Why?"

"He couldn't find another teaching job."

"What a pity."

"I hear the restaurant job pays better."

Isabel said, "What price culture!"

"Ah, culture! Jesus, I have only a couple of weeks to finish that paper I promised Stoneface."

"When are you going to Washington?"

"March thirty-first. Just overnight. Are you coming?"

Isabel was flustered. She pressed a forefinger against her lips for an instant. "God. I forgot to tell you."

"What?"

"Kevin called. That's why I phoned your office. He's in a bad way. Emily's left him. And the Artists for Peace rally has fallen apart."

"I never thought that would get off the ground. Too lofty."

"Kevin's accused of misusing some of the funds raised."

"Oh?" With his mind's eye Conrad looked over the objects stolen in his offices, including his own hidden bottle of Scotch. "*Did* he misuse them?"

"I don't know. But he's a good manipulator. He'll land on his feet. He'll go on to greater glory. But he is broken up about Emily. She's found another man. He feels all alone."

"Maybe he should meet Vivian Kirkill."

"I don't think that's funny."

"Sorry. Why don't you ask Kevin to come here for a visit?"

Isabel exclaimed, "That's exactly what I did! And then I phoned your office to say I hope you wouldn't mind."

"Not at all."

"Well, he's going to drive. He thinks he'll take the southern route; that means ten days or two weeks, so I'll have to be around here the thirty-first. I won't be able to go to Washington with you. That's a shame. We'll go together another time. But I am worried about Kevin."

"He'll be all right." Conrad realized that one always feels that way about others. Why didn't he feel that about himself?

Again they slumped into the silence of their private thoughts.

Over dessert, Conrad, rather sadly said, "Mrs. Todd will be leaving early in April. She's expecting her baby fairly soon."

Ignoring that last statement, Isabel said, "I have a confession to make." She lowered her head; when she looked at him again, without the fixation of a stare, her sapphire eyes were clear. The tone of her voice was husky. "For the past few hours, I've been living with a very uncomfortable feeling. I've been ashamed."

"Of what?"

"Of how I felt when Mrs. Todd told me she heard a shot fired. I didn't know if you were hit."

Conrad had to urge her to continue: "Yes . . ."

"I didn't know if you were killed."

"Yes."

"I felt—" Now she cleared her throat and said softly, "If Conrad is dead, then I'm free."

"Ah . . ." Her jigsaw puzzle would have fallen apart and she would be free to put the pieces together into a different picture. We overlap into each other's picture of ourselves, each trying to see what's at the center—but we can't because we're at the inside of it.

Isabel continued: "I didn't feel sorry for you or disbelieving about how it happened. It lasted for less than a minute. But in that minute I was happy to be free. Then I was so ashamed, I burst into tears." She was dry-eyed now as she told him this straightforwardly. "I thought, Free?—for what? to do what?— without you. And I suddenly realized what it would mean to lose you, for you not to exist anymore. Freedom isn't what mattered. I'd be smaller somehow, I'd be the lesser. There is more to me because of you. If you were dead, I'd . . ."

Conrad smiled and concluded for her, ". . . shrink a little."

"Even then I wasn't grieving for you," Isabel went on. "I was only sorry for myself. And that made me feel ungrateful." She paused. "I know now that I'm not; I'm not ungrateful. Of course, I know I'm not the ideal wife for you . . . but then . . ."

"Ideals are wishes," Conrad said, "wives are people."

"When I phoned your office again and you told me you weren't hurt, I felt the opposite of relief. I don't mean regret. Of course, I didn't have any regret that you were all right. It's just that I knew then I wasn't going to be free and there was no relief in that. I was glad not to be 'relieved.' Still, I didn't quite understand what I was feeling then. Remember it all took place within an hour of my hearing from Kevin that Emily had left him. He sounded so bereft. I felt neither free nor bereft—but very clearheaded, suddenly, about how lucky I am and how much . . ." she groped for the right word to name the meaning she felt. ". . . how much I am thankful to you for."

Conrad reached across the dining room table to stroke her fingertips with his. "You've just made the kind of speech one imagines might be heard at one's funeral."

"That's it!" Isabel agreed. "I suppose almost no one says this sort of thing to anyone while he's alive. That's why I'm saying it now—because you almost were dead. I know you feel I rub you the wrong way some of the time; that's just my way. But it's rotten if I never tell you how much I like you— and want you alive."

"That's marvelous!" Conrad beamed.

"It doesn't mean I'll be any different for you than I've been in the past," she smiled, but she was not kittenish. "It means—I don't wish to lose you or be free of you or have to miss you." She took a deep breath. "I think I'm confessing that I'm happy with you. I don't believe I've told you that before."

"Understood," he replied. "And I'm happy with you."

She admitted, "It's not ideal . . ."

" I D E A L S !" Conrad almost shouted away the burden of them. "Ideals," he repeated more calmly, "are like road maps—in contrast to any ground you actually cover." He was simply savoring the fact that his wife had just told him she loved him.

"But you're an idealist—always imagining how things should be at their best."

Conrad thought for a moment before saying, "I am an idealist who spends most of his time working for a pragmatic fulfillment—of as much 'ideal' as can be got."

"And what are you the rest of the time?"

He said, "An ideal pragmatist."

Openly, she asked, "What's the difference?"

"A pragmatist tries to get the best out of a situation. An idealist makes matters worse in the hope of realizing his own dreams."

Isabel said, "Now I think I'm aware of what I must always have admired in you unconsciously."

"What?"

"Your self-satisfaction. You're even more smugly self-satisfied than I am."

They both laughed. "I'll tell you one thing I'm sure of," Conrad declared: "*Half-truths* are all of the truth that any human being can ever hope to know."

Conrad had never visited his assistant's apartment before. He found it with a little difficulty. The address on Park Street near Crown was easy enough to find, but in the entrance lobby the appropriate bell to ring did not carry an occupant's name; rather, it read Under the Mushroom. There was no elevator in the building. It was a three-flight walk-up. The door was opened by a rangy young blond in a gray sweat shirt and faded blue jeans.

"Christian?" Conrad asked uncertainly. The boy had grown a mustache.

"Hi." His tone was indifferent. He did not step back, open the door any wider, or attempt to show Conrad in.

"I'm looking for Tom Spofford."

"Yeah. He lives here." Christian Kirkill pulled one end of his scraggly mustache between his teeth and chewed on it.

"You live here too?"

"Sure." Only then did he move back from the doorway and allow Conrad to follow him into a square, tan-colored living room filled with early spring sunlight beaming through windows without curtains. "Is he expecting you?" Christian Kirkill asked in a manner that mocked the civility of the question.

"Yes. I spoke to him on the phone."

"I'll see if he's up. Make yourself comfortable." When he turned his back and strolled down the hallway, Conrad, recognizing that he was barefooted, wondered whether he owned a pair of shoes.

Conrad tried to imagine under what conditions he could make himself "comfortable" in such a room. There was no chair. There were three former army cots covered with khaki-colored blankets; in the center of the linoleum floor, on a tripod of brass legs, stood an Indian brazier burning a few black coals and emitting a cloyingly sweet fragrance—like a combination of heliotrope and cinnamon. Scattered everywhere were newspapers; articles of clothing churned with paperback books, towels, and beanbag ashtrays. There was a huge poster portrait of Mao Tse-tung on one wall and a plaster sculpture of Buddha opposite it. Between them, on the far wall, up and down two stacks of shelves made of unpainted boards resting across pillars of brick were dozens of clear plastic jars under the pale purple light of a long, narrow fluorescent bulb. Each jar contained a yellow or greenish growing thing floating in a pool of chemicals. Growing their own organic food, no doubt, Conrad thought. Without sunlight and without soil: just like Christian Kirkill himself.

Tom's girlfriend Rhoda appeared, rushing down the hall, pulling a plaid jacket on, saying, "I've got to hurry. Hello." Her straight pale hair was pulled back tight and hung in a ponytail swishing behind her thin neck. "I've got to get to work." It was twelve noon. She looked at him apprehensively and then darted away through the front door that slammed shut behind her. She knows, Conrad thought; she knows from Tom why I have to confront him.

Christian returned. "Tom's just putting some clothes on. Want to have a beer?"

"No. Thank you." He stood stiffly with the backs of his calves touching the low edge of a cot, turned away from the bright daylight coming in through the window behind him. Wearing a navy blue blazer and gray flannel slacks, he felt completely anachronistic in this infantile welter. He felt that he was standing in that one room the brother and sister lived in, that one sanctuary of chaos in Cocteau's *Enfants Terribles*. How prophetic Cocteau's film of decadence turned out to be.

"How's Caroline?" Christian asked—as if he'd just remembered her existence and her connection with the man standing before him.

"She's fine," he lied.

Christian showed no further curiosity.

"*You* look well," Conrad said, not concealing his surprise, trying to find something to say to this boy he disapproved of, whom he hadn't seen since that frustrating evening in London in his daughter's flat.

"Why not?" Christian asked.

"Your mother told me you were ill."

"My mother?!" Christian barked out a short laugh. "Before or after she started her 'new life'?"

"I haven't seen her 'after.' "

"Neither have I." He brought out of his back pocket a can

of beer, pulled it open, and took a gulp. "Sure you won't re-consider?" he asked, offering Conrad the same can.

"Rhoda goes to work at noon?" Conrad asked idly.

"Second shift in the hotel. She's a chamber pot. I mean a chambermaid," he laughed, charmed by his own wit. Conrad was dismayed to see how gray his teeth looked when he smiled. "But here comes Tommy now," Conrad said in a sing-song manner, like a fraternity brother pledged never to take anything seriously.

A bandage covered the stitches on Tom's upper lip. The clothes he had just put on were a pair of pajamas. They ap-peared to be brand-new. Five-and-ten-cent-store pajamas, stiff cotton with an imitation paisley print in bronze against a baby-blue background. It made Tom look like a teenager. Tom Spofford in his leisure attire, Conrad thought; Tom Spofford "at home"—knowing that I was due to arrive at noon, had been naked, making love to his chambermaid when I arrived. Did he wash before he put on the pajamas "for company"? or is a piece of his tail still wet? Why not? He should be worried about this meeting. It's good to make love, for reassurance, when you're frightened.

"I didn't realize the time," Tom said.

"Has to sleep late," Christian explained. "Doctor's orders." It was forty-three hours since the "accident" with Vincent Hugo. Christian made no gesture toward leaving them alone together; the three of them stood awkwardly amid the debris.

Tom asked, "Would you like to come to my room?"

Now Conrad caught a glimpse of the space in Tom's upper jaw where the boy had lost two teeth. He nodded, and then followed his assistant into the dark hallway, past a bathroom and a kitchen, and finally into one of the two bedrooms at the rear of the apartment. There had been nothing on the floor in the hallway, but the bedroom again was sloppy with dishev-eled clothes: the happy dream of irresponsible children—a combination of Tom's clothes and Rhoda's. There was no chest of drawers in the room, only a bed, with a blanket and sheets thrown back, and two straight chairs. Conrad and Tom sat down on them, facing each other. On the wall behind Tom's back, Conrad saw picture postcards of Madonnas and the Child. Not reproductions of Raphael or Bellini, but the rankest Italian kitsch. There was a photograph of Pope John XXIII, his hand raised in universal blessing; a black and white drawing of St. Peter's Church; and a pastel of Rhoda's head in profile which must be a product of Christian's hand.

"Are you Roman Catholic?" Conrad asked.

"No, no. I've had all that. But Rhoda's considering it."

Trying it on for size? Conrad thought. Comparison shopping? What he said was, "I hope you're feeling better."

"Oh, I'm fine. It did shake me up." He covered his mouth with his hand for a moment. "But the stitches come out in a couple of days and I start seeing the dentist about new choppers tomorrow." They both tried to laugh at the word "choppers." Then they looked at each other in silence. Conrad got up to close the bedroom door, but by the time he sat down again it had creakily swung halfway open.

"It doesn't matter," Tom said, lowering his eyes.

Conrad thought of Christian at the other end of the hall. The radio sound of a cool rock song seeped down the hallway from the living room. "Why do you live this way?" He immediately regretted the patronizing tone; to cover it up, he added, "I mean, with your salary and Rhoda working, can't you afford to live by yourselves?"

Tom shrugged his shoulders. "This is Rhoda's apartment. There were other people living here before we met. They change." He tried to smile. "It's fun. We help each other out— a lot."

"You never mentioned Christian Kirkill."

"He asked me not to."

"He used to know my daughter."

"He speaks very well of her."

Conrad suspected he'd invented that. He looked around the room again, thought of Rhoda's squinting eyes, Christian's bare feet, the kitsch on the wall, and said, "I had hopes of better things for you."

"This is only temporary," Tom replied cheerfully. "We're thinking about finding a place for ourselves. Maybe this summer."

"If you keep your job?" Conrad asked.

Tom paled. The remark had surprised even Conrad, who hadn't known it would come out so bluntly. He had no desire to lose Tom. That was exactly why he suffered anxiety over this meeting: he desired to keep him, to go on "shaping" him, "influencing" him as he believed he was doing—at the same time that he knew everything was changed by the discovery of the thefts. How were they to go on from that? Conrad stared at the youth before him—bright-eyed and bushy-tailed—so strong and willing and healthful-looking in his adolescent's cardboard-like pajamas and terry-cloth slippers. Now he was watching the healthful color of the high cheeks fade with fright. Tom licked his lips and touched the bandage over the stitches with his fingers. Conrad asked himself, Isn't he my protégé? How can I protect him—develop him, cultivate him—now?

Tom asked, "You mean—I can't keep my job?"

"I mean we have to talk about it."

"After all I've done . . ."

Conrad was grateful that Tom didn't make the mistake of adding, ". . . for you."

"It's just one thing you've done that puts the job in jeopardy."

"As soon as I return to the office, I'll put all those things back where they belong!"

"And we'll pretend that nothing ever happened to them . . ."

"Could we?" Tom interrupted, hopefully.

"And that *I* never knew what happened to them?"

Conrad made that sound impossible. Tom rested his hands on his knees and hung his head. Barely audibly he said, "I suppose not."

"What did happen to them?" Conrad asked.

Tom looked up at him suddenly with moistened eyes as if wondering whether he had heard correctly. "Don't you know?" he asked in a whisper.

"I know they are in your office. Did you take them?"

The boy is thinking of lying, Conrad imagined, but at length he heard the confession: "Yes."

"The question is *why?*"

"I don't know."

"Did you mean to sell them? For the money?"

"No."

"Then what did you plan to do with them?"

"Nothing."

"You just wanted to keep them?"

"I guess so." There were no tears in his eyes now; he was trying to understand what had gone on.

"How did it begin?" Conrad asked.

Tom scratched his head. "I think I got the feeling that day, when you scolded me for looking at the picture of La Rochefoucauld behind the . . ."

". . . silk hanging . . ." Conrad supplied.

"Yes. I wished I had that picture."

Conrad tried to laugh. "Is that gone too?"

"No. I didn't take it."

"You started taking other things instead."

"Yes. I didn't mean to."

Conrad pressed the fingers of both hands against his temples, knowing that he should not go on like this, that he would have to turn Tom over to a psychiatrist, to Jerry Rosenblatt, perhaps; someone who could treat him professionally. All he said was, "That's very neurotic."

Tom looked at him as though he had never heard the word before.

"Do you know what a neurosis is?"

"No."

"When you do something you don't want to do, or know is wrong, but still can't help yourself from doing it. Or—if you're

not able to do something you want to do or know is right."
Conrad knew that was telling more than he needed to say. It
reminded him of how much he liked being Tom's "teacher."

"Yes," Tom agreed. "It was something I didn't want to do,
but I couldn't keep from doing it. I'm sorry. I'll put them all
back," he repeated.

"That's not good enough."

"What else do you want me to do?"

"I can't let you continue at your job," Conrad began in measured tones, "unless you are willing to see someone—an analyst or a psychiatrist—who can help you with this . . ." Weary
with the burden and doubtful of the outcome, Conrad compromised and called it, ". . . this problem."

Neat as a pin, Tom said, "I'll be glad to."

"Not that I know how it will turn out," Conrad added. He
was aware of how put upon he felt now. This was his responsibility. Instead of firing Tom, let alone turning him over to
the police, he was going to harbor him—conceal what he
knew—and give the young man a second chance. He deserved that, Conrad told himself, for all the good he had done.
But Conrad felt the undertow of making a false step in this
way, as if it were bound to turn out badly and that it would be
his fault. Was he indulging himself, out of the longing to have
a substitute son or a pupil, someone to "influence"? Or was
he justified?

"I can't stand to see you look so sad," Tom said.

"It makes me sad," Conrad admitted. He stood up, needing
to get away. "Come to the office day after tomorrow."

"Please don't go like this. I can't bear your hating me."

"I don't hate you."

"You're angry with me. You're sore as hell. Get it out. Get it
over with." Now he was sounding like the teacher.

"I'm very disappointed," Conrad said.

"Oh, damn, that's not enough. What you should do is what
my dad used to do. Give me a good strapping. I can take it. Go
ahead—spank me—and then we'll both feel better."

Conrad backed away from him in dismay.

"Here," Tom said, bending down to the floor and removing his leather belt from a pair of blue jeans, "take this," forcing it into Conrad's hand. "You spank me as much as you want; it'll make things better for both of us." He pulled open the snap on his pajama bottoms, let them drop to his feet, and bent forward on his knees and elbows against the mattress of the bed; he covered his head with his hands. Conrad stared down at the rounded pink flesh of the exposed buttocks, fascinated and repelled at the same time. He was no Pentecostal father in a woodshed in South Dakota.

Christian Kirkill emitted a long, low, suggestive whistle from the entrance of the bedroom, where he stood slouched against the frame of the half-open door. He gazed first at Tom's upturned, naked rear end and then at the leather belt in Conrad's hand. "I had no idea," he declared lasciviously, "that you were so versatile."

"I'm not," Conrad snapped out. He threw the belt down to the floor where the brass buckle made a slapping sound. Otherwise there was silence. Tom took his hands away from his head and looked up in surprise, without changing his position on the bed. Christian leered, with the private satisfaction of a potential scandalmonger. Filled with disgust, Conrad pushed past him and strode down the hall toward the doorway. As he pulled the door shut behind him, he heard Christian consoling Tom: "He doesn't have the guts."

Later, calmed down by the walk to his office, refreshed by the smell of clean air after the suffocation of incense in Tom's apartment, Conrad tried to exorcise the distaste of the whole scene—the sloppiness of their lives, the make-believe of their escape from responsibility—by immersing himself in his work. There was paperwork to be done, reports to be read, forms to approve, but he recognized that he was constantly distracted by the image of Tom Spofford exposed on the disheveled bed, prone on his elbows and knees, with the vulnerable flesh of his pinkish buttocks in the air waiting for punishment—to set things straight, to even the score, to make it all right again between them. Conrad grimaced with repugnance. He telephoned Jerry Rosenblatt to ask if he would take a patient as a special favor to him, perhaps on a crash basis, or at least see him frequently for the next few weeks, because the future of the young man's job depended on immediate treatment. When Dr. Rosenblatt agreed to, Conrad, slightly more relaxed, asked, "What do you know about kleptomania?"

"As much as you do," his friend replied lightly. "Why do you ask?"

"Because of Tom Spofford. That's what I'd like you to see him about."

"Just give me the facts, man. I'll make the diagnosis."

"Of course." Feeling properly put down, Conrad recognized that he did not want to let go of Tom even as a patient let alone as a protégé. He remained silent.

"When did your father die?" Dr. Rosenblatt asked, although he knew.

"Just after I started college."

"And you have no son . . ."

"Is this consultation a professional courtesy or will you send a bill on the first of the month?"

His friend laughed. "A word to the wise . . ." and hung up.

Conrad stood at the side of his desk, with one hand resting on top of the receiver he had replaced on the telephone, remembering the plane flight from Chicago to St. Louis, after the telephone call that told him his father was dying. The sight of his mother's face as she waited to meet him at the airport was all he needed to see to understand that his father was dead. He felt, when he fainted, that his head was a solid globe plunging into the pool of water that his body had become. He no longer had a father protector and he never did have a son protégé. But he too was susceptible to make-believe.

He began to feel faint now, for the first time in years. He sat down, grasped his ankles with his hands, and lowered his head between his knees, took deep breaths slowly until he felt himself recovering equilibrium. He would regain his balance without the fantasy of a son substitute. That was merely a subjective conceit doomed to be withdrawn from him.

At the end of the day he strolled home sadly, determined to concentrate on the position paper for Senator Stonefort regarding American culture.

The Isabel who greeted him was especially beautifully dressed.

But that night Conrad was impotent. It made no difference how fiercely Isabel tried to stimulate him at first or, later, how languidly sensual she became—he remained flaccid, limp, and he felt dead. In the darkness of the bedroom as they lay side by side on their backs, no longer touching, he said to her, "It's as if the electric current's been turned off and I don't have any idea where the switch is to turn it back on." Isabel propped herself up on one elbow, leaned over, and kissed him on the shoulder. "Don't be so upset. It happens all the time to other people. I know. Women talk about it."

"Men don't."

"Oh, they think their whole 'manhood' is concentrated in having a hard-on at will, like always having a weapon available to beat someone with."

"That's not the way I feel about you."

"Have you been 'spending' your resources at some other gaming table?" she asked lightly.

"No."

"Oh, Lord, you look so grim. It's the first time this has ever happened to us. . . ."

Concerned only with himself, Conrad had thought of it "happening" to *him*. "But it has nothing to do with you," he quickly replied.

"It's *me* you're not able to make love to."

"It's only *you* I want to make love with."

"It isn't the end of the world," Isabel concluded, got up to put on some clothes, and urged Conrad to come downstairs for dinner.

Later that evening before falling asleep, he failed again to raise an erection.

"How lucky women are," Isabel consoled him, perversely. "They can fake it, if they have to. Men can't. Do go to sleep. Stop thinking about it."

After the third day of the same frightening sense of loss and deprivation, Conrad went to see his internist. The doctor examined him in a sterile white cubicle, large enough for only a high, sheet-covered table and a sink in the corner, and then led him into an office where they sat comfortably facing each other across the doctor's desk. "There's nothing obviously wrong with you. I'll call you later in the afternoon, when I get the results of the urinalysis and the blood tests. But I suspect there's nothing organically the matter. You're in good physical shape—would you say so?"

"I feel fine, otherwise."

"Except for exhaustion."

"I'll admit to a little exhaustion . . ." Conrad tried to smile.

"And tension? Are you under extreme tension these days?"

Conrad watched the doctor remove his pince-nez spectacles, breathe on them, and then polish the lenses with a linen handkerchief. He reminds me of Franklin Roosevelt, Conrad realized. Or am I seeing "father figures" everywhere these days? Am I trying to behave as if there are father substitutes to please—who aren't doing right by me? and worrying about what kind of father figure I have been for Tom Spofford? He thought of not knowing whether he would be appointed provost, of not hearing a word from Caroline, of not yet having completed the paper for Senator Stonefort, of having nearly been shot by Vincent Hugo, of knowing that Mrs. Todd would be leaving and have to be replaced. He thought also of his recent telephone call from a woman who said she was the Washington bureau reporter for the *Chicago Times-Herald* and asked if she could interview him. A reporter for Grant Hannover's newspaper. A sense of "falling away" all around him and a vagueness of demands on him that were oppressive but unclear. "Yes," he admitted, "I feel more than usual tension these days."

"Impotence is almost always psychological," the doctor said quietly, and replaced the rimless eyeglasses on the bridge of his nose. "Medicine knows next to nothing about it. Of course, if you drink too much and work yourself too hard, that's likely to contribute to it; but that's not the whole story. We don't know the whole story." He chuckled. "I'll charge you very little for this visit! Because the best I can tell you is to rest, slow down—and get your confidence back."

"Confidence comes from *doing* things, not from doing less." Conrad was snappish.

"How about doing it with someone else?"

"I see; the 'blood of a virgin' prescription?"

"Something like that."

"I hadn't realized I was that old."

"You aren't. It isn't a function of age, anyhow. But to use your own metaphor—you said you feel as though the electrical current has been switched off—well, then, you've overloaded your system; it blew a fuse. You can't press yourself this hard. Your body is saying 'Stop it!' and 'Give me a rest.' "

Conrad thought, I don't know how.

The doctor continued: "Of course, you're an overachiever, but then vegetables don't get ahead." After a pause, he said, "Sometimes, when people try to do more than their bodies will allow them to do, they turn against themselves. What it means is that they're trying to withdraw from the conflict *out there* and fight it out *in here*. This time, it hasn't turned into an ulcer, Conrad; I know you. We've been through that before. Consider yourself lucky. Impotence in someone like you is temporary. Don't make yourself miserable about it."

"So easily said . . ." Conrad muttered.

"You have a young wife. And you have a big job. But you must be driving yourself too hard."

"Funny: I'm stuck back at your saying something about what one's body will allow."

"That's right."

"As if it's a separate 'party' to be satisfied."

"It is! Think of all the pleasure your body's given you over the years. Where would you be without it?" he laughed. "Now you show it some consideration."

"What do you want me to do?"

"Rest. Cut out the drinking. Cut down the smoking. Wait. Take long walks. Wait. Your sex life will reemerge."

Conrad walked out of the office, into the early spring fresh air, thinking that, by the twentieth century, medicine had made fantastic progress in surgery and pharmacology; dentistry was now capable of miracles; but as far as his impotence of the moment was concerned, he had just received the identical advice that any Cro-Magnon man would have got if he'd taken himself into the prehistoric cave of the wise man of the tribe.

In the ten days that followed, he tried to act on the advice, nevertheless. He spent only half-days at his office. After lunch he took a nap on the sofa in his study, then worked at the position paper on American culture; Isabel went alone, or with someone else, to three evening engagements—one a concert—while he read or watched television; he slept alone in the guest room each night. Without explicitly saying so, Isabel and he had agreed not to talk about it further, assuming that when he had recovered they would be reunited the way couples come together again after having taken separate vacations. While he tried to think about it as little as possible, Conrad did find himself remembering his doctor's use of the word "withdrawal." To withdraw from conflict *out there*— amorphous as it was; from combat—as ill defined as it was. But if competition is not the be-all, and conquest the end-all, of life—there wasn't much fun without it. An unknown, un-named power within his own body overcame his will and he was doing penance to placate it. Only once did he wonder if he should see Dr. Rosenblatt, but he knew how busy Jerry was, knew that he'd forced Tom Spofford onto his schedule, and, worse, he doubted the methods of analysis for help in what he wanted to believe was a—briefly—temporary psycho-somatic condition. If he saw an analyst, he would be made to examine his resentment toward Caroline's pregnancy; he would have to confess his ambivalence toward Isabel's refusal to have a child; he would explore the questions of what in secret he felt guilty about and—*therefore*—punished himself with this special way of humiliating his masculinity. And by the time the strands of a story had been woven tight enough to carry the weight of that "therefore," the condition would be gone: he would be able to have erections eight hours a day if he wanted—and no one could ever know whether the analysis had cured him or if the unknown power within his body had simply "changed its mind." He did not call on Dr. Rosenblatt. Maybe the caveman advice would be enough; maybe he just needed a rest. He was tired of continually proving himself.

With regard to the paper on American culture: he came to understand he was tired of trying to prove himself an excep-tional man, or original mind. He would do an ordinary job of it: workmanlike, competent, useful but not superior. This was not a *Discours* to beat out Rousseau's prize essay on whether civilization confers benefits; this was to be part of the argu-ment for a bill submitted to Congress. Still—there was one afternoon, while the assignment was only half finished, when Conrad awoke from his nap with the vague recollection of a dream about the presentation to Senator Stonefort and his staff. Conrad entered the senator's office followed by a porter who wheeled in a stack of materials four feet high, a great sheaf of papers which turned out to be a series of translucent acetate overlays upon a base map of the United States. Each map showed the distribution of a separate aspect of culture in

America: the first being the locations of Indian reservations throughout the country. Then the sites of Protestant and Catholic churches, Jewish synagogues, Moslem mosques, Buddhist temples—each overlay in a different color. The next dozen showed the distribution of elementary and secondary schools, secular and parochial, colleges and graduate schools for higher learning, institutes and academies for specialized research. After that: the location of libraries, public and private, the sites of concert halls, theaters, motion-picture houses, art galleries and museums, dance halls, nightclubs, bars, saloons, whorehouses, gambling casinos, racetracks, summer resorts, and the last—his favorite—a map which showed throughout the length and breadth of the land, for the spring of 1974, how many adolescents hadn't heard their mothers call them down for dinner because they were lost in the world of *Huckleberry Finn*. As he riffled quickly through the high stack of colorful overlays, they shed the brilliant rainbow light that spelled "American culture"—and it was the brightness of those gaudy, colorful lights that woke him up.

The paper he finished and carried to Washington in his briefcase contained no such vision. It was a fifty-seven-page typescript surveying the activities of the arts, the sciences, and the humanities (with appropriate statistical supporting evidence). It came to the conclusion that the primacy of political freedom under the Constitution of the United States, resulting in absence of federal demands for conformity upon the culture of its citizens, had resulted in the most fertile field in which the vigor and originality of the life of creative spirits has ever had the opportunity to cultivate themselves. It was cliché-ridden in just that manner. "Variety" was the predominant concept, "freedom of choice" for the consumer, "self-selection" for the creative types. It was a review document, not a personal evaluation and criticism, that could be used for Stonefort's purposes. Conrad had not used it for his own. None of his reservations appeared in it. There was no radical distinction made between high culture and low culture, so the

senior senator for Missouri need have no worry about allega-
tions of elitism from the populists. On the contrary, throughout the document was the implication that all the manifesta-
tions of cultural life are accessible to all the citizens of the
Republic. No question of differences of capacity or training or
interest cast any shadow of "unfairness." While Conrad reassured himself that nothing in the paper was actually false,
nevertheless he kept to himself the belief that his skepticism
might make up the other half of the truth in the long run.

He held the briefcase on his lap protectively during the
shuttle flight, thinking of how apt and how vivid is the image
for those latecomers who scrounge among the leavings of what
had been food for the spiritual lives of others—"culture vultures," they're called, carrion birds who swoop down to de-
vour dead flesh. Whereas, to be cultured, to have a culture, for
it to be alive in you, is—when you're told your wife is having
an affair—being able to bring to mind a story out of Rabelais
to console yourself with. Conrad chuckled quietly to himself:
one's culture is one's source of consolation.

The plan had been that Conrad would hand over his paper
in midafternoon to the senator's staff and be given the addi-
tional specialized reports to read overnight; he was to have
dinner with the Stoneforts in Georgetown, stay over at the
Hay Adams, meet with the senator's staff in the morning to
make revisions in his own paper, and then give an interview
to Grant Hannover's newspaper reporter over lunch at the
Sans Souci restaurant. It did not work out that way.

William Stonefort was unusually testy. Conrad stood alone
with the senator in his office. "The situation is much worse,"
Stonefort said in an edgy tone of voice.

"You mean with Nixon?"

"Nobody really cares about his cheating on half a million in
taxes . . ."

"Nobody?"

"What everybody's worried about is what's on those tapes."

"He'll have to turn them over, won't he?"

Stonefort blurted out, "If he doesn't have them destroyed!"

"What do you think he'll do?"

The Senator sighed. He turned his back and looked out of his office window toward the Capitol building.

Conrad wanted to know if there was any hope of putting through the legislation to establish a Department of Culture under these circumstances. He looked around the high-ceilinged office, at the monumental mahogany furniture, the comfortable armchairs, the thick carpet, at the flags that framed the broad window: the flag of the United States on the senator's left and the flag of Missouri on his right. "Don't you think . . ." he began gently.

"I can't think," Stonefort said fiercely. He turned to face Conrad; he was pale and tense, his fists clenched. "There are all those forces marshaled against us—but we can't tell what they might turn up."

Conrad smiled to himself. The battle of the politicians and lawyers turned into detectives.

"Our own top people don't know—"

"Senator Scott said on television, 'The White House has evidence clearing the President of . . .' "

"He doesn't know," Stonefort interrupted. "He's the one who called for the meeting tonight."

"Tonight?"

"Oh, my God, Conrad. I haven't told you. I can't make dinner. I should have let you know. This evening meeting: all the members of the party in the Senate. A kind of self-examination. Goldwater and Scott want it. As if we can find out where we stand by looking at our feet."

"That's all right." Conrad was less bothered to be given short shrift than by the sense of foreboding that such a meeting suggested. All those senators "in the dark." And his own situation in Washington all the more uncertain.

"But, of course, about dinner—you could go to the house. Ruby would love to have company. I just can't make it."

"No. Give her my love," he added quickly. "But no, thanks."

"Very embarrassing."

"Don't give it a second thought."

"I did invite you for dinner."

"I can take care of myself."

"I wish I could say that about the party. There'll be elections in the fall . . ."

"You can't control things . . ."

That was how the interview with the newspaper reporter came about sooner than Conrad expected it to. Once he returned to his room at the Hay Adams, he telephoned the Washington office of the *Times-Herald* and asked for Miss Eleanor Saunders.

She answered accusingly, "You're not canceling tomorrow, are you?"

"You've jumped to the wrong conclusion. I wanted to ask if by any chance you might be free this evening. I've just been disinvited to dinner. Are you free for dinner?"

"What luck! I am. But I'm not really dressed for dinner."

"Well, then, let's try the restaurant here at the hotel."

"What time would you like?"

He read 5:15 on his wristwatch. "How would six-thirty be?"

"Excellent."

"Oh, by the way," she added, in a tone of preparatory warning, "I think you ought to know—I'm black."

Miss Eleanor Saunders could not have been more than thirty, very handsome, and not very black. She was milk-chocolate colored, with sculptured features, strikingly smooth, as if carved out of walnut. Her lips were painted a warm rose red that matched her fingernails, and her eyelids were touched up with a lighter red shadow. Long, wavy, black hair fell around her head, under a tan velvet beret, and her dress was made of cashmere wool that looked like old ivory. She carried a large woven shopping bag from Guatemala over one arm and held out her other hand in greeting.

"How good of you to change your plans," Conrad said.

They ordered martinis in the lounge where a pianist played music from Broadway musicals. She told him how pleased she was when she phoned New Haven to learn that he would be coming to Washington and she could interview him there. But why did she want an interview at all? he asked. Because Grant Hannover—whose paper it was—said Conrad might become the next provost and we should have a "scoop," with the first in-depth portrait ready to go, if that happened. Then why not a reporter from the New York office? Ah, Mr. Hannover didn't think anyone on the staff there would be as "sympathetic" as Eleanor Saunders. A subtle man, Mr. Hannover, Conrad suggested. "Mr. Hannover must be a very interesting boss."

Knowingly, Eleanor Saunders said, "He's marvelous . . ." She brought out of her bag a compact tape recorder no larger than a desk calculator, and placed it on the small table between them.

Conrad looked around the lounge and toward the dining room. There was a convention atmosphere—with men speaking loudly back and forth among the tables. "Don't you think it's a little too noisy here for an interview?"

"A little."

Conrad asked a waiter if there wasn't a table in some quiet corner.

"Full up," was the reply.

Miss Saunders suggested, "Why don't you order dinner sent to your room? We'll have all the privacy we could ask for." And he agreed.

Despite the erotic undertone in her manner, it was the interview that Eleanor Saunders worked at.

Over dinner, as she switched on the tape recorder, she appealed to Conrad: "Tell me the story of your life." He was surprised to discover he felt at ease with her, despite the un-likelihood of the whole situation, and spoke freely, if modestly, about his professional career.

"I take it that you love your work," she concluded.

"As you do," he smiled.

"That's right, I do."

They ate chicken cacciatore and drank Vouvray.

"Tell me about yourself," he said.

"Oh, that's not important. We must get on with it." Conrad ordered a bottle of champagne to be brought up by a waiter when he came to wheel the dinner table away, and, as he poured them each a glass, Eleanor Saunders checked the tape recorder.

"It's intimidating," Conrad said, as soon as they were alone.

"Don't think about it. Just make yourself comfortable." She placed the recording machine on the lamp table between them; they sat in those yellow-pigskin-covered armchairs facing each other. When she leaned forward to see that the tape was moving correctly. Conrad watched the folds of her dress, crossed to make a V-shaped neckline, fall forward. She was not wearing a brassiere. That, he supposed, is what she meant by not being dressed for dinner.

"Well, just think of what all that tape-recording across the street . . ." nodding his head toward the White House on the other side of Lafayette Square, "has resulted in."

"We're not doing anything illegal," she replied.

A smart girl, Conrad thought, and very, very pretty. Perhaps it was not the presence of the tape recorder that was intimidating; he had never been alone in a hotel room with a black girl before. She crossed her legs, she leaned back, he lit a cigarette for her and one for himself; they sipped the champagne. She went to work: "Who runs the university?" was her first question.

"Lots of people." He chuckled. "Legally, the trustees own it. Operationally, the faculty mans it. Professionally, the administrative staff is responsible for it."

"That sounds so cut-and-dried." She was disappointed.

"It's anything but that. There's a constant struggle over what ought to be done, and how to do it."

"So who makes the decisions? I mean does everyone get into the act?"

"No. It's splintered up. You can't have a majority vote on everything." He chuckled. "Most couples can't agree on where to go out for dinner tonight; imagine a democracy on every issue from faculty appointments and curriculum planning to the choice of toilet paper to buy for the johns."

"All right. That's hard to imagine. So—?"

"Anybody might think that, if *he* were running things, he'd do a better job. Well . . . different people are responsible for the variety of things that have to get done and, even if their choices are not entirely rational—and can't be justified in every instance as reasonable and fair—there are enough checks and balances to keep them from being purely arbitrary, merely playing favorites." Conrad began to speak more slowly now, realizing that he had named precisely what he was afraid of. "It is a question of trust in the judgment of the people who have to make the most important decisions. Trust that they will act out of concern for the good of the university as a whole."

"What is the university *as a whole?*"

That stopped Conrad cold. He had been thinking that Eleanor Saunders's eyes were the color of bitter chocolate and her eyelashes were exceptionally long and tightly curved. He began to grope for an answer. "As a *whole?* . . . Well, it's a condition for trying to realize intentions—intellectual intentions. It's made up of everything from the professors and the students, the buildings and the grounds, the libraries and the laboratories, its history and its prospects, from the goals in the minds of trustees and administrators . . ."

"To the toilet paper in the johns."

"Right." They laughed together.

"So it's something different, *as a whole,* depending on

who's trying to keep it all together in his mind." He nodded; she then asked, "And still it's one and the same school?"

"Oh, it's not a school." Conrad poured more champagne into each glass and didn't continue until he'd forced the green bottle back among the ice cubes in the shiny metal bucket and sat down again. "The university is not a school," he repeated.

With surprise she asked, "It isn't?"

"No. A school has a single purpose—like the Law School or the Medical School—and a fairly high degree of uniformity in its principles and methods. But a university has many purposes as different from each other as the Divinity School's are different from the Chemistry Department's."

"And they're all supposed to get along somehow?"

"Yes . . . somehow. In a kind of fruitful disparity—all based on respect for variety in the life of the mind." Conrad could feel the champagne warming his cheeks; he wondered if he were blushing. He was being asked much more serious questions than he had anticipated.

"How do you keep it all together in your mind?" she asked.

"With one paradox," he answered. "Don't lose sight of your ideals, but don't idealize the facts." He thought of the earnest student dressed like a monk, reading, as he trudged through the snow, a book that turned out to be pornography.

Eleanor Saunders recrossed her legs in the opposite direction and started questioning again. "But the whole purpose of the university is for education, isn't it?"

"Well, *research* and education. There's no knowing in advance what any scholar's inquiry, experiment, or speculation might lead to . . ."

"For the good of the country, or the good of the world?" she supplied.

"Oh, that . . ." he brushed aside. "Of course, there might be some practical advantages, especially for technology." He fell silent again: seeing clearly the secret truth pulsing at the heart of the university as a whole. "It exists," he began "in its essence and its ultimate goal," seeing all of the buildings, the ceremonies, the flag at half-mast, the annual budget broken down into direct costs and supporting benefits, "it exists in order to make it possible for individual scholars to pursue their own interests."

"*Wow!*—but I have to go to the bathroom," she said, and then excused herself and walked through the bedroom, leaving him alone to refill the glasses again. He stood in front of his chair looking out through a window offering a view of the White House at an oblique angle. The lights had come on. The Washington Monument stood tall and pale to the left of the Executive Mansion from this point of view. But he was not absorbed by the sight. Rather he saw again all the functions he was aware of being performed—from fund raising and admissions of students, the janitorial services, the athletic and recreational resources, the acquisition of priceless libraries, the dormitories, the dining rooms, the studies, the offices, the classrooms, the pageantry of convocations—all, all of them were established and supported and carried out in order that Brom Kirkill might enjoy the mystical poems of Rumi, David Bach analyze the surface of the moon, and Walter Webster revel in the glory of a painting by Poussin.

Eleanor Saunders had combed out her wavy black hair before she returned to the room. The tape recorder continued to whir through the silence. Trying to draw the threads of the interview together, she smiled. "If the university is not a school, and it exists to let scholars cultivate their private interests—where do the students come in?" They raised their glasses and seemed to toast each other before they took their seats again.

"Students have the opportunity to discover what they might become most interested in. And, by the way, don't think of scholarly interest as 'private.' It's not. Not the way interest on a savings account is private. Research results in something that everybody else who's interested can share."

"What?"

"The advancement of knowledge. And the assumption that

it will be shared—made available through lectures or publication—is what justifies all the support it gets from the people who put their money or time and intelligence into making it possible."

"I'm interested in you," she said.

"Now, that's a private interest." They laughed. She took off her shoes—lizard skin shoes for a very small, high-arched foot—and wiggled her toes.

"But a scholar's interest is public," she said like a sober schoolgirl trying to learn her lesson.

"It is in something other than himself. It might be in discovering the origins of cities through archaeology in the Middle East or finding a cure for cancer. It's not a personal interest like making a pile of money."

"Everybody needs money," she said.

"But not everybody is interested in something outside himself."

"I figure," she began—as Conrad realized both of them were slightly tight— "there's a fortune to be made by some chemist who comes up with the right pill. Dropped in a glass of water it will make it taste exactly like a martini but it won't have any calories. That will be the greatest invention since the birth control pill." Then she added, "I wish I had been your student."

"I couldn't have taught you much." He thought sadly of Tom Spofford and the portrait of La Rochefoucauld hidden behind the silk hanging.

"Why is anybody interested in any of those obscure things?"

That gave him pause. "There is no greater mystery," he replied. "Interest, genuine interest, of an intellectual nature— the formulation of a question and the search for its answer— the kind that can be tested with some degree of confirmation or verification . . . that kind of curiosity satisfied by that kind of resolution: ah! why anyone has it—wants to know what the surface of the moon consists of or how best to appreciate a painting by Poussin—that is inexplicable. What we do know is that it can't be created artificially, in the faculty any more than in the students. For example, I knew of a man who taught German history, and was good as a teacher, but who had no *interest* in German history the way a true scholar has; he didn't want to find out anything about it on his own. He didn't have any of the passions of an explorer or a detective. He actually tried to fake it—the results of original research that could be shared—by plagiarizing a book written by someone else. He was 'interested' in his job, but he wasn't interested in 'something other than himself'—for its own satisfaction—so he wasn't able to contribute to knowledge to the satisfaction of the university."

"Did he get the ax?"

"He will be leaving soon."

"So the people the university keeps on are all doing something to satisfy themselves?" She was intelligent and playful at the same time—just what he liked.

"But not only for themselves. Because their results can be criticized, evaluated in the public arena—the give-and-take of scholarship, which creates the possibility of objective judgment."

"Isn't it always objective, a matter of The Facts?"

"No. The 'facts' of events seem objective, but what they're worth, what they *mean*, is debatable."

"And the 'give-and-take of scholarship' . . ." she repeated.

He completed the sentence for her: ". . . carries on the debate."

Conrad lowered his hands toward the floor, untied his shoelaces, and slipped his feet out of the brown cordovans. "Now," he said, "the 'fact' is that I've taken off my shoes. The debatable question is what that 'means.'"

"That we're going to play footsie." She chuckled, brought her stockinged feet up to his, and wiggled her toes against his toes.

"And what does that imply?" he asked.

"That you are 'interested' in me."

"But this is not an issue of intellectual curiosity."

"I should hope not."

"What if I'm only teasing?"

"That can be tested," she said, broke the warm contact between their feet, got up, switched off the lamp between them, and lowered herself onto his lap. Her arms went around his shoulders, her cheek pressed against his cheek.

Between the inner warmth of the champagne and the outer warmth of her body against his, Conrad luxuriated for a moment in the promise of pleasure. He brought his arms around her and stroked her back. Then, a chill of fear made him aware that he might not be able to perform. He had been impotent for more than ten days. Slowly he said, "I don't know if I can . . ."

"Keep your eyes closed and pretend I'm white."

That startled him. "What a bitchy thing to say."

"Is that a 'fact'?" She was confronting the history of her life head-on against her assumption of the history of his life.

"I wasn't thinking about that. But I haven't been able to have sex for a little while."

"You're not missing anything necessary right now," she observed, moving her thigh against the hardness of his crotch. "And that's a fact."

Conrad lifted her up and carried her to the bed. He removed her clothes hurriedly and dropped them on the chair. He undressed in the darkness; only a pale light from the White House filtered through the thin curtains into the hotel room. Naked together under the covers, they kissed and fondled each other. Having never been in bed with a black girl in his life, Conrad said, "I've never known anyone like you before."

"Lie to me," she responded cheerfully, "lie to me good."

She was the stranger, the other, not necessarily the enemy, but The Foreigner—the Native Foreigner, the American Black. He had lived his whole life in a world of white Americans, descendants of emigrants from Europe, and of black

Americans whose ancestors were Africans—with so few bridges across that gap between them that his daughter had gone to Africa, had offered herself to be a bridge, had thrown herself into that gap. His fury at that thought all the more excited his desire to ravage Eleanor Saunders. He made love with the sharp edge of hostility—with a weapon to beat someone with; goading her to further exertions and submissions— thrilling them both and leading them to exhaustion, to falling asleep in each other's arms.

When the ringing of the telephone woke him suddenly in the morning out of a deep pit of sleep, Eleanor Saunders was gone. He wondered when or whether she had turned off the tape recorder. He lay quietly in the warm bed, not ready to let go of the impression of their lovemaking. As after an ocean voyage one still feels his body listing to the motion of the ship, Conrad felt his loins, his groin, his thighs swelling and retreating with the memory of intense intercourse. He would go through the meeting at the senator's office that morning, but he had a hard-on and he was eager to get home.

PART 5

ORDEALS AND GOOD DEALS

A FEW WEEKS LATER, Caroline sent a collect telegram announcing "it's" a boy, asking Conrad if he'd like to celebrate the event with a gift, and supplying an elaborately worded Native American address around a post office box number somewhere in Arizona. Isabel's brother was the first to contratulate him on becoming a grandfather. Kevin had been staying with them since the beginning of April. Having driven across the country in a weary Volkswagen, he was self-pitying and morose at first, but within a few days of resting and enjoying Isabel's easygoing sympathy, his amiability revived.

Isabel told Conrad not to fret. "Don't think about Caroline and the baby as 'tragic.' Don't worry. She's tough."

"I'm not worried about her," Conrad said, not knowing what he felt.

Isabel, who had been standing at the bar, came across the room to his armchair, bent over, and kissed Conrad on the cheek. "I don't believe you," she said, "but I'm proud of you for saying that."

"There's no point in worrying about Caroline."

"Very economical of you, darling. Do worry only when it leads to a point."

Conrad was unsure of where to find the cutting edge of that remark, but Isabel had been drinking more than usual since Kevin's arrival. He had plenty of other things to worry about:

discontentedly, irritably, without any immediate relief in sight—conditions to be borne rather than problems to be solved. Tom Spofford had returned to work pretending that nothing had happened. That made Conrad even more uneasy than if he had been abject, still longing for quick woodshed justice to make things all right again, because he was aware that Tom was seeing Jerry Rosenblatt for an hour every other day. Conrad was formal, proper; there was no margin for familiarity let alone confidences; he felt deprived—waiting for a verdict of some sort to be brought in by the jury. When Tom attempted to ask him for a favor—as in the old days—wondering if Conrad would consider Rhoda as a replacement for Mrs. Todd, Conrad actually recoiled. There was no basis for favors anymore. Fortunately, the spring weather meant that Conrad could play tennis outside at the Lawn Club each noon with an old friend, so the fact that he no longer invited Tom to play squash with him in the gym did not seem unnatural. All this "biding time" . . . Conrad had made a formal appearance before the Search Committee which turned into a seminar on the ideals and operations of the university.

Since he had come back from Washington—and with Kevin in the guest room—Conrad had returned to his own bed. The first night they were together again, Isabel's head against Conrad's shoulder, her body pressed along the length of his, she must have sensed him tense with anxiety, for she played her hand along his chest, past his hip to his leg, in a soothing rhythm, repeating, "Relax. Relax. A little affection goes a long way," gently rousing him.

He hugged her closer to him, whispering, "I hadn't thought you'd be 'taking care of' me."

She may have been put out but she did not sound irritated. Levelheadedly she judged, "You hadn't thought I'd be equal to it."

He made no reply.

Isabel continued: 'You don't give me enough credit. Didn't you think I'd learn something from living with you?"

"Like what?"

"Like: aim for what you want, but don't pretend things are other than they are."

"Oh." He sounded disappointed.

"Find out *what* they are first. I've been reading. Impotence is to be expected occasionally. Hormonal changes, that sort of thing: biological. But then it's reinforced by fear—the dread that it might be permanent—that part's psychological. Variety helps. Change helps. We ought to go away—for a weekend or even a night."

His shoulders slumped. "I've just got back from Washington . . ."

"I wasn't thinking of going far," she replied. "How about Caroline's room?"

Both of them burst out laughing. They rolled around with each other like puppies, nipping, cuddling. Suddenly they made love even more happily than if there was nothing to worry about.

Enormous with child, Mrs. Todd was celebrated at a farewell party in the conference room for which Cameron McNeill made a rum punch and, having tested and tasted enough of it, danced a highland jig in her honor and kissed her many times on her forehead. Mrs. Todd covered her face with both hands. She was barely more than a child herself and now she was leaving the company of adults for an unpredictable length of time. Isabel and Conrad Taylor had their gift of a crib delivered to the Todds' apartment.

Mrs. Todd's replacement was Miss Frangle (who, it was later learned, had started life with the name of Miss Finkle but who was given to renaming everything; she called her new Oldsmobile a "Youngsmobile"), a middle-aged, unmarried lady. She had been Walter Webster's secretary when he was dean of the humanities, and, assuming that sooner or later she would Know Everything about her new job, she tended to be slow about learning what document was located in which files. Gone was the brisk competence of long, brown, straight-haired Mrs. Todd.

The Search Committee met weekly, but no news came through to Conrad. He knew that whatever he had left undone in making the decisive impression on the president, in all the years that Blackwell had held that office, could not be made up for in the few weeks or months before he chose his next provost. This was a stretch of time in which those past ten years could be reviewed and all the incidents of working well together or points of friction between them could be reevaluated. There was nothing more to be done, Conrad told himself; all the good and all the damage that counted had already been done. He himself was unable to imagine the relative weights of each as they were measured up against each other upon the president's palms.

For a few days, early in the month, Conrad showed Kevin around the campus, the local bars, the rest of the town. In the end, he left him with a sketch pad in his hands in front of fragments of Greek sculpture in the old museum, but after a week, Kevin spent most of his time making sketches of eighteenth-century horses from the Mellon collection in the new museum. He had no desire to be introduced to the university community or any of the Taylors' other friends; he refused to allow them to give a cocktail party for him. He was brooding. He drove into New York for the opera or a play, or to see an old acquaintance or relative, but otherwise kept to himself. He longed to come up with a new scheme that could make even more of a splash than the aborted California—and then national—Artists for Peace rally might have done. Something that would redeem him, reaffirm his effectiveness as a planner—an activist, someone farsighted—a leader. But he kept alluding to the fact that Emily had walked out on him, as if each time he closed his eyes he could see her back moving farther and farther away from him. What had he been unwilling to do to keep her? He was arrested in his self-pity. He, too, wanted to believe in a world where no one made mistakes, and no one suffered for misplaced kindnesses.

Isabel took Kevin riding on a borrowed horse almost as good as her Champion. She helped him buy a wardrobe of Eastern summer clothes. She asked him to supervise the planting of new flower beds in the backyard at the Hillhouse Avenue house. Toward the end of the month, Conrad was able to take his brother-in-law out to the country club one afternoon. Kevin didn't play golf but he loved to swim, and Conrad left him at the pool.

Conrad was off to play his first full foursome of the spring with Henry Warner, Dr. Connolley, and Judge Jackman. These were his friends outside the university—town, not gown. Good friends for a number of years. Warner's store was a New Haven institution and Warner was a man of superior taste; although Connolley practiced at the Yale–New Haven Hospital, he had no connection with the faculty—a gynecologist and obstetrician—but an alumnus who contributed, through his wife's largess, to the university fund-raising campaigns; Judge Jackman was a local magistrate, Lincolnesque in appearance, a discriminating book collector, and an amateur cellist. His most prized possession was an autographed photograph of Benjamin Cardozo of the Supreme Court—for Jackman had been his law clerk a long time ago.

They spoke little as they moved from the first tee down the fairway. The green earth was spongy in stretches and still almost frozen in other spots. The weeping willows around the water hole—number four—were beginning to grow new leaves long and thin as early string beans. This was where Henry Warner had landed a hole in one the year before.

They paused at the fifth tee to light cigarettes. "Pretty impressive story about you in the newspaper this morning," Dr. Connolley said, sharing the pleasure. "One million dollars. Jee—sus! How did you do it?"

"I didn't do a thing," Conrad replied.

"What are they talking about?" Henry Warner whispered to the judge.

"There was an announcement in the *Journal* that somebody named Hugo in Salt Lake City presented the university with a gift of a million in unrestricted funds 'in honor of Conrad Taylor.' There wasn't any explanation."

"There isn't anything to explain," Conrad stated with false modesty.

His friends shook their heads in disbelief.

"Okay. The truth is I did his grandson a favor. That's all. I've never met the man. I didn't ask him for the money. He gave it out of the goodness of his heart."

Conrad's three companions applauded.

"Bully!" Henry said. "Old Blue!" was the doctor's cry. The good judge admired: "A million-dollar favor."

"I had no idea at the time that it would result in any gift to the university at all."

"Sure, sure," Connolley said. "Just one of those little happy accidents."

"Yes," Conrad replied. The whole thing was unmentionably silly. The telegram to the newspapers making the announcement public; the check to the president making the reference to its being given "in honor of . . ."; the personal and confidential letter from Chancellor Drake saying that Vincent Hugo would be starting at Brown in the fall, as if Conrad had been awaiting the information.

"Let's tee off," the judge demanded.

They put out their cigarettes, broke them apart, and scattered the fragments into the grass.

The azure sky was soiled with the streaks of gauzy clouds, like the traces of a sloppy cleaning woman's polish on a glass table. The sun was spring-warm. Henry Warner, always dapper, wore knickers and knee-length argyle stockings. Conrad warmed himself with the thought: These are my friends; they are neither of the university nor of the government, neither ivory tower nor pork barrel. They don't live either for theory or for action alone. They are the merchants and the professionals of Plato's Republic. Not the guardians. The academics think only of *ideas;* those in government, only of *action*. These friends are in the happy medium—their fulfillment depends on a reasonable combination of theory and action, every day, in every encounter in business, law, and medicine. Senator Stonefort hasn't had an idea of his own in twenty years, and Walter Webster wouldn't know what an "action" is. But the former lives to make his mark through directives for other people to act on, and the latter can justify himself only through the originality of his thought. But these three have one foot in each realm and they stand square and sound: know what they're about and make things happen. No matter how the government abuses them and the university perverts what they sponsor and support—they will go on making the government and the university possible.

"What do you think of how the investigation's going?" Conrad asked.

"In Washington?" the judge replied. "Fascinating. Absolutely fascinating. It's all makeshift, you know. The game is called 'Find a Law.' "

"Find a Law?" Henry Warner repeated.

"As the problems have never occurred before," the judge answered, "the solutions depend on how to use existing laws to manage them. There is no history of tape recordings in the Executive Branch as government records, let alone as criminal evidence; everything now turns on the rights to The Nixon Tapes."

Dr. Connolley said, "The White House refuses to turn over any more . . ."

"But Judge Sirica has ordered the President to obey the subpoena," Henry Warner said.

"And if the White House refuses," the judge explained, smiling, "the House Judiciary Committee might finally agree to that as grounds for impeachment." They strolled down the sloping fairway toward the next green. "We have a President who's secretly undermined the constitutional system of the country by reaching for 'total power,' and we'll probably get rid of him because he refuses to comply with a subpoena. That's like putting Al Capone in jail for income tax evasion. The worse your crime—the smaller the mistake it takes to do you in." He laughed. "The efficacy of legal strategy is not to be confused with 'justice.'"

Dr. Connolley and the judge won by a combined 160 to Conrad's and Henry Warner's very close 168. It was a wonderful way to start the golfing season.

Just before the end of the month Conrad received an invitation to a dinner party at the Baird-Lloyds' home in Manhattan. It was planned for the members of the Search Committee, the president, and the Taylors. "Dress Optional." The sky was still brightly lit at five in the afternoon. Standing before his leaded windows, Conrad held the invitation card in his hand and tried to anticipate that dinner while gazing out to the green lawn of the quadrangle, the dark red brick of the nineteenth-century buildings around the courtyard; students strolled along the diagonal paths. Tom Spofford knocked at the half-open door of his study. "I wondered if you'll be leaving now or if I could speak with you, privately, for a few minutes?"

Conrad looked over his shoulders to see the young man in his green plaid suit—the hick's clothing which he hadn't worn in half a year—and took that as the sign of a declaration. Conrad measured the word "privately" and relented enough—for the first time since the missing objects had been returned to their places—to offer a drink of his Scotch to the youth "after hours," not in hope of reestablishing the broken pattern, but in nostalgia for loss of it.

Tom returned with the glasses, ice, and the pitcher of water. They remained silent until they both had drinks in hand and sat facing each other across the desk. "What do you want to talk about?" Conrad asked in his professional manner.

316

"I'm not going to see Dr. Rosenblatt anymore."

"Is that his decision or yours?"

"It was mutual." Tom smiled for the first time. Conrad noticed his new teeth and the pale scar on the upper lip. Everything about him was repaired. He was restored. He was moving again from self-confidence to self-esteem. The young man on the make. "We came to the necessary conclusion."

"What is it?"

"That I ought to leave."

"This job?"

"Yes."

Conrad felt rent, torn, but that, of course, this decision was right. It was inevitable, inescapable. He was not relieved, only acknowledging the loss. He wanted to shake hands, wish Tom well, and have it over with, so that the source of this hurt would go away as fast as possible, but he knew this interview would not end so simply. They would have to talk it out. "Why is that?" Conrad asked, giving him the invitation to discuss it that he obviously desired.

"Well, it was very strange and surprising—the meetings with Dr. Rosenblatt, I mean. Until I finally came to see why I'd taken all the things."

"You did come to see that?"

"Yes. *I wanted to get caught.* I wanted to be found out."

"Why?"

"So that I'd have to think through what it is I *really* want."

"And that turns out to be different from what you're doing?"

"Well, somewhat. You see . . ." Tom took a deep breath, preparing to be instructive: "I'm grateful to you for all you've done for me—taught me—helped me with, but you've come to expect too much from me. More than I want to—" He waited, openmouthed, trying to remember a phrase.

"Live up to?"

"Right. Actually it's not so much what you expect from me, it's how much you thought I ought to expect of myself."

"Oh."

"I don't want to get a Ph.D."

317

"I see."

"You overestimated me. From *your* point of view," he said defensively. "I want to get ahead, but I'll have to do it in my own way."

"Of course."

"Naturally," Tom quoted Jerry Rosenblatt; it was the doctor's favorite word—"naturally." "In other words: according to *my* nature."

"And how does one find that out?"

"Trial and error. I tried it your way. Reading the books you admire, wearing the kind of clothes you like, planning to take the courses you thought were appropriate." He raised his glass— "Drinking the kind of liquor you like."

"Which you don't like?" Conrad asked.

"I don't really approve of liquor."

Conrad remembered the smell of incense in Tom's communal apartment, the organic foods floating in their chemicals, the "natural" disorder of clothes and newspapers and empty beer cans on the floor. Caroline disapproved of liquor, too. The Puritan slobs. He said, "I was 'expecting too much' of you?"

"Well, you were showing me your way and I thought I was following it. I was trying to follow it. I just couldn't say no."

"Outright," Conrad added.

"That's it! I couldn't say no outright. So I said no in this indirect way—this cadging away of things from the office until I got caught, so I'd have to confront why I wanted to get caught."

"Which is?"

"In order to face—*not* wanting to go on doing it your way."

"Ah!"

"I can gets lots of different kinds of jobs," Tom said with no self-consciousness. "I'm a good mechanic, a carpenter, a statistician—I could be an actuary or an accountant; I'm strong. I can do manual labor."

"I thought you wanted to be an administrator, an execu-

tive," he said with a smile, "if I remember correctly." Conrad
refilled his glass, but did not offer Tom another drink. He
wanted to calm his own anger enough to discover exactly what
he was angry about.

"I thought so, too." Tom lowered his hands and pressed his
fingers together. "But I was wrong. And this roundabout
means—of getting caught and having to talk it over with Dr.
Rosenblatt—was my way of finding out that something deep
down inside me says this isn't right for me. I've got to get
out."

Conrad felt himself put down. He became petulant and
asked, "Want to go hitchhiking cross-country?"—disliking
himself instantly for allowing his annoyance to be expressed.

"No. I don't know what I'll do next. But I had to explain this
to you. And apologize. And give two weeks' notice."

"All right," he said brusquely. "Two weeks' notice," he
repeated, accepting. Conrad assumed Jerry Rosenblatt had
coached Tom for telling his story. Making it "perfectly clear."
This was the tale that explained him: what Tom "really"
wanted. Oh, to be interpreted! Conrad assumed that Jerry Rosenblatt had rehearsed the boy the way an attorney prepares a
defendant.

Tom said, "It's not all that bad," seemingly sensitive to Conrad's feelings of loss, without their having been expressed.

"I am sorry if I put too much of a burden on you."

"No way to find out," Tom said brightly, "without trying."

Conrad saw Tom so far removed from his hopes of a protégé
that the youth sitting opposite him appeared to be an impos-
tor.

Breaking the silence, Tom said cheerfully, "I understand
from Mr. McNeill that your daughter's had a child. Congratulations!" In the past, Conrad would have taken the remark to
be heartfelt; now he recognized it as chitchat. "Thank you,"
he replied, yet resenting: How could you disappoint me like
this?! Why aren't you equal to what I'd hope of for you? But
that was unfair. Half the responsibility was Conrad's. The

question for him was: Why did I expect it of Tom? What misled me to imagine a potentiality that turned out not to be there? He watched Tom moistening the corners of his mouth and his lower lip with the point of his tongue. "Do you want another drink?"

"No, thanks."

Conrad looked out to the rooftops and listened to the chimes of Harkness Tower strike five fifteen.

"You don't necessarily have to continue here for two weeks if you don't feel like it."

"I know this isn't a bad time for me to quit."

"Well, then, you just take off when you want to. You'll be paid for the two weeks in any case, and check with Mr. McNeill about how much you have coming from accumulated vacation time and any other fringe benefits."

Tom's firm face broke into a smile. "You've always given me *good* advice."

Wiser now, Conrad laughed. "Not always," he corrected. "Sometimes."

"Almost always." Tom's tone was that of a student about to evaluate his teacher at the end of a course. "Except, maybe, that time you told me not to file a complaint against Vincent Hugo." He patted the left side of his mouth. "I probably could have collected a bundle . . . Rhoda thinks . . ."

Conrad interrupted him. "Sorry, Tom." He looked at his wristwatch. He dismissed him by saying, "I have to leave now."

His judgment had been called into question enough. Whereas he thought he'd been effective by encouraging Tom to bring out the best in himself, he had miscalculated. A clear-cut error of judgment. But he did not need to be shown that Rhoda would make Tom an ingrate. He turned his back. Tom closed the door behind him.

Earlier that afternoon Jerry Rosenblatt phoned to ask Conrad for a drink at the Faculty Club at five thirty. He must have known that, sometime during the day, Tom would tell him about the decision to leave, and he would take it hard. He would take it badly. It would be a blow to his pride. Not merely because he had made an error of judgment. That has to do with intellectual vanity, or how well he carried out the duties of his office. But this failure would diminish the sense of his personal power. Conrad consciously had wanted to exercise his influence to make Tom into something other than he was. Not a purpose he was charged with, not a function of his office; it was not within his control—administratively—as part of his responsibilities. It was a private wish to gratify his sense of the effectiveness of his will. It may have been "according to his nature," but it remained to Tom to show the error of the trial. The depth of the disappointment lay in how far the wish was kept from being satisfied. He was misled by his wish to his own disappointment.

And how do you live with your disappointments? By accepting the fact that they prove the limits of your powers. What the fact declares is: you can't have it your way. Conrad's influence was arrested by Tom's resistance. He felt spurned— not his judgment criticized, as in dealing with a David Bach or a Henri St. Cyr; those issues were official and impersonal. His character disdained, not his office; his personality declined—not his position challenged. Formerly pleased to think he was extending himself, he was made now to feel diminished for having overstepped his bounds—implying that he had undertaken to carry out a project somehow improper. He was made to feel guilty by having been rejected.

Conrad was a little late for their appointment at the club; Dr. Rosenblatt sat at a small table along the wall opposite the bar.

"I've ordered a martini for you," he said.

"Why?" Conrad asked.

"Because I suspect you need it. Medication," he replied.

Conrad asked, "When did the word 'medicine' disappear and 'medication' replace it?"

"Did Tom talk to you today?"

"Yes."

"You need a martini."

Conrad looked at his old friend with gratitude. "I'm sorry that you know me so well," he said.

"No you're not; you're glad."

"So you've 'interpreted' him, given him a 'likely story,' " Conrad said, "and now he will try to 'get high' in some other way."

"You are well rid of him. He didn't have the kind of staying power it would have taken."

"Why didn't I see that?"

"We see what we hope for."

Conrad sipped the cocktail and then shook his head—tired of himself.

Jerry Rosenblatt announced: "I'll tell you something I shouldn't tell—because you need a lift. Promise you won't tell anybody. This will cheer you up." He took a deep breath, looked around at the few others in the room, and softly said, "The Search Committee met for the last time today."

"You mean you've exhausted the list of all the handicapped black Jewish women qualified for the job?"

"We unanimously recommend Conrad Taylor be made provost."

Conrad broke into a smile. Dr. Rosenblatt patted him on the knee. "It's only a recommendation, mind you. The choice remains with the president and the trustees . . ."

"I know, I know . . ."

"For second choice, the committee named Grant Hannover."

"That's a surprise. He's a trustee. He's on the Search Committee himself."

"It was Baird-Lloyd's ploy. The 'new blood' argument. Thought it would please the trustees to have one of their own in the running."

"That's a new twist."

Dr. Rosenblatt asked, "Do you really want the job, Conrad?"

"You're big today on what one 'really' wants."

Jerry Rosenblatt laughed. "You ought to know what's good for you—and what you're good for. You've been in charge for a long time."

Conrad was meditative, remembering the moment in Marguerite Yourcenar's *Mémoires d'Hadrien*—when Hadrian finally learns that he will be made Emperor of Rome he says of himself: "my own life no longer preoccupied me; I could once more think of the rest of mankind." Conrad faced his friend squarely and asked, "In charge? You know what I've realized about how an administrator is 'in charge'? The way a traffic cop is in charge. They're both prone to the same mistake. Cops think they make the cars go, but all they have the power to do is make them stop."

Kevin was ebullient that evening—having met an art student in the museum, whom he was taking out for dinner. They had talked all afternoon about the need of a forum for artists to express their ideas for peace and prosperity. If the California rally hadn't been ambitious enough, and the American Artists' plan fell through—it was only because, Kevin saw it now, the idea had been too parochial. It should be conceived on a global scale. There should be a direct route by which artists anywhere and everywhere in the world could make their presentations to congresses and parliaments in their own countries and to the United Nations and other international bodies. Kevin said it had the "rightness" that made it "inevitable." Here was a purpose he could get behind, invest his talents in. He was dressed in a white suit as if for Palm Beach, and, now, despite his limp, he walked with a springy step. He saw a new goal for himself, and he had picked up a sympathetic fellow artist to discuss it with.

Isabel and Conrad dined alone. In a low voice, fragmentarily, he reported to her some of Tom's conversation and decision to leave, without going into details about his kleptomania and the sessions with Jerry Rosenblatt.

"Why are you taking it so hard?" she asked. He did not know how much to say in answering that question. "You'll find another assistant. You found another secretary."

"It isn't the same."

Isabel dropped her spoon into the soft dessert. "You're tired of your job. You need a change. Why don't you take something in Washington?"

"I'm not tired of my job." Why do so many people want a change all the time? "Shall we hitchhike across the country?" he asked.

"You ought to have a different job," she repeated.

"I have a career. On the other hand, I'm strong. I could do manual labor."

"What about going to Washington? *I* want Washington!"

"Just for a change. You'd want it only a little while. Then Washington would pall, too. I think you need a new horse."

"I'm not joking. Why don't you ask Stonefort what's happening?"

"All right. I will." And Conrad walked quickly around Rosalie as she cleared the table, strode across the hallway to the telephone in the corner of the living room, looked up the senator's unlisted home number, and put through the call.

While he waited for the senator to come to the phone, Conrad heard the voices of a group of people in the background. He was momentarily embarrassed.

"Conrad," the senator asked forcefully, "how are you?"

"I'm fine. I hope you don't mind my calling you like this?"

"Certainly not."

"We haven't spoken since I was in your office. How are things coming on the bill."

Cautiously, the senator said, "Almost ready. But I have to sound out some more supporters before I take it to the floor."

The noise of voices in the background seemed more pronounced. "How's the political climate?"

The senator said, "Everybody's appalled by what happened in West Germany. Can you imagine? One of Willy Brandt's top aides turning out to be a spy for East Germany."

"Perfectly natural mistake," Conrad said somberly. "He saw a potentiality that wasn't there."

"What's that?"

"We see what we hope for."

"Well, I met Willy Brandt a number of times. A remarkably good man. His resignation means a terrible loss . . . I can't understand a mistake like that. A scandal. One of his top aides!"

"Is it true about Maryland *disbarring* former Vice President Agnew . . .?"

The senator was silent.

Conrad said, "I'm afraid I've interrupted a conference."

"That's all right."

"Let me know how things go with the bill."

"Of course. There's still a good chance. I'll keep you posted."

"Thanks. Good-bye."

Isabel was standing in the middle of the living room when he put down the phone. "You didn't say much about your going to Washington."

"You have to read between the lines. If there's to be a government job offered me in the foreseeable future it depends on Stonefort's pushing a bill for a new federal department. All I could gather is: he's not ready to and he wouldn't say why, or he *couldn't* because of whoever was there in the room with him."

"All right. It'll come sooner or later. Want an after-dinner drink?"

"Cognac. Please."

She poured the brandy into snifters and brought them to where Conrad remained in the S-curved love seat by the telephone. They faced each other. "You look so anxious. You're not sleeping enough." Conrad thought of telling her about the recommendation of the Search Committee but he had promised not to. "Why do you take everything so hard? I swear, I think you're even more upset by Tom's walking out on you than you are about Caroline."

Conrad held the cognac glass up to his lips with one hand and patted Isabel's arm with his other hand. He looked through the dark windows of the sun porch toward the lights of the house next door.

"What are you thinking?" she asked.

"Maybe we feel more sharply the loss of something we had no right to expect at all than we feel when we're deprived of something we have every right to expect."

"Darling," she sighed, "I don't follow."

"Well, maybe we're more hurt if an unexpected gift has been stolen away from us than . . ."

"Can't you be a little more direct?"

"I'll tell you a story." He looked at her golden hair, the smooth line of her jaw, the sapphire of her eyes, but he was trying to call up a distant memory. "According to one of Madame de Sévigné's letters," he began, pacing his speech slow, "the Duc de La Rochefoucauld was at Madame de La Fayette's on the night news came to Paris of the battle on the Rhine in which his eldest son and heir, the Prince de Marcillac, was wounded. He showed very little emotion. Then word arrived that the Comte de Saint-Paul, the son of the Duchesse de Longueville had been killed. He was their love child and La Rochefoucauld adored him. The duke restrained any expressions of his feelings. Only later, when word arrived that his fourth son, the Chevalier de Marcillac was dead, did he break down, dissolved in sorrow. He did not care for his son the chevalier, but it was because of him that he could weep openly for the loss of the Comte de Saint-Paul."

"You amaze me," Isabel exclaimed. "You literally make mazes for me to zigzag through in order to find your meaning." She was both in awe and chastising him at the same time. "Now, why couldn't you just have said, 'It's not that I'm taking Tom's leaving so hard, it's that his walking out reminds me of

326

how bitterly Caroline disappoints me, and that's what I'm grieving for'?"

Conrad answered with a smirk. "It wouldn't be half as civilized."

Alone in the living room, having put out all the lights, they made love on the carpet, without taking off all of their clothes—with an other than civilized intensity.

Miss Frangle visited the hospital the third day after Mrs. Todd was delivered of a son, and brought back to Conrad the most unexpected reward of his life, a handwritten letter from his former secretary which read:

Dear Mr. Taylor,

I don't know how to tell you this, so I'm going to blurt it out. It will probably sound crude and that is too bad because, if I learned one thing from working for you, it's how much you enjoy expressions of thoughts and feelings being "polished"—but I learned a great deal more, as well.

I've never respected anyone more than as much as I respect you. I'd never before seen at close quarters anyone carry out work that entailed so much responsibility, and I never imagined anyone could do it so fairly. That's why I admire you more than I do my parents or my teachers or anyone else I've ever known (with the exception of my husband—although I admire him for entirely different reasons).

I'm writing this in the hospital the second night after my baby was born. The lady in the other bed is asleep. I've said good night to my husband who was here all evening. We talked about what to name our son and he agreed with my desire to call him—Conrad. He will be Conrad Todd. Don't you think that sounds grand?! As he grows up—and all during his life—I'll be able to keep in mind the other Conrad—

Conrad Taylor—who is the model of what kind of man I hope he will become.

I cannot tell you how grateful I am to have worked for you—and to have been privileged to see how you work. I believe it will stay with me as long as I live: that combination of dignity and well-meaning and good spirits, all at the same time. Or rather, I believe now that I can tell you how grateful I am—by naming my first child Conrad. Please don't think this presumptuous of me. It is a greater way of showing my thanks than any other way I can show.

She signed the letter, "Your friend," and Conrad thought, I had a friend in her all this time and I did not know that; I had a secret friend. Otherwise, standing alone in the center of his study—holding the letter out at arm's length in order to read without his glasses on—he felt all his ability to articulate response had disappeared. He was dumbstruck, as if he'd lost the power of speech. He was elated—wordlessly—for he could not immediately relate this news to the rest of his life.

He had sent a check to Caroline at her address in Arizona but did not know whether it was received. She had not been in touch with him since sending the telegram, and he did not know what her baby—his grandson—was named. It certainly never had occurred to him that she might name the child "Conrad." It was not something he had ever thought about. And here he was disjointed with elation by the totally unexpected gift of gratitude from Mrs. Todd—whom he had never consciously tried to impress or influence or "win" for himself. Suddenly the idea of having a child named after oneself struck him as a profoundly basic human aspiration that had been smothered by all the arguments for the independence of one generation from another. A child named for you! If by someone you were conscious of having helped—a daughter, a protégé, perhaps—that would be appropriate; whereas he had not thought of Mrs. Todd in any such way. She worked for him and they worked well together, while all along she was mak-

*We invite you to visit our
two shops in Buccleuch Street,
open especially for students.*

text books

27-31 BUCCLEUCH STREET

Our textbook shop stocks
basic works in most subjects
housed in the David Hume
Tower and George Square.

Open an account there today.

paperbacks & stationery

7-11 BUCCLEUCH STREET

ing judgments of him, shoring up appreciation of him in a way that he was unconscious of. Should he have seen in her the potentiality for cultivation that he had mistaken in Tom Spofford? For her to have named the child "Conrad" was like being awarded first prize in a contest he was unaware of having entered.

Conrad Todd. Three days old. They would have the same initials! Conrad thought of presenting his carnelian cuff links to the infant as a gift for the future.

He had spent so much energy in caring about what people like Clifford Rostum or Senator Stonefort thought of him, brooding over what impressions his work had made on them, it had not occurred to Conrad he might be celebrated with such an expression of appreciation from someone who, in many ways, knew him better as a person than either of those men. The warmth of acknowledgment, of recognition—of acclaim, even—radiated through him. It gave him the well-being of a man who is at peace, who craves nothing more; one other human being, who had a sense of his worth, considered him a model for what a person should become.

He was fulfilled.

Tom Spofford appeared at the open door. "I've come to say good-bye."

Conrad turned the letter in his hand facedown on the desk. He thought of announcing, "Mrs. Todd's naming her baby after me!" But he repressed the urge, resenting Tom: he is too raw to know what can fulfill a man over fifty. Conrad held out his hand. "Let's shake, then, and let me wish you good luck."

"And good luck to you," Tom replied, as if he were an equal.

Conrad was reminded of how much respect he had lost for Tom, and how much that cost him in self-respect. "What are your plans?"

"Not quite sure yet. We'll take a vacation first. Go camping in the Berkshires. We're leaving tonight, as soon as Rhoda finishes work at the hotel."

"*The* hotel," Conrad repeated. That wiped the formal smile off his face.

"Yes."

Suddenly Conrad demanded, "Was it Rhoda who pasted up that letter about my wife and another man?"

Shamefaced, Tom admitted, "I did it. I'm sorry. Rhoda saw them together. I thought you ought to know."

"Why?"

Tom stared into Conrad's eyes, uncomprehending.

"Why did you think you ought to tell me anything of the sort?"

"I thought you had the right to know what other people knew."

"But you didn't think *you* had the right to tell me."

"I didn't?"

"That's why you sent an anonymous letter."

"Oh."

"You didn't want to be held responsible for your actions."

"I didn't want you to know that *I* knew."

"Because, if I did, I'd be embarrassed before you. I wouldn't be the man to look up to that you thought I ought to be?"

Quietly Tom said, "That you thought you ought to be."

Conrad scowled viciously. "You're a rotten kid. You're a sneak. You want more than you've earned, including knowledge of someone else's private life."

"I thought I was doing you a favor."

"You thought you were lording it over me. You wanted to hurt me and not own up to it. You didn't know how to mind your own business because you don't know what your own business is."

In a rapture of self-absorption, Tom said, "Maybe I wanted to get caught at it."

"Dr. Rosenblatt has given you an all-purpose alibi."

"I think I'd better go now."

"Yes. I believe you've got everything you could out of this situation. Damned little."

Tom was contrite. "I'm sorry."

"I'd like to believe that you are."

At dinner, Conrad called for celestial blessings on the occasion of naming Conrad Todd. Isabel was pleased for him but did not seem as impressed as he hoped she would be.

Kevin gratefully said, "It's been very good to be here. I thank you. It was just what I needed. But now it's time to leave."

"Already?" Isabel was sincere. "Are you ready to go? I'll miss you."

Conrad added, "So will I."

"And I'll miss all this. Your New England house. 'The Glorious East.' Especially this dining room. You've painted it exactly like the dining room in our house in Jamaica. . . . A long time ago. You even have the same groups of gloxinia in all four corners. Did you plan it this way deliberately?"

Isabel said, "Yes." She had never mentioned that to Conrad. Wonderful! her husband thought, how we are able to satisfy more than one need at the same time.

Kevin—as departing guest—laid out his plans. He would sell his car and leave by plane for Europe. He meant to canvass the existing organization for artists in seven or eight major countries there and if he generated enough enthusiasm for establishing International Artists for Peace and Prosperity, he'd carry on through the Mideast and the Far East, on his way back around the world to California.

Conrad slumped in his chair, silently thinking that Kevin was a throwback to the personalities who believed they could stop wars by personal diplomacy—Henry Ford's Peace Ship in 1914, William Benton against the Nazis. Hadn't Kevin once retraced the footsteps of Jesus?

"Incidentally," Kevin added, "I'm taking a souvenir of New Haven with me," as casually as if he had in mind absconding with the pair of white porcelain candlesticks on the dark blue tablecloth.

"What?" Isabel asked.

"The art student I met."

"Oh . . ." Isabel's tone was a mixture of amusement, remembering the Israeli camel driver—and of apprehension.

Kevin laughed. "I need someone to carry my bags and arrange reservations."

"What will you do with him when you get back to California?" Conrad asked—remembering Yato and his tiny wife.

"You forget he's an art student."

Isabel urged him: "Bring him over first. Let's meet."

"No. I suggested that. He'd rather not. He's shy. Besides, he knows who you are. You met some time ago."

"We did?" Conrad asked. "What's his name?"

With a certain pride of appropriation, Kevin answered, "Christian Kirkill."

Conrad said, "I don't believe it!" and instantly regretted not controlling himself.

"He told me you don't approve of him. He's very sensitive, and very talented."

He must be, Conrad assumed, to act out this new role so convincingly. "It's not a question of approval," Conrad began, but he could not let himself tell his brother-in-law that he didn't trust Christian, that he considered Christian untrustworthy, an opportunist. "Will he work in the house for you?" was all Conrad let himself say.

"Well, he'll be an apprentice in the studio. He draws very well. He wants to learn how to sculpt."

He wants a free ride, Conrad imagined, for a few weeks or a few months. But then we have no right to judge what's good for someone else—we don't know what's best even for ourselves.

In the dark, they lay in bed side by side, barely touching. Conrad said, "I'm sorry for Kevin."

"You shouldn't be. He isn't sorry for himself."

"Perhaps we could have done better by him while he was with us."

"That wasn't in our power."

Conrad moaned. "It seems I'm being shown more frequently than ever what the limits of my powers are."

Isabel sighed. "It isn't in my power to give you a son who could be named after you."

Conrad reached for her hand and held it in his. "I understand that. I don't ask for that."

"But you must have thought about it, when Mrs. Todd . . ."

"I didn't think about it at all."

"Are we never going to know what each other is thinking?"

In a measured cadence and self-deprecating tone, Conrad said, "I know you are more thoughtful for me than I would have given you credit for."

With compassion, not putting him down, Isabel said, "I know you are uncomfortable when you are not in command of a situation."

He laughed. "One doesn't always have to be comfortable."

Like the teacher's pet, she demanded, "What does one *always* have to be?"

"Able to recover."

For dinner at the Baird-Lloyds in New York, the Taylors took Walter Webster and Jerry Rosenblatt in their car. Mrs. Rosenblatt chose not to come.

The Baird-Lloyd mansion on Fifth Avenue, just north of the Metropolitan Museum of Art, had been built by the grandfather of the banker's wife in the 1880s. It was a Venetian palazzo in Vermont granite; the sculptured casements around each window rose to a flaming point in the gray stone. Waiting to enter, the group stood under a permanent awning of fluted glass. When both the double doors were open, the entrance was wide enough for all four of them to enter abreast. Somehow, instantly amused by that idea, all of them locked arms and passed through the doorway in unanticipated good humor.

The first impression of the house was that nothing in it could have been changed since it was first occupied. There was dark oak furniture in the baronial hall, a huge Oriental rug on the floor, massive mirrors, a tapestry worthy of Maria de Medici, and a full-length statue in medieval armor holding a jousting spear. Jerry Rosenblatt stared at it. "They always make me think of skeletons in medical school."

Walter Webster said, "You know, this country is so new—even the family skeletons had to be imported."

The butler led the way up the stairs, to a sitting room where most of the other guests awaited them. A maid moved about carrying a tray of glasses filled with champagne or orange juice. "How European," Conrad whispered, and Isabel responded, "New Yorkers are discovering the joy of *not* getting drunk before dinner."

Conrad pretended shock. "I hope it doesn't catch on."

The room was so large it was difficult to estimate how many people were present. At least, it was not dark and weighty and pseudoantique in the way the hall had been. The walls were white with gilt-framed panels between high windows; the chairs and sofas were delicate looking, though hard to sit on, and covered with elaborate floral designs in needlepoint. It reminded Conrad of pictures he had seen of drawing rooms in Buckingham Palace. Professor Evats was there in his perennial grays and shiny bald head; his Czechoslovakian wife stood slightly before him as if to keep him from harm. She talked with Mrs. Marvin Flower. David Bach brought his new wife—a girl of eighteen, who was all eyes, apparently having just awakened into a fairy tale. Mrs. Baird-Lloyd, the descendant of Peter Stuyvesant, looked as though she disguised a barrel under her black lace evening gown—a very heavy woman, whose small head and thin arms bore no relation to the heft of her torso. Her white hair, swept up into a high pompadour, had been tinted blue. In greeting them she explained that the host, whom she referred to as "Baird-Lloyd," was showing the gallery to Professor Flower and Mrs. von Bickersdorf. She then introduced Mr. and Mrs. Grant Hannover to the Taylors. Gregory Blackwell and his wife stared out of a window at the evening traffic on Fifth Avenue and toward the trees of Central Park.

The conversation centered on the fact that the President of the United States was about to spend much of the month of June abroad. "He's off to the Middle East, Brussels, and then Moscow," Walter Webster said.

"And why not?" Jerry Rosenblatt asked. "Nixon's last fling. He's doomed."

Mrs. Blackwell tore herself away from the view. "Oh, I wouldn't say that. What a terrible thing to say! He's on a diplomatic mission. Nobody knows if he'll be impeached. You have to keep an open mind."

"Would you buy a used country from a salesman like that?" Conrad asked.

Only David Bach thought it was funny.

Mr. Baird-Lloyd arrived with Brita; Marvin Flower entered the room behind them muttering, "Oh, woe, woe."

Conrad studied the Grant Hannovers. He stood erect, tall, and well made, in an elegant dinner jacket of black velvet. His dark hair was clipped in a dome close to his head and led down to the narrow chin beard that circled his strong jaw. He made Conrad think of the nobleman in the French film of a generation ago—*Les Enfants du Paradis*—the aristocrat who married the actress and ends up murdered in a fashionable Turkish bath. Mrs. Hannover was pretty: petite with a peaches-and-cream complexion, dressed in mauve satin, clutching a silvery metallic handbag out of the 1920s. She could not conceal the somewhat haunted look of a person who has always been expected to put herself forward more than she felt equal to.

No further round of drinks was offered after all of the guests had assembled, and the host led them back downstairs to dinner, with Mrs. Blackwell on his arm. The dining room was completely unexpected. It had all the grandeur of a banquet hall, but it had been "renovated," modernized. The seventeen for dinner were seated around a large squarish table covered by an immense white linen tablecloth, under what only could be called spotlights—aluminum cones along steel rods on the ceiling, which threw dramatic circles of light, interlocking along the table, shining brilliantly on the silver, the porcelain, the crystal. It was as though a Broadway set designer had been hired by mistake, instead of an interior decorator, and he had produced an atmosphere for operatic arias with no apparent appreciation of the kind of people the Baird-Lloyds were or the kind of guests they were likely to entertain. The Baird-Lloyds seemed to be lost in this mistaken decor: she sat between strangers at one end of the table opposite him. He continued to impress Conrad as the image of a corpse, colorless, waxen; the flesh around his lips was faintly blue; though Walter Webster had called him wily. The table was so large that even with four or five chairs on each of the four sides—brass chairs with doeskin-covered seats—one could stretch out an arm at full length and barely touch the shoulder of the person next to you. Conrad was seated between Mrs. Marvin Flower and Brita von Bickersdorf. There were name cards. At each table setting, an inscribed guest's name had been slipped into a small, silver, rectangular frame, which made Conrad think of the labels before bushes and trees in a botanical garden.

The sequence of conversation at table followed the pattern that Conrad had observed at any number of ceremonial dinners connected with university functions at which the wives or husbands of the faculty or staff members were also present. The ladies would ask the gentlemen next to them questions expressing some interest in their professional concerns. Mrs. Hannover, at the moment, asked Marvin Flower whether he preferred teaching to writing, and he was launched on an assessment of the proportion of the time that he thought one impeded or contributed to the other. Then the scholar or administrator would arrive at the awareness that the person who'd asked the question either did not follow or couldn't care less about the answer, at which point he asked her about her renowned garden or her children or how the summer house she and her husband planned to build was coming along. Conrad listened to David Bach at the moment actually asking Mrs. Blackwell whether the fritillary bulbs she'd imported from Holland last fall bloomed in her garden this spring. With seventeen people at the table, there were at least eight separate conversations being carried on at the same time. Only when Clifford Rostum was in charge, host at his own table, would he strike the wineglass with a knife and demand, "*One* conversation, please." Isabel always resented that; it meant shop talk for the men and silence from the women. At a dinner party Conrad and she had given at their own home once, as Isabel became aware that everyone was focusing on what she and Judge Jackman were talking about, she struck her wineglass with a knife and called for, "*Six* conversations, please!"

Opposite him, Conrad could see Grant Hannover trying to sound out Isabel with the usual familial and domestic questions, regarding her appraisingly. He was a good-looking man with long dimples on each side of an open smile—like long parentheses that appeared and disappeared in the vivacity of his facial expressions. Conrad turned to Mrs. Flower, on his right, to ask how the building of their summer house was coming along; then, with relief, he could turn to Brita, on his left, and listen to strong, sharp comments about her current experiences at the United Nations. The food was excellent and there was too much of it; the servants moved soundlessly in and out of the room, bringing and taking away one course after another, filling and refilling the glasses. It appeared as though it would be one of those evenings in which nothing is articulated and everyone is left with the frustrated assumption that some function had been performed, some ceremony carried out, although no one had given a name to it. But, when

337

cheese and fruit had been served, and the port was being poured, Mr. Baird-Lloyd stood up and called for attention so that he could propose a toast.

"My wife and I appreciate your having accepted our invitation for this evening," he began. "This is our modest way of showing thanks—on behalf of the Board of Trustees—to all of you who have labored long and hard on the Search Committee in the duty of helping President Blackwell find a successor to Clifford Rostum as provost." There was an instant of silence in memory of Cliff Rostum. "The committee has done its work. It has presented the president with two recommendations—of the highest order of eligibility—and both of those candidates are here with us this evening. I wish to express my thanks to the members of the Search Committee, my congratulations to the two men who have been recommended, my best wishes to the president in his further deliberations, and, as ever, my love of the university—for whose glory we all do whatever we can." He raised his glass, everyone else stood up, raised glasses, sipped the port, and sat down again while Baird-Lloyd alone remained standing. Isabel caught Conrad's eye and winked.

The host, for all his deadly pallor, allowed a calculated, tight-lipped smile to crease his face. "The glory of the university resides first and foremost in the education that it offers." He paused to let that debatable point sink in. "My grandfather used to say to me," he continued, "that one measure of an educated man is that, if he is called upon to make an after-dinner speech, he can do so at a moment's notice—as long as he's given a topic." He chuckled. "He told me what the secret of success is. Since any educated person knows *something*, he can always turn the topic around to whatever he knows something about. For example—if he is a structural engineer, and he's asked to talk on the topic of shooting elephants, all he has to do is start out by saying, 'Shooting an elephant is not the same as building a bridge.' And then go on to talk about how to build a bridge." Everyone laughed.

"We have with us this evening two well-educated men, whom I would like to call upon to give us after-dinner speeches: Mr. Taylor and Mr. Hannover." Conrad was startled; he would have to sing for his supper, with no forewarning. Baird-Lloyd nodded from one of them to the other. Grant Hannover was smiling at the host, contentedly. "These are the candidates the Search Committee have recommended for consideration for provost. I offer as topic—'The Nature of the University.' Let's see you think on your feet! Grant Hannover," he commanded first, with a flourish of his waxen hand, as he sat down.

The heir to a real-estate and a newspaper fortune, publisher of the *Chicago Times-Herald*, husband of a Du Pont, flier of his own plane, stood up, erect, slightly amused, moved around his chair and rested his hands on the back of it. "Ladies and gentlemen," he began, turning his gaze from side to side, "the university," he said slowly, "is not like shooting an elephant." Everyone but Conrad chuckled. Walter Webster applauded.

"I'll tell you what else the university is not," Grant Hannover went on. "The university is not a school." Conrad felt the hairs at his nape begin to stand on end; he stroked the back of his neck. "The university is not a school, because it incorporates many schools within its realm, and many conditions for research and discovery that are nowhere near representing the single-minded purpose that characterizes a school. It is the richest resource for mental innovation, for experiment, for investigation and speculation—a fruitful diversity whose main character is its good intentions for intellectual curiosity, its respect for variety in the life of the mind, and its support for the interests of genuine scholars no matter how seemingly obscure their interests may be." He paused, he looked to Gregory Blackwell at one end of the table, to Mr. Evats at the other end, and then leveled his gaze on Conrad Taylor seated opposite him. "The key term," he said to him, "is *resources*. For the riches of the university which I referred to are to be found in the knowledge and wisdom of the faculty, the wealth of conditions for learning in the libraries and the laboratories, the intelligence the students find in their fellow students. And the function of education is to learn how to make the best use of one's resources—through one's own assets and the powers put at one's disposal by the university. The aim is always toward achieving The Best: the best results from what you've taken command of from your resources. If learning can be measured, the gauge of it is: how well have you come to use your own assets and the resources made available to you. This, then, is the essence of the university: that it makes possible for the scholar-teacher the opportunity to make the greatest possible use of native talent and interest; and for the student to be introduced to and indoctrinated in how best to make use of native and communal resources. The success of the university can be measured by the degree of efficiency in the use of all of its resources, of its faculty and staff in the present, and of its students and graduates in the future. It is the role of its leaders and administrators to maintain that goal. And more power to them!" Grant Hannover broke into a broad smile, gazed from side to side, bowed his head slightly—more to indicate, Conrad thought, that he had terminated, than that he had concluded. All of his listeners applauded. Hannover tossed his hand forward, with a gesture of challenge, indicating that it was Conrad's turn, and sat down.

Conrad Taylor rose slowly. One of the waiters pulled the chair back behind him. Conrad rested his fingertips on the edge of the table before him, spread his feet apart, stood firmly. "Ladies and gentlemen," he began. "The university is not a school," he agreed, nodding to the operator, the manipulator, "but it is a seat of learning. There are different things to be learned; some are taught explicitly and some indirectly, implicitly."

He paused. He was in no hurry. He felt the attention rapt. "A generation ago, a student here in New York tried to sue Columbia University for misrepresentation. He argued that he

340

had enrolled to learn wisdom but all the university offered to teach was knowledge. He wanted his tuition money back. He did *not* win the case." The audience chuckled.

"It is acquired knowledge, and the methods of discovering what may come to be accepted as knowledge, that the university offers to teach explicitly. That would appear to be exclusively an intellectual enterprise, the total academic endeavor. But there is more to it than that. The moral and aesthetic dimensions of learning—the ethics of scholarship—are what is taught indirectly, more by example, by the performances of the models to be emulated, than by directives. For the ground rules of scholarly discourse are all unwritten. The thinker does not operate in a vacuum; his peers, his superiors, and the highest authorities in his field make up the human context in which his work is developed and tested—and appreciated."

Conrad's eyes turned from Gregory Blackwell, to Marvin Flower, to Brita von Bickersdorf, to David Bach. "I believe that the professors of our university who are present tonight will confirm my belief that this interdependence constitutes the social nature of the world of learning. And its psychological principle may be reduced to one question: by whom do you wish to be appreciated?

"Let me begin again. Not long ago I read a work of cultural history called *The Diffusion of Civility*—a translation from the German. It shows how the manners of the courts of eighteenth-century principalities vied with each other in cultivating their individual styles, how some came to predominate, and how their set of styles was imitated and spread wider and wider along the social scale. Styles of government, of dress, of table manners, of conversation, even of courtship. Any style is an expression of values and of power, or—as Mr. Hannover put it—of interests. A leader is one who initiates or sustains such a style and whom others emulate, because, by conforming to his values, they hope to receive his approval.

"I submit that there is an analogy between the social and political world described in *The Diffusion of Civility* and the moral world of the university. Students try to achieve the recognition of those they admire, the leaders of their field, by doing things in their style. The leaders—in whatever seat of learning—are the authorities in their subjects by virtue of their erudition and the originality of their thought; it is they who set the standards to be maintained. The diffusion of the style of scholarship in any field is what takes place indirectly, by good example. Through it one learns how to be intellectually honorable. In contrast to personal ambition, it cultivates ambition for the enhancement of the field of study one hopes to serve. That alone can save one from abusing his assets or taking unfair advantage of his resources. One must be accurate about facts; one must know where other people's ideas end and one's own begin; one must be happy to make one's hypotheses or theories available to others for their evaluation.

"All of this is the learning of scholarly fairness. Leaders in their fields have no higher authorities to appeal to. They must—as all of us must in the other parts of our lives—depend on their own self-criticism. They are not leaders because of military or political power, because of wealth or charm. They are simply those who understand more or appreciate better what it is.they study. To help bring the best out of any potential scholar is a purpose of the university, but to 'deliver' it through the methods that conform to the intellectual standards of scholarship is another purpose. The morality of that style is the closest approximation to wisdom that the purveyor of knowledge can aspire to teach. It is born of, and imbedded in, the respect of one human mind for another; and, while that cannot be taught, if one has any sense of it to begin with, it can be cultivated: which is the ultimate function to be performed by the university." Conrad added, "I thank you," to the hushed audience, and sat down.

It was Marvin Flower who shouted, "Bravo!"

Conrad looked at Isabel and saw in her gaze that she took pride in him. The rest of the guests applauded enthusiastically.

Mr. Baird-Lloyd expressed his heartfelt appreciation that a good education "pays off" in two such fine after-dinner speeches and then bade them to coffee in the library. Mrs. Baird-Lloyd led the way across the hall.

As large as the sitting room above it on the second floor, the library ran the length of the house along the Avenue, with a view of Central Park. The books on the inner wall were divided by generations: there was a section of contemporary works that the host and hostess must have bought for themselves; there were the complete works of revered authors that had been the gathering of her parents; and there were the valuable first editions in leather-bound boxes that Mrs. Baird-Lloyd's grandfather had not only treasured but read.

A maid served Turkish coffee in china demitasses, each differently decorated. As the guests gradually filed into the room, Conrad overheard Mrs. Baird-Lloyd talking of her eldest son to Mrs. Blackwell. "He's at the Berlin branch of the Clayton Bank. They've just had their first child. His idea of saving money is to fly to London when he sees an ad for baby carriages on sale. Would you believe it? He actually did it!"

David Bach said to Brita von Bickersdorf, "Well, I suppose Mr. Nixon is one of the few people in the whole world who can go to both Cairo and Jerusalem."

"Publicly," she added.

Isabel approached Conrad. She neither kissed him nor stroked his arm; they did not show affection "publicly," and said, "It was a wonderful speech."

"Thank you." He knew that she thought well of him and he felt prepared for whatever else might happen next. He had yet to see Hannover enter the room.

Mrs. Evats was asking Jerry Rosenblatt about Brom Kirkill. ". . . in a terrible state," she said. "Didn't you know? His wife ran off with one of his students, and now his son's involved with some sculptor who's practically kidnapped him."

Dr. Rosenblatt said, "No, I didn't know."

"I think he's headed for a nervous breakdown."

Jerry Rosenblatt's eyes wandered the room for a route of escape. "When did you see Brom last?"

Mrs. Evats said, "At eleven this morning."

"Well," Dr. Rosenblatt said, "maybe he's had the break-down by now," and moved away to talk with Marvin Flower, who was gaping at the leather-boxed first editions.

Conrad took a cup of coffee, made his way to a far end of the room, and sat down in the corner of a large cushioned sofa. Grant Hannover materialized before him and asked, "May I join you?"

"Of course."

Like a tough small boy, who has played his prank, caught—as he had planned to be—with his hand in the cash register or with the evidence that he had cheated on an exam, Grant Hannover bluffly asked, "Are you very angry with me?"

"No." Conrad thought it peculiar that he could feel contempt without being angry; he was not amused. What he said was, "I'm always impressed by a general statement that embodies its own specific example. You use the resources at your disposal most efficiently."

"Isn't it funny that only you could have understood all of my speech?" He placed his empty coffee cup on the end table next to the sofa.

"And you mine," Conrad replied.

Grant Hannover smiled sheepishly. "Isn't imitation supposed to be the highest form of flattery?"

"Yes. But it's not a compliment." Grant Hannover made no comment. "Tell me," Conrad continued comfortably, "what would you have done if I had been asked to speak first, and if I had made most of the statements that you—presented?"

"Oh, I had another card of notes. I would have switched to the other line."

"I see. Very resourceful. Very well prepared."

"Your wife is as charming as she is beautiful," Hannover said.

"So is Eleanor Saunders," Conrad replied, and then abruptly stated, "I had no idea you wanted to be provost."

"Neither did I. It came as quite a surprise to me, too."

Conrad asked, "Did you listen to the whole tape?"

"Enough."

"First-rate reporter—Eleanor Saunders."

Grant Hannover agreed. "First-rate. Been working for me five years."

"Would you be willing to give all that up?"

"New challenges!" Grant Hannover whispered intensely. "That's what excites me. Taking on new challenges. That's what life is all about, isn't it?"

"A happy warrior," Conrad said. He did not find it easy to dislike the man, although he was appalled by him.

"I'm a happy man," Grant Hannover countered modestly.

"My dear!" Mrs. Baird-Lloyd barked out, looming above them, "you must come settle this argument about Chicago that your wife is having with Walter Webster—something about the Art Institute." She took Grant Hannover by the hand and led him away.

"Excuse me, please," he said over his shoulder to Conrad, now like a polite child who wished to endear himself.

Conrad reclined in the corner of the comfortable sofa, gazing at the separate knots of humanity disposed about the room, stroking or pulling away from each other, feeling he had been left with one detail of significance only: Grant Hannover knew he would be called upon to give an after-dinner speech; Conrad did not know. Baird-Lloyd had forewarned Hannover but not Conrad. He was not quite ready to see the fullest implication of that fact. He simply focused on the detail—the way, at the moment, he regarded Baird-Lloyd—merely centering all of his attention on the left ear in which was located a snail-like plastic hearing aid. Gradually, only very gradually, the larger impression of the whole man developed into the fullness of perception that he was Baird-Lloyd. By the same token, very slowly, Conrad was able to see from the single detail that Grant Hannover had brought with him notes for two possible after-dinner speeches that Baird-Lloyd wanted Hannover as provost. The idea did not crush him, although

345

the discovery was a distasteful surprise. Baird-Lloyd had told
Grant Hannover he would be called on, and not told Conrad.
It was as simple as that. And now Conrad Taylor was watching
Baird-Lloyd whispering into the ear of Gregory Blackwell. He
felt abysmally tired. He was glad to be sitting down; he
wanted to go away.

They fulfilled their duties. Isabel and Conrad drove Walter
Webster and Jerry Rosenblatt to their homes and then, finally,
reached Hillhouse Avenue themselves. Just before they got
out of the car, Conrad said, "I don't believe I'm going to be
offered the provostship."

"Attacked by swans?" Isabel asked.

"Something like that."

"Good!" Isabel was cheerful. "Let's go to Washington!"

"Let's go to bed."

Instead of tennis and lunch the following Monday at noon-
time, Conrad left his office, walked through the quadrangle,
out the gate that faced the Green, and across it to Henry Warner's store. He was planning to visit Mrs. Todd, back in her
apartment now, and to see Conrad Todd for the first time. He
had the pair of initialed carnelian cuff links in a trouser pocket
of his tan gabardine suit. But he wanted something more as a
present for the infant's parents.

Browsing through the elegant store, his eye was caught by
what appeared to be a stack of eight scallop-edged salad plates
with some green olives and two stalks of celery on the surface
of the top plate. It turned out to be a cookie jar of Italian
pottery, a trompe l'oeil, a visual double entendre—which delighted him. While the salesman tallied up the charge, he
wrote on the card to go with it: "May your plate never be
empty." And then asked to have the cuff links boxed separately as another gift. "I'm afraid I can't put them in a Warner
and Son box," the salesman said.

"Do you have one without a name in it?"

"I'll try to find one, sir, if you'll excuse me . . ."

Alone at the counter, he heard "Conrad!" called out from behind him and turned to see Henry Warner approaching from the staircase. "What a good idea—starting to spend that million-dollar gift in your honor right here. . . ."

"Fat chance," Conrad replied.

"Are you being taken care of?"

"Yes. Very well indeed."

"I'm just off to lunch."

"Instead of golf?"

"Not today. But we'll see each other at the Connolleys' later in the week—right?"

"Yes." Conrad had forgotten about the birthday party for his friend Warner that the Connolleys had invited them to weeks before. But, of course, they would be there.

They signaled good-bye to each other. The salesman returned, holding an anonymous black jewel box, with white satin inside the lid and black velvet along the bottom of it. "That's perfect," Conrad said thankfully, laid the cuff links into it, and snapped it shut. "If you'd wrap both of them as gifts, I'd be very much obliged. I'll even pay for them."

On Tuesday the boom fell—twice. First in the president's office. Gregory Blackwell postponed the weekly staff meeting and asked to see Conrad alone, at eleven that morning. He entered the president's office on a balmy June morning; all the windows were open. A bough of flowering dogwood stood in a pewter vase on the floor in front of the empty fireplace, and the two men seated themselves facing each other on opposite sides of the hearth. Silent for a few moments, Blackwell, more than a little uneasy, announced, "I'm going to recommend to the trustees that Grant Hannover succeed Cliff Rostum as provost."

Conrad said only, "I see."

"No, you don't," the older man retorted edgily. "Even I'm

not perfectly clear about why I'm doing this, but I'll try to explain." He crossed his legs; he wove his fingers together and pressed his hands against the vest of his blue suit. "From where I sit, there are two kinds of problems: the internal organization and operation of the university—and the relationship between the university and the rest of the world. We have to maintain excellence internally in order to justify the financial support that we need from outside.

"You are of inestimable value in contributing to the way the university is organized and operated, self-critical and self-evaluating, vigorous in its internal watchdogging. I don't want to lose that! And I don't want the problem of having to find someone to replace you to be in charge of the college.

"But we're in a deficit position. We need to raise much more endowment money annually than we've been doing. I need someone to help me raise money more than this university needs someone to keep it running well inside. I think Grant Hannover can do that. He'll be a new face in the academic world. He has the right connections. He's ambitious."

Conrad stared at Blackwell, thinking: Clifford Rostum deserted you, but you need someone to tell you what to do, and so you have fallen into the clutches of the honorable Baird-Lloyd. Nevertheless, your days are numbered and Hannover's are unpredictable. What is he after next? A governorship? Head of the Ford Foundation? To be appointed an ambassador? This is an interim, isn't it, just a few years before a whole New Team takes over?

"I want . . ." Blackwell continued, "Grant Hannover—so as to help me as much as possible on the fund-raising frontier."

Conrad had an instantaneous impression of the two of them as Lewis and Clark discovering the Northwest.

"But I don't want to lose you," Blackwell continued. "Moreover, Mr. Hannover has made it clear that he sees no way of accepting the offer—if it's made to him—unless he has the assurance that you will stay on."

"Oh," was the flat sound with which Conrad punctuated the

pause—in a tone between personal surprise and objective curiosity.

"I hope you understand why I've reached this conclusion," Blackwell said tentatively.

"I understand," Conrad reassured him. Because you want it both ways—a new face to help you to raise funds, a new name as provost with all sorts of unusual panache, while the actual work that the provost should be performing "internally" becomes part of my job without its being spelled out.

"Of course," Blackwell went on, as if reading his mind, "it would mean an increase in your responsibilities and a concomitant increase in your salary."

Conrad couldn't keep himself from saying, "A bad precedent."

"Don't let that bother you. Such arrangements are always flexible."

"I suppose so." Meaning: errors can be corrected in the next administration.

"You must know how I value your devotion to the university."

Conrad said, "Please don't . . ." Suddenly wondering if this interview was being taped, to be played back at future private consultations.

"Conrad," Blackwell started up again, "Grant's here with us now. He's in the next room. He'd like to talk with you. Let me bring him in. Is that all right?"

"Surely."

In a moment, dressed in gray flannel and a university necktie, no less, Grant Hannover's dimples and chin beard, his verve and cleverness, swept into the room. Smiling, he shook hands. The aging, self-effacing Nobel Prize president excused himself.

"I understand you're willing to become the next provost," Conrad said, as Grant Hannover lowered himself into the armchair where Gregory Blackwell had been sitting.

"Only if you'll help me," he replied.

349

"How?"

"I think I know how to improve the university's image with the outside world, and how to raise the money that's needed. But you alone can keep order and equilibrium inside or show me how to make it better—because I don't know A from B as far as that's concerned."

"You want me to be your adviser for university affairs?"

"My mentor, my teacher, my guide!"

"What makes you think you can't do it on your own?"

"I don't know the ropes. I know a lot about public relations, about publicity and public information, about fund raising and alumni interest—but I don't know shit about the faculty or curriculum; I don't know a tinker's damn about personnel policies."

"You haven't tried yet."

"I couldn't make it. I don't have the fine tuning it takes. If I heard about a homosexual who wanted to take off six months to go back to his lover in France, or a guy who'd plagiarized a book, or a kleptomaniac—I would have fired each one of them on the spot. I don't know how to handle problems like that."

So you know about all of them, do you? Conrad thought. And you feel called upon to prove your powers to me with three *more* examples of the efficient use of your resources. It pained him only to think that Jerry Rosenblatt must have betrayed him. Walter Webster had probably been lured into sharing a confidence; St. Cyr had probably blabbed about his own situation, once he had the promise of a new job; but only Dr. Rosenblatt and he knew about Tom Spofford's problem.

Conrad asked, with all the coolness of a disinterested observer, "Are you trying to win me, or get rid of me?"

"I'm trying to tell you," Hannover answered hurriedly, "that I've been finding out about things I've never had to cope with before, and that I wouldn't know how to handle—without advice from someone like you."

Someone *like* me? Conrad wondered, or *me?* What he said was, "Would you take the job if you knew I'd quit?"

"No."

So he knows my wife is wealthy, Conrad thought, that I can live without keeping my position here. At the Baird-Lloyds' dinner he showed me how he could make use of his powers—he wanted me to take the measure of those "assets"—and now he is showing me his needs, his estimation of the degree of help he must call for. He is asking for my aid because he wants the status of being provost without all the responsibility. He wants it only as a stepping-stone, not as an end in itself. He wants to make use of it for how long? two years? three years? He is an operator on his way to someplace else. He is a transient, and I am a stalwart.

As if suddenly embarrassed by memory of his speech at the Baird-Lloyds', Grant Hannover asked, "Will you forgive me . . .?"

Conrad wished he could say, Would a strapping in the woodshed make things all right? He merely nodded affirmatively, reserving his words to himself.

"Then you will stay!" Hannover concluded.

Conrad held up a hand in the sign of: Halt. "I'll think about it," he agreed.

"How long?" Hannover asked with a smile.

Some years ago, Conrad remembered, Clifford Rostum had told him: on decisions that you'll have to live with for twenty years, wait at least forty-eight hours; on those that matter for the next five years—at least twenty-four hours.

Conrad said, "Twenty-four hours."

Hannover nearly shouted, "That's a deal!" as he stood up and firmly shook Conrad's hand again. "I'll be back in Chicago by then. I'll expect to hear from you."

"You will."

Conrad Taylor closed the door of his office-study behind him, remained standing in the stillness of his isolation, his privacy, wondering what to think next, wondering what news his mind would bring to him. On his desk there were inter-office memos to read, forms for signature, reports, outside correspondence, bills, newspapers, magazines, journals. He turned his back on them and moved over to the silk brocade wall hanging, drew it aside, looked at the stylized portrait of La Rochefoucauld and thought, Like a crab, one must go sideways, sometimes, in order to get ahead. And yet, he did not suffer the passion to get ahead. He would have preferred simply for things to have remained as they were—but immediately recognized the delusion in hoping that things might ever be allowed to remain as they are. The intercom buzzer sounded. He let the wall hanging drop back into place, and walked across to the telephone.

Miss Frangle announced a call from Senator Stonefort.

Conrad pressed the lighted button. "Hello, Bill."

A female voice said, "Just a moment for Senator Stonefort."

As they exchanged greetings and asked after each other's family, Conrad listened to the muffled tones of old Stoneface's restraint; he was not ebullient, he was not his hearty self. He was in low spirits. Soon he got to the point: "On the bill for the Department of Culture . . . I just can't rally enough support to take it to the floor."

Conrad said, "I'm sorry," but he was indifferent.

"You labored so hard and well for it . . ."

"I have no pride of authorship about that; don't give it a second thought."

"It's not that *I* haven't worked like a dog, and the White House damned well knows it! But . . . the climate here, right now, is so *down* on Nixon, there's no predicting what will happen next."

"He's getting a great reception in Egypt," Conrad said, glancing at the newspaper headlines on his desk.

Sourly, the senator said, "The Egyptian vote doesn't count here."

After a pause, Conrad could think only of, "So the bill is dead?"

"On ice. For a while. No way of knowing what the climate

will be at the end of the summer or six months from now. The whole situation could turn around any minute."

How? Conrad wondered. Has Nixon ever considered becoming a Cistercian monk? He said, "Yes, of course."

"In the meanwhile, there is an interim suggestion. That is, there's a possibility we could get some mileage out of a sort of compromise. If we can't gather enough support to establish a new department and a Cabinet post, we could go the route of setting up a Bureau of American Culture by executive order, without a Congressional vote."

"I see."

"I'll be talking with people at the White House about it."

"Yes."

"What I want to know is whether you'd be willing to run it, if I can get it off the ground."

"Where?"

"Here in Washington, of course."

"You'll have to let me know more about it. What you'd expect me to do with it, what kind of budget it would be given, how long I'd be expected to commit myself for . . ."

"Yes. Yes. It would be a lot more modest than the department would be, but it still might throw some weight around."

"On behalf of American culture?"

"On behalf of the Administration, you clodhopper."

Both of them laughed, but there was no pleasure in it.

"I'll be honest with you," Conrad said, "there are new developments here, coming to a head right now. I can't be of any help—for a few days, at least. I'll get back to you, and we can talk more about this in a couple of days. Okay?"

"All right. Life is full of surprises, isn't it?" the senator concluded.

"Too full."

So, there was a choice to be made. But as a Viennese purist once wrote: When given the choice of the lesser of two evils, choose neither. Support Grant Hannover or support the Nixon

Administration. And the alternative to both is what? Conrad sensed only that, in the jigsaw puzzle supposed to show him the portrait of himself, all the pieces had come loose and were gradually moving farther and farther away from supporting a center; would the center be missing forever? Isabel was off to Boston with Ellen Connolley to visit Ellen's mother and to see polo games. The maid and the cook were out. He planned to have dinner alone at the Faculty Club. No one home, and the person at the center cannot see the center. But, then, this is the world I love, he told himself. This is the life I can be "at home" in, even if I am alone. What would become of me if I were to take a temporary job in Washington? What flag would fly at half-mast if I died?

It is not a question of having a job; of course, I can always get some job. It is a question of whether or not you have the luck to live with what you love. Conrad recognized that he loved doing what he did and being where he was more than he loved Isabel—which was only a confession that he approved of himself. But, then, if he didn't, he would not be any good for someone else, no matter where he was. If he went to Washington, in one situation or another, it would be merely temporary and it would please Isabel even more temporarily—although there is so little in life that is not only temporary.

Conrad recognized that he could not be better off. He had no ambition for something different, either for the sake of change itself or for Grant Hannover's "challenges." It was like recognizing the foolishness of the sex manuals that promise you "a better sex life," when what matters is only whether it is good or not. It is like the foolishness of Caroline wanting to keep in touch with the "depths of her existence" when it is the surface that is of greatest importance. All the mythological make-believe is only for compensation when the surface of life is not good.

And if this surface is lost to me? Conrad considered—what depth is there to fall into? Isabel says, "It's so silly of you to identify yourself with what you do; it's what you are that counts." But the two are related as a theme and its variations: your theme and your variations. The relationship between what you are and what you do is like the relation between a score of music and performances of it—when each performance must result in a variation. One cannot know the score unless the music is played.

He looked out of his study window at the statue of the first president of the university. No one raises statues to commemorate anybody anymore. Conrad did not long to become a statue in the quadrangle. What did he long for? To be of as much value—and to enjoy himself as much in doing it—next year, as last year. He was on his plateau, and if that degree of self-satisfaction had to be bought, for an interim period, by acting as secret provost within the university while Grant Hannover was public provost outside the university—that was not too high a price to pay. It's a lucky man who knows what he loves as clearly as that. And still, and still—there was a drawback.

He would be in the service of an unscrupulous man. Compromised. He had not felt forced to compromise in the past for his self-protection or self-advancement. Conrad was experienced in arranging compromises among other parties, but he was not used to making such adjustments himself.

Perhaps he was wrong in his suspicions of Grant Hannover. It was possible that Grant might be of unexpected value to the image and the substance of the administration of the university. Perhaps there was a benefit to be gained from the collective wisdom of a Baird-Lloyd and Gregory Blackwell that stood beyond Conrad's imagination; he might be seeing things from too limited a point of view. Should he, instead, martyr himself by shouting from the rooftops: Grant Hannover is a horse's ass! as if that were a more noble way to behave? Hannover wasn't a horse's ass. He just wasn't Conrad Taylor.

Senator Stonefort suggested a compromise that had no attraction for him at all. Thinking: all that power—always only temporary. He had no need for it—unless Isabel made his going to Washington the condition of their remaining married; but that was a paranoid thought. Washington was merely a whim as far as she was concerned. In the long run, whether they went to Washington would have next to nothing to do with whether they remained together.

As at the end of the evening in New York at the Baird-Lloyds', he felt exhausted. It was not so much that he was thinking through the problem of his future at the university as preparing himself to admit that he would do almost anything—even against his better judgment—in order to stay at the university. It did not make him like himself more, but it gave him a more accurate measure of himself. To leave his position of authority in a pique of disapproval of Hannover, or to leave in order to take a place in Washington to please Isabel, were equally secondary to his own desires; he was not willing to sacrifice himself to them.

Wearily, he left his office, said "Good night" to Miss Frangle, and wandered down Broadway to the Faculty Club.

Rodney Booth stood at the bar talking with an unfamiliar black man about his decision to move on from studying the American Indian to doing fieldwork with the Ashanti in West Africa. Conrad strolled into the candlelit dining room. Walter Webster sat at a table by himself. "My dear fellow," he asked Conrad, "why are you alone?"

"Isabel's in Boston."

"Come join me."

"What about you?"

"My sister isn't feeling well and asked me to disappear."

"What luck," Conrad said pleasantly, sitting down opposite him.

"Despite your good speech, that was a rotten night at the Baird-Lloyds', wasn't it?"

"You didn't like it?" Conrad asked.

"It was ridiculous."

"I found it entertaining."

"You can put up with more kitsch than I can."

"That's part of the job."

"I'm glad I don't have your job."

"You know—Grant Hannover is probably going to become the next provost."

"That's unlikely—even if he is attractive."

There is a remark somewhere in Pascal's *Pensées* which reflects that even the length of Cleopatra's nose had its effect upon the history of the world. Conrad told himself to look it up. The course of his own life was about to be influenced by the curve and depth of the dimples in Grant Hannover's cheeks.

"You don't really think he'll become provost, do you?"

Conrad said, "Yes, I do."

"Well, he's nobody's fool. *You*'ll stay on, won't you?"

"Yes."

"Good. Then we'll have the best of both worlds."

"I suppose you'll be going to France for the summer," Conrad said, looking over the menu.

"No. I won't."

"After what you gave up to stay for the Search Committee?"

"Gave up?"

"Not taking the six months' leave. The fireman . . ."

"Oh!"

"I was deeply impressed by your loyalty to the university. You sacrificed your pleasure and stayed to be part of . . ."

"I didn't sacrifice anything. I was asked *not* to come. My young man had found someone else—most unexpectedly, of course, within days after I'd left Paris. I called to ask you to forget the leave of absence just at the time the Search Committee was formed, but it had nothing to do with sacrifice; it was only because my cable brought the reply that he didn't want me to come back just then."

Walter had thought of it as his last chance. Maybe it was. "I'm sorry," Conrad said.

357

"I like you for that. Here, have some of this wine."

All about them various stray members of the faculty, with or without wives, had taken places at other tables in the dining room. Conrad sipped the wine, tasting again the thought that, while Grant Hannover was "nobody's fool," he just wasn't Conrad Taylor. But then Conrad was *somebody's* fool, often enough. He had misconstrued Walter Webster's reason for staying at the university through the winter and the spring; he had misjudged Tom Spofford's character; he had mistaken Baird-Lloyd's power to influence Gregory Blackwell; he had underestimated Mrs. Todd's devotion to him. He had to stand corrected time and again. Even Sigmund Freud had said: "I'm no judge of human nature"; but he thought well of himself.

"What are you beaming about?" Webster asked. "You look as if you're savoring a delicious idea."

"I was just thinking—I can't imagine how anyone can bear not being me."

They laughed out loud. Walter poured Conrad another glass of wine. "You *are* all pervasively irreverent."

Conrad felt his face go cold—touched by a ghost. "Where did you hear that phrase?"

"Gregory Blackwell used it at one of the Search Committee meetings." Webster showed he saw how this upset Conrad. "He certainly wasn't being nasty about it."

"What else—critical of me—did he say at the time?"

Webster thought for a moment. "Only that you are a prima donna."

"A real prima donna or a fake prima donna?"

"It wasn't qualified."

"Was he quoting anyone?"

"No."

But Clifford Rostum had been present at the meeting, nevertheless. So he had misjudged Rostum as well. The late provost had come back from the dead to cast his vote against him. Had he decided he'd seen in Conrad a potentiality that was not there? Rostum was Blackwell's guide even beyond his death.

"I'm sorry I told you that," Webster said.

"It doesn't matter. Funny what you find yourself touchy about."

"Yes."

They fell silent as a waitress served the soup. We are being judged and guessed about by others, Conrad thought, all the time, and just as inaccurately, as we are trying to see *them* whole and clear, always trying to get each of them exactly in focus—but they keep moving and we have to keep adjusting the lens. The only thing the eye cannot see—without a mirror—is itself. But what is the mirror for one's whole life? We live part of the time in an objective world, as I am sitting here now across a square wooden table from Walter Webster, and part of the time in an experience of the imagination that is nowhere in space. Even at this instant, where is Walter's mind: inside a portrait by Clouet, or wishing to regain the presence of his sister, or longing for the Paris fireman? Conrad gazed about the dining room, identifying some of the faculty members. There was a mathematician chewing on a piece of steak, who was probably contemplating his theory of rings and fields. There was a Sinologist who might be retracing the route of "the Monkey" in *The Journey to the West*. The musicologist in the corner, digging into his salad, might be listening to Solti conducting Mahler. The difference between them and ordinary people is only in how very much further away from the here and now is what takes place in those imaginations, and how much more of the time they spend there.

"What plans do you and Isabel have for the summer?" Walter asked.

"What? Oh, we haven't decided yet. Everything's been up in the air since Clif died. Although I think of spending some time in northern Michigan. I'd like to show her Charlevoix," thinking: I'd like to visit my childhood, as Isabel had wished to decorate their dining room with a memory of her childhood.

"And then maybe drive down to some Indian reservations in the Southwest."

Walter Webster did not ask about Caroline.

Alone in his bed in the empty house on Hillhouse Avenue, at dawn, Conrad awoke to discover that he could sense no sexuality. It was as if his genitals were numb. So the impotence returns; it comes and goes. No memory of passion shared with Isabel—or with anyone else—could stir him; no pornographic image, flashed on the screen of his mind, made any difference. He lay there limp and sorrowful, assuming now that he was no longer in charge of his erotic life, that his sexuality would fluctuate according to the rhythm of a waning physical power, no longer at his command. He was no longer in control. But when he was very young it was not in his control either: then, he could not "turn it off"; now, he could not "turn it on." How long would his marriage survive that?

He could no longer read without glasses; he suffered lower back aches. His body would gradually follow a predestined schedule of its own dissolution. But for the time being, for the meanwhile, he remained in a position of authority. He thought of the small, smooth, silver frame with his name slipped into it as a place mark at the dinner table of the Baird-Lloyds'. The name card could be slipped out; someone else's name could be inserted. As he had been put in office, so could he be removed from office. The possibility of loss is what gives the edge to pleasure. Neither his office nor his marriage was a stepping-stone to something else. Each was an end in itself. But nothing is to be taken for granted. Everything will be taken away. The only thing that matters is to carry it out with dignity.

He shaved and dressed, made his coffee, listened to the news over the kitchen radio, carried on in his ordinary ways, knowing that nothing was changed by his accepting that someday he would die; but in the meantime, he was determined to live as well as he could.

For the first business of the day, he asked Miss Frangle to send a telegram to Grant Hannover in Chicago. It read:

IF YOU BECOME THE NEXT PROVOST OF THE UNIVERSITY, I WOULD BE HONORED TO HELP YOU IN EVERY WAY I CAN. YOU HAVE MY PROMISE, AND MY VERY BEST WISHES.

As an afterthought, he dictated another telegram: "To Mrs. Taylor in Boston. Just say—'DROWNED BY STURGEON.' "

Isabel did not take it well at all. She was offended that he should have made the decision without discussing it with her. He was not able to show her, from his point of view, why there was no worthwhile option.

"You can always give up this job and not work at all."

"I'm not ready to retire. I am what I do."

"And what will you *be* when you don't have anything to *do?*"

"The music will be over."

Isabel became petulant and continued to drink martinis until she fell asleep on the sofa in the study. He covered her with a light blanket and left her to stay there overnight.

Her mood of sulky dissatisfaction had not altered when they met late the next afternoon. Conrad had showered by the time Isabel returned to the house. He was pulling the long plastic cleaner's bag off his summer dinner jacket when she entered the bedroom.

"You haven't forgotten about the birthday dinner for Henry Warner at the Connolleys' tonight, have you?"

"No." She was tight-lipped and distant.

"You're awfully late."

"I had a drink with an old friend from New York at the hotel."

" 'The hotel?' "

"The Park Plaza."

Conrad did not ask who the friend was. He finished dressing while Isabel bathed. He went down to the living room and paced back and forth, nervously smoking a cigarette.

When he returned to their bedroom he found Isabel in a long white dress, with pearls at her throat. She was standing at her dressing table and caught sight of him in the mirror. "Don't rush me," she said. "I haven't put on my makeup yet. I want to wear lots of rings!" The long curved drawer of her dressing table was divided into sections holding bracelets, necklaces, rings, earrings—most of which she'd inherited from her mother, some she'd bought for herself. The most spectacular things left to her by her parents were kept in a bank vault.

Conrad watched her choose or reject one ring after another. His eye was caught by the sight of a black jewelry box at the front of the drawer—exactly like the one he'd been given for the carnelian cuff links. He picked it up and opened it. There was no name in it. Emerald earrings with diamond pendants lay on the black velvet. "I've never seen these before," he said.

"Oh, I've had them for years." She walked past Conrad to the bathroom.

He snapped the box shut and replaced it in the drawer, not wanting his suspicion confirmed. It was easy enough to imagine Isabel meeting a lover at the hotel that afternoon and coming back with the gift of these earrings. He judged that his own encounter with Eleanor Saunders held no more significance than a good-night kiss. What benefit was there in thinking about Isabel having a fling? She had never promised to behave otherwise. If he had been wrong in a judgment of Isabel—as he had been of others—it was in not believing she would keep her word. Nor was he sorry that she refused to bear a child.

Conrad turned toward the fireplace in the bedroom, rested

a hand on the mantelpiece, and stared at the jade tree overhanging the pool of rippled, pine-green malachite, the pearl-moon caught in the petrified leaves. He said to himself: How sweet it is to fall in love, as a sardonic thought. Just at the point where he imagined he had arrived at a clearer assessment of his strengths and weaknesses, he wondered whether he'd confused the two.

The windows were open to the June breeze. Conrad asked himself: Is this the taste of swallowed pride? Acrid. But not unbearable.

Isabel drove the car. The light at sunset was clear and the color of the sky soothing.

"You never did answer my question," Isabel said.

"Which one?"

"Remember New Year's Eve at the Connolleys'?"

"Yes."

"Did you marry me for my money?" She was less than half joking.

"How would I know?"

"What?" For an instant she turned her eyes away from the road to look at him with surprise.

"I know a lot about myself. Some of it pleases me and some of it doesn't. In fact, I continue to learn new things about myself all the time. But the answer to your question is not in my store of knowledge."

Isabel shrugged her shoulders and said, vaguely contemptuous of the whole academic world, "Knowledge is its own reward!"

"Self-knowledge," he proclaimed, "is its own punishment."

But Conrad had come through. He looked out at the suburban houses as the car approached Ellsworth Avenue. He was beyond regarding himself as compromised by accepting Grant Hannover's proposition, compromised by Isabel's infidelity; he felt justified in wanting to keep both his job and his wife for what they were worth to him. Justified in the sense that he controlled those decisions. That also is only a half-truth. We ski down a mountain and remember only our skiing, not the mountain.

To ease back toward a more sympathetic rapport with his wife, Conrad tried to smile, and whispered, "I, too, have just done Corviglia."

ABOUT THE AUTHOR

Morris Philipson has published two previous novels in addition to several scholarly works and numerous short stories, articles, and reviews. He holds a Ph.D. in philosophy from Columbia University and has taught philosophy, cultural history, and English literature at Juilliard, Hunter College, and the University of Chicago. A former editor at Alfred A. Knopf, Random House, and Basic Books, Mr. Philipson has been the Director of the University of Chicago Press since 1967. *A Man in Charge* is one book in a group of four interrelated but independent novels that Mr. Philipson is writing.